C000183202

K]...

TALES FROM THE TWO SPOONS

Bíonn siúlach scéalach

(*Travellers have tales*)

Holm Oak Press

Dedication

For Joyce: Heartfelt thanks for the miles and smiles, the family tales, your incredible imagination and wonderful gift of storytelling. Now there really is a Two Spoons.

This story is for Kate and David. From the Two Spoons with love and the few important things to remember on life's journey.

I am truly blessed to be the continuation between my wonderful parents, Ann and John, and my two children. We are the flow of an ancestral stream of wisdom, with every moment a part of the jigsaw of life.

With much love for you all.

KINSHIP

TALES FROM THE TWO SPOONS

Bíonn siúlach scéalach
(*Travellers have tales*)

Deirdre O'Sullivan

FIRST PUBLISHED IN 2022 BY
Holm Oak Press
Jamesbrook
Midleton
Co. Cork
Ireland

British Library Cataloguing in Publication Data
O' Sullivan, Deirdre.
Kinship, Tales from the Two Spoons.

www.twospoonscafe.com

ISBN–978-1-7396751-0-3

Design and typesetting by Paul Whelan
Typeset in Adobe Garamond Pro

Printed and bound in Ireland by
www.printmybook.com

Front and Back cover art: Watercolour by Joyce Elizabeth Byrne

ACKNOWLEDGEMENTS

The characters of the *Two Spoons* stories originated as children's tales for Kate & David, imagined by Joyce Byrne. The inspiration to build those stories into something greater arose while walking through the walls of forgotten masons in the ruins of Rostellan Estate. Jesus Josephus married the threads together. The narrative was released beyond the confines of my own imagination and sprung upon my First-draft readers. I was surprised in their response and had my initial encouragement. Thank you all, from the overwhelmed to the unresponsive!

The work continued until it was my unequivocal fortune to meet the careful, guiding hands of WordSmith editor Peg Smith. Peg raised the bar to lofty heights for which I am eternally indebted. By way of their eagle eyes and incisive literary minds, Second-draft readers took me to the home straight—Anna O'Connor, Una O'Sullivan, and Seamus Quirke. Sincere thanks to you all.

Finally cast into the hands of Paul Whelan for layout and design, the "polishin' and dustin'" was completed. Thank you also to Jon Waterman and all the team in Carraig Print. For the wisdom of their words over many years, my gratitude extends to Dr. Christine Page, Dr. Dan McKeown, and to my own yogi, Lal Rice. I listen deeply to the dharma of Thich Nhat Hanh and the Plum Village Community.

The story and characters are wholly fictional, the historical snippets are fact.

Deirdre O'Sullivan
Aghada 2022

follow the cast ...

Jesus (Jesús) Josephus
Narrator, from Cadiz, Spain; born 1966
Daniel Samuel Joseph
Father to Jesús Josephus, from Cyprus; born 1937
María Joseph née O'Sullivan
Mother to Jesús Josephus, from Cadiz, Spain; born 1940
Abuelo Sean Seamus (Grandfather John James)
Father to María, from Cork, Ireland; born 1915
Abuelita Rosa O'Sullivan (Grandmother Rosa)
Mother to María, from Madrid, Spain; born 1919
Samuel Hadrian Joseph
Father to Daniel, from Bristol, England; born 1900
Mama Tia
Mother to Daniel, from Cyprus; born 1910
Dr. Lou Zhao
Friend of Abuelita Rosa & mentor to Jesús Josephus in Cadiz, from San
Francisco, California; born 1914

Philomena Sowersby
First cousin to María, Blackrock, Cork; born 1955
Ambrose Stanley Sowersby
Philomena's Scottish husband; born 1954
Bridget McCarthy
Philomena's friend in Cork; born 1954
Michael & Emily O'Sullivan
Parents of Abuelo Sean, Rostellan, Co Cork; born c.1878
Jerry O'Sullivan
Brother of Abuelo Sean, Rostellan, Co Cork; born 1918
Mary & Frances O'Sullivan
Sisters of Sean, Rostellan, Co Cork; born 1925 & 1927
Kenneth & David O'Sullivan
Sons of Jerry, first cousins to María; born 1942 & 1944
Timmy O'Brien
Friend & Fellow Musician to Sean in Cork; born 1914
Kathleen
Young employee of Two Spoons Café
Robert
Young employee of Two Spoons Café
Maureen Doherty

Philomena's stalwart support at The Two Spoons

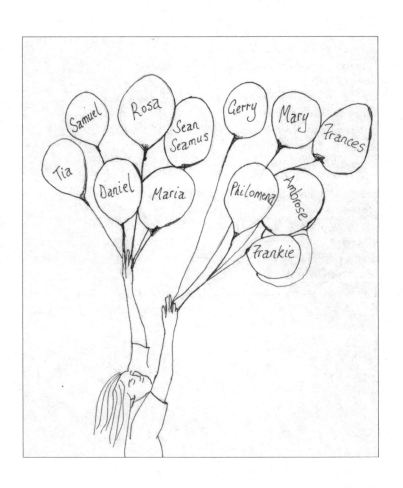

Cove of Cork, 1938

A glancing blow knocked him sideways towards the low quay wall.

"Jesus, Mary and St. Joseph," his father cried, grabbing his son's arm, steadying him until he regained his balance. "Ya big awkward eejit," he shouted at the back of the sloping boy, pushing a handcart along the busy quay. "He nearly had you in there, son."

"Not even off dry land, Da and I was on my way into the drink."

They found a quiet corner in Barry's, away from the commotion of the sea front, nodding a greeting at old Danny behind the bar. In silence, they supped their pints.

"Do I have to go, Da?" His voice trembled. "I don't want to leave. I did nothing wrong."

"It's best," was the short answer, "for awhile anyways. 'Til things calm down." He wouldn't look at his son.

"But where am I going?"

"Bristol, maybe, or a bit further than that," his father muttered into the back of his hand.

"What? Bristol? England? Ah Jaysus, I can't, Da."

"We'll see what Captain says," his father answered crossly and nodded towards the door. "That's him there."

∞

"On that?" He was incredulous. "On that? I can't get on that thing. Sweet Jesus, Da I'll die!"

"You won't." His father spoke sharply, his back to the pitching boat below the wall. "You won't die. He's the best boatman there is." He pressed two pound notes into his son's hand. "Go now, and may God go with you, my boy."

They shook hands and turned away from each other, into the roiling throng.

∞

Two Spoons Café, Blackrock, Cork

"Ah Jesus, 'tis yerself."

"It is indeed." We share this more often that any other form of greeting.

"I made you currant scones last night," Philomena said smiling, jerking her head towards the box on the counter. "Every day, I bake. Except Sundays. Your father up there said we all deserve a break." Philomena concurs with my mother on the subject of my miraculous birth, and likes the insinuation that I am the real Jesus.

"Oh, wonderful, cousin! Thank you. I'll put on the coffee."

I like baked goods; any combination of flour and water, with anything added—grains, seeds, nuts, cheese, dried fruit, sweet or savoury. I choose this above all else, an entire meal in flour. It makes travelling very simple; I find a bakery and that's it, no reservations and always the early morning, for the best stories rise at dawn before the onslaught of mainstream living.

"What's that tennis joke? Dan's one. I can never get it straight in my head."

"The first mention of tennis in the Bible?"

"That's the one." Philomena smiles again, trailing floury hands high over the Mason Cash bowl.

"Mary waited, while Martha served."

She laughed heartily, her belly shaking the steel table into a rhythmic creaking sound. "Whuh, whuh whuh."

"And the first mention of the high jump? Jesus cleared the Temple.

And what about this one; where was Noah when the lights went out? In d'ark!"

"Oh Jesus Josephus, she laughed, "you're a wonder alright."

∞

It is just a name, Jesus Josephus. My parents, I believe, gave little consideration, in 1966, as to how I would manage this in life. My forename, Jesus, or Jesús (Hay-zoos, it is pronounced in Spain), was a foregone conclusion, for my birth was due on December 25th. I was named before I was born, regardless of gender. My mother, María, had been strongly warned after an adolescent medical misadventure, that she would possibly never bear children. So whatever I was going to be, I was mi niño milagro, her miracle child. The overtly male connotation of the name did not perturb her. Nor did she ever conceive again. I am her real Jesus.

I do not have a middle name. My family name, Josephus, was a clerical error on my birth registration that went unnoticed for many years. My father claims the registrar was hungover after New Year festivities and he lamented the less-than-efficient Spanish bureaucratic system. That, or a failing in communication between the Naval Base hospital where I was born and the Cadiz city authorities. My father is Greek by birth and half English, so lamenting anything Spanish that did not please him was acceptable. My parents used the hospital registration for all of my Catholic sacraments and when I required a passport, they were no longer responsible for my documentation; I just had to go with it. Jesus Josephus it has remained. Daniel Samuel Joseph is my father's full name, so Josephus is a reasonable errant form. I have never tried to change it.

My family pronounce my name in Spanish, Jesús, Hay-Zoos. In English-speaking countries I hear myself pronounced Geeesuss, short with two syllables in the biblical way and I often draw a pause on introduction; the religious connections and the dominance of Christian faiths play their part here. Of course there is the hesitation at the thought that I may not actually be serious and no one wishes to be taken for a fool. When I am in Ireland, in Dublin, I seem to be Jaaayyy Zuss, colloquially hanging onto the Jay for a micro-second too long, followed regularly with a dollop of Irish wit: " 'tis the second comin'." In the Two Spoons café in Cork, Bridget McCarthy half closes her eyes and slightly inclines her head between the Jee and the suss, just like the nuns would have taught her. I try not to smile.

∞

"What would be your favourite food, Jesus?" Philomena asked, cutting butter from her palm into the bowl of flour. It was dark, still early, the winter sun not yet at the window. I was chopping carrots and onions for the soup pot.

"Oh I love your scones, Philomena. I loved Mama Tia's cassoulet. I love my own mother's paella." I paused, waiting for my digestive system to give me the answer. "I always think if I was really hungry, I would just like two poached eggs on toast with butter."

Philomena laughed. "I don't hear foie gras, or boeuf bourguignon, pommes de terre Dauphinoise et le crème caramel on your list. Oh! The struggle I had in college with the ould crème caramel. And those awfully fiddly petit fours they were the death of me."

"No indeed," I said, "too many words and much too much effort." I stick to a vegetarian diet mostly, thanks to the Buddhist monks and nuns in a monastery I attended when I finished school.

"Since the mid-'80s, Philomena, the world has voraciously embraced the habit of meat-eating. It is incredible how it has consumed the world. And now the West is convincing the East that they should have dairy products? Having survived millions of years without them? It seems insane. We are so bad at thinking for ourselves. We get in our own way all the time, my friend Dr. Zhao told me a long time ago." I paused while she crumbled her dough. "I fast intermittently as well, Philomena."

"Like in the desert? Forty days and nights?" She smiled, pushing at her spectacles, leaving a floury streak on her cheek, her fingers returning to the light, lifting movements of pastry making.

"Not quite! Even the real Jesus probably struggled with that! No, every second or third day, I finish my food consumption at say 8p.m. and break my fast the following day at noon. A full 16 hour break to give my digestive system a rest. I find it improves clarity of mind too."

"I could use that for sure." Philomena fingered her flour mix like falling raindrops. "And shift a few spare pounds in the process."

"But you know, Philomena, what really is best of all? Good fresh bread with butter and a cup of strong coffee. Oh yeah. I can go miles on that."

"Isn't that the truth of it," she agreed, " 'tis best to keep it simple."

I recite for her, " 'Coffee, that wholesome liquor that heals the stomach, makes the genius quicker, relieves the memory, revives the sad and cheers the spirit, without making mad.' Someone wrote that way back in 1760-something when coffee was making popular inroads in England."

"Oh I'm more of a tea person myself, Jesus." She added after a thought, "I have the ould Cona pot there for when we're busy and I use the little cafetières otherwise. The rep from Bewley's Coffee sent me off to learn all about it one weekend. Gosh I never knew there was so much palaver and history to coffee and tea. Anyways, my eyes eventually glazed over with all the boom, boom, bash bash, crashing about, what's it called, barristers or is it bannisters?"

"Barista," I corrected her.

"Yes, that's the stuff. He even put in a machine here but shur it took Kathleen half the day to make one cup and a queue a mile long waiting for everything else. You'd want to have nothing else to be doin'. Poor ould Biddy was as high as a kite after an expresso thing. Just a tiny cup and shur I nearly saw the hair lift off her head. 'Oh it's just a little one, just an itsy bitsy teeny tiny one, so small you'd hardly notice it at all,' she kept saying over and over, teetering on top of the stool. In the end I sent her to the shops for bread, just to get her out of the way."

I laughed at the thought of Biddy high on her stool, high on a coffee.

"So I keep good, ground coffee and make it fresh. But oh do I love my Barry's Tea."

∞

My first encounter of the same Bridget McCarthy, Biddy, was perched on her high stool eating a Rich Tea Biscuit. "Jus' the one," she said "is all I need. But don't spare the tea." She turned her gaze towards me, adjusting her swinging leg from left to right, "Hey, Jesus, how does Jesus, the real Jesus I mean, make tea? Hebrews ih! Tee, hee, hee." she giggled.

I had to smile. "That's one I haven't heard yet Bridget, and I thought I had heard them all. If anyone else asks me to turn their water into wine, I might have to take them up on the offer."

"Oh Jesus in thy mercy, come to me tonigh'... ," she intoned piously, eyes closed, clasping her biscuit to her chest, then tittered at her own frivolity.

"Biddy!" scolded Philomena coming through from the kitchen to hear her friend's words, "That's sacrilege!"

"I'm sorry, Jesus," she said, bowing her head towards me.

Philomena cried, "No Biddy! Sacrilege to the real Jesus!"

"But I am the real Jesus," I countered. "You'll be lucky if I come to you tonight, Bridget."

She bowed her head, giggling. "Sacred heart of Jesus, I place all my trus' in thee."

Bridget was in every way a thin woman. She epitomised the word: thin to look at, thin lips, hips, size, and thighs. A thin line of eyebrow, thin line of nose. A thin, tinny sound to her. Her hair was thin and hung carefully coiffured to chin level, the thin tip of her tongue flashed to the side of her mouth in a habitual way. And she tripped along gaily in low-heeled court shoes, always chattering and humming her own tune.

On her high stool, her crossed legs hung limply one over the other in an almost indiscernible way. Her eyes were sharp, her eyes missed nothing, gazing in a way that engulfed you, drew you in until you expected a soft voice of wisdom but were more likely to encounter something like, "So Jesus, where have you been? Did you meeh anyone interesting? Have you any news?"

I rarely see her eat a meal—a Rich Tea Biscuit, a soldier of toast, wafer thin ham in crustless bread. Half a finger of Kit Kat could take her an hour. She sips tea from a mug Philomena keeps on the shelf for her, 'Biddy's Mug' in fire-engine red paint around the lip.

"She had it painted for herself at some folk festival in West Cork," Philomena told me, "and she presented it as if it was a gift. Then she howled with laughter and took glee in telling me that there were no short roundy ones that she could have got for me. She's a cheeky little bird. But we go back a long way, she's been around forever." Philomena nodded, her lips pursed. "Don't get me wrong, Jesus, I'm genuinely fond of her. We have shared many a laugh over the years. But she lives in the rarified atmosphere of one—one squared actually. It's mostly all about her. And then there's the occasional glimmer of something richer, then poof! It's gone. She's maddening all right, but very entertaining." Philomena paused again. "Sufferance, comes to mind. She has an irritating persona and dropping her tees adds to that. I shouldn't let it bother me, her little ways, but occasionally they do."

∞

"I was with the nuns once, Jesus," says the same Bridget McCarthy, "in a convent up in County Wicklow, awhile after my mother died, Lord res' her."

She did the flashing hand effect that many of the Irish do, a Formula One version of the Sign of the Cross—more like swatting a fly. This includes replacing the solemn hand movements to the left and right shoulder with a series of rapid taps on the breastbone. I guess at this stage of human evolution, God doesn't mind.

"The aunts sen' me to Sr. Benedictus, to see if I could have a calling, a vocation. Saints preserve us, I had no idea wha' they were looking for, or wha' they wanted me to find. The pries' lih a smelly incense thing and talked on 'invocation' so I though' all tha' incense was for me. For my cause d'you know. In truth, all I found Jesus, was things to polish. Floors, seats, walls, windows, candlesticks, prayer books, confessionals. I spen' nearly two year dustin' and polishin' and cleanin'."

She nibbled at the edge of her plain biscuit. "The nuns looked after me alrigh' ah y'know, food 'n a comfy bed and all those prayers. Buh I loved the cleanin', it was very satisfyin' and I had never been much good at anything before ih. And," she stressed, waving her chewed biscuit towards me, "I could sing as much as I liked. I think that's what goh them in the end—the singing. Fa-te of, our Fa-a-der-ers, livin' still, we will be true to dee til death," she sang off-key mournfully, eyes closed, biscuit clasped to her breast.

"What d'ya think, Jesus? D'you think the real Jesus would be impressed with all tha' polishin' and dustin' an' singin'?"

I shrugged cautiously. In those early years of my visits to the Two Spoons I was not yet sure if Biddy could be offended. "Possibly?" I ventured.

"More possibly noh," she sighed. "Somehow the nuns weren't for me they decided. So they sen' me back to Auntie Lohhie in Cork."

"Are you not from Blackrock?" I asked her.

"Oh dear Lord no, I was born and reared until I was seven years old in Ballylickey, Wes' Cork. My father, God res' him," she paused, eyes downcast and did her sort-of-Sign-of-the-Cross, "gave into the drink early on buh noh" she stressed, waving her biscuit, "before there was nothing left to drink. My mother struggled on for a while, until one of her four aunts took pity on her and took us in. Tha' was Kihhy. Then Mam got sick and gave up the ghos' too." She paused. Mam had already had the Sign of the Cross religious moment. There perhaps is a condition that it doesn't require repeating?

The café was quiet. Philomena was out on errands, Maureen Doherty taking care of business. Biddy had my sole attention.

"So when did they send you to the convent in Wicklow?"

"I stayed with Kihhy but she didn't like me for some reason tha' I never could figure ou', so she sen' me to Lohhie, then Behhy who sen' me to Pahhy who lived here in Blackrock. By then I should'a been back at school, so they sent me to the Ursulines. And Philomena was the firs' person I meh in there and the firs' person to ever, really look after me. Oh I can't tell ya how long ago tha' was."

"Ah! I see." I had finally found the connection. Non-colloquially speaking, with her 'tees', Biddy's aunts were Kitty, Lotty, Betty, and Patty. The best of my Spanish English was duly challenged by Bridget McCarthy's stories.

"She still looks after me, I don't know where I would be withou' Philomena Sowersby. Oh I had three or four year in the school with the Ursulines and then Pahhy took sick and couldn't look after me and I couldn't look after her, so Kihhy and Behhy and Lohhie goh together and the next plan was Lohhie kep' me 'til I finished school." She paused again but not for long, as very little could interrupt the flow of Bridget McCarthy.

"After tha', she had a friend, who was Mother Superior of a conven' in Wicklow so I goh sen' there. That's where I learned the dustin' and polishin' and singin'. And Philomena says I left me tees behind me there in Wicklow and brought away a drawl. I'm noh sure I ever knew wha' a drawl was Jesus. It sounds like a bih of a shawl and a drawer. I never found ih in me suitcase." She tittered in a high pitched voice, "tee hee hee."

Some of Biddy's oddities were making sense to me now. We sipped our teas.

"Anyway after me time there in the conven', she sen' me to Boston to her brother's son, Manus and Helena, and a streel of chil-der-en. I though' I was goin' on me hol-days. They had seven chil-der-en."

She said chil-der-en. I had only ever heard my grandfather Sean Seamus say chil-der-en.

"Her sister nex' door had another five and they though' I could be the 'aw-pear'. I didn't even know wha' tha' was, Jesus," she whispered, her eyes wide. "Timmy and Tommy were immediately naughty, so I used my own mother's threa' and banged their heads together. I migh' have overdone tha' " she mused, "it took a day or two for Tommy to speak proper again and his left eye seemed to do funny things. They sen' me to the store for candy. I didn't know wha' the store was, an' if I found ih, I didn't know wha' candy was."

Biddy paused, nibbling delicately on a biscuit, her eyes constantly alert to movement in the café. I tried not to be reminded of a furtive mouse. "Then I had to take them on a 'walking bus' to school. Buh they took me in the wrong direction and we were still walking after an hour and a half, three babies in a pram, one on a skeeter board behind, and eigh' walking. Their father was going to work and saw us like, what's her name, Julie Andrews and the Von Trapp Family, nowhere near the school and he had to load the school-going loh into his 'stay-shun-waggen' and sen' me home with the res'. Oh shur Jesus, I didn't even know where home was."

I laughed, although I shouldn't have, for the image of Bridget McCarthy wandering the streets of Boston with twelve children in her charge was unnerving. She didn't laugh with me, not even a wan smile at the memory.

"Todd had an allergy to egg, so he ended up in the hospital with, wai' 'til I think wha' he had, the doctor told me, 'anna-filla-ack-tick shock'. Have you heard of tha' on your travels, Jesus?"

"Indeed. Not a pretty thing to witness, Bridget."

"I though' he looked a bit surprised alrigh' to find egg in his tea but Lohhie had showed me how to boil eggs and not much else. The other chil-der-en said he had a special pen for his shock but I couldn't see how writin' anything was going to help him." This for some reason tickled her and now she laughed, a high pitched tee hee hee, covering her mouth and scrunching her eyes closed in her mirth.

"Did things improve at all?" I asked, admittedly in an effort to shorten the details, for Biddy was in full flow, awash with tea and Rich Tea Biscuits.

"Ah they sen' me home after a few weeks of this but they asked me again the nex' year to give ih a go. Maybe I had grown up a bih they said. They promised ih would be a holiday. The Aer Lingus girl says 'welcome to Logan International Airport' and I goh an awful frigh' cos I didn't know tha' was Boston. I thought I'd be in trouble already. Then I goh on the bus like Manus had writ to me in a lehher and the driver said something like 'wareuwannago' so I jus' looked at him and he said it again 'wareuwannagomissi' so I jus' said 'waddawaddawadda' back to him. He though' I was bein' funny and threw me offa the bus."

There was no stopping this incessant flow of comedic disaster.

"Then one day I took Teresa for a haircu' and the wan said 'waddawaddaeigh' dollars', an' tha', I'm tellin' you Jesus, seemed like a loh a money to me? Nineteen-seventy something in Boston?"

"Eight dollars?"

"Ya, that's ih, tha' was still a heap of money. I put a colander on her head and pulled through some of the hair and chopped the other bits. She though' it was grea' fun and the other boys Timmy an' Tommy were cheerin' me on and sayin' they wanted theirs done next. Well she looked like a mop head buh they were thrilled cos we spen' the money on candy. An' there was a pile of candy for eigh' dollars. I hid it everywhere in me bedroom, in the bed pos', in the wardrobe, in the pillows. I though' I was doin' a fine job of this aw-pear business, the chil-der-en liked ih, buh Helena was furious when she saw the haircuh. Manus drove to the hairdressers an' they said they'd never seen her so I lied an' said we must've gone to the wrong one. Then I had to tell him we bough' candy and when I wen' to geh ih, the chil-der-en had found ih all and ih was gone. Eigh' dollars of ih. Jesus forgive me, I don' know wha' I was thinkin', lyin' 'n' all tha' but I though' the chil-der-en liked me an' everything would be okay. I cried and cried."

She blessed herself again. "Oh holy God in heaven. Sometimes I think I'm noh very brigh' Jesus."

I let that be the statement she made and didn't make it a question for replying.

"They were goin' away for two days to wha's it again, The Cape I think, ya, and I was to stay with the chil-der-en. Todd was naughty again so I put him in a hole in the wall that Timmy said was for bold chil-der-en, but turns out it was a thing for the laundry an' I couldn't find him there when I opened the cupboard. So I forgot about him. No one else seemed to notice. Then I wondered where he might be at tea-time and Tommy said he knew an' goh him back from the basement. Shur he couldn't speak, he was hoarse from shoutin' all the day and no one heard him."

"Oh dear Lord Bridget. Was there any part of it you enjoyed?"

"Oh yeah of course. Ih was all an adventure to me Jesus. Tha' we all goh to the end of every day in one piece was a, a wha', wha' can I say?"

"A success? An achievement?"

"Ya, tha's ih! A success." She seemed pleased with herself. Success, a lovely word. A miracle was actually what came to my mind, but I would never have wanted to upset her. Or anyone for that matter.

"They told me the cod liver oil was for their tummies so I rubbed it on them at nigh' until their mother wanted to know why they smelled of fish. I was more than eighteen and Manus though' I could drive an' I was afraid to say no, so he gave me the keys to the 'stay-shun-waggen'. It was HUGE!" Biddy's eyes widened over her tea-cup at the memory.

"HUGE. An' of course I goh in the wrong side and there was no steerin' wheel. And the stick thing had lehhers on ih. So Tommy said he'd steer if I did the stick thing but I think there must've been an angel that stopped me Jesus. I like to think tha' a' tha' very moment an angel stopped me, 'cos I remember sittin' there thinkin', do noh do this Bridget. An' Manus came over to the car and looked at me and he said 'hey I guess I might be wrong about the driving Bridgeh. Let's leave that for now'."

I smiled and breathed slowly with her pause.

"Then I met Himself."

"Himself?" I asked

"Oh the fella I was married to. For a while anyway. We'll leave tha' for another day."

∞

The Great Trip, East Cork 1977

Sometime after his passing, when I was just about ten years old, my mother set out in search for the family of her father, John James O'Sullivan, Abuelo Sean to me, Abuelo being the Spanish word for grandfather. My mother, María, Spanish-born, half Irish and Catholic, had an account of everything and everyone he had ever spoken of recorded in several school copybooks—and in a small parish in Cork she unearthed it all. In truth, my travelling began there, in Cork, poking around lanes and graveyards, my unattuned ear following the lilt, the fall and rise, the turn of phrase of my mother's family. We traipsed the county, she with her copybooks and concertina, I with wide eyes, for every one relative led to another, every other to the next, as she pursued her father's tale.

The Rostellan estate walls his fathers had built were ivy clad when I saw them. The woods had grown around and through the walls, giant beech trees with great tumbling roots, whiplike ash saplings piercing the shattered and collapsed remains of greenhouses. Fallen trunks rested on crumbled sections of mortared stone, but in their wholeness, the walls stood strong. The fires in the great heating vents were long burned out, the ice-house remained perfectly formed in an earth bank, the forged arch gate closed by a rusty lock, to keep us from falling into the brick-lined chamber. And as Sean had told us both: miles and miles of walls, miles of them. Everywhere, along the shore, across the causeway, around the old gardens, up to the old farm and in the abandoned demesne, slowly choking on creeper with a gnarly hoop of briar to catch you, hook you, and trip you. Whitey-grey craggy limestone lumps, scattered along the shoreline, tossed amidst the pinks and purples of the coastal sandstone. Tall sentry footings sticking out of the sand where layers had crumbled under the might of the harbour tides. I touched the stone, the mortar, the work of my grandfather and his father before him.

"See this?" says Mamá. "1727."

We were on the shore line below the new football pitch, looking north to the Great Island and East Ferry channel. The wall was shaped by a mason's hands to look like the prow of a boat, built into the sea wall of limestone, pointing fiercely north, its date of construction softened by weather and carved forever.

"Papá said they were the first to have sailing races here, from here to the naval island out there." She waved a hand to the west, across the stony lines sparkling in sea greens, a pink hue to the sand-spotted shore. The oystercatchers rose in a synchronised chorus.

"Haulbowline," I could tell her. "Abuelo told me too." The word had a sing-song to it that I had memorised tripping along Cadiz cobbles, Haul bow line, haul bow line, hurry up now ain't got spare time, pull it up and we'll be just fine. Abuelo Sean had laughed then and said it was not the nautical term at all but meant the Norman place of eels.

"The old boathouse. He used to meet with Hazel here."

"Hazel?" Nuts? Trees? He never told me about hazel here. I misunderstood her, and she let me misunderstand.

"Oh Jesús, Jesús!" She was uncharacteristically short-tempered with me. "You cannot possibly remember everything he said," and she turned on her heel and walked away. Her outburst stung deeply, for even then, I felt I had remembered exactly that—everything he had ever said to me.

On the causeway, a marker dates to 1734, carved in limestone, the miles and furlongs to many Cork places. That was over two hundred years ago, nearly two hundred and fifty.

"Hun-der-ed," says Mamá, smiling at his memory.

"Did they really build all of this, Mamá?"

Mamá nodded, "Sí. Everything is exactly as he told us."

"Why did he leave, Mamá? Why did he leave Cork?"

She watched the swans on the lake beat their wings furiously to prepare for flight. "He would never say, he would not tell. Even Mamá Rosa never knew. I will find out someday, for it always made him so sad."

The wing beats lifted the great birds over our heads with a swoosh of salt air.

∞

Mamá did learn Sean's story from her aunts, but I didn't hear it for many, many more years, for it never seemed important to me. I knew him in my way, long hours of watching his hands, building walls, fixing things, carving in wood or stone, playing the concertina. Long hours of wandering and stories, laughing with him playing the eejit Corkman in a foreign land. I had my own version of Sean Seamus O'Suilleabháin, his voice, his sounds, our trailing through old Cadiz.

At his funeral I had stood between Abuelita Rosa and Mamá and sobbed. Long dry sobs, for when he passed away I had cried every tear a ten-year-old could. His wracking breaths tearing me asunder, his soundless blue lips voiceless, searching for something he could no longer find. Once he had smiled, then whistled, a clear content sound that startled me and Mamá. She had smiled then, saying to me, "He is remembering 'The Maid Behind the Bar'" as she softly fingered the notes into the lifeless white hand she held. "I love you Papá," she had whispered through streaming tears.

∞

West Cork, The Great Trip, 1977

Our exploration of East Cork was diverted by extended family to the west, so we left by public bus to meet Brown Dawn on Bere Island. I peered shyly from behind my mother at this huge man in a bulging shirt and thick red face from which I assumed he was speaking Irish, for they were not natural sounds to me in all three languages to which I had become attuned. Why was he Brown Dawn? I have seen only a handful of dawns and I can't ever remember one being brown. Maybe it was a Bere Island thing? How did my mother know what he was saying? What is he saying? I wanted to ask. Is it Irish? Did he know my Abuelo, Grandfather Sean?

Brown Dawn played his fiddle in Denis' Bar. So fast it was a blur to my eyes and a wave of streaming notes like no other to my ears. My mother played chords on the concertina and watched his fingers move. There was nothing big about those moving fingers; they were deft and accurate and lightning. I found I was holding my breath, I was afraid to let it go in case I blew it all away and it would be just a dream.

Men drank dark black beer from bottles with a brown label. Maybe this had something to do with Brown Dawn? They smoked pipes and thick cigarettes stuck to their lips as they laughed or talked, and they ground the stubs with big black boots into the floor. Blue pipe smoke clung to the glass light bulb over the bar. So, between the furious fingers and the exhaled smoke, my eyes may not have seen what was really real.

A young girl stood to dance, and Brown Dawn changed his musical rhythm, a polka, a Kerry polka I heard someone say—as if it were an intrusion to this island in County Cork. And if the fast and furious fingers of Brown Dawn had been mesmerising, so too was the effortless grace of this dancer. "Move now, move now," shouted Denis—at least I think that's what he said, for men stood away to the walls, giving room to the dancer who kicked the sawdust motes to rise and join the smoke-laden air. My mother rested on her concertina and in the half-light I watched a tear run down her cheek. Oh! Abuelo Sean Seamus you have left us.

Later in the dim light, I remember curling into the arms of a warm soft body, an aunt or cousin. "Ah-woy-ra," was what I heard, murmuring softly that we wouldn't be much longer now, that my mother would soon be learnt. It meant nothing to me and I was beyond trying to understand, for my eyes were heavy with smoke and noise. My mother leant closer to her tutor, Pod-rig, a young bearded man with a guitar who led her through chords as he played and sang. I closed my eyes to their sounds of falcons flying on silver wings, twisting and turning in blue sky.

∞

On the mainland the next day, we went to Mass in the biggest church ever, huger than you would think in a small Irish place and full, full, full at ten o'clock on a Sunday morning. "We'll get Mass," a cousin had said and my mother had nodded, "for the love of Mary."

It was May, of course, I realised many years later, the month of Mother Mary. But my childish mind held tightly to the love of Mary and my hand held tightly to my own mother in the vastness and shuffling of a May Sunday in a foreign country. It was so very different to Brown Dawn and his fiddler's reels of the previous night. My mother wore her mantilla. I kept my gaze to the floor, counted the diagonal crosses on the red tiles as far as I could see, without lifting my head so that the Holy Ghost would not see that I was not listening. In Cadiz, Sister Dolores had told us so often and for oh so many reasons how we would go to Hell. I am certain not really listening to a foreign priest in a foreign language in a foreign country would be one of them. I tried not to think of her stories of Hell and pressed against my mother's side, feeling small in this place.

When I tuned in again, there was singing from away up high behind me; I could not but look skywards to the rear where from the gallery, the voices of a hundred angels were singing, "With sweet tones announcing, the secret of A. Of A, of A, of A, María, of A, of A, of A María." Now what could THAT be? Along with the love of Mary we had singing girls telling my mother A had a secret. I had a lot to ask Mamá.

∞

On Dursey Island, three weeks into our journey, she turned to the south and declared our time to return home had come. We gathered our stories—her Span-Irish collection of notes, her new tunes of love and loss—and we made our way home to my father. As we sat in Cork airport to depart, Mamá scribbled furiously in her New Copybook for Ireland. I did not like to disturb her, listening to her sometimes as she would stop and click her pen against her teeth, recalling this or that.

"Hola, Jesús, what was the name of the, aah, hmm, el castillo near the town, you know, right on the water?"

I was watching the television above my head, where men were running furiously back and forth with sticks and sometimes there seemed to be a very small ball. This must be the hurling game my grandfather had talked about. They wore shirts like stripy tigers of yellow and black and it then seemed the men in cross stripes of yellow and blue liked something, for they were throwing their sticks in the air and jumping on top of one man. I was anxious because I knew he could get hurt.

"The O'Sullivan castle? It is called Dunboy, Mamá."

"Ha! Yes, gracias, Jesús."

"Mamá?"

"Hmm?"

"What was the song you learned on the island? With the falcons? I fell asleep with Ah-woy-ra."

"Pod-rig with the guitar?"

"Yes."

"The name of the song? I think it was 'Song for Ireland'."

"What were the falcons doing?"

Mamá clicked her pen and smiled at me. She turned the copybook pages backwards a little bit then said, "Ha, ha! Here it is!"

She hummed and swayed, pulling me to her lap, "Key of D. La, la, la, la, lala, la, tall towers la, la, la, la, lala. Silver, do, do dodo, they, hm hmhm, hm, hm, hm, their breasts. Si, si lo tengo ahora. I have it. I wrote the notes for the concertina but they were building their nests if I remember the English words correctly. La, la, lala, la la hmm, sang a song for Ireland."

"You like this?" She held me away from her, smiling, pleased that she could recall it for me.

I nodded. I wrapped my arms around her neck and breathed her smell, the smell of her hair, her skin, the smell of her suede coat. "I like it. I liked Ireland, Mamá."

"Yo también. Me too, Jesús."

∞

Bristol 1977

In my memory, there is not much time between returning from our trip to Ireland to my father in Cadiz and his need to equal her efforts. A tall man, he looms large in my mind's eye to this day. Adored by my mother, they were together in the wholeness of that word—two, one, two, infinite, inseparable, separately each in their own right, for the greater part of both their lives.

On his insistence, and carried by a somewhat forced vigour on both our parts, he and I boarded a naval frigate bound for Portsmouth. My trepidation this time knew no limits. Travel again, by sea, travel alone with my father, and my first departure from my mother's sacrum. I choose that word carefully, for I had never been separated in any sense from the presence of my mother. That, was what I felt most keenly on that journey.

We were in search of the world of my paternal grandfather to whom I owe my British passport. Samuel Hadrian Joseph was an officer of the Royal Navy, a Bristol man, a seaman since a boy, as had been his male lineage before him, serving the Admiralty through a succession of Crowns. Samuel followed his ancestral line somewhat without distinction, through the ranks to officer. While on a period of leave at home in Bristol in the mid-1930s, he learned more of the accelerating dissension in Europe, the political heat rising through the misery of what would be the interwar years. In a breath, he exchanged the North Sea for the Mediterranean, where having survived the Abyssinian Crisis, the British Navy were about to establish a permanent defensive base in Cyprus.

His posting to Cyprus was apparently a relief after seasons of patrolling the seas of the north. "Biting cold Baltic winds, where every vessel looked the same, looming from greyness, grey of sea and sky, grey ships, grey food. Day into night into day," my father recounted to me in a stiff and forced monotonal British officer's accent.

I cannot imagine it could have been so dreadfully dull. Perhaps the tale I heard was embroidered for my father's ear, or eclipsed by the subsequent service closer to the equator. I was never to meet this man. "He was in daily demand, checking shipments, supplies, ordering victuals, prepping, stripping surpluses, dockets and tabs, bolts and buttons." These are my father's memories, of a man he knew little about. Samuel Hadrian's war years were all served in the Mediterranean, with a few sporadic leave returns to Bristol. His mother, by all accounts, succumbed to her weak heart upon reading of his marriage to his Grecian sweetheart Anastatia. A simple affair, the Naval chaplain and his Commanding Officer in attendance, with the bride's mother and brother as witnesses. His bride wore French brocade and lace, their union blessed under hot sun and the strong liquor of the taberna of Mama Tia's family. And not a Joseph relative amongst them.

"Undoubtedly," my father says, "I was immediately conceived. They hardly drew breath."

My father was unusually silent as we explored yards and lanes of Portsmouth; the Naval College, The Mount, the dockyards. Unlike my mother, he had scarcely a word of his father's story, just the scantiest of bones on which to hang a life. Was it Portsmouth or Dartmouth? He pored over lists and registers, endless days of Naval history, his preciseness deserting him for lack of clarity of fact. He did not know his father. We journeyed by train and coach to Bristol and, oh, the wonder of that place! His joy standing at the stage door of his father's birth, striding across Clifton Downs to gaze at the Avon Gorge below. "The ships! The ships!" he cried. "From here he could see the ships!"

There in Westbury Park, Bristol, he found old school records: Joseph, Samuel H., age 14 years, of Joseph, Edmond Stanley, Officer HMRN. He was finally real, an entry in a school record showing he had once been a boy in this place. In a wildly untended corner of the Canford Cemetery, the carved Bath stone façade of the Joseph family was all that remained of my father's lineage. My wearied feet weaved through Clifton lanes, down hillsides to Hotwells, the Lock and Swing Bridge, Underfall Yard, Harbourside, through warehouses and channels of old Bristol Harbour, every pylon and wharf breathing history, the magnificence, the wonder of movement and commerce, the splendid Bridge.

But no living soul to remember him, all gone. His brothers perished at sea in various conflicts, his sister and her unborn child caught in an epidemic of influenza. In the Bristol Museum Papá closed another ship's manifest, rolled an ancient chart, and announced it was time for home. I did not disagree and I felt my innards release with relief.

∞

Cadíz 1947

There was postulating and reshuffling, the winners and survivors of the Second World War. Samuel Hadrian's wartime accomplishments, or possibly his mere persistence in maintaining life, was rewarded with a new posting to Cadiz to assist in the rebuilding of the Spanish Navy. My grandmother and father were Cypriot residents, which did not deter him. "Come along now, come along now," my father remembers, as he hustled them to a naval troop ship. He settled Mama Tia in a taberna of her own—Casa des Angeles in old Cadiz, a home to inhabit that wasn't Royal Naval married quarters, a livelihood for herself and less time to be lamenting her Greek losses. My Grecian Cypriot father was ten years old, without Spanish but with public school English and plenty of courage.

"I am the son of Mama Tia in the taberna, Casa des Angeles," he recalls telling my seven-year-old mother and, without hesitation, she replying "I am the daughter of John James—la hija del hombre con el concertina." The daughter of the man with the concertina. My ten-year-old father was struggling with the Spanish tongue, my mother knew no Greek, so they spoke in English. In the streets of Cadiz she taught him all about Spain and they were together forever.

I was curious in later years about the Hadrian element to my grandfather's given names. I failed to find any other significant reference, so I can only surmise the choice was related to the famous Roman Emperor, of the also famous northern English wall. Hadrian was born near what we know as Seville, only a hair's breadth relatively speaking from our home in Cadiz. Despite the written adage of Hadrian (omnium curiositatum explorator), who was an explorer of everything interesting, he too, like Samuel, was apparently difficult to like. He too, like my father, was shipped off to another country at a young age. There may have been none of this knowledge in my great-grandparent's choice of his middle name, but a curious sensation arose in me when I read one of Hadrian's poems, nearly nineteen hundred years after he had composed it on his death bed.

> *Oh, loving Soul, my own so tenderly,*
> *My life's companion and my body's guest,*
> *To what new realms, poor flutterer, wilt thou fly?*
> *Cheerless, disrobed, and cold in thy lone quest,*
> *Hushed thy sweet fancies, mute thy wonted jest.*

This is my heritage, of these places, these people.

∞

Cadíz 1949

In a few short years my naval Grandfather Samuel was gone; he slipped in the bath and drowned above his own taberna, while below him a mason Corkman with a concertina played "The Maid behind the Bar." The Naval Base physician attended to certify his death. The clientele asserted he had not partaken in the taberna, had appeared and disappeared being not inclined to "dancing foolish jigs and folly reels." Having carefully examined the body and, finding no evidence of struggle, the physician announced that my grandfather was already unconscious before he drowned. He most likely slipped and struck his head, whereupon bruising was discovered below the left ear. A tragic occurrence. My twelve-year-old father, Daniel, observed these proceedings from where he was asked to assist the physician in the tiny upstairs bathroom. The demise of his own father. Accidental death by drowning was recorded, and the Royal Navy paid a pension until Mama Tia's death many years later. My grandmother, my father told me, removed Grandfather's bottle of rum from the bathroom cistern and sold what was left of it to the Naval officers after the funeral.

The Navy took my father to their bosom, schooling him until he was made a junior Naval cadet at sixteen years old. In Rota Naval Base, the British Royal Navy were by then working with the U.S. Navy, who from 1953 were back on European soil so to speak, assisting the Spanish Navy to rebuild their military, in Spain. And Papá was a Greek Cypriot. It was an interesting situation.

In the taberna Casa des Angeles, the recently widowed Mama Tia found herself quickly adapting to life without a husband. The Naval pension made life easy, she ran a good and popular taberna, with a quick eye for trouble and a handful of reliable customers to help her out. She continued to wear her wedding ring, spoke warmly of her son, Daniel, intimating to careless drinking strangers that her husband was merely absent.

My father learned well with the Navy, and also kept order behind the scenes at the taberna—fixing, shifting, making. All of his spare time outside schooling and helping his mother was spent with my mother, María, in the Cadiz streets, finding Abuelo Sean at his masonry work, or watching the boats in the port, or the old men fixing nets, throwing dice, smoking cigarillos.

Abuelo Sean liked Cadiz, said it reminded him of Cove and Cork Harbour. He liked to watch, but never, ever wanted to be on the sea. He recalled stories of the gentry at Rostellan Castle back in East Cork, sailing their big boats to the Naval Base at Haulbowline, the first sailing races. He laughed telling me of his own great-grandfather, who was caught by the British forces smuggling spirits from France to West Cork and lost his farm on Bere Island as punishment. "Faith, and you know they said he could keep his boat but they confiscated his twenty acres and his sheep. Three days later he sailed his sloop to Cork with all the family on board and got a term carting stone across the harbour to Haulbowline, to build the new Naval Stores. One day they left him penniless and three days later they started paying him more than farming could ever have. Isn't that the twist of life?"

∞

I have no memory of my drowned paternal grandfather, my childhood was filled by the living. Now, as an adult, when the opportunity arises, I like to take a hot bath. "As hot as you can bear it," my maternal grandmother, Abuelita Rosa always said. "Add a fistful of rock salt, leave everything you no longer need in your body and your mind seep out. ¡Déjalo! Let it go!" I breathe into my body, all my cells, empty my mind, fill my heart with love, peace, compassion for all living things. I breathe out all that is past and give thanks.

Sometimes I submerge my head until my ears are underwater; I listen to my heart beating. My digestive system gurgles; I imagine organs floating—kidneys, bladder, all the pipework, liver, spleen, pancreas, all weightless. I inhale and my body rises from coccyx to crown, exhale and I fall to the bottom. Shavasana, Corpse Pose, with which we end our yoga class, allowing one hundred trillion cells to absorb. Occasionally a gurgle turns to a fart, rectal bubbles which makes me laugh. I think of Bridget McCarthy in Cork, most apologetic after celeriac soup, reddening and muttering "pardon me." I kneel in Balasana, Child's Pose, my genitals reflected in the shiny surface. The water drains and as the last dregs run down, I relieve my bladder into the plug hole. Everything gone. God bless Samuel Hadrian.

∞

Cadiz 1970s

I could hold several passports—Greek and Spanish from my parentage, British from my Grandfather Samuel, Irish from Grandfather Sean. A musician and stonemason, John James O'Sullivan jumped on a ship leaving Cove in the south of Ireland and months later fell off in Cadiz, south-western Spain. Collapsing on his knees on the harbour wall, he vowed to never, ever step foot on the ocean again. He had not a word of Spanish and little other than his mason's tools and his concertina, a small bellows propelled musical instrument. He fixed walls, then built houses and played tunes for pleasure, learning to weave his Irish sounds to Spanish ears. Grandmother Rosa danced to these tunes of his, and Sean Seamus, as he became in his new life, was smitten. When I knew him, he was often drinking wine or sherry from a small glass, smoking a cigarillo. "Sean Seamus O Suilleabháin," he would say grinning at the sun, "how far have you come?"

He had been as good as his word—he had never sailed again, so my first ten years of life were spent, as much as possible, in his company. He always had a story or a tune and he invariably made me laugh.

"Dear God all the things I was called when I first got here." He drew a loud chord on the concertina and burst into a deep voice, "Shawn John, Say moose, o sool i vawn," he repeated in a sing-song voice and I joined in in a different key: "Shawn John, Say Moose, Yo seff, Ya mez, Hi May." We came together in a chorus of "UN GRAN HOMBRE, O SOOL I VAWN."

"I can't helpit," he started to tell me—this was just one word to me without context or meaning, helpit. Maybe it was hell-pit, meaning it was too hot in Spain? Most of my grandfather's tales contained Cork colloquialisms that my Spanish ear had to untangle.

"I was a good mason and with God as my judge, a good man. Your grandmother loved me, she got me, then the church got me. First the nuns, then the monks, and then no one else could have me. It was eternal, working for the church. The nuns loved me, the monks loved me." He paused to smoke a bit, started a tune, pulled it up, laughed, and stopped. "They wouldn't approve of that one, the monks," he said, "that's the 'King of the Fairies.'"

"What's a fairy, Abuelo?"

"Oh what's a fairy indeed," he laughed. "That's for another day, there's just too many stories of fairies to start now. Back then when I first got here, I built the monks a garden wall, an outdoor privvy, a greenhouse, a shed, a chapel extension, a new refectory, repair the tower … 'twas endless but I smiled and winked and played my tunes." He drank tea from a flask. "Níl mé ach an duine. Soy sólo un humano. I am only human."

He spoke Spanish with a Cork accent, passable, understandable in the everyday. He was a man of few words anyway, unless it was a story, so Spanish or English was modest, carefully thought, often witty with direction. He was not misunderstood. My mother wrote his letters to his family in Cork and he eagerly awaited their replies. He said all their time and energy went into living and staying alive. "There's not a bob to spare." My foolish youth never knew what a bob was and I imagined it to be a bop, the sound of a drop of water in a bucket. "Boip." They must have no water in Cork.

∞

Living in Cadiz, Abuelo Sean kept learning Irish tunes, often meeting other musicians off the boats at the quay or in the tabernas. He was always happy to play, trying anything a fiddle, or accordion, or guitar threw at him. Sometimes Scottish or French, maybe Breton, sometimes far away Canadian, Nova Scotian, versions of his own sounds. Unvocal tunes mostly, although I often heard him sing but never with the concertina, more usually when he was working, cutting stone or mixing mortar. He had a soft, high voice when he sang but I am certain now this may have been the cigarillo effect.

Oh I would climb a high, high tree
And rob a wild bird's nest,
And back I'd bring whatever I do find
To the arms I love the best,
—she said,
To the arms I love the best.

His father's songs, although he hadn't many of them to recall, were in the old Gaelic tongue. "Old Irish," he used to say, "Irish before we had English. Irish had a great way, an ancient way of expression that never really translated across to Béarla." I didn't know what he meant until many years later while travelling in Beara, West County Cork, where I remembered the similar word Béarla and had to enquire. "Arra one is heaven's own doorstep," I was told; "the other is that tongue foisted upon our ancestors by the King's men."

"We sing in quarter tones and untempered scales," said Abuelo Sean, "anything to be Irish."

She casts a spell, oh casts a spell,
Which haunts me more than I can tell,
More dear because she makes me ill

Than who would will to make me well.
She is my store, oh, she is my store,
Whose grey eyes wounded me so sore,
Who will not place in mine her palm,
Who will not calm me anymore.

"Pentatonic scale. They always began in B flat, intervals of the octave and the fifth, and a B flat end."

I admit I didn't memorise this, for it was just a mumble of sounds to me in my childhood years. My mother, María, recorded all these words in her School Copybooks of Sean's Sayings and Tunes. Mamá plays the concertina and also the fiddle. My father played an above average guitar, but to Abuelo Sean's horror, preferred the twang of a country tune to any polka or reel. Sometimes Papá picked at Spanish classical tunes but more often relapsed to tunes he would hear from the Naval Base radio station or his American colleagues.

Mama Tia was happy to let anyone play music in Casa des Angeles, and as a child I would sit by her at the long black countertop and watch them play. Always, I was fascinated by their movements, their expressions, the raised eyebrow and knowing looks they exchanged, as they moved seamlessly from one tune to the next. The "The Ninety-Eight March" moved to "The Ninety-Nine March" to the "Lakes of Sligo." I drank in the names, the sets they repeated and, when I didn't remember words or misheard the exchange in Irish accents, I would later take Mamá's copybook of tunes and read what she wrote, often with the opening bars drawn across the lines. She would note the date and who had brought the tune to them. When playing a set of tunes, "The Sailor's Jacket" went to the "Come to You Tay" reel to "Lilies in the Field" to "Kitty in the Lane." Sometimes "Kitty in the Lane" became "Ladies Pantalettes" and "Dogs Among the Bushes." "Rocks of Brae" became "King of the Fairies."

In truth, I couldn't say on hearing them which tune was which, but I did write a list of the titles and, as best I could, a corresponding list in Spanish. It was a difficult task. My school friends Rodriguez, with Pedro and Margarita, lay on my bedroom floor and howled with laughter as I read them my list. "Woman of the House," "Will you will me a Fiddle," "Jug of Punch," "Gaily we went and Gaily we came," "Ducks in the Oats," "Shoe the Donkey," "You broke my Cup and Saucer," "Dusty Windowsills," "O Pulse of my Heart, Why do you frown?" We made up story lines, acting scripts, played games, meeting each other in the schoolyard, cheering and saying, "I Wish I never saw You." Or "Drag her around the Road," "Toss the Feathers" at "The Drunken Sailor," hooting with laughter, as our class mates would ask "¿Qué estás diciendo?" "What are you talking about?"

My childish fun was encouraged by Abuelo Sean. "Here, Jesus, 'Where is the Cat' on 'Many a Wild Night.' " Or he would stop me in the yard coming from school and say, "I Buried my Wife and Danced on Top of Her." Or " 'There's Sheep in the Boat' on 'The High Part of the Road' but 'Paddy Fahy Doesn't Care.' " Mamá would frown and say sharply, "Suficiente ahora, tiempo de tarea, that is enough now!" as if our fun was displeasing, perhaps a mockery of their music. It was for me a childish fascination with something that was not mine, that I could but watch and listen and absorb.

"Reels, Jesus, listen." Abuelo Sean sat in Casa des Angeles early one Sunday morning drinking coffee with Mama Tia. He drummed the tempo out on the stone floor with his foot, one-two, one-two, one-two. "They're the hardest to play fast AND get the rhythm," he stressed. "Now here's the jig, one-two-three, one-two-three, but you got to get the ONE-two-three, ONE-two-three. The stress on the one is the important bit. Then a reel is one-two-three-four, one-two-three-four." I nodded and listened, for it hardly mattered as I would not be a musician but it mattered that I heard him tell me these things that were from his heart. He picked up the concertina, fiddled the straps to his hands, and pulled it to life. "A hornpipe is like a reel but we vary the rhythm, light and heavy, heavy and light. Hear the first note heavy, the next one light, de-da, da de da da da, this is 'The Cuckoo' now, an ould one for sure and we'd follow that with another which is a bit slower but the same rhythm. This one's 'Chief O'Neill's Favourite.'"

I nodded again and looked at Mama Tia, her lips pressed together as she threw her eyes upward impatiently. I guessed she couldn't tell me who Chief O'Neill was and why that tune might be his favourite.

"And here's 'Drops of Brandy' that'd be a slip jig, le la le la le la la la, le la le la le la la la."

He played away happily, eyes closed, cigarillo smoking over his coffee mug.

"Now then," and he struck a new chord and tempo, "'Give us a Drink of Water.'"

Mama Tia heaved herself off the countertop and went to the back of the bar, returning with a tall glass of water. Her Greek never took to his English; she just hadn't the sound of Abuelo Sean that I had. I took the glass from her, "Gracias, Abuela, para Abuelo."

Then, often in the later part of a Sunday, in the dark cool of the taberna, I would stare at the almost frowning, studied concentration of the musicians as they watched their own hands fly through single notes or run them together like sunlight on dripping honey. The smell in the dusky taberna: deep ochre richness of sherry casks my father made into tables; three-legged stools Sean had turned on the pole lathe in his yard; and four-cornered stools Mama Tia had seated with spun cord in yellows and blues—intricate twists of threads and crossed designs. Everything we owned came from somewhere or something else. Fabricated, turned, carved, cut or stitched, weaving our story-lives.

Me-hall and Meek-a-leen were cousins of someone, connected in a way that I never understood and for many, many years never associated my phonetic spelling with the Gaelic version of Micheál and Mhicilín. They came on Sundays, or when the fleet was in from fishing for a few days. Big, tall red-haired men with furious accents that raced into an indeterminable string of sounds when they conversed with Abuelo Sean. They played music with him, tune after tune after tune, pausing only to tweak a string or spit tobacco from a cigarillo into the drain. They drank beer in small glasses that Mama Tia hauled through a big steel tap. It seemed to me that the more beer they drank, the faster they played, the faster they spoke, until this whirl of moving parts became an unsteady planet on its own orbit and I would be sure that it would crash. Then Mamá would appear with her fiddle and the tempo would change, the voices would soften, a lull, a hush as she played solo and Me-hall would suck his teeth and whistle along " 'Tis a fine girl y'are, María." Mamá would eye him over her fiddle neck and smile and say, "Give us a song, Miguel," and open a chord of invitation.

My father would come for me, short-tempered and making noises about school on Monday or "time for bed" or "no place for a child." Walking furiously, muttering to himself, I follow him the short walk home, smelling of cigarillos, a headful of noise and fizzy orange drink, the sound of Abuelo Sean, the Irish light in his eyes. Later I would hear my grandfather in the yard between us, for they lived adjoining our house. Sometimes he would whisper outside my window, "Jesus, are you listening? Didn't we make music up to God in there? Faith, wasn't that just the craic." Sometimes I heard him relieve himself into the drain; he knew Abuelita Rosa would cluck and tut-tut to that. If I sat up in my bed I would see him standing there, weaving his own tune in the night-time air, whistling softly or coughing up cigarillo, draining the tunes from his head to his feet, before softly stepping home.

∞

Cadíz 1970s

"Your great-grandfather was a also a stone mason, Jesus. In Cork, on a big estate." Abuelo Sean Seamus tapped at a lump of stone with his big hammer.

"What's an estate, Abuelo?"

"An estate? Hmm. A big house, land, farm, gardens. Where the rich people live."

"Did your grandfather live there?"

"Oh Lord he surely did not child! But he worked there. He built miles of walls, miles. They walled in the whole place, hun-der-eds of acres, with one long wall from the causeway all the way around the harbour. Big limestone walls."

"Could I see those walls, Abuelo Sean? If I went to Cork?"

"Shur faith 'n' I couldn't say, Jesus. I haven't been there since, but I see no reason why not? They were built to last forever. They were huge. Walling in what was theirs. Walling the rest of us out."

I did not know walling, I could not say in any language what a verb was.

"Then they had the gardens, twelve-foot-high walls in two divisions, each five-hun-der-ed yards long and two-hun-der-ed yards wide."

He said hun-der-ed in a way I loved but back then had never heard anyone else say, so I would make it mine, running around the narrow Cadiz streets saying, "five hun-der-ed of them please, sir; a hun-der-ed thousand welcomes to you, ma'am" to anyone, for anything.

"And bee boles. Holes built into the back wall of the garden where they hung a hessian cloth across the front and kept a swarm of bees there. Lovely it was. Full of apple and pear trees too. Y'have to have honey bees for fruit trees. Y'have to have bees 'n' insects for all things to grow."

He stopped to smoke his cigarillo. I was sing-songing this in my head: Boles for holes. Bees for trees. You gotta have the honey bees, for fruit trees, you gonna get no pears, if they ain't there.

"Incredible it was. Slate-topped walls, greenhouses heated by fire, like the Romans had, hypocausts." He said it like hy-pe-custs. I imagined insects like locusts buzzing around, keeping the greenhouses warm, having flying races with the fruit bees.

"Follies and bridges, garden walls, paths for perambulating. They cut the limestone from the ground in the estate and carted it by pony. The big blocks for the more important buildings came from the quarry miles away, at Carrigacrump or Castlemary, by teams of four or six horses. The estate was so busy it kept a team of six masons in full pay."

"I want to build like that," my young self proudly told him.

"Indeedn't you do not!" he cried. "For it killed him. And it nearly kilt my father. But faith 'n' it didn't kill me."

What did eventually kill him was the cigarillos. He died grey and smiling and desperate for air, his lungs making their own concertina tunes. Pálido. Ashen-faced is truly a real thing. I tried not to look at him, but held his hand and sang him Spanish songs from school. "Jesus," he gasped, "have mercy on my soul, 'tis a long way to Cork." In what would be nearing his final days—although I did not want to think that, and as of yet did not know it—I wrote what he said phonetically, for I had no understanding of his words. Inside the back cover of one of my mother's copybooks of his life and stories and tunes, I scribbled what I thought I heard.

> *Toime assen t'olive Jesus,*
> *assen t'olive.*
> *Is chock sen t'olive a reesh Jesus,*
> *le ku nav day.*
> *Le keowl ma nom an. An keowl.*
> *Gur rev moh agud muh ah her.*

I knew it was Irish. There was no one to hear him but me. On Bere Island during The Great Trip, Mamá asked Brown Dawn to translate it for her:

> *I'm out of the ground Jesus,*
> *out of the ground.*
> *Into the ground again Jesus*
> *with the help of God.*
> *The music of my soul. The music.*
> *Thank you my Father.*

∞

My Great-Grandfather Michael O'Sullivan left Rostellan in East Cork having learned his mason's skills from his own father. Michael was impetuous, not to his father's liking; they just did not get on well together.

"He was a funny ould fella my father," Sean recounted. "I can't really say I knew him that well. He tells me he needed to leave, get away from his ould man, so he took a collier ship to Wales, to work in the mines. Some fella in a bar in Cove told him 'twas the best thing to do to get out of Cork. But it was long, dirty work in the mines and he hated it. He walked out one Saturday after his shift and kept walking, walking, all the way to Swansea Port and beyond—again west along the sea, to an end, any end, so as he might get a boat somewhere, anywhere. He trailed the lanes with not much in his pockets, his tools in a bag and faith whaddya know, under a great thorn tree, he met a man digging a cart out of a ditch where the pony had took fright. So he put his shoulder to the wheel, helped him clear it. He had a way with horses, so he was able to calm the pony back into the shafts. He was offered a ride, and I suppose grateful for the lift and a compassionate human ear, for his worn-out feet and worn-out boots didn't know what was next."

Sean trailed a few notes on the concertina, drew in the cigarillo, and was silent.

"What next, Abuelo?" For I didn't know anything at all about Wales or coal or mines or ditches. I knew what he wore under his trousers he called britches. He sometimes played a polka for me because it made me laugh, "The Britches Full of Stitches." How can you make a song from Abuelo's underwear?

"Oh it was a car-penter he aided. They took him in, to the Master Car-penter's house. He said he was given a real dark bread with cheese and dark beer not unlike porter and they gave him a bed on the summer hay in the loft. And janey, he awoke the next day and they asked him if he would work with them. The task of building and fixing more walls and houses, this time on the Pen Rhys estate, up above Oxwich Bay."

I write with a pencil or pen, so in my small and limited mind Pen Rhys Estate must be to do with letters and maybe this estate was like the other estate in Cork. I would have to ask my mother. And what was a car-penter? Maybe he used a pen too?

"Oh shur, he never minded hard work and a more beautiful place he couldn't have found. He took me there when I was a lad, 'bout your age I suppose. He told me he was on his knees in his cottage every night, giving thanks to his God for taking care of him and, although the days were hard and often bleak and cold in the dark months, the work was good and his new work-mates kind and caring. He fell in easily with them, a common rural background, a love of horses and cards, and an eye for good masonry. Shur why wouldn't he? He had a fine voice too, with no compunction to see a ballad through to the end." Sean laughed. "Indeedn't I remember my mother throwin' her eyes to the heavens and she'd cross herself prayin' to God for his 'mournful dirges' as she called them, to be done."

I said nothing, for it somehow struck me that my very real grandfather was talking about his own real mother and father whom he never saw again since he had come to Spain. I suddenly had an urge to see mine—and they were right here, just through the next door.

"Well, as the century ticked over, he was happy out amongst his Welsh friends and he thought no more of any other life."

He played a bit, we were quiet and thoughtful, both of us. "That's called 'The Parting Glass'," he whispered to me. "Hear that pull on the C note. Wouldn't that break anyone's heart?"

A sea note. Gosh how will I remember to ask Mamá all of this? I can ask Abuelita Rosa or my father some of the things, Mamá was the best though.

"Well, anyways, after a period of a decade or so he longed for home; the odd letter got to him, told him of his father's death, his mother's middling health and all that was changing in Cork. So he took his chance, bade his farewells to those with whom he had fondly shared his time and sailed for home. Now things were a bit different, the Brits were after long wars in South Africa and now there were more war coming in Europe. He sailed into Cove, and everywhere there was talk of uprising, of freedom and independence."

Sean paused again, smoking, not playing. Sometimes the old concertina would wheeze a bit herself, let out a reminder that she was idle. He would fiddle a button or idly pull on the strap around his wrist until I saw him come back to me in his eyes.

"He returned to the great Rostellan Estate and continued where his own father had lain his tools. And y'know, the harbour was busy with trade, ships arriving and departing, goods loading and unloading from all of the five quays at Rostellan. There were coal boats to the port in Ballinacurra. The walled gardens his father and forefathers had built were in full swing and supplied fresh produce to all manner of vessels and crew. The place was rich and well looked after and provided a livelihood for many of the local inhabitants. His bosses in the Big House were fully aware of the political talk, and carefully reminded their numerous staff of how their bread was buttered."

That meant nothing at all to me. Who would be paid in bread and butter?

"And where did he meet your own Mamá, Abuelo? Was she from Wales too?"

"Oh she was the school mistress there on Holly Road, Rostellan, an O'Keefe girl. They got together as people are wont to do and I was born there in Rostellan, John James O'Sullivan myself. But pretty quick then, he took the King's shillin'." Sean stopped there. Whatever the King's shillin' was, it must have been important, for he neither smoked nor played, just stopped. It took him a few silent minutes to pick up his tale in which I was afraid to ask anything that might distract him.

"He had a few letters from his Welsh friends telling him about the Great War and if he was joining up for the Great Cause. I think my father was torn between his life back at home, his wife and babe son, and the desire for something greater, some great adventure.

But shur the talk was everywhere. Joining up, or rebelling while the English were busy, talk talk talk of fightin', fightin', fightin'. And whatever he was, he wasn't a fightin' kinda fella at all."

I watched the cigarillo hiss and spit as it glowed between his lips. He played a few random chords that didn't seem to take his mind to a tune so he stopped again.

"Off he went in his new uniform on the back of a lorry, left me ma and me. I don't remember any of it of course but I always remember her saying later, it wasn't the same man that returned."

I had absolutely no idea what a lorry was.

"Then after a few years he came back from the War and after awhile Jeremiah was born, I just remember that, the excitement of having a brother. My own brother! Then after that there were the twins who were sickly and didn't survive too long. I must've been five or six then. Mary was next, then a couple of years later finally Frances, the apple of my father's eye. And so, Jesus, the threads of life are woven."

He pulled suddenly on the concertina so it gave a loud whoosh and with a big squeeze, he was off on a very fast clip. "Yahoo!" he cried as he played and rattled out the words as he might remember them, "do-de-doo-de-doo-da-double-in, ye-de-ya-de-yadadeda, ya-de-da-dedadde-double-in, yootle-de-doo for Lanigan's Ball!

Six long months I spent in Double-in
six long months doin' nothin' at all
six long months I spent in Double-in
learnin' to dance for Lanigan's Ball
 Yeehaw!"

Double-in. Is that an Irish dance move?

"My father took me to Wales y'know, Jesus, when I was about your age. It was the summertime, my mother was grieving the twins who passed very close in time to each other. They just were never right. Mam stayed at home with Jerry and I suppose she was possibly expecting Mary, so my grandmother was keeping the eye."

Dios Santos! Where would I begin? Who was Mary that Mam was expecting her? And why was her mamá keeping her eye? I never asked Sean these things for I was afraid he would forget the story, so I stored my queries for Mamá or Abuelita Rosa. I watched him sipping sherry as he remembered.

"We went on a boat from Cove, father knew the captain and they would be putting into Swansea with a load. So off we went, with not a lot between us I can tell you. My mam jammed some bread. Granny gave me a bottle of milk and half a crown."

Oh! I did have to ask him this one. "Why only half a crown, Abuelo? And why did you need a crown?"

Of course he laughed and laughed, "Oh! That's a good one, child," he wiped his eye. "Half a crown was the money then in Ireland and Wales. And Granny most likely never had very many full ones."

"What's Wales like, Abuelo?" I diverted, slighted a little by his mirth.

"Er shur, I was so happy to get off that bloody boat I hardly remember the first bit. 'Twas all fine 'til we passed the end of Ireland at Wexford and got onto the Irish Sea and ochón, oh Lord, she bucked and brayed like a sick horse. I thought I might just die and never live again. And my poor father—I have never seen a man be green. He was as green as grass, the two eyes in the back of his pole."

Men from Mars are green, or so José had told me, and what could have happened to his eyes? Some of this was very difficult to keep up with.

"Anywhich ways, we pulled ourselves together right enough. We stopped that first night in Swansea near the port, my father got us lodgings and some food. It was all so busy to my small self, just noise and not a word did I understand, neither English nor Welsh. I remember laying on my bunk and somehow it still seemed to me to be moving so I had to keep saying in me head, no boat, no boat, no boat, dry land here. My father drank beer so he just snored the night away."

Abuelo Sean stretched his legs out across the yard, spilling a drop of sherry onto his leg, which was followed by "Ah whisht! What a sinful waste." He flicked his cigarillo ash into an empty cup, all the time whittling away at a piece of white wood, turning and peeling and shaping and cutting, a pile of shavings on the toes of his boots, the flashing silver blade of his pocket knife bright in the sun.

"We walked a bit the next day, he showed me buildings and big, big houses. I had seen a bit like it, in Cove, but leanbh, I had never been anywhere else in the wide world. Horses and carriages and carts and motor cars. I had only seen a couple of those ever."

I was wide-eyed. I never thought of a world without cars or vans or trucks. "But Abuelo, why had you no cars in Cork?" We didn't have many in the narrow streets of Cadiz.

"Faith and shur they were hardly invented. The combustion engine was a new thing when I was a lad." He smoked and whittled, spat into the drain and smoked again.

"Go on Abuelo, go on about Wales."

"Oh we walked a bit, my father's a funny fella, all talk one minute then nothing for an age. I suppose a lot had happened to him since he left Wales, the War, marriage, and child-er-en. Now that I am an old man, I know you'd be remembering things that you did, roads you took, how life moved you. Played its tune for you to dance. Mebbe he was wondering how it would have been had he stayed. Who knows? He didn't say and I wasn't of an age to ask."

He paused, sipped. I paused, afraid to breathe in case he forgot to go on.

"We got a charabanc then."

Oh! I couldn't let that go. "A what?"

"A charabanc, a big carriage, with a motor engine, like your school bus but a lot older. This one had a soft top. Oh Lordie, I was so excited by that. Full of people with bags an' boxes an' even a box of chickens. That took us west awhile, 'til we got to the moors, big hills of grass and heather on the right and the sea fell away on the left. I can still see it now." He waved his hand vaguely, wiping the memory haze of blue smoke. "I'd never seen anything like it," he whispered. "Cliffs and sand and more cliffs, and then all this moorland with sheep and ponies here and there. 'Twas nothin' like Cork. Then we got to Oxwich, a great curve of sand and sea." He paused, his free hand waved the cigarillo in a wide arc, the expanse of Oxwich Bay. "An' a little church stuck on the cliff in the trees." The ash fell on his knees.

"D'you know, Jesus, I've been to Cork and Wales and Cadiz and a couple of stops in France and Spain in between. I have been nowhere else in my life. It isn't hard to recall the look of just a few places you have been. The sun was low then and the whole place was golden." He touched my head. "Dath do cheann: the colour of your hair. You'd be richer than the man with all the money just looking at it. And then father was talking and shaking hands with someone and a fella in short trousers said something to me that made no sense at all at all but he pulled at my shirt and took me down the sand to a few other fellas and a football and shur I was made up."

What was made-up? Componemos historias. We make up stories at school. I knew it was best if I remained silent. I watched his hands working, his foot was tapping, which meant he was thinking of a tune, which meant he would start whistling soon enough. I wanted the story, not the tune.

"What next, Abuelo?"

"Ah, we had a week of it. Those lads were the child-er-en of the car-penter. We went home with them and in the whole week I understood about a half of what they said to me. So I made up the rest." He laughed. "They must've thought me an awful gobshite from Cork. But what a place! What lovely people, singin' and talkin' and feedin' us up. Me da fixed a few walls with them and he showed me all the bits he had built while he was living there, before I was born. He was especially proud of the big repair job they did at the fish croft at the mill, so we'd walk through the woods of an evening to see it. And the church, just sitting there by the green where the sheep grazed. He had repaired the church tower after a storm. We went to mass there too except it wasn't Mass at all but the Welsh version 'cos they're not Catholics. Though I can't say I would have known the difference."

Abuelo Sean pared his piece of wood—short, careful movements with a gentle flick of his wrist. "For the first time in my life, I was in the spotlight. The laddeen from Cork with the funny way of talkin'. Oh I lapped it up, I can tell you. Cream off the milk it was."

He turned and worked the wood 'til I finally saw the tail on the little dog he had made. " 'Twas great to see my father smiling and happy. 'Twas just us and none of the pains of life."

He gave me the newly carved dog and fished in his pocket for a bit of rubbing paper. "Give Jack Russell a rub there and take off his hairy bits. Go aisy on the nose tho' in case he takes a snap at ya."

Then he was laughing and whistling his tune. "This one is called 'The Night Poor Larry was Stretched.'"

What that could mean to anyone, in any language?

∞

"The garden walls were all a-topped with slate flags." Sean was fixing a drain at the back of Casa des Angeles for Mama Tia. He cut small blocks of stone to fit around a square metallic grille, each stone set in dry sand and cement mix, carefully laid through a haze of blue smoke drifting upwards towards the sun. His hat was stained with sweat around the rim, worn to the shape of his hand where he pushed it back on his head.

Atopped. Atopp-ed. A-topped? My mind drifted on the new word.

"They laid slates up atop those huge high walls. Sloping outwards you know, to carry off the rain water. I never asked my father where they got the big slate from, could be Bangor in Wales I suppose, or could be Valentia in Kerry."

He said Val-en-see-a. Like a Spaniard.

"I never asked him that. Big, they were. Two-inch-thick flags, some of them three foot long and near three foot wide too. Imagine getting one of those yokes to the top of a ladder, or scaffold of sorts, I suppose."

My mind rested on yoke.

"What's a yoke?" I later asked my mother.

"Yellow inside an egg, Jesús."

"Goes on the neck of a donkey," said my father.

"Oye, Jesús," Rosa laughs, "Sean, he says 'yoke' when he does not think of any other word."

"Jesús," my mother called after me as I turned away. She was laughing with Abuelita Rosa. "Ask Sean what a, em, 'wetherick' is?"

I stared at her, for there was fun on me in this, I knew by them. Darkly muttering "idiota," I made to leave, but Mamá called again.

"No, no, truly Jesús. A wetherick. He tells me, oh, where, Mamá?" She looked at Abuelita Rosa. "Where does he say? Kill someone? Kill a boy's name, hmm, Kilkenny. Kilkenny! Michaleen says a yoke in Kilkenny is called a wetherick. Ask him. Tonto! Silly Irishmen!"

I fled to the sound of their laughter.

∞

Cadiz was my playground. There was always someone about, friend or neighbour and it was our heaven. The alleys, our bicycles, dodging cars and buses, street-sellers. We would kick a football in the evening sun on our own street. Sometimes Abuelo Sean would join us. He was a small man, small beside my father but not a lot larger than some of us. He loved a football, often causing a riot amongst us by tipping it up and down on his foot, then up to his hand before fist-passing it. Or running along, bouncing the ball before kicking it high over our heads to catch it again. A meleé would ensue about rules and hand-ball and he would laugh and say, "That's the Irish way." After a while he taught us some more of the Irish ways, the rules of the Irish game which suited our narrow streets. Or we would get him on his bicycle and take him to Plaza San Antonio or Park Genoves, where we would form teams and score 'a point' over the beautifully sculpted hedges. In the wintertime we used the beach—the visitors not so plentiful then, the city was ours.

I was immensely proud of him; my grandfather was good with a ball and he was fun too, enjoying teaching young players new tricks. When they protested that his skills would not be allowed in their football games, he would laugh and say, "Tell 'em 'tis good enough in Cork."

"I am no good anymore at the running, Jesus," he gasped at me one evening, "I'm flahed out."

I never heard the word flah, and could only guess what flahed out was. When he had got himself sitting on the beach wall, watching the rest of them playing, I sat with him. I was never much of a soccer or fútbol fan and never have been a runner, so messing around playing catch for a while suited me fine. I also don't ever remember them calling desperately for my participation.

"I played a lot y'know, Jesus," Abuelo Sean was saying. "We used a field in Ballinrostig and another in Corkbeg and shur we'd run about in any open space and kick a ball. I suppose I was a little older than you, mebbe in my teens, still at school mostly. Unless there was work to be done and there was always work to be done."

He was sipping water from a glass bottle, wiping his forehead with his handkerchief. "They were hurling a lot in the '30s, I never took to that."

"Hurling, Abuelo?"

"Oh yes! Not something you will see in Cadiz I can say for sure. Long ash stick and a small ball, size of your tennis ball."

I still couldn't visualise it, so I said nothing.

"I took to the music then and as you get bigger and stronger as a lad in Ireland, you get more work and less school. And that's just what happened. Less carrying books and more carrying stones. I am the stone carrier of the universe, Jesus. But the music was great and shur I still rode miles on me bike to play or hear music. So between that and the stone-carrying, I stayed fit. The fags will kill me though. My runnin' days are done."

I was young enough to hear that with no presumption. I did not think of ever losing him. We sat cooling slowly in the evening haze.

One of his favourite times always, was watching the sun retreat on another day. "Sin é, lá eile déanta," he would say, which to me always sounded to me like shin-ay-law-ella-day-on-tap. I would wonder who Ella was and why the day was on a tap. He would wave as it sank to the sea and softly say, "Wishing you all the best in Cork." I did not then understand the poignancy of his Irish words; that's it, another day done. Another day far away in another land.

I would ask him of his family or he would bring a new letter for me to read. I have no memory of him writing a letter, but perhaps my mother would have done that for him. "Brother Jerry went to join the guards, de policía. Yer not allowed to be de policía in your own home place, so they sent him to Waterford first, that's the next county to Cork. He had been to Dublin to do his training whilst I was still there, you know, living in Rostellan."

He said "double-in" again and this time I knew it was the capital city of Ireland. Sister Dolores had taught us that.

"Mary and Frances were school-girls at home when I left. Lovely little things they were too. I missed Jerry when he left for his training. We were great buddies growing-up together, he was bigger than me and he use to look out for me. But I was older, so I could cop the wiser part of the team. It would be my idea to rob apples from the priest but I'd need him to carry out the plan." He laughed to himself, remembering.

"Where's Jerry now, Abuelo?"

"Ah, I think his last letter said Waterford still but he was hoping for a posting back in Cork. He can retire y'know when he is sixty. Shur that can't be far away."

We sat quietly. I listen, sometimes prompting him with questions, but he usually just likes to talk.

"We had a pony in the back field that we'd ride around on. My father used her for carting things about on a small two-wheeler cart."

I could guess at that, I suppose.

"Sometimes we'd take the younger girls around the field, sittin' up together. When she was older, Mary was a natural on a pony, she could stay up longer bareback than any of us. She would ride out on a nice horse old Shanahan the coal-man owned."

"What's a goal-man, Abuelo?" I thought we were talking about football.

He looked at me oddly, as if there was something amiss with what I asked.

"A coal-man, Jesus?" He sounded perplexed. "Just what he sounds like? He sells coal."

"Coal?"

It dawned on him just then that coal was not a thing I would have experienced, ever, in sunny Cadiz, in my eight or nine years of life.

"Coal. Remember the mines I was talking about in Wales?"

I nodded.

"Coal is black stuff that comes out of the ground, hard like a rock. Millions and millions of years of buried vegetation and fallen trees that goes hard and carbonises. Then they dig it out in the coal mines, ship it around on collier ships and we burn it in the fire in small little lumps." He made a ring of his forefinger and thumb to show me. "And it's black as black and dirty. But that's what kept us warm. That and any bit of an ould tree that fell down and we could cut up with a saw for the fire. That's what I mean about there always being work to be done. Always jobs. Always work to stay warm and alive."

I tried to picture it. Football in the field and the pony and a fire with coal and saws and trees. I couldn't put it together. It was all just too far away for me.

"But this ould pony anyways, you couldn't get her to go after it had been raining. She'd trot along 'til you met a puddle and faith she'd just stop. Stop and stare into the puddle."

"Puddle?"

"Well, let me see. Un charco de agua. Oh there were plenty of them. More holes than road I can tell you. Lookin' at herself or the sky or whatever it was she saw. Mebbe it was ghosts. Drove my father half-cracked." He laughed. "He'd get all wound up, flickin' the reins and shouting at her but 'twas never any use. But Jerry? Jerry would climb down and walk up to her, scratch her behind the ears and whisper something and faith she'd lift her head to listen to him and he'd lead her on a bit an' she was ready to take off again."

"What would he say, Abuelo?"

Abuelo Sean spluttered and coughed until his eyes were red and running wet. "I asked him once, I says, 'Jerry, what do you say to the pony to get her to move on again?' and d'y'know what it was, Jesus?"

I was already smiling knowing it would be fun, for he was still chuckling himself.

"He told me he says to her, 'The one-armed bandit drivin' the cart, stick a pistol up yer arse an' make ya fart,' real quiet-like, so my father wouldn't hear."

We laughed together.

"And shur you could say blah, blah, blah to a pony real quiet 'cos they won't understand ya anyway. Or another one he'd say, 'Pony, pony, go a bit faster, or I'll put a stick o' dynamite up yer blaster'."

Abuelo Sean was much more fun than running after a ball.

"Then we had a dog, lovely little thing, Tricky. We had lots of dogs, or always had a dog of one sort or another. But I remember this little doggie because the girls found her up the back field. I think meself it was old Mrs. Murphy's and when she learned that the girls were looking after her, she left them at it. We'd had the doggie for some time and I remember then it was summer and I got home from the estate real late one evening to find a hullabaloo at home. Little Tricky was gone missin'. Oh! the wailin' an' goin' on." He laughed again, I don't know why, it can't be nice to be missing your doggie.

"So no sign of little Tricky for a few days and then me dad found her under a hedge, along the field. Little thing had picked up some poison I think and just crawled in an' died under the hedge."

"Aw! Abuelo. They must have been so sad." I imagined little girls like Marissa and Aziza in the younger class in school. I was thinking of these if they were sad and how I would feel for them but also I was watching Rodriguez and Filip kicking the ball into the hedge. They would get it stuck there.

"Well the girls were right upset. When I got home, Jerry had dug them a hole to bury the little thing. I washed up in the yard, quick like, 'cos they had to take me to show me the grave and say a prayer."

He started to laugh again.

"What's funny now, Abuelo?"

"I asked them if we would make a little cross for the grave, so they'd be able to find it in the field when the grass grew again. And shur they were delighted with themselves 'cos they didn't need one, they told me. They had thought of something even better." He stopped to cough and cough and he squeezed his eyes closed with his fingers through his gasping mirth.

"What had they done?" I have to laugh when he's laughing. He just folds up like his concertina and wheezes away.

"They'd buried the little creature on her belly with the tail sticking straight up in the air as a grave marker."

"Oh! That's no good really, Abuelo, is it?"

"No, Jesus," he wheezed, "even with prayers to God, 'tis no use at all."

∞

Abuelita Rosa. "My little love." Sean would say of my grandmother, a gorgeous woman, in my mind always smiling. "If it wasn't for Rosa I could go home to Cork," he'd pull a chord on the concertina and say, "but shur I could never leave her or I'd leave my heart."

He would fiddle a few notes, run up a scale, before drawing a long high melody.

"What's that?" I'd ask.

" 'Blue-eyed Lassie, There's a Tear in my Eye.' "

I pictured the TV dog, bounding across the field to rescue another day. I didn't know Abuelo knew a song about him.

Abuelita Rosa was a nurse in the Rota Naval Base Hospital. Her English was colloquial Cork from Sean, or American twang from her patients. She spoke English and some Spanish with Sean, my father, and me. She spoke Spanish with my mother and Spanish and some Greek with Mama Tia. My father spoke Greek with his mother, English and Spanish with my mother and Sean, and mostly English with me. We blended like a small European summit. My father's English was Cambridge Public School from a Naval Officer in Cyprus, clipped and correct, tainted by his Greek-Cypriot tongue and Spanish upbringing.

From his Naval colleagues, my father later assumed Americanisms, turns of phrase, their twang and a love of country music. "Country music?" Abuelo Sean was aghast and would loudly play off-chord on the concertina, to exhibit his disapproval of what he told me he thought was "just-shite."

There's another word I bandied about Cadiz, racing my friend Rodriguez along the harbour wall, swinging our gangland kendo sticks, calling, "Justshite, justshite, play that music and you die!"

∞

La Mañana desnuda, el diamante purisimo del dia …
vale más despertar.

My grandfather Sean would start this recitation in his Cork Spanish, Abuelita Rosa would smile and say it was the only real Spanish she ever taught him.

"Naked morning, the purest diamond of the day;
It is better to awake."

"La mañana desnuda," she would answer him,
"árboles, altos pájaros, el invierno, el otoño … Paz."

They would look at each other.
"La luz es alta y pura para cuanto respira."

Naked morning. Trees, high birds, winter, autumn … Peace;
The light is high and pure for every breathing thing.

I loved them both and I was still so small and young.

∞

"Did I tell you the about American Navy in Cork in 1917, just after I was born? My father was back from the Great War late that year, his head in bits and missing the use of his left arm. He walked with a stick ever after and didn't much speak." Abuelo Sean was pulling on the concertina with both hands while buttoning with one, as the other held a burning cigarillo. His fingers were short and misshapen from the stone-work, and watching them move and bring such sound was a miracle to me. He'd laugh and say, "That's a bum note from the broken pinky." Smoke weaved through the sounds, drifting through the blueness, the movement of notes through the bellows blew it in every way.

"Nearly two thousand of them Yanks, living up on the hill, in tin huts and timber bunkhouses. Timber Town on the right and Tin Town on the left. The road up the hill was called Yankee Road. They came to East Cork to build sea-planes, to stop those German U-boats destroying the Allied shipping and supply lines along our coast. Those U-boats could get anything, submarines they were. The place was full of military."

That word sounded like mil-tree. I wasn't sure what to do with it.

"There was a big command at Cove town, English military and navy, American soldiers on their way to the Front in Europe and more of them based in Cove. They were a breath of life those American boys, to the Allies, y'know, the English and French armies. Those lads had been stuck in stinking trenches for three years in Belgium and France, fightin' Jerrie. In came the Americans, all gung-ho, with their new gear, new weapons, young fellas just freshly trained, still wet behind the ears. The new American army, their first fighting abroad. They helped Tommie shove Jerrie back along east to Germany."

Abuelo Sean didn't say who Tommie was, or who Jerrie might have been, but I imagined him all muddy and smelly after three years not washing behind his ears, getting pushed along by fancy, clean soldiers with flashy new guns. "Hie, hie, move along now."

"He told me that the Yanks ruined it for everyone in Cork, 'cos none of the girls wanted to look at a local fella in his dowdy ould baggy trousers and peaky caps. They cut a fine dash in their smart uniforms, chewin' their gum, drawling their words. But shur, in less than a year the war was over, the huge sea-plane base was dismantled and auctioned off and them young Yankee boys were all shipped off back home. But y'know, 'twas never quite the same again in East Cork. Oh no sir! Like pedigree dogs the Yankee boyos had left their mark. They would have come from miles around to dances in the ould YMCA hall between Tin Town and Timber Town. Bikes and ponies, donkeys and Shank's Mare."

I wondered who Shank was. Shank the Yank, he drank and stank, fell over one night and drowned in a tank of beer. I could make up these lines forever to go with Abuelo's tunes.

"The priests did their nut. All these foreign heathen boys would be getting good girls into trouble. And of course nearly all of them young Yankees had never ever been outta the U.S. of A.—'twas like life from another planet for all of them. Boatloads of them. I often wonder how many of them ever got home again."

∞

"Lemme tell you about the Cork Grand Prix of 1937." Abuelo Sean sat opposite me at the bench at in the yard, where I was trying to do my schoolwork. "Have I told you this before?"

"No, Abuelo. A Grand Prix with racing cars? Like Monte Carlo?"

"The very thing. We had an early start that morning from Rostellan, piled into Tommy Mac's ould lorry. Gosh it seemed to take hours to get anywhere, we were eight or nine of us, piled on the back, off to see car-racing in the big city of Cork. We had a flask of tea and sandwiches at the Glounthaune railway bridge at seven in the morning and chugged on to the city to get a good viewing spot. The best lookout would be the Carrigrohane Straight, but shur the crowds were immense. Tommy left the truck at the new greyhound race track and we walked the last bit. Oh! The craic Jesus! It was mighty. Paddy Flynn hopped on his wooden leg. Michael Roche was there with one arm. He had a left arm and my ould man had a right one so they kinda strode around together making a pair like a three-legged race."

This confused me greatly. A pear is for eating and a three-legged race? And I still didn't know what is a lorry? It was certainly better than homework I thought.

"The noise! Some of these cars could do eighty and ninety miles an hour y'know? We had never seen nothing like it. This was Formula One racing. There was Prince Bira of Siam in a Maserati. Lovely, yellow and blue."

I could only listen in wonder. I knew what a prince was, I didn't know Siam. And a Maserati? I interrupted him.

"Abuelo, what's Siam and Maserati?"

"What? Siam? Like Siamese cats from Africa. Maserati is an Italian car, this was a White Mouse."

Oh no! Cats and a mouse! None of that really helped me so I would have to ask my father later.

"He smashed it too, the Maserati, so Charlie Martin won in the Alfa. But more than anything my eyes were open to the world, Jesus. People, money, cars, and the speed of them."

He paused, smoked a bit, carving a spoon from an olive piece for Mama Rosa. His hands were always moving.

"We went to Costigan's on Washington Street for a plate of grub and a pint or two of porter. Tommy threw us all into the lorry after dark to roll on home and d'you know I woke in Rostellan with the carts and the horses and the baggy trouser brigade and I could only think there must be more to life than this and the lumps of limestone in my hands."

"And what then, Abuelo? Did you get a car yourself?"

"Indeedn't I did not!" he laughed. "Shur no one but the rich fellas had cars." He whittled and spat cigarillo threads.

"We went back the next year too. 'Twas supposed to be a great event which it wasn't, because of the war I suppose, but 'twas exciting all the same. The Prince had fixed up his White Mouse and he came second. A big ugly lookin' French thing called a Delahaye V-12 won and another lovely French Delage came third. Tommy had passed away in a farming accident—he fell hard from a hay rick and never recovered, so his brother Finn drove the Ford lorry but he was a bit of a dry ould shite and wouldn't stop for porter. We landed back at the Pump House Pub in Rostellan about eight o'clock, full of noise and smoke in our nostrils, chomping for action like young yobbos."

He quietly drew on his cigarillo; it made its own hissing noise as the paper burned brightly and illuminated his face, which was turned to the ground. He turned the spoon over and over in his hands, without a word more.

"Abuelo?" I asked, after enough time to know something happened to the story. "Abuelo?" I ventured again.

He looked up and through me, his lip trembling, his eyes wet and red.

"Abuelo?" I asked again, and having never ever seen him in this way, felt compelled to jump off my bench and go to him and take his hands in mine. His eyes came back to me and a tear rolled through the grey stubble of his cheek to his moustache and hung before falling to the wood shavings.

"Jesus," he muttered, "Jesus have mercy on her soul."

"Abuelo?" I was alarmed now. "Abuelo, what is it?" I whispered. There was a long silence.

"Ah child, the stuff of adult nightmares. All long passed now but still an ould scar on my ould heart." He squeezed his eyes through his fingers, rubbed the heel of his hand across his nose and inhaled deeply.

"Ah shur, they never raced in Cork again and right soon I took the boat to Cadiz anyways."

∞

My own father built soap-box cars in Cadiz. "A box, two pieces of two-by-two from a fish crate for axles. We carved out the outside face to take a bearing plate from the garage, popped a wheel onto the bearing plate, repeat the other side. A three-by-two for the cam, a small bike wheel and a fisherman's rope for the steering. Fantastic. We had great races around the Cathedral, down to the harbour wall, no cobbles. A few bruises and bangs and incidents, no deaths of course. The worst incident was Benoit tipping sideways and breaking his spectacles, which bloodied his cheek. It looked a damn sight worse than it was, pardner." My father said this with an American drawl; he did this quite often when he was telling stories, and Mamá told me many years later that it was a result of the Americans mimicking his British English, always in a condescending way. As if their way came first and was best.

But José's mother was a loud and complaining woman so the soap-box cars had to stop for a while. My father and Sean built a car for Rodriguez and me and our friends Ana and Isabel, but somehow it was not the same for us. Rodriguez was all about soccer and bikes and bike stunts. I was never particularly comfortable with my feet off the ground. We sold the car to Pedro and his sister Margarita for six cans of Coca-Cola and a dozen Mars bars which they stole from the Naval Base kitchen.

∞

We were sitting on crates inside the harbour wall, late sun above the sea. Abuelo Sean smoked a cigarillo, working a piece of whitened driftwood that I had found lodged in a drying fishing net.

"When I got on that boat in Cove in '38, y'know I had no idea where I was going. My father arranged it all. He had served some of his war-time with the captain and I was just to get on with it. He shook my hand and pressed a few bank notes into my fist and turned on his heel and was gone. That was the last I saw of him, although for sure I didn't know that then. I am certain he muttered a thing about Bristol. I heard nothing about France and had no idea that I was off to Spain. Shur it was a lifetime away from Cork."

"Hola. Cómo estás?" he would sometimes greet the fishermen, mending pots or nets, peeling sunflower seeds from their husks. "Buenas tardes." Sometimes he would elbow me and say, "Ask him what that fish is." Or, "Ask him if he had a good day." I would laugh and say, "Abuelo, you know how to say that," and he would laugh too and say, "Yes, but it hurts my ould head to think about it."

"El mar y el cielo se ven igual de azules y en la distancia parece que se unen," I say to him.

He laughs. "Ah, you're the clever one, Jesus. Let's see. Hmm … okay, the sea and sky look the same blue and in the distance it looks like they join together. El horizonte."

"Sí, the horizon."

We sit watching the life around us, the noise of the docks, the fishermen calling, the circling gulls. The rhythmic scrape of Abuelo Sean's little knife.

"I thought I would get off in Bristol. I can tell you I had had my fill of ship life already but ole Captain laughed at me and said he was keeping me 'til I found my sea-legs and what would a Paddy boy like me do in the King's realm? I told him right quick we'd be around the world before I found sea-legs and he laughed again and said, 'Right so, we'd better get on with it.' "

I didn't understand much of this: Paddy boy, King's realm, sea-legs. But I knew he hated sailing or being anywhere except looking at the sea, so it must be about that. "Were you really sick, Abuelo?" I had only been seasick once—only once because I had never sailed a second time.

"Sick? Oh boyo. Oho boyo! Sick wasn't innit."

Innit. Hmmm. That one would have to wait.

"I was so sick once we passed the Wexford coast, they had to hang me over the rail to stop the mess. I retched and reached on every wave. The boat didn't stop heaving and neither did I. Oh boyo. You know, I actually prayed to Mother Mary the boat would sink, for drowning would be preferable. Oh yes! See this?" He pointed to a small ragged scar above and through his left eyebrow. "That's my sickie scar. I wasn't of the mind to notice that every time I heaved up, I was abrading my head against a crack in the glass. One of the mates found me with a bucket of puke and blood running down my face. They thought I had vomited up my innards." He laughed loudly—but at all, at all, I didn't see how that could be funny. As if he understood my reaction, he clapped me on the shoulder and said, "I'm laughing now, Jesus, but I can tell you there was not a thing funny about it then. And then we had to do it all again, down the coast of France. Ah, Jaysus."

I knew that wasn't me, that was the real one, in the prayers.

"Oh Jesus, Jesus. Never ever again. I came right a bit about the place where France became Spain. Then down Portugal. And this was Maytime y'know. The days went on forever. I showed my face eventually and the captain laughed and said was I fit for work yet? So he tied me to a capstan on the back deck and gave me short lengths of rope to splice together."

"Splice?"

"Yes, splice, like knittin'." He poked a fishing pot on the pier with the toe of his boot. "There? See? Two ropes knitted together to make a strong connection. I had no idea why I was doing this but it took me mind off my welfare."

"Welfare?"

"Condicion. Nada vomitó."

"Was it a big boat, Abuelo?"

"That's the very thing, Jesus. Not big at all, not even sixty foot."

I knew by now what a foot was. Abuelo and my father were always arguing feet and inches. The Spanish used metric, my father used Imperial, and the Americans used their own version again. I had heard many stories of confusion in the Naval Base.

"She was a fine thing if you were lookin' at her, instead of throwin' up on her. 1936 Miller Custom, built like a fishing trawler. 'Twasn't the captain's y'know and I really had no idea where he was going or what was happening. We refuelled a few times, stopped at ports for getting things off or putting things on, but the journey was ever on. Shur I was a small East Cork village man. I had no idea in the world about Spain, or the war or what was coming next. We get to Cadiz after what felt like months and he says, 'That's you boyo. This is your port of call.' He shook my hand and right then I was a Corkman alone in Spain."

I was silent. I couldn't bring myself to begin to imagine it.

"Just over there." He pointed with the end of a cigarillo in his yellowed fingers, which he then flicked to the sea. "Just over there, he docked and that was that. One of the mates walked with me. I could hardly walk and the whole world rocked for another few days anyways. He asked if I had pesetas and guess what I thought he said, Jesus?"

He didn't give me time to guess. "I thought he said potatoes." Abuelo threw his head back and laughed loudly. "Potatoes! What in the world's use were potatoes to me here? When he found I knew nothing at all at all about Spain, he carted me back to the boat and I refused absolutely to get on board again. So he threw me down the gangway like a sack of the same spuds." He laughed again. I laughed with him this time, although I remember thinking how it really wasn't very funny. I didn't like it much at all.

"So they gave me a bit of a grounding in all things Spanish. Told me about Franco and the war and the war that was brewing in northern Europe. Told me about pesetas and how to look in a newspaper and see what it was worth to the English pound shilling and pence. I didn't have very many of them anyways. They fed me that night, then the mates took me for cervezas, which was nothing like porter, and me ould guts weren't up for much. I slept on the deck. 'Twas hot. I remember that all right. Real hot." Abuelo whittled steadily, the setting sun catching pink and orange flashes on his blade.

"Indeed, indeed. A Corkman in Cadiz. Oh boy I could sing that tune for you. The captain took me the next day to get some potatoes and then up the city there, to the nuns. One of them had English enough for us to get on. I understood from the captain that they would keep me for one ten-shillings-a-month worth of pesetas, until I got myself together. He told her I could build walls. And the rest, as they say, Jesus, is history. And faith my child, she never once took ten shillings from me for lodgings. Not once. My first lucky break."

I was silently processing this information. My grandfather, arriving to all I knew in the whole world, Cadiz.

"I got on okay after that. I don't know what I would have done without the nuns. And then the monks. They were all so good to me. One of the nuns took me the second evening I was there and opened a grammar book. She taught me my first Spanish words. Say this and this and hello and how are you and what time is it. All that kinda thing. I would play them tunes in the big room where they sat in the evening after their prayers. And oh my word, did they have a building programme?" He whistled through his teeth, shaking his head back and forth. "They'd had a fire in '36, so there was a lot of work for me. And no shortage of potatoes it seemed to pay me."

He shook his head again. "All the way to Spain and working for potatoes. And there on the very peseta, Franco's coat of arms and on another one the earlier Spanish coat of arms. And 'twas all new to me, Jesus. 'Twas all learning. And if I thought life was dull and slow in Cork, I got my wish for something else. I shoulda wished it wasn't so far away though."

He looked down at the wood shavings in a pile on his boots, reached for a handful and let them slip through his fingers. "How quickly an oul' piece of nothing wood drifts far away and becomes something else entirely."

He handed me a dolphin. "Delfino. Graceful creature of the sea. Which I, let me tell you, was not."

∞

Mamá was of the first generation to teach as a lay person in the convent school, for the call to serve God as a sister had faded and, in truth, they were short of staff. There was an Irish nun who spoke very good Spanish, Sister Dolores, reasonably newly arrived when Mamá went up there. Sister Dolores taught me in my late primary years. Why a Wexford woman was in Cadiz I never asked. Full of enthusiasm for sewing and stitching, knitting and crochet, she thought both boys and girls should know these tasks. She was not so enthusiastic for physical education which I loved, so we fell foul regularly over my needle on the wrong side of a gingham square and being utterly unable to tell the difference between tacking and hemming. My final-year knitting project was in two distinct uneven fractions: the bit I had aspired to and the larger bit that Abuelita Rosa had completed in order that I not be flayed alive and that I would graduate to senior school.

I left junior school with a tremendous love of reading, of all sorts of books, and a commanding vocabulary in English and Spanish, for which I owe Sister Dolores eternal thanks. That and a swathe of Catholic hymns which regularly come to mind, or may be prompted upon hearing a chorus or church choir. She pounded on a piano key to keep us in tune or blew a note on a melodica to start us off. My mother much later commented on how she could hear the broad Wexford accent from three rooms away. "No, no, no, NOT flat!" As for the tales of the rebellious Irish against the dreaded Sassenach in Wexford, we had them in bucket loads. The Irish 1798 rebellion was her personal soap box; I think perhaps she fought it alone and came back especially to tell us. Even if a history period started in Rome or Madrid or our own Nationalists or Fascists, it finished in New Ross or Vinegar Hill. Perhaps this was the origin of her regular, most profound prayer, Jesus, Merry, St. Joseph.

My mother was the junior teacher everyone remembers; her softness, her quiet way, her likability. She would make mathematics a song, spelling a game, history a drama, geography a story. She had enough Catholicism to satisfy the sisters and the bishop, but not so much to sour the children. And she sang. And she played music. Wasn't that a gift to any school? She taught me when I was six and seven. I truly remember being in awe; this is my mother I thought. MY mother and all of these children are NOT hers! I have to share her? I rebelled somewhat and had crying fits and sulks.

"Jesús," she told me firmly, "there is only one child in that school that comes home with me, only one child that I kiss good night, that I kiss good morning, that comes to the market with me on Saturday and Mass on Sunday. On Monday when we go to school again all the other children have a little bit of me. Just this … ." She pinched her thumb and forefinger together in front of my nose. "Just this, is all they get of me. But you get THIS." She opened her arms wide and I ran into them, and sweeping me up to her, she whispered, "In every big thing that is wrong, there is a little thing that is right. That is what you look for."

∞

I am strong, I am of strong build—good bones, Abuelita Rosa said. Teachers would ask me to lift, or carry, or do odd jobs. Strong and reliable, my middle names. I was also tall. "Jesús Josephus will just … ," was a catch phrase I heard more than once, usually from my own mother as she volunteered my physical abilities, if not my willingness.

In the old convent in Cadiz, I regularly did errands for one of the elder nuns, often taking me from my classes or my meal breaks. Of course they all knew Sean was my grandfather and they all knew Sean. We were muted and compliant for it was a different time then; there were no job descriptions or insurance laws that said a student couldn't carry a box of papers or books up three flights of stairs. "Gracias. Momento por favor," she said, and to my stunned, silent horror she lifted one side of her long skirts to reveal copious quantities of white material underneath, which I took to be her equivalent of Sean's britches. Petticoats or slips or such like. I stared, mesmerised, and after the longest moments of rustling and fishing about she gleefully produced an orange. "Ah! Gracias."

My strength of course was unknown to me: What teenager knows themself? I just was, or was there, a human being in the world, learning about life and school, ducking and weaving all that was thrown at me. I went to the Shotokan Karate Club, only because it was there and something to do. Rodriguez came along and we pretended we were Bruce Lee, jumping off walls and crates on the quayside, rolling off Roman Amphitheatre remains in our black Moroccan leather jackets, tight jeans, and sneakers. In the dojo I liked the training, we were also muted and compliant. We accepted it. I liked the discipline, and I was always good at instructions and following commands. Abuelita Rosa had shown me my body, how it works, my anatomy, my sees-tems, so the application of martial arts came easily: block, deflect, strike, attack, and defence. There were Americans from the base: dee-fen-se they called it, making three syllables. Rodriguez stayed for a few early grading belts, then he drifted away one summer to the bike park. I stayed in the dojo, drinking in the language, the commands, and thus I found my strength without knowing it. I was strong mentally, physically lithe and flexible, fast and fit. I doubt if any fifteen-year-old is self-aware. We do not see ourselves.

In my travelling years I have stayed lean and long and strong. Able, capable. Able to manage a heavy backpack into an overhead bin, or onto the top of an African bus. Able to pause a Canadian minivan driver on the overnight run from Montreal to Boston and say, "Your luggage load requires rebuilding, Monsieur, or we will be crushed." So somewhere I assumed strength and ability and a confidence that grows with it. I say this only insofar as it has assisted me through life.

I wear large in a pullover or T-shirt or jacket. Not XL, not medium, for all of the large is in my height. I am six feet tall exactly. A precise precision my father would say. He too, was six feet tall in his prime, until those intervertebral discs relented with age and I remained above him. He liked Imperial more than decimal but knew every weight and measure to the zillionth, sizing things with his eye, apportioning proportion, soothing his military mind. I am unlike him in this respect, for my mind favours my mother's inexactness, her man-ya-na as her Cork cousins would laugh, mañana. Tomorrow, it suits me. I am like my father in build, in skin tone and in colouring; more brown now than black of hair but blue-eyed not brown. It is a less than usual combination in southern climes to be blue-eyed and brown-skinned and it has been to my advantage in the travelling world, for I am immediately of nowhere, uncategorisable other than loosely Caucasian.

Abuelita Rosa was a steady presence through my adolescence, with her reminders of how important it is to stay healthy, to respect the myriad happenings within my skin on a constant basis, even at rest and sleep. Her hands would clap together, "Oye, oye," she would crow, "sit and eat, sit and eat, stop and chew, slowly, slowly, make it like water in your mouth." Then, running her hand from the throat to her navel, she would croon in a sing-song voice, "Take it slow, your eating system for all of your life. No exchange, you wear it out too soon. Part exchange, not so simple," her finger wagging at me, "and costs you mucho, mucho. The business of eating, no thing else going on in your head while you chew."

She taught me how my body works. "Every individual see-stem makes up the whole. In here," she says, pointing to her mouth, "travel very long way through here." She ran her hand along her upper body, "Out here," pointing to her bum. "Mind what you ingest, Jesús."

Rosa mixed almond and orange oil flavoured with cinnamon. She would knead my big leg muscles after training, cooing soothing noises while she talked about cleansing and clearing, moving waste, igniting electrical charges in my sees-tems.

I would nod and drowse and sleep the sleep of the dead.

"Jesús, Jesús," she would croon, "lighter, lighter on the foots, tread gently the earth for she feels your every step and you have so many more to make." Her hands intuitively on my feet, pressing, moving from bone to bone. "From here," she says, feeling the top of my big toe, "all the way to here," working her deft fingers along the arch to the heel. "This is your spine too. This maps your body, your organs, your bloods, your lee-quits. Always mind the foots."

It was only in later years that I learned where she had accrued her vast knowledge, to me always beyond that expected of a well-experienced nurse.

It was in '86, after the burial of Mama Tia. Mamá, Abuelita Rosa, and I were en route from the chapel at the convent to Casa des Angeles. We had taken a ride in a funeral car to near Plaza Viudas, when Rosa had asked to walk the remainder. My father had travelled ahead of us with Tia's caring couple, Eva and Micha, who would serve drink and food to guests, including customers of the taberna and Naval Base personnel, colleagues of my father and Abuelita Rosa.

Stopping suddenly near Calle San José, Abuelita Rosa clasped her hands in prayer and bowed over them before opening her eyes and arms in greeting to a gentleman who was crossing the plaza. "Rosa, Rosa, Rosa! Amor mío!" he called.

They embraced, murmuring with warmth and tears. Mamá stood slightly aside to give them time to make their greetings, smiling broadly, respectfully, watching her mother in an adult place that was seemingly unconnected to either of us. She then stepped forward as the gentleman reached for her hands and shook them warmly.

"Ah María, hermosa hija. Bellas damas."

Mamá, still smiling, responded, "Mucho tiempo, Dr. Zhao."

I remained aside. These were my dearest mother and grandmother with someone whose name I had often heard, yet had met only a handful of times.

"Esto es Jesús," my mother stated simply. I smiled at the man, shook his hand. "Encantado de conocerte."

"Ah Jesús, Jesús. It has been too long." He looked up at me, holding me by the hand, and we paused briefly, unspeaking, smiling, our eyes fixed on each other. It seemed he could see my soul. "Jesús. Just splendid. How tall! You got that from your father."

His accent was American, his ethnicity Eastern, his Spanish perfect.

"Come with us, Dr. Zhao," my mother was saying, explaining that Daniel was at the taberna and we were returning to funeral guests. But he was not to be persuaded; our meeting would be another day.

"Amor mío, Rosa." He kissed her hand and stepped away, blowing kisses as he departed.

There was silence between us. Mamá linked arms with her mother, squeezing her close.

"Es hermoso."

"Sí. Es hermoso."

And that was that, for now.

∞

"Abuelita Rosa?" I sat beside her at a quieter part of the taberna. The funeral was in full swing; Mamá played the fiddle, two more musicians flew along with her, on a mandolin and guitar. Someone beat a bodhrán. There was much whooping and cat-calling as my mother swept them in with her eyes before returning her gaze to the fiddle neck that demanded her concentration. A Greek fisherman puffed on a harmonica.

"Abuelita? Dr. Zhao?"

"Dr. Zhao?" She chuckled warmly. "What is it you wish me to tell you, Jesús?" She sighed deeply then laughed again. "Hombre hermoso. The beautiful man." Dipping her finger in her sherry glass, she put it to her mouth and sucked delicately at the taste. Alcohol was not usually in my grandmother's day.

"Ah! The most extraordinary human being. It is from he I learned the sees-tems, the lee-quits, the chi." She shrugged. "The flow, the energy of being alive. Nursing was just reading libros de texto and feeling for el pulso and looking at the colour, and then Dr. Zhao came to the hospital. After the second war. He came to us from America, San Francisco. His family went there from northern China. He knew everything of Western medicine but also of Eastern. He knew what to press on suela de su pie. Here." She clasped the underside of her foot in her hand.

"Sole of your foot."

"Sí, so your em, las tripas, bubbling would calm down."

"Nausea, indigestion?"

"Sí. What to stroke in round like so, like a clock so the pain departs. I see him, hmm, el gopecito?"

"Tap." I tapped the table top with my finger.

"Sí, sí on the skin here," she pressed her four fingers below her right ribcage, "outside the appendix, young sailor who in the face, turned red, like el tomate, then vomited. But no more pain. That was Dr. Zhao, una y cada vez."

"Every time."

She ran her damp finger around the rim of the sherry glass until it hummed. I smiled. It was something Abuelo Sean asked me to do as a child, to make me laugh because he would say, "I'm tuning the concertina now to your sound."

"Our bodies are sin costuras. What is that word?"

"Seamless. No joining."

"Sí, seamless. He show me this with acupuncture, shiatsu, bone and sinew and muscle, where does one stop and the next start? Nowhere. One become the other. What does your heart know of your kidneys? Everything. Every little bit is together as one. We are a whole."

"So you learned your medicine from Dr. Zhao?"

"Sí Jesús." She stopped and tasted some more sherry, then smiled coyly at me. "But a bit more too."

I snorted on my mouthful of beer. "Rosa!" I actually was surprised, for it had never occurred to me that there had been anyone in her life except Abuelo Sean.

"Oh Jesús!" she laughed at my astonishment. "Why you surprise? I was solo, hmm, fifty-something when your grandfather smoked himself to his, el lecho de muerte, sí, bed for death." She tutted and shook her head, her face darkening. "He would not listen, Jesús. For nearly twenty years I say do not smoke those things, they will kill you. And for the next fifteen, I did not say again." Her lips pursed defiantly.

"And you know? I tell you, a man who smokes like that and does not want to hear, he wants to die. Or a man who drinks like that," she gestured to the bar where Pedro Martinez weaved unsteadily to an Irish reel, "he wants to die. Quiere beber hasta que muera." She shook her head darkly. "John James, no tanto beber. Not so much beer. He needs his hands and here," she tapped her head, "for his work. His music." Her fingers played the air at concertina width. "So he punished his lungs instead." She crossed herself and kissed her thumb, shaking her head somewhat angrily.

"Cabra vieja obstinada. Idiot."

I was silenced by this outburst for I had never heard Abuelita Rosa speak ill of my grandfather. I put away my childish memories to be an adult in the lives of adults I had inhabited in a child's way. "His stubbornness angers you even now?"

She looked at me. "I loved your grandfather. But he was never really, completamente, for me. He kept a part of him en otro lugar, elsewhere. Somewhere in his music. His Irish stories that he did not tell me. Para mí, no. He gave it to María. After he passed on, I went to my work. No one say *Stay at home*. No one say *Retire*. So? Lou and I worked together for more years at the Base, then he retired, bought la casa in old town, not so far from here. He lived sometimes San Francisco, sometimes in Cadiz."

She paused, silence sitting between us, she remembering, me processing this new vista. I sipped my beer and caught my mother's eye, as she lay her fiddle carefully on a red silk scarf in its cracked wooden case. She released the tension in the bow, winked at me, and picked up the concertina.

"Abuelita Rosa, I love you dearly. You are the wisest, most wonderful grandmother anyone could have. I also loved my grandfather, but I was still a child."

"Oh, Jesús, he loved you too. What happen in my life after he died, was mine. No secret. You were a child, then teenager, young adult, sometimes not here, then here. I chose not to speak of Dr. Zhao when he retired from hospital. But we did not drift apart. En los últimos años, just in the last years, when he stayed long time in America, his family. Then life … whoosh … changes. Moves on."

She watched Mamá playing. "See how she throws her head like your grandfather? Mi hermosa niña." She played again with her sherry. "It was, la sopresa to meet with him on street, Jesús. Lou. I did not expect it. Han sido tres o cuatro años since we met. Three, four years."

I nodded.

She gestured towards Mamá. "I tell you the story now, Jesús. María was fourteen, fifteen, no bleeding. No menses. No pains, no difficulties, just simply no bloods. The doctor at base say it's okay, okay, el tiempo but after some times, I knew maybe it is not okay. Lou, Dr. Zhao he is in the U.S., on leave. He had been to Korea just then, a hospital ship, the big war there." She shook her head again. "Terrible things. Those wars. He suffered so much, he cried, many times, for mucho tiempo, muchos años. Trying to, em, ayudar, em, assist all those poor leetle soldiers and sailors. All those big men in suits and governments they are throwing away young lives. For what? Pfff." She snapped her fingers.

I breathed slowly. She wiggled her finger, furious with history, in her sherry.

"Lou came back to Cadiz, María fifteen, nearly sixteen. I say him my worries, he examines her. My lovely baby girl, mi hermosa niña. Just something not right in her sees-tem. Here." Abuelita Rosa tapped the bridge of her nose.

I frowned at first, then remembered. "Pituitary gland?"

"Sí. Amen-horrea. No hormone come, no menses. Lou, he says, I needle her but you cannot see me. Ask Francesca to be the nurse. Your grandfather take our lovely girl to Lou one night, quiet, at the hospital, and he use the needles. I stay home. Make bread and pray."

"Acupuncture?"

"Sí, sí acupuncture. But he not want me to see. Francesca, she tell me, lots of needles all over the face, the feets, the spine. Then he tell me rub here," rubbing the top of her thumb nail, "and same on foots, big toes. And here." She pointed to her heel, the back of her sandal. "Here. So I use the oils and the prayers. And your grandfather he say, 'Rosa you mad, and that Lou is mad too.' But he went to the nuns, lit the candles and prayed at their altar. And Lou was not mad at all, Jesús, for here you are."

I laughed. "So I have Dr Zhao to thank for my existence?"

She nodded. "Lou Zhao. He knew. Dos, maybe tres menses, then a little bloods. Then he come to the house and he give María el regalize, what is this?"

"Liquorice?"

"Sí, liquorice to chew. He put small needle in her feets and thumbs and he rub round like clock, here to here." She pointed to her navel, down to the pelvic bone. "Then slowly, maybe takes another year, bloods, every month."

I looked across the taverna at my mother, who lifted her head, raised her eyebrows and smiled at us. "For Jesús," she called to the crowd, as she broke into "Jesus Merry Joseph." Through the smoky air, I winked at her knowingly, for Mamá had written this tune for me when I was still a child at school. I asked her one day why Sr. Dolores often shouted 'Jesus, Merry St. Joseph' if she got irritated or cross. I thought it was personal to me; that I might have been the harbinger of her fury. Mamá laughed and explained it was a form of frustrated prayer, so we made up a song there and then, for me to think of whenever the Irish nun started to overheat. Mamá had set it to the tempo of a reel.

"Your father, Jesús, he knows this, but also he does not know how. He was being the young sailor just then, living on the Naval Base. Then helping Mama Tia here in taberna. María and he, always together when children, nearly together later, sometimes alone, sometimes she with her friends, he with his. But no amor until later, until he bigger sailor. She come from teaching college, in Seville. Amor espera. Love waited."

I did not know this of my parents. I had not asked either of them about their courtship. "And there was another love for Mamá in Seville, at teaching college?" I queried her.

"Yes, Antonio, muy buen chico. Very nice boy from Nerja. They did the amor together," she smiled at the recollection, "but I think perhaps it was always amor for Daniel."

I raised my glass of beer. "To Lou then?"

Abuelita Rosa smiled at me. She stuck her finger in the sherry glass then raised it high. "To Lou. And you. For you truly are, Jesús, el milagro."

"Sí, Abuelita. Every day of my life is a miracle. I have you, my parents, and so much more."

She smiled again and played with her sherry glass before taking my hand in hers and clasping it to her breast. Pulling me towards her, she whispered into my ear. "No, Jesús. I mean this. Everything about that time was so special. From the moment María knew she was carrying you and Lou says 'a Christmas baby. Expect a child on December 25th or soon afterwards.' And he say to me. 'This child Rosa, this child is special for this world.' He knew, Jesús."

I frowned, not understanding. She released my hand to her lap but kept me close to her, continuing to whisper.

"Lou say to me, this is different, Rosa; somehow this child is different. Un propósito especial, a special purpose. And remember Jesús, this is long time ago, long long before Lou and me, hmmm, you know, come together. I did not know why he said that but when you are growing and being the child, I knew he was right, Jesús. I knew you were different, you are especial to the world. You have a message to carry."

She sat back momentarily before pulling me to her once more.

"All you need to know, everything is inside you, Jesús. Inside every cell of you," she tapped her breastbone. "You are born with the knowing all the things. All the things you need. It is, la tarea, ola, hmm, what's this?"

"Task, job."

"Sí, your task, your job to teach others. To show them. You need to remember all that you know. You need to learn más y más, more, more. You need to keep well, eat well, sleep well, train your mind well. And you need to trust tú mismo. Yourself. When a question comes up, up from here," she pulled upwards from her stomach to her throat, "stop. Stop, listen for answer. Trust, trust that this is correcto. You have been born to show others the truth of Life."

I was unsure, but this was Abuelita Rosa. She had always spoken the truth to me. "I will," I told her solemnly, "I promise."

"It is just amor makes the universe. Love. Comprende? If you get, hmm, ola, greed, anger, or hatred or la posesíon, it no lasts long. It soon, hmm, eh, desplomarse."

"Collapse. Fall down."

"Sí. Sí. Collapse. El amor ser el solo camino. Love is the only way. No te olvidamos. No te olvidamos."

Never forget. Oh if I could recall a fraction of what she taught me. Abuelita Rosa, life lessons and learning the wisdom of those who have lived. She sowed the seed of knowledge that, deep inside my soul, was really the Real Jesus.

∞

Aceptarte tal como eres es el primer paso y el último paso.
Tú tienes que ser quien tú eres.
Lo que debieras ser no es importante.
Quien sea que seas, eres único.
El universo te ha hecho así
La Divindad te ha hecho así.

Accepting yourself as you are is the first step and the last step.
You have to be who you are.
What you should be is not important.
Whoever you are, you are unique.
The Universe has made you that way.
Divinity has made you that way.

I shared this Buddhist sutra by Sri Amma Bhagavan with Abuelita Rosa much later, much, much later when I was an older adult, for I had somehow absorbed all her words by osmosis. Divinity had given me the greatest springboard from which to step onto the stage of my life.

∞

Cadíz 1986

In the way of the same Divine Universe, the accidental encounter prompted both Abuelita Rosa and Dr. Zhao to reconnect, their journey together was now also to be mine.

"Come with me, Jesús." It was a command, not a question. Abuelita Rosa was outside the door of our house at a very early hour. I had been to the sea and was washing salt from my face in the yard, preparing to sit for meditation. "Now?" I responded.

"Sí. We will see Lou."

I did not question her. She was not one to ever question me in the unfolding of my young life. We walked together in the early silence, the sharp air of spring, starlings chattering busily on a line, the city awakening.

"He will teach you. You will learn all that I know, all that he knows, and that is a buen comienzo."

I laughed. "A good start? Pensé que había comenzado. I thought I had already begun?"

If I had begun my learning in life, Dr. Zhao's house became my college. My library, my dojo, my laboratory for the next two years, my academy. He took my young adult self and built upon my school and martial arts training, studying deep anatomy, physiology, biomechanics, kinetics, the science of movement, of physics, the invertebrate world. We practiced Qigong, Tai-Chi, the fields of yoga, bodyworks. We looked at organised religions, their sources and courses, their influences, their parallel flow with health and healing. My life, my head, filled with new knowledge, my body bending to new shapes, my spirit still, like filling a deep pool in old Cadiz. I learned and, as I learned, Dr. Zhao would laugh and say, "Thank you, Jesús, I am re-learning or I am learning anew."

In the way of a teacher, he examined my knowledge, set me tasks, made me work at the disciplines I was not drawn to. "The wise learn the habits of the fools. Do not just read what you agree with; learn to read what you disagree with more, to understand."

Dr. Zhao's physical stature and mannerisms often reminded me of the character of Mr. Miyagi in "The Karate Kid." The situation was not dissimilar, although I was spared the physical tasks of waxing a yard full of cars or painting long sections of timber fencing. He was quite tickled, bowing deeply, hands in prayer, when I shared my thoughts with him.

Behind my studies, I might hear Sibelius playing his second symphony. I would be thrown smatterings of his biography: an isolationist in Finland, another victim of wine-sipping and smoking. I might hear Jean-Michel Jarre synthesising "Rendez-Vous" and I remember how Lou had been moved, recalling the NASA connection to Jarre's concert in Houston—astronaut Ron McNair should have played the saxophone at that concert but was killed in the Challenger crash, in January 1986.

Perhaps it would be Webern's Cello Sonata, found abandoned in an attic in 1965. Or I might appear at the door and be greeted with a life history lesson on Shostakovich, culminating in why he composed "String Quartet No. 8." Or, without speaking, I would be directed to my yoga mat and we would descend to that place between being asleep and being awake in yoga nidra. The breadth of the man was astounding. The variety of my accumulating knowledge was breathtaking and I absorbed it all readily.

When Dr. Zhao travelled back to San Francisco, which he did three or four times in my twenty-eight-month tenure, I continued to visit his house to learn, or maybe to water his aloe vera plants and fig trees. I recall him quoting Christopher Columbus: "Four vegetables are indispensable for the well-being of man—wheat, the grape, the olive, the aloe. The first nourishes him, the second raises his spirit, the third brings him harmony, and the fourth cures him." Then he laughed when I para-phrased it to the acronym W-O-G-A. Wheat, olive, grape, aloe.

I would cast my sleeping mat upon his porch and lie there to absorb his absent energy. He would telephone while I was there and tell me of his America sojourn, ask me about his plants, the daytime temperatures, or the timer on the nightlight, such little things. The cat didn't belong to him, as he laughingly told me. He belonged to the cat. While he was away, someone else belonged to the cat.

"I have sons in the world, Jesús, three engineers—roads, electronics, and computers. I have a daughter who is a skin surgeon. Their mother was a domestic science teacher and a gifted pianist. They all have different knowledge to me. We all share a love of food, Monopoly, and stimulating conversation. And, of course, California wine. I have lived for seventy-two years, Jesús, and I am lucky to have nine grandchildren—from fifteen years all the way down to three. I eagerly watch their interests unfold."

I remember him just then, winding a thread through the gyroscope on his desk, setting it to spin and placing it on the head of a rook chess piece. We watched silently, no sound but the hum of the spin, the vibration of the air conditioner, and the faint sounds from the street outside.

"Simple. Greek, you know, gyroscope: gûros—circle, and skopéo—to look. Input, output, spin. Simple, but so much knowledge, so many places to be useful.

∞

"Your body is not a vehicle to carry you around the earth."

Dr. Zhao was easy to listen to, a quiet California drawl, carefully chosen words without pauses, ems or ums, and too old for the insidious interjection of like or so, that had crept into everything American and subsequently worldwide. A clear and concise communicator, obviously comfortable with his knowledge and in having it questioned or challenged.

"It is not some static place in which we live. It is the place of wisdom and magic," he continued.

This was early in my studies, maybe the first weeks or so. Dr. Zhao was pouring coffee for a mid-morning break while I sliced warm bread from his bake oven. Handel's "Water Music" played high above us from the Kilpsch KG-4 twin speakers of an American hi-fi system. I used to look fondly at this engineering marvel, for we barely had a radio and TV in our house and a soft-eject twin tape deck was my sole luxury item. Abuelita Rosa was with us this day, as she was on occasional days when my studies would often become a discussion class. Lou would invite her to choose a topic and we would begin from there.

"Your body is a recognisable form for others to identify you. It is the friend of the soul, not of the personality. A network of fascia glides and slides beneath your skin, moving you through life. Every day when you know how, you can listen to hear what it tells you. It is a masterful triumph of universal engineering, that is your body."

He took my hand. "See here? Pink nail-bed, strong healthy nails. The worriers and anxious chew their nails, pick away at themselves, their own self. Clear skin, strong hair. The nails, the strong bones, the hair, they are our presence, who we are. Skin is our interface with the world around us. Hair carries the memories, sometimes we need to let them go to make more room. Yet some cultures do not ever cut hair."

He stood up and lifted my own hair from the nape of my neck. I laughed.

"That's right where I feel Abuelo Sean, Dr. Zhao, when he has something to say to me, or tell me he is about."

Lou leaned into me. "Ah! Next time tell him I said Hi, and that I am most definitely looking after his lovely wife."

Abuelita Rosa clucked and tutted, then playfully pushed at Dr. Zhao. "Yo no! He will say she is not needing the looking after."

We laughed together.

"See? Strong spine. The skull on cee-one of the spine, the atlas, neatly, beautifully fitting into cee-two, the axis to form … ?"

"Atlantoaxial joint."

"Right. And allows you to? With some help of course from all the surrounding tissue, muscles, nerves, et cetera."

"Nod in agreement, or shake in disagreement."

Rosa chimed in, "El punto inicial. That is just the beginning."

"But perfectly formed. Perfectly engineered." Lou nodded, lowering my hair again and laying his hand upon my head.

"You are a collection of integrated parts, integrated at a level of seamless genius that the human race dismisses daily, or fails to comprehend. I cannot understand why every child in junior-school does not start with these lessons. More than any book-learning, letters or numbers, they need to understand their own bodies, how they function so supremely." He paused, his feet tapping a rhythm on the floor. "Did you know that your autonomic nervous system automatically controls your breathing, so you actually change which nostril you use every ninety seconds or thereabouts? This is a chemically controlled process that we are unaware of. Just one such example of," he shrugged, "what can I say? Perfection? Exquisite perfection?" He returned to his seat.

"When I was in junior-school, then junior high, we had physical education four times a week. We were encouraged to join teams, clubs, societies. This taught us tolerance, kindness, praise for others through teamwork, sharing, encouragement. Those who did not shine academically could be outstanding in sports or another genre. They too, could glow with success and garner praise from their peers. Enhance their own self-esteem, you know? We carried this to high school and then into life. Somewhere between then and this, someone, probably in a suit in an office, decided it was better to learn abstract math, or graphs of social geography, than it was to be loving and kind to your little classmates." He shook his head wonderingly then leaned towards me.

"If I can be wide-eyed at the genius of a combustion engine, or the genius of an engineered super-structure constructed from applied math, how can I miss the genius of the human sum of parts?" He sat back again in his chair, watching me as I moved. I nodded, thinking of my axis and atlas performing their primary function of allowing my skull to move. I lifted the milk jug to my coffee cup.

"Now what?" asked Lou. "What did your body need to do there?"

"Em, well," I shrugged, anxious not to appear unknowledgeable, "process many bytes of data before functioning, then functioned?"

"Exactly. So emotion engages requiring action, brain engages requesting action, muscles respond producing action, senses inform brain, brain monitors action, action is performed until emotion is satisfied."

"As in, that is enough milk in my coffee? So all of that in a six-, maybe seven-second performance?"

"Right. That's exactly right." He seemed pleased with my response.

"Every day you are using the sees-tems, Jesús. You know?" Rosa chimed in. "Lo que sucede, when you sit down? Stand up? Eat? Excretar los residuos? All the basic human functions. Mirar esto, look." She stood up.

Lou continued. "Okay, Rosa will raise her right hand above her head. Ignoring the mind and brain functions, data processing, et cetera; which muscle will respond first?"

"Em," I faltered, scrambling in my memory for an answer, "I would guess, the muscles of the shoulder joint? Deltoid, supraspinatus, biceps brachii, also?"

"How about guessing tibialis anterior?" Lou smiled.

"Ah! Balance correction?"

"Exactly. To raise her right arm while in a standing position, Rosa's brain will tell her feet to first correct her balance. In a single microsecond. Isn't that just something?" He paused momentarily, lost in the perfection of this moment, this revelation. "Now," he said as he leant forward a little and clapped his hands. "Tell me all the things you do for yourself?"

"For me? What do you mean? My activities?"

"Indeed Jesús! You know, tell me your daily routine?"

"I sleep well, I eat well, Abuelita Rosa always tells me if I am too fast or too busy. I swim in the sea. I do my exercises, my yoga, my meditation. Not every day but four times or so in a week.

I no longer do karate, but I remember all the training and the stretching exercises."

"And any ills? Ailments?"

"No, very little. I have a fungal infection between two of my small toes that does not seem to clear up. I have a recurring something-not-right in my right quadricep muscle. It pulls on my knee."

"So, start with this fact, present in any school of medicine. Your body wants to be right, always wants to be well. Your body does not want to be out of sync, or in pain. Pain is telling you something is incorrect."

"My sees-tem is unhappy." I laughed. "Abuelita Rosa told me this when I was twelve? Thirteen?"

"That's right!"

"And Lou teaches me." Rosa declared.

"Many of the answers are in Eastern thought; Western thought likes to fix symptoms. A symptom is what? An indication of something else, often deeper, or seemingly unrelated. Skin issues are usually the body's last line of trying to tell you something is upsetting you."

"And it is very específico. Exact." Rosa nodded. "Small toe, kidney and bladder, insecurity, ansioso, this is?"

"Anxious," I replied, slightly puzzled, "but I don't think I am?"

"It is very specific, Jesús," Dr Zhao continued. "Anxious or insecure may just be this particular phase of your life, not a personality trait. Just right at this time, maybe relating to your path after school, your writing, things that niggle at you. Your meditative or yoga body may be saying *Stop worrying*, but your brain is saying *Worry, worry. What will you do?*"

"That's about it, Dr. Zhao, that's just what it is like."

"And skin, weeping?—Why am I sad? Itching?—Who is under my skin? Hot, burning?—Why am I irritated? Why am I burning?"

I recalled just then as he spoke, recounting to my mother the woes of unfair judging in one of my many karate competitions—an errant judge who made a call against me. She had nodded knowingly through my tale then merely asked of me, "Well are you mad, sad, glad or bad?"

"What? What use is all of that?" I queried her furiously. "What is bad?"

"Bad. Afraid, Jesús, fearful. Know how you feel, for healing truly comes from feeling and only you are responsible for all that you are." I smiled now at the memory. All this wisdom, a constant in my life. How could I worry about anything?

"And your quads?" Lou continued. "Large muscle body between hip and knee joint, too big to be specific, so you need to examine exactly which part of the quad is causing problems. And of course the symptom may be in the thigh and knee, but the origin may be in the hip or pelvis. Or in the feet, in the gait. If the hip is restricted, the knee will try to compensate. Palthi posture for meditation may irritate the insertion of the sartorius muscle here." He pressed onto the inside of my lower leg, below the knee joint.

"When they sit down to eat in India they generally sit cross-legged, which is also of course a posture in yoga. Padmasana calms the mind and applies pressure to the lower spine, which may facilitate relaxation. Helps digestion." Lou paused, Rosa intervened.

"Injury, pains look at left side, right side. Male or female, inside we are both."

I nodded. I had understood this concept from her many years ago.

"Hips? Pelvis? Stability and security. Rock-solid core of our own self. Base chakra of energy flow. But also the reservoir of negative emotion. It's where we store our ills with the world and others."

I paused in my thought and closed my eyes. "I have very much to learn. I think there will be many coffees!" The enormity of their knowledge filled the air around me.

"I will be your teacher, Jesús," Lou spoke softly. "We will teach you. We need someone young to know and Rosa here knows more than I know."

Rosa lowered her head as she brushed my cheek with her hand. "I am always the student. I am always doing the learning, every day. I read. I listen and look. I meditate the information that comes to me. From the world. I breathe and ask cuestino la verdad? Where is the truth? You know this, Jesús."

"Observe, listen, learn." Lou smiled at her and took her hand. "My beautiful Rosa. What a pleasure it has been sharing with you."

I held my breath. Half-breath. Sip of coffee, pause, breathe. The hair was prickling on my neck, tears pricking in my eyes. Abuelo Sean, "my little love," he used to say. But he left her, he and his cigarillo musical lungs. My heart beat for him. I knew he would he happy for her, wherever he was.

"It is too easy to follow The Thought Collective." Lou was standing now, adjusting the volume of the hi-fi, changing the compact disc in the drive.

"In 1955, U.S. President Eisenhower had a heart attack. He went against his advisors and made it public, said, 'Stop smoking, cut down on fats and cholesterol.' There's a long intervening story of physical and other ailments, then he died in '69 of heart disease." The room filled to the sound of Karen Carpenter—clear, beautiful sound—"We've Only Just Begun."

"And so began this raging war about fat and cholesterol. Ancel Keys in the U.S. said fats, et cetera, were the baddies; John Yudkin in the U.K. said sugar was the killer. And, as sure as eggs are eggs, the food industry waged in as it suited them. So in the U.S. they shaved off the fats and piled on the sugar. Then sugar became sweeteners—aspartame, saccharin, sorbitol. And everyone believed someone, or of course followed The Thought Collective. Why?"

His question caught me off guard so I quickly shrugged, scrambling for a reply. "Propaganda? Misinformation? Safety in numbers?"

Dr. Zhao nodded. "And opposing forces, personalities, everyone with their own agenda. That," he shook his finger at me, "and this is before mass communication of thought, other than radio or newspaper. TV was only just beginning to carry some weight. So that, and the burgeoning inability of people to read widely, think carefully, and form their own opinions."

I nodded my understanding. I had no concept right then of how much more nodding my understanding I would do, in Dr. Lou Zhao's University of Life.

"Sometimes there are tribalistic instincts, behaviour patterns from family origins, or division of political or ideological tribalism. Folks learn to suppress their thoughts, avoid conflict, condition their responses to what they learned growing-up, avoid competition, confrontation, or be passive, passive-aggressive. All that stuff." He waved his hand vaguely to the sky.

"What I need you to know before we really do this, Jesús, is that you need to listen to your self. You can read anything you like in this room, you can hear me pontificate on any subject on those shelves." His hand swept an arc around him. Rosa laughed from the kitchen. He called to her. "Hey! You are not here to wash up coffee cups. You too are here to teach."

She came through wiping her hands on a towel which she playfully flapped in my direction. "You have nothing to worry about, Lou. Jesús has been listening in here," she tapped her head, "and here," she tapped at her heart, "for all of the years. Since I remember the first words we shared." She kissed me on the head.

Lou smiled. I smiled. This would be a new dynamic for my grandmother and me, for her and him. I felt the hair at the nape of my neck stir again. I heard Abuelo Sean in my ear: "Now for you, Jesus. Aren't you the lucky one?" Karen Carpenter moved to another track, "Close to You."

"If you have, what?" Lou was saying, "Approximately a hundred trillion cells in your physical body, firing on electrical energy, electrical current, Jesús, if you have sees-tems that function every micro-moment keeping your physical and mental body running like a Swiss clock, then why does science say you have fifty percent junk DNA? Or that your appendix is no longer of any use? There is nothing junk about any part of you. You operate as a seamless whole. Unless you stop, reflect, meditate, listen, you will not hear the cause and will think treating symptoms will suffice. This is what happens in a large proportion of the world. You need to know, to tell them there is a better way."

"And know onion layers," Rosa reminded him.

"Onion layers?" Dr. Zhao looked at her quizzically.

"Nuestros cuerpos. Bodies, like an onion. We are layers. Physical outside, then etérico, astral, mental, el alma, el espíritu, et divino."

"Ah! Layers from skin to core. We are not just a bumbling, mumbling bag of tissue, Jesús. We are real to the world, we are real to the universe. Rosa's layers—physical, ethereal, astral, mental, soul, spirit, and Divine. Different frequencies."

There was a silence, a pause in all of our lives. I felt overwhelmed, out of my depth; but very quickly that feeling subsided, to be replaced with calm. A calm intent. Later Dr. Zhao was to tell me that all feelings last only seven to ten seconds, to be replaced by something else. When we learn to recognise them, accept them, then it is easier to react.

A dog barked out on the street, the passing sound of conversing voices like an equaliser graph, faint, faint, loud, louder, louder, loud, faint, fainter, fainter, silence.

"There is a living library, Jesús. Here, around us, if we choose to hear. We are wise beings, wise and knowing souls. We choose carefully where we are born, the blueprint we will follow, this inner knowing, this connection, it comes only from the heart." He placed both hands over his left breast. His eyes were closed. "Inner knowing, inner connection, always listening to your own truth. Never lonely, never afraid. We only do what brings us peace. Everything else is harmful to our selves. It is from here we begin now to learn."

I looked at Rosa. She smiled, nodded, placed her hands in prayer under her chin.

"Amen, Jesús."

Karen Carpenter moved along a groove to "It's Going to Take Some Time."

∞

I am of no faith per se. In my travels I have experienced them all, from the extreme to the benign. In my young adult education in Cadiz, I extensively read the history and beliefs of many, their foundation, their growth or decline, their role in the history of the world as it evolved and as we know it. I am aware of their place in everyday life, in the shaping of human-kind from the compassionate acts of mercy to the callous acts of violence in the name of faith. I have to remain mindful, of not engaging on occasions, of engaging carefully on others.

But I have also experienced the joy and freedom of discussion and expression, the exhilaration of debate, of acute learning from a human being with an opposing view. Communication without conflict, opinion without dogma. I have learned to disagree in a way that is instructive, constructive, respectful and kind. Oh above all else kind, kindness and compassion at all times. But agreement comes with heartfelt gratitude and joy.

I meditate, a practice I learned in my days of martial arts and continued through my early adult years, as I naturally evolved to practice gentler forms of discipline such as QiGong, Tai Chi, and yoga. I spent eight months in the mid-'80s in the Buddhist monastery of Thich Nhat Hanh in south-western France.

I have only twice found myself in meditative practice in the presence of the Real Jesus, as Biddy McCarthy would say. At least that is what I have come to accept it must be, for the light is white but not blinding, the silence is peaceful but not mute. It is whisper-like, and as I journey every fibre of my being feels alive. I have watched souls arrive, in a steady stream, sometimes in waves, sometimes alone. Every faith or creed has a death-related belief. Abuelo Sean told me the Irish Catholics believed that it took three days for the soul to depart the mortal body and travel to the Pearly Gates. Biddy laughs and says she would take at least twice as long as that because there would be so much news to catch up on along the way.

I have heard many faith or religiously instructed similarities. I like the three days concept, like the story of Jesus from burial to rising. In my meditation the souls are always peaceful, not whole like a human but an energy recognisable as a human form, presumably because that is how my mind needs to see them. Always they are surrounded by angels, guiding, minding them. Always they are ageless, having lost their earth-borne façades. Almost always they meet with other souls, perhaps those they knew in their incarnation who passed before them. The feeling is warm and always there is a soul departing as one arrives; in the out door, out the in door. There is calm, order, light. Always angels.

I think I see this to understand life on earth, not to be disillusioned or saddened by the act of death—be it natural, accidental, medical, criminal. It's a difficult image to convey when so many see death as a finality. It helps me to not become overwhelmed in my travels through stories, endless eons of war and outrage and protest. Humans have forever fought: what's yours, what's mine, where I draw the line that I own.

I continue to read the books of Thich Nhat Hanh, repeat his wisdom, his questioning words: When does the stream become the river, the river become the sea, the sea the cloud, the cloud the rain, the rain the stream? The eternal cycle.

I see Jesus watching, touching, murmuring, moving amongst them. Once a wave passed my unseeing eyes and I observed Jesus looking at the earth, suspended like a beach football. How do they think that this is what I meant? It seems so simple. Love one another. Do unto them as you would have them do unto you. Love God, whatever you perceive that to be, with all your heart and all your mind and all your bottom. I add that last bit for Philomena; Biddy would titter and say: "Oh you have enough bohhom for all of us, Philomena."

I see Buddha with Jesus. They embrace and remain close while they, well, while they nothing. They just are, as if their combined energy could change things like a catalytic force. The stream of souls move around them, through them, a swirling river of pure, white energy. After that particular meditation, I could not sleep for three days.

∞

Spain 1984–85

I enjoyed my studies at Dr. Zhao's, unique as the situation may have been. My school-friends were also learning: at university, teaching college, or el aprendizaje. I understood my journey was also an apprenticeship and, although not official, it was entirely suitable. As I reflect from later years, my life took its own course, its own rhythm, and I am fortunate not to have struggled against the flow.

My father had loudly and strongly voiced his concerns, preferring that I would attain a college degree than attend Dr. Zhao's on an informal basis. I had overheard or been party to several arguments between my parents on the matter, Mamá always finishing with "Jesús will be writing, Daniel. You know there is nothing else needed." Eventually, somewhat soothed by the confidence displayed by Mamá and Abuelita Rosa, he had withdrawn his complaints, but not without conditions. Despite the difficult and disharmonious time, in hindsight, his dissension was essential; I needed that strong voice of debate in order to give weight to my decision-making. It was otherwise easy for me, insofar as I had no other desires to proffer. Papá stomped about for quite some time, then finally acquiesced and nodded his support.

I had completed my secondary schooling and then my bachillerato, along with the general subjects, also studying anatomy, history, and art. I read what I could in English: My Great-Uncle Jerry, the Waterford guard, regularly sent me books that he thought I might like. John B. Keane, Frank O'Connor, Sean O'Casey, Maeve Binchy, and school books that belonged to his grandchildren. Philomena sent me history books, travel snippets from the newspapers, her children's poetry books as they became obsolete in the educational system. I practiced reading in English. I constantly consulted The *Oxford Dictionary of English Etymology*, edited by Mr. Charles Onions. Papá's sixteenth birthday present to me, always making me smile, for he had inscribed on the fly-leaf: Jesús, Onions for your writings and travels. My Love, Papá.

After school, I travelled within Spain, Galicia, Basque to the Pyrenees, through south-western France to the monastery of Thich Nhat Hanh in Dordogne. I studied Buddhist teachings there, working along with other lay members and monks of the sangha, building the kitchen gardens, planting the plum trees that eventually gave the monastery its name, Plum Village. Here I slowly deposited the aggressive martial art practice for a slower pace of movement. I released the combative muscular tension for a grace synonymous with a more natural flow.

It was here I truly learned to breathe. It was here I learned to pause and listen closely to the voices I heard, instructing me, directing me if necessary, those guiding lights from within. I learned to trust myself, to trust the wisdom of my own unfolding life.

∞

In my third month at Plum Village I was struggling, I was homesick, I was unsure of my presence in this place. Truly my work in the gardens was keeping me sane, keeping me grounded. The summer visitors had departed and I was invited to remain in autumn, preparing the ground for winter, saving seed for spring. In September, we would enter the 90-day Rains Retreat, what seemed to me a gruelling schedule of meditation, prayer, and dharma talks. This traditional retreat went back to the time of the Buddha, in 500-and-something, b.c., when monks could not travel from village to village because of the rains in northern India. They would spend the 90 days together praying, chanting, learning, gathering their energy for the months ahead.

I sat under the shade of the vine in a quiet corner of the monastery, contemplating an audience with Thay Nhat Hanh and requesting his blessing on my leave-taking. I understood completely that somehow my life was not mine, that every moment was Divine. My task is to decipher these moments. One of the lay sisters whom I had met once or twice passed by on a walking meditation. She smiled and I bowed over prayer hands to acknowledge her presence. On her next round, she diverted and came to sit with me. I smiled wanly for I was not sure I desired company. I could hear my mother, "In every big thing that is wrong, there is a little thing that is right. That is what you look for." I welcomed my companion.

"You don't look too happy?" Her accent was English.

"I am struggling with the concept of ninety days of retreat. I have had nearly that much time here already and I am unsure of whether I need to stay."

She nodded. "Have you somewhere to go?"

"Oh yes. My parents and grandmother are in southern Spain. I can go home."

"That is good then?"

"Yes, I am ready to see them again."

"So that was an easy discussion? Sounds like you have it sorted?"

I laughed. "Yes it does. Thank you."

She sat swinging her legs, her sandals flapping against the soles of her feet. "But?"

"But?"

"There's a but?"

I sighed. "Yes of course. That is just too simple an answer. A part of me wants to stay, to experience this. I do not think my life is destined to be a Buddhist monk, so this may be my time to learn. This may be the closest I get to the silence of learning my true self."

She nodded. We sat quietly, not a difficult thing to do in the largely silent monastery of Plum Village.

"My father was a diplomat in Vienna, Ugandan, like me, living the dream after Amin's regime. Jet-setting and hobnobbing. My mother had long since fled from his meteoric drinking lifestyle, leaving three of us with him. We were dispatched to English boarding schools. Only the best education, perfect English, this is your ticket from African hell he told us. I was seven years old." She plucked at the sleeve of her robe, her toes constantly lifting and falling in her sandals. Sometimes it is easier to tell a complete stranger your story, but it does not ease the tale.

"I wet my knickers on the flight home for the Christmas holidays. I was so terrified of him you know. Absolutely terrified. My brother Maz, all A's; Henry, all A's; and me? I got 'could work harder', 'could try harder', 'needs to pay attention'. I was seven years of age. He lined us up in his study, 'well done boys and you? You are just a stupid, silly girl, go and get a stick.' He beat me so badly I bled for three days."

I took her hand, which was now pulling a little harder at her sleeve. I held it carefully, hearing Abuelita Rosa the compassionate nurse, "Como un pájaro en un nido," like a bird in a nest.

"No mother, no mercy, Christmas in Vienna thank you very much. The maid tried to help me and he threatened to throw her out of the top window. Dear God, I was seven. Now I am thirty-seven and I am unwinding myself from this mess my parents made that I had to grow up in. I am a black African from Uganda, with an English public school education, living in a bed-sit in London and belonging absolutely nowhere."

The silence sat between us. "Maybe I could go home to your parents and grandmother and you could stay here?"

I looked at her. She was smiling wanly, then she laughed. "I'm kidding you. I need to stay here if I am to be ever, ever able to go anywhere, ever again." When she looked at me again, I was crying. Then she was crying. I put my arms around her and we cried together.

"How do you manage?" I asked her.

"One tiny step at a time."

"So a ninety day retreat is just one moment after the next with no thought for anything except the moment we are in?"

She nodded. "In my life, there is just this moment that you and I are sharing. I know I have somewhere to sleep, the bell calls me to prayer or dharma, to gather for a meal or tea, to meet the sangha. If I can manage for just a little while, not thinking about or hearing anything that has happened to me, then I know it is my own voice in my head and not the countless voices I have heard in the intervening thirty years. I know if I can do this, I will eventually be able to look at things differently."

"The sun sets, the sun rises."

"Every day. Regardless of who we are, or where we choose to be. We can choose the pain of it or see the beauty. Finally here I have the space to see the beauty, the pain diminishes."

We watch the sunlight on the vine leaves, dappling, dancing.

She laughed shortly. "I'm not stupid of course. I got my degree, I read English and Art at Cambridge. I read everything else I could lay my hands on. Endlessly. I could earn a living without resorting to selling myself or anything illegal or dangerous. I can thank my father for that, for my top-class education, for my terribly good English manners. I can lay a table for an eight-course diplomatic dinner, you know?"

"Splendidly useful in life and not something you will get to practice here." In Plum Village we ate once a day, with our fingers.

She laughed with me, then kicked off her sandals, scuffing her bare feet in the loose soil of summer. A faded love-heart tattoo adorned her big toe.

"Now I need to learn to forgive him, my cuss-ed father, forgive her, my cowardly mother, for what I have considered unforgivable for thirty years. And figure out why I had such a hellish start to my life. This is my path and ninety days may not be long enough."

The wind rose a little, blowing our robes. Cuss-ed she had said, in two syllables.

"Cuss-ed? Cuss, the verb, is American for cursing. I have not heard it pronounced the way you did?"

"Ah! Miss Gibb, A-Level English. She ate and regurgitated the dictionary. We had four new words every day and I absolutely loved her. Cuss-ed is American-English also, for a contrary or troublesome person or animal. My father was both."

I stretched my upper body and uncrossed my legs in the sunshine.

"I would be honoured to assist you on your ninety-day journey if I may? My name is Jesús Josephus."

"Seriously? You came here with a name like that? And you are contemplating the incapacity to stay for a month or three? What about forty days in the desert? Are you stitching me up?"

I laughed again, guessing the meaning of her words. "Truly no! No. It is a name. It just happens to carry some weight." I shrugged. "The real Jesus got to thirty before he knew what to do. I have a few years before that."

"Well, give it a good go before running back to your mother."

∞

Cadíz 1987

Abuelita Rosa accompanied me to Dr. Zhao's about once every month or so. We would take churros, or buñuelos de viento to have with coffee. Sometimes he would have bagels that his friend Dr. Ehrlich baked. On this day we had Roscón de Reyes, a Christmas treat that Mamá had made, so it must have been early January, maybe our first class after a Christmas break. Dr. Zhao joined his family in the U.S. for major holidays.

"Medicina, the healing art. Now let's poke about in history a bit," Dr. Zhao announced, once our greetings were complete. "Billroth?"

In chilly weather he closed the windows and lit a small wood-burner in the central room. The coffee-pot would simmer there, wafting brewing odour through the book-lined walls. Rosa smiled at him, maybe remembering this lesson from her own tutorials. I could but raise my eyebrows questioningly.

"Billroth. Theodor, Austrian, 1870s. From Dr. Billroth we have the Cords of Billroth, filtering the red blood cells in the spleen, essential maintenance of the red corpuscles." He followed on quickly. "Willis? Circle of Willis, Thomas, English, 1650s. Arterial junction at base of the brain in most mammals including humans. Henle? Jakob."

"Yes," I responded enthusiastically, "Loop of Henle in the nephron in the kidney," a spark leaping from the memory recesses of school biology.

"That and probably ten other anatomical parts. He was quite the anatomist, Mr. Henle, German, 1840s. He has a fissure, ampulla, ligament, membrane, all called after him. Rosa?"

"I go back, Lou, to the ladies quizás," she smiled. "Okay, Jesús, very young Italian girl, Alessandra Giliani, trece-oh-siete, morte trece-veinte-seis. So very early, sí.?"

"A doctor?" I asked. "She had a short life. I did not think a girl would be a doctor in 14th-century Italy?"

Dr. Zhao nodded, "Prosector, preparation of corpses for dissection. University of Bologna."

"Then later," added Rosa, "also Bologna, Anna Morandi Manzolini, diecisiete-catorce. Artist in la cera."

"Wax?" I asked puzzled.

"Yes, anatomical models," replied Dr. Zhao, "supremely beautiful, even nerve endings, capillaries and vessels, that level of perfection. She learned from her husband and continued after he died. She was mid-18th-century."

The coffee-pot sang. Dr. Zhao retrieved it from the stove. Rosa laid the Roscón de Reyes on a plate. Lou's eyes widened. "Ah! The Three Kings have come again," he laughed. "The perfect gift to a hungry mother in a stable."

We happily settled into coffee and cake, before Dr. Zhao continued.

"Okay. Once we were past the really ancient history, which mixed shamanism, pagan beliefs, and cures with pure misadventure, we get to Babylonia, Mesopotamia, then the great Egyptians. Merit-Ptah, lucky lady, 2700, b.c., by all accounts physician in the Pharaoh's court. Twelve hundred years later, Hatshepsut, female pharaoh, and known as Queen Doctor, looking for botanical cures. Hippocrates, Father of Medicine, 460, b.c.; Mary the Jewess, Gnostic alchemist, first century, and an endless stream of wisdom compiling a line of learning to the present day." He paused, for homemade Roscón de Reyes is not to be swallowed with large chunks of conversation. We ate silently.

"There are countless names, Jesús, attached to bits of body parts, body functions, body disorders—many, many of them European names. That really just means it is how we understand them. It does not," he stressed, leaning his elbows on his knees and looking at me directly, "does not mean that the Eastern or other civilisations had not seen or understood them before us, or knew them by a different term. Every civilisation played its part, added to the knowledge, and as the world opened up through travel, so did the wisdom. It merely means that is how they were named for our learning in a Western tradition." He sat back in his chair, thoughtfully stroking his goatee.

"William Harvey was the first to establish a pressurised blood circulatory system driven by the heart. That was the 1630s. John Houston, an Irishman trained in Scotland, 1830s, has the Houston's Valves to his credit. Do you know the Houston's Valves?"

I shook my head. "I couldn't venture a guess. Nothing to do with space travel I imagine?"

Dr. Zhao laughed loudly, slapping his thigh. "Houston, we have a problem. Very good, Jesús. But no, it is part of one of our everyday bodily functions. Houston's valves are skin-folds in the rectum that keep the faeces from falling into the anal canal and then the anus. They are so beautifully designed and functionally perfect, they are a devil to get past when performing a colonoscopy. They did not plan to have anything coming at them from the opposite direction." He found this amusing and chuckled to himself for a moment. I imagine he was recalling performing a colonoscopy, or similar procedure, manoeuvring past some unnamed soldier or sailor's Houston's valves.

"Katharine Bishop, Berkeley, University of California, 1920s, discovered in her lab rat experiments the function of Vitamin E. I attended a couple of her lectures in San Francisco between the war and Korea. Can't remember too much—histology probably sent me to sleep, but I knew I was in a room with one of the great names."

"Choh Hao Li? You have his papers, remember, Lou?" Rosa nudged him.

Dr. Zhao nodded. "He was also Chinese-American, born in China, moved before the war. A couple of years older than me. He was in Berkeley too. Pituitary expert, endocrines."

"Hormonal sees-tem." Rosa looked intently at Dr. Zhao. He smiled at her then looked at me.

"I would have met Dr. Li socially in our community in San Fran. We lost touch in the war years, then Korea. I telephoned him in … 1955 or '56, was it Rosa?"

I knew what he was referring to. "My mother, no menses."

"Yes." He smiled softly, taking Rosa by the hand and shaking her gently. "But I didn't tell him about my method of treatment."

Somewhere just there was the briefest of held breaths, between life and no life, between being and becoming. Somewhere just there, Dr. Lou Zhao had inspired my soul's existence. This part of my journey I already understood from my Buddhist teachings. Without any effort a series of unconnected sentences filled my mind.

What prompts a caterpillar to become a butterfly, an acorn to become an oak? What transforms must be alive.

A dead caterpillar cannot become a butterfly.

From outside time, space, and matter, is life.
Matter cannot become nothing. It is always present.

Birth and death are only doors through which we pass,
sacred thresholds on our journey.
Birth and death are a game of hide-and-seek.

This body is not me; I am life without boundaries, I have
never been born and I have never died. Since beginning-less
time I have always been free.

I smiled at Dr. Zhao, for without words comes understanding.
All three of us, wiping sticky cake from our fingers, knew in our
unspeaking hearts the connection among us.

"Well, Rosa," Dr. Zhao patted his lips with a handkerchief, "please
pass my sincerest thanks to María. That was just delicious."

I cleared up the coffee ware, Rosa sitting quietly by the wood stove,
while Dr. Zhao had left the room for the bathroom. "He lost a
young girl, Jesús, same age as María, about same time. American
girl, la hija of a sailor. I was in the ward that night, with Madeleine
and Federico. She was young, in trouble, as María, but different
trouble. But she had bad heart. He could not fix it."

Dr. Zhao returned to the room. "There have been many things
I could not fix, Rosa. But it is important to a doctor, well to a
human being, to know that you tried your very best."

She reached for his hand as he passed by her chair, squeezing him.
I felt the countless stories they must have shared, as colleagues,
lovers, friends. The endless death of war.

"Gaia is our Mother Earth, Jesús. I have seen so much of the trampling of nature that man has inflicted on her. I have seen the destruction of one war become the more clever, scientific destruction of the next war, then the next war. How we used chemistry and science to inflict greater and greater ills upon others, as if we were really, really clever." He paused, shaking his head sadly.

"You know, they fire rockets into the ground for testing, nukes into the sea-bed and monitor the results. Scientists. People who should know. How can they possibly not think that sending a nuke into the sea won't have a rippling effect elsewhere?" He shook his head again, more angrily, before breathing deeply and closing his fingers together at his forehead.

"We are guests on this earth, not any contrived idea we have of ourselves as anything wonderful. We are another species, no different, no more important than the creepies beneath our feet. We all have a role. We are equal in her eyes and, oh my word! What will we do before we understand this?"

His words haunted me frequently during the next thirty years.

"We ourselves, our complete bodies of all parts—mental, physical, emotional—we are a small part of Mother Earth. She too is on her journey. If we look after ourselves first in a wholesome way, then this is our first step to looking after Gaia. All of those great scientists, all through the ages, all across the planet, in every civilisation. Wonderful people naming and understanding things that were never intended to have names or be understood but were somehow perfect in their formation and function."

He stopped, swinging his relaxed leg across his knee. "I am in awe. Daily."

∞

"Close your eyes, Jesús. Now think of brushing your teeth, okay? Got it?"

I nodded.

"Now," Dr. Zhao continued. "I want you to visualise the back of your teeth in the upper layer, unmoving, rooted in their sockets, fitted perfectly to your maxilla, just one of the sections forming what you know as your skull. See in your mind now, the roof of your mouth, you know what it looks like in the mirror?"

I nodded again.

"You know why it is all bumps and ridges, what they are all called?"

I shook my head.

"Lots of things!" he laughed. "Those bumps and ridges are formed by many things. I guess you could say it forms the shape of your mouth, assists in vocal sounds, is an opposing force for your tongue to assist with chewing your food. Now use your tongue to feel where the hard bony section becomes the soft palate. Palatine raphe, to the uvula, that hanging down bit. You won't get that with your tongue, but you know where I am?"

More nodding.

"Now move your tongue to the right, like you would with a toothbrush, to where the teeth in their gums join the inside cheek. Move down your cheek to the lower teeth. Are you following me?"

"Wow! I have to really concentrate." I tried to smile.

"Yes, now you can run your tongue along your lower teeth, set in the mandible. What's it called where they meet the inside of your lip? Right in there."

I shake my head briefly, for there is little other I can do.

"Lots of things!" he laughs again. "I guess you could say alveolar part. The muscle between inside where you are and the skin under your lip is the orbicularis oris. This is the moving section of your face, embedded in the hinged jaw, temporomandibular joint. Now behind those teeth you meet the lower gums and you can just turn the tip of your tongue to the floor of your own mouth, where it is anchored? Okay? Yes?"

Nodding again.

"If you blow out your cheeks now," he stopped to laugh. "It's impossible to give that instruction without performing it myself! Now that, is essentially the entire buccal cavity. A million cells, blood vessels, nerve endings, tissues, all those perfectly, functionally laid teeth, enamel, dentine, pulp cavity, root canal. If I were to start listing even the anatomical sections of your tongue alone, wow! This allows you to chew, produces saliva, enzymes for digestion, taste buds for eating, smiles, form words. Where even does your tongue start? Hmm? The hyoid bone. But how far down your pharynx is the connection? When does your pharynx meet your larynx? What flesh is what? How can any of it be separate to anything else? This," he stressed, his hands thrust palm upwards, "this is the seamless whole. Okay? Okay? The thorax contains all of the seamless layers, everything we are, passes through this section of the body."

He held my head, manoeuvring it minutely to move freely in his hands.

"For once I am not doing the nodding like a mute idiota." I laughed.

"Relax. Relax now," he smiled. My head glided with his small gentle manipulations, minute rotations in all directions. His fingers moved to the hollow at the rear of my skull, his thumbs under my jaw.

"Cerebellum, deep in here, top of the brain stem. Gives you balance, emotional alignment to our own truth. It is the middle of do-ing and be-ing, the centre of the left and right brain. This is where you live your own truth. Keep your mind open always to your own fluid truth, your own flow," he whispered. "This will give you a light heart as you live in integrity, true to your self." He paused his movements.

"Atlas, axis, here. Posterior transverse line, cervical spine, down seven vertebrae to thoracic spine. So what we know as your neck is what? Vertebrae, all connected, changing minutely in shape one to the next, from cervical to thoracic." His fingers pressed my spine down to my shoulders.

"Muscles of the neck, trapezius, rhomboid, splenius, scalenus, longissimus, levator, and related tendons and nerves. Hmm? Ligaments to hold your skull to your clavicle, spinal formations, mastoid tendons. Then how about carotid artery, jugular vein, occipital nerves, thyroid cavity. And of course what we refer to as the Adam's Apple, which is only in the male of our species."

He paused. "That's just five minutes and a fraction of what we simply call our mouth and neck. Incredible, yes? In the space of washing your teeth and rinsing your mouth, you can reflect on all of that. Focus on that knowledge and give thanks. Brush your teeth and try to *not* think about tomorrow."

He gently manipulated my head in his hands. "You knew this though?"

"Yes," I agreed, "in a less defined way. The monks in France, Thich Nhat Hanh, would have had us observe all of our movements as we performed them, in a meditative way. Mindfully, to be with ourselves at every moment and to give constant gratitude for our entire selves. Our awareness in every function. I am breathing in, I know that I am breathing in."

I inhaled slowly and deeply. Dr. Zhao inhaled with me, still holding my head in his hands.

"I am breathing out, I know that I am breathing out." We exhaled together.

He smiled. "I have a Russian friend who says, 'The man is the head of the house, of the family, but the neck is the woman. Only she can get the head to take a direction.' "

He chuckled softly, then releasing my head, kissed the front of my shoulder, saying, "Hola, Sean!"

∞

There were days when our teachings or discussion were random and informal. He would prune his bonsai bodhi tree or move through Tai Chi poses in his living-room, telling me this or that. Sometimes we would knead dough for Dr. Ehrlich's bagels, tend to Lou's patio plants, de-leaf the vine, or trim back dead growth over the arbor. Occasionally, he would employ my greater strength and height for tasks such as adjusting the ceiling fan or changing light bulbs. Between us, we could clear gutters, fix a window sash or loosened shutter. The exchange of story and learning never ceased, even in the silences.

The mài network in our body could open a discussion on the river and tributary flow of qi relating to acupuncture. This was just one gem I pencilled into my own stack of copybooks, followed by the Chinese characters defining those words and, as he would routinely say, "Not readily translated to an English concept."

Or a yoga nugget might be, "After shoulder stand, let your blood flow back to its place, and your organs find the space in which they reside."

He often seemed invigorated by my presence, as if the unlocking of knowledge gave him impetus. He would sometimes rise from the table, select a book and, pushing his glasses to his forehead, exclaim "Ah! I had forgotten this." Or, "It is here somewhere, somewhere I have that."

In late spring or early summer afternoons when the sun was hottest, we would often sit with our books on the shady patio, overlooking his yard and garden. I might hang the hammock for him and he would snooze, and I would read or study to the sounds of his soft snores.

On this day we were still ruminating on the lessons of the morning. He sipped his iced tea and asked quietly, "Hey, Jesús, where do you think Abuelo Sean goes when he isn't on your shoulder?"

I was surprised by his question and had to smile as I inserted my notepad and pencil to mark the page of my book. "I haven't given it much thought, Dr. Zhao." I paused to reflect, recalling my own Buddhist teachings on soul and self. "Anywhere he chooses, I suppose?"

"Have you asked Rosa if she hears him? Or María?"

"No. Nor have I told them that I do."

He nodded thoughtfully.

I never asked the why of his questions. Or his thought processes. Or the flow of our work together. It all just happened, each day, something new, something different.

He tipped off the hammock like a ten-year-old and disappeared indoors, returning after some few minutes with the cloth bag of letters from the Scrabble board. Seating himself across from me at the patio table, his bare feet and legs crossed under him, he opened the bag of letters.

"No questions okay?"

I smiled in agreement. "It would seem silly to start questioning you now."

From his shirt pocket, he produced a selection of crystal pieces—rose quartz, amethyst, and a pale blue crystal I did not recognise.

"Celestite. Drawing celestial power. And amethyst, améthystos—the Greeks believed it would prevent intoxication. I am a man of science, Jesús, with the extreme fortune of also being a man of the ether. I realised quite early in my career that every learning opportunity I ever needed arose just as I needed it." He wagged his finger at me, "And that includes the ones I would wish to forget." He shook his head.

"Sometimes that was death, in the cruellest manner, largely humanly inflicted you know, war and stupidity. But sometimes it was nature, or illnesses, accidents, or violence." His fingers tumbled the crystal pieces in his palm. "And I had excellent teachers, wonderful parents and grandparents who struggled, yet gave me their wisdom and learning too. They are why my wisdom must not die with me."

"But you have your own children?" This was the first time I had voiced this thought which had occurred to me on many occasions.

He waved his hand vaguely. "Engineers. They were not interested. And my daughter listened for a while then succumbed to the rote way of learning. Now she is so busy with conferences, meetings, skin pathology, blinded by science." He shook his head somewhat sadly and shrugged. "It is how it is. It is who they are, where they chose to be. It's okay. I have the one student I needed."

He laid the crystals in a semi-circle between us at the edge of the table. Opening the cloth bag, he rolled down the mouth, exposing the loose pile of wooden letter tiles, and placed it in the centre of the table.

"Now, close your eyes, Jesús. Breathe as you will, then short breath in, long breath out, and again, you know how it goes."

He sat quietly for some moments. I recall the heat, the smell of that lingering heat, the cicada clicks, and hum of hot life.

"Now pick a letter as you will and just put them on the table in front of you, in the order you choose them. Take your time and you will know when to stop."

I felt for the cloth bag and, rummaging softly, slowly selected a letter, then a second. My hand stopped, poised over the bag.

"Okay, and do you feel that's it?" he asked.

"I feel that's it for that time." I breathed once, then twice, "But I am not finished."

"Okay, follow your heart, Jesús."

I reached again and randomly selected one, two, three, four, five more letters and laid them as I drew them. I knew that was it.

"Okay now, breathe again for a moment or two. If you are sure that's it, give thanks to the Universe and come back to me."

I did as he asked. As I opened my eyes, he removed the cloth bag to the edge near the crystals and placed a half-sheet of paper in the centre.

"Now the first two."

One was facing me upwards: L. I turned over the second and righted it: H.

"Leave them together here," he instructed, pointing to the paper. "Now line up the next five all facing you correctly."

I fiddled the wooden tiles about until I had a line of letters: L, W, R, N, C. Then I moved them also onto the paper.

"Leave some space between them. Now Jesús, use your third eye, your inner vision, your own wisdom to make two forenames from the letters as they lay there." He handed me the pencil.

I was puzzled at first, but as no direction we had ever taken had disappointed me, I trusted his guidance. I took my time, unfocussing my eyes as I would in meditation, or sitting in Plum Village with the monks. Having loosened the grip on the present, the notion of time, my mind finds what it needs. Between the L and the H, I wrote E and A. LEAH.

I studied the long row of five letters, once again unfocussing my vision, allowing my mind to bring me the answer, then shifting the tiles apart, I filled in the missing vowels. LAWRENCE.

He clapped his hands together excitedly, in pure delight. "Bravo Jesús! Fabulous!"

"Leah and Lawrence?" I enquired.

"Yes. Your guardian angels, Jesús. You won't know why, but as you age and experience life, you will get to know who they are. They are always there for you, they always want the best for you, always, always want to guide you. You just have to ask."

I imagined telling my father what Dr. Zhao had taught me today. This was certainly not on any curriculum he, or any of us, could have foreseen. "Will they share riding my shoulders with Abuelo Sean?" I queried.

Dr. Zhao clasped his hands gleefully as he squeezed his eyes closed. "Oh Jesús! I can just imagine those conversations."

∞

Devon, England, 1990s

He was right of course, Dr. Zhao. Once you acquire that kind of knowledge, it never leaves you. In the course of the years, both names would regularly pop into my head, the cliché perfectly describing the event. Presenting themselves to me in moments of need or uncertainty, moments of joy or peace. I became aware of their guidance, and anything or anyone I met or learned from, did not refute my belief in the existence of existential guides that we all have.

A Dutch traveller and I were the lone guests of an English Youth Hostel one winter's evening. Thea, was several years older than me, with nearly perfect English, and for two days we shared parts of our daily explorations, our touristic off-season experiences. Thea was a commercial photographer, so winter suited her exploits. We very quickly passed the this-and-that phase, wonderfully circumventing the mundane, as it often is with passing encounters. There is, of course, no such thing in my world as chance, or coincidence. My life unfolds, trusting the perfection in every moment. We shot straight to the essence of being questions.

On this evening we were sharing our combined supplies and the cooking facilities, preparing a meal to eat together. There seemed to be no discussion, or division of labour, much as happens in the Two Spoons with Philomena.

"Why did I always choose selfish people to love? Why in a handful of relationships, with only two of lasting consequence, did I choose selfish partners to love? Who briefly gave and then spent the next years taking. Taking, I mean, of me." She stopped, her knife poised. "Even in Dutch English that makes no sense," Thea laughed. "I mean taking of me. They took a part of me, a little every day, and gave back nothing."

"And then were surprised when you had had enough?" I guessed.

"Yes. Yes, as if I were a, what can I say? A forever stream of acceptance of essentially bad behaviour from another adult, another human being. Even without labelling, you know, partner, spouse, girlfriend, I was a human. Someone who claimed to love me but showed little interest in me, or my thoughts or feelings, in my be-ing. Why? Why such poor behaviour to another person?"

"Why?" I could only shrug. "Why? In your responses you were giving and loving, you showed love?"

"I think so. Maybe that was my error, maybe I should have been more, em, angry, upset perhaps about their behaviours, their actions?"

"No, no!" I countered. "Love is the only way. In honestly showing love and understanding, you are true to yourself. If the other person's choice is to not learn from you, you cannot change that. That is for them to deal with, their journey. You reach a point where you decide for you, that this is enough, this is the end of trying, or trying in different ways and so you stop, or change roads, or often that is the time you meet someone new. Then wow! All hell breaks loose and it becomes the new person's fault that it wasn't working."

She laughed. "Exactly! Someone new the first time, so that brought its own, hmm, well, good English phrase, 'bucket of sheet'. The second time I had grown up enough to just say, this is enough now."

We continued our kitchen tasks, preparing food, chopping, shifting pots, adjusting temperatures.

"I went to the counsellor the first time, when you are trying to work things out, and she said, 'seven to nine years', that is what a relationship takes for you to know quite a bit about the other. The length of time it takes for a human to learn what it is another might teach them. Seven, nine years, then you choose to remain and the relationship takes on a slightly different route or you decide, okay, this is done now. You need to part, learn from another person, or be alone to absorb life."

"And of course the first lesson is trusting your self, trusting that life brings you exactly what or who you need. Not what you want, what you need. When we learn that, life is easier for everyone." I stirred and tasted. "What we need is a tipple of red wine to improve the flavour here. Anything on the shelf?"

We searched through the remnants in a communal kitchen; motorway services sachets of salt and pepper, dregs of olive oil, a can of beans, scattered bits of sugar in bags or paper twists, quarter pint of milk in a fridge door but nothing of contributory value to the pot. Life never gives what we want but we always get what we need. Maybe we needed for nothing else right now.

"So they appear selfish?" Thea was saying. "Or they are truly selfish in taking, not giving?"

"I think some people are lazy. If they know you love them and are always there, reliable, strong, then unfortunately they tend to take it for granted."

"Granted?" she was puzzled by the word.

I thought of Mr. Onions' Dictionary: Old French graanter or creanter; Latin credere, believe; then English: to assure, promise, guarantee, regard as not requiring proof. "They expect it from you, every time. And there will be parameters where you may be unwilling to give but they learn how to work around that, to make it happen anyway."

"Ah! Yes, yes, so as long as I am giving, they are taking?"

"Yes. And if you are strong, self-reliant, happy with your own self, then you absorb their failings, as much as they draw the best out of you. You may think, that was not nice, or that was rude, or that was out of order, but you tend not to complain or say. Then having played this part for sometime, you think Enough! But that requires courage. Honesty. And now you have to be honest. You have every right to say Hang on a minute here, this is how I feel and my feelings are just as valid as yours. You have behaved badly towards me and this is how I feel. You then create the opportunity for them to change. Or not. Then you have the right to be true to you, and say That is enough now!"

She was silent, her hands busy with salad-making. I drained pasta, stirred sauce. "But that's not all, is it, Jesús?" she said, shaking her head.

I smiled at her questioningly.

"There is something in me that I need to learn, isn't there? There is a reason that I choose this."

"Yes," I nodded. "You choose your own reality. There are always two of you in a relationship of any sort. There will be something in you, your life as a child, your understanding of how love relationships work, that you choose this role. A bigger picture you were playing. Sometimes we choose others who like to keep us, well, small. On a tight leash, if you like. It gives them control and stature. "

"Mothering. I always felt I was mothering, minding. My love was a place for them to anchor, to safely hang out, maybe hide. I am the rock. Smothering, perhaps?"

"So you both hid? You both took on a role. But don't be hard on yourself, this is life. And we live to learn."

"After the honeymoon period, you know, the excitement, the sex, the fun, it never felt equal, but I thought that this was love, this is how it was supposed to be. I did not know."

"We manufacture all sorts of realities in our head, Thea. In the reality you created, you allowed them to be selfish, to be less than thoughtful to you. Our head leads us many places. Only our heart has the answer. Unfortunately, as humans, we are very bad at listening to it. We are oh-so-good at getting in our own way. Sabotaging our own happiness. So you have to be thankful to these persons for the opportunity to learn and make your peace with them and with your own self."

She laid plates at the table. The hostel warden stuck his head through the door. "Smells good! Need anything?"

"No, thank you, all's well. Would you like to share with us?"

"Thank you but no, I will dine with my family." He departed, returning quickly with three-quarters of a bottle of red wine. "Last night's guests forgot this. It is all yours. Enjoy!"

"Thank you, we will." I smiled at Thea. "Just got what we needed!"

In his absence, his kindness and cheeriness lingered, while outside the sea pounded the groynes holding a battered beach in place, a winter greyness of a leaden sky.

"It was grief, relief, grief, relief in equal measures," she continued. "But never guilt. I was never guilty. She made a mess of things all on her own. By the end, I was just an onlooker in the life of another. But the relief. And then the grief. And sadness. I had truly loved her once."

I waited for her to continue.

"That was my mother. She suffered all her life from, well," she shrugged, opening her hands wide, "they called it depression, sometimes dysthymia, sometime, someone said aandachtstoornis, een bipolaire stoornis, what's that in English?"

"Bipolar disorder."

"Yes, and attention deficiency. But I lived with her long enough to not believe any of that, to see her on the better days, when she was so lovely and was my mother. I had brothers and sisters but somehow I was the one who saw her at her best. I could brush her hair, or paint her toenails, little things to brighten the day. We would walk together in the forest but the good days never lasted for very long."

I nodded, "Yes, usually there is a stronger connection with one off-spring, for no known reasons. Or at least a scientific one. So already you were minding, mothering your own mother?"

"And my father. My sisters were good at meals, shopping; but they were older and were busy with school and boys. I was the youngest and when I was in my last years at school, they were all gone except one brother working with my father. So I did everything for him at the home and in the office. My mother then had long times in em, the instituut. Then it was different at home, happier, but always the grief or sadness that she was missing our lives."

We sat to eat, clinking glasses of reasonable mid-range supermarket Merlot.

"She then had very bad, hmm gewrichtsontsteking," she rubbed her finger joints, "here and in her back. Pain in the joints."

"Ah! Arthritis."

"Yes. She died eventually of too much morphine. Too much pain."

"Aw. Always, grief is difficult, Thea. We have truly lost someone's presence, even if it is a relief to them, to the family." I squeezed her hand and she smiled, her eyes bright.

"It was a long time ago, Jesús. But I knew the difficulty was mostly in here," she tapped her chest. "My grandparents were not good to her. He was a Nazi supporter, a very difficult man, very unkind to her and his family but a model citizen in the street. Pretending to be deeply religious, yet betrayed the Jewish families. Bekrompen fanaticus. Huichelaar. Pretending one thing, then being something else?"

"Bigot and hypocrite."

"Ya, yes. Bigot. And violent, beating my grandmother. This is what my mother grew up with, pain and hurt and blood. Watching her mother try not to make it difficult. Learning to always stay out of the trouble with him. Everyone always pretending everything was okay. I think this is what drove her crazy."

She stopped. "Ach Jesús! My mutterings must not spoil the lovely meal in the winter English weather."

We laughed, for there was nothing to be seen beyond the windows on a darkening evening. Then we were silent as we ate. As we sat over empty plates, the conversation ranged on, flowing as it will without interruption or dissent—lives, living, learning, and loves.

"And of course there is the possibility that we have done it before, no?"

She brought me pause, my glass raised to my mouth.

"Indeed." I sipped at the last mouthfuls of wine. "Reincarnation you mean?"

"Yes. Yes! Oh I knew it would not be strange for you. Let me tell you something, Jesús. I was a princess somewhere. I know it. I feel it. I look at Diana here in England and," she waved her hand, "Beatrix at home in Netherlands, Charlene in Monaco. It's like, I knew that life. The showmanship, the façade, the power. Is that too much Merlot?" she asked with a laugh.

"Not at all. I studied with the Buddhist monks. They will tell you that you have had hundreds of lives." In my head I heard hunder-eds, I heard Abuelo Sean. "Lifetimes. We are in every lifetime, collecting pieces of our selves." Ain't that the truth, I heard somewhere to my left. Maybe it was the Merlot. The thought made me grin.

Thea returned my smile. "I have never spoken of this, Jesús. Maybe it is the Merlot, but more it is you. I do not often meet people who listen, who absorb a story without needing the details or crashing in with their own version of things."

I raised my nearly empty glass. "Why thank you."

"I was brought to France on a ship, this is like a dream but not a dream if you can understand that?"

"Yes, I understand that. It is a cross between a dream and a memory with a dollop of reality."

"Yes. It is just that. I am then taken to the mountains, high mountains. I see this sometimes at night, but always, for oh I can't say how many years, the same picture, the same mountains, the same forest. I can even smell the air. And I was called Leah."

∞

I was in the snow-muffled woods, the Chamonix Valley in France, Les Houches. Some of our group were on the slopes—snowboarding, skiing. I was hiking the higher streets of the town, mostly cleared of snow by the ploughs and the local residents with winter tyres, getting to and from the main thoroughfares. The edge of the town gave way to the forest, Route de la Griaz, Chemin des Longues, and this is where I had chosen to spend my day, walking and listening.

If I stopped and quieted the crushing of my boots on the powder, I could hear the sounds of the novice slopes, the rhythmic clang of the tow-lift as it crashed through its mechanics, the whirr of the driving-wheel pushing bars through the leverage. I climbed above the noise, the slopes becoming a distant visual array of skiers in a rainbow of movement and colour.

I reached an old tree, out of the regimented, planted conifer line, the long branches weighted, minuscule drops of melting snow at the tips in the midday sun. I pushed and worked myself against the trunk until the pack snow made a perfect seat, the shafts of sunlight breaking through to my legs. Taking off my glove, I let the sun dance forest-shadows on my palm. In the silence and the absence of others, I could tilt my head to my right shoulder and say Leah, this is for you.

∞

Two Spoons Café, Blackrock, Cork

"I had a woman in here once, Jesus," Philomena started. "I'd never lain eyes on her before and she asked for a pot of very strong tea. Do you remember her, Biddy?"

"Oh tha' wan, shur I do o' course."

I couldn't see how they could possibly know which "wan" on the strength of that exchange, for every second customer asks for a pot of tea; maybe "very strong" was the clue. But they seemed to know well enough between them, all of the time. A wan I understood to be somehow close to one, or another person, usually female.

"And Biddy here says, 'Oh tha'll fix everything, a poh of strong tea.'

" 'Well,' she said, 'indeedn't it won't, and I'll tell you a good one. My young fella got into trouble at school, then again, then bigger trouble, then trouble at the football field, so this went on a while, my wayward 18-year-old boy, behaving like a kicked pup. So I bailed him out of the same sort of trouble one Saturday night or near enough to Sunday morning in the town, after more of his madness and says I to him—Listen here boyo, that's enough now of yer carry on, ye've met your line. So he broke down and wept and wept like a 6-year-old in the front of the car. Sobbed until my heart broke for my own boy. "Arra, mam, whatever it is it won't go away and I'm in bits and all over the place. I can't get straight in me head at all."

" 'So what do you say except, it's okay love, it's okay. Everyone goes through it and we come out the other side and wipe the tears away and say look love, your father and I are here to help you. So he stops the sobbin', still holding his head in his hands and I say c'mon now I'll go in and put the kettle on and we'll have some tea and a chat.

" 'Okay so,' he says, and I go in and after ten minutes there's no sign of him and I go out to the yard, the car's gone, my boyo gone. So I called his father and we called the guards and they said they'd put out a call, pick him up and bring him back.

" 'And there's nothin' you can do but wait. So I threw a few turves on the fire, pulled on me blanket, made the tea, knitted like crazy, said the Rosary. Multi-tasking, like all good mammies. Waiting. The telephone rang at near three in the morning, the guards in Adare, Co Limerick. Boyo took off, foot down for an hour or so, came to his senses and turned the car for home. Then the guards spotted him and he panicked in the blue lights, rolled the car three times and what do you know, he walked out of it without a scratch. He ruined me lovely car. His father's patience lasted long enough to go and bring him home, where he was always going to be safe and looked after. But he told him that was the end of pots of tea and chat with mammy for some time to come. Buck up now boyo. Get a grip on your life.' "

"Wasn't he one lucky fella, Jesus? Noh a mark on him she said." Biddy was on her stool her foot swinging at a great rate, shaking her head left to right. It was hard not to see her becoming unseated.

"He was one lucky fella all right," said Philomena. "There were stars out for him that night. She was one lucky mammy and one lucky boy. Oh for all the unlucky ones." She blessed herself, more slowly than I have seen her do and paused, her head bowed. "Oh my heart for all the unlucky ones."

"Is it not all in God's hands?" I asked, "Although that is probably unhelpful to anyone with a broken heart. We know not the hour, which is all the more reason to be right here fully in every moment."

"It's hard to tell a poor mother I think, that it is all in God's hands. That Mammy didn't lose her son, that time." Philomena leant on the café counter-top. "She took him outta school, and she sent him to the local nursing home as an unpaid assistant. More tea 'n' toast than any fella could look at in a lifetime." She chuckled, "He wasn't long atoning or mending his ways and she said the ould wans straightened him out quick time. So he lived to help others and they to help him. Isn't that the way of it?"

∞

"Here Jesus," Philomena called out to me one day, "look at what Wilhelmina found for you."

Wilhelmina, living true to her name as fierce protector, was Philomena's twin sister, older by ten minutes, louder by ten decibels, alike to a tee, except for less stature than Philomena. Wilhelmina was a golfer of great merit where she lived in Co. Clare and was married to the owner of a haberdashery in Miltown Malbay, Walsh's Gentleman's & Ladies Outfitters, Purveyor of School Attire. I rarely met Mr. Walsh and had only met Wilhelmina a handful of times.

Philomena proffered with floury hands an old black-and-white photograph, instantly recognisable as my mother and me, Philomena and her mother, Mary, and Mary's sister, Frances, my great aunts. I was immediately drawn to the likeness between my mother and Philomena and could remember Sean Seamus in the open smiling faces of his sisters. I remember the picture being taken, for it was a rarity even then for anyone to produce a camera, or to even pass the thought that it was a photo opportunity when your brother's family appeared from Spain with little warning.

"How old were you that time, Jesus, when you came with your mother on the Great Trip. After John James passed away?"

We were drinking tea in the Two Spoons, one of Philomena's favourite tea sessions of the week, a Thursday afternoon after the carvery lunch was cleared away and the tarts were in the oven for the morrow. Maureen was behind the counter taking care of things; Bridget was perched on her stool, her crossed leg swinging like a metronome, keeping a time only she knew. About every twentieth swing her shoe would just about nearly fall off her foot, so she would stop and adjust it with the toe of the other foot. It was mesmerising.

"Ten Philomena, I was ten, ten and one-quarter. That would have made Mamá thirty-six."

"I was twenty-one," she said. "I remember you well. I was already married to Ambrose, his mother worked for old Mrs. Farquharson at the big house on Duchess Hill, where Biddy's apartments are now."

"I remember meeting Ambrose," I said, "He was so tall. Taller than my father and that seemed huge. He knelt on the floor and said, 'I'm very happy to meet you,' very slowly, thinking I didn't understand English. My English was just fine, but HIS English sounded like a foreign language. I had never heard Scottish."

Philomena laughed, "I don't think he has ever heard that in all these years. My father had a terrible time understanding him too, unless they were on the whiskey. My father's hearing seemed to improve greatly under the influence."

"I remember you dancing," I told her. "You took me to the Sunday afternoon dance."

"Oh!" she cried, "Cecil Fitzmaurice at the Arcadia. Oh! Dancing with Cecil. He was just air on legs. Do you remember, Biddy?"

"I do, I do indeed. Cecil, huh," she sniffed disdainfully. "He was a real nudi-nadi."

"A what?" I had to ask. I had not heard this descriptive term before.

"A nudi-nadi, y'know a wishy-washy type of lad."

"Oh Biddy!" exclaimed Philomena. "Bad cess to you. He was the loveliest man in Cork and he still is."

"My fella was jus' a lummox," Biddy sniffed again.

"A what?" I had to repeat, for this was another new one for me.

"A lummox, a, well, there's no other word for ih really. A lummox on two fee'. I'd a been behher off with a brush. And I love to dance as much as I love to sing. The world hasn't seen the bes' of my talents ah all. 'One day ah a time, sweeh Jesus,' " she crooned into a dessert spoon, "tha's all I'm askin' of you … .' "

"Just give me the strength, to stay every day, away from you," finished Philomena.

"Oh Philomena, you don't mean tha' ah all and y'know ih. Wha' about a bih of Cah Stevens instead? 'Ih's noh time to make a change, la la la, take ih easy, la la young … .' Oh I can'h keep tha' up. Young is jus' not quite righ' for you. Tee hee hee hee."

"Spare me, Jesus. Say a little prayer for me."

∞

I was once delayed at Nairobi airport for six long, very hot hours, so it truthfully wasn't difficult to have conversation with any English- or Spanish-speaking fellow travellers. My companion latterly was African-American from Boston U.S.A. I loved his turn of phrase, his Bostonian colloquialisms, his paraphrasing each new idea with "Now here's the thing … ." We meandered from Africa to Asia, politics to population, travails of travel, backpacking, hitchhiking, climate, customs, beliefs, history, herstory, boredom. The source of humans, the course of humans. He enquired as to my occupation. "I travel and I write," was the best way to put it. He owned a travel publishing house with several well-known series of guidebooks and authors.

"Can you write all that you just told me about Africa and the history of humankind from the Rift Valley? Was it all historical fact or mixed with supposition and pseudo-science?"

"Yes, all factual," I replied. "Historically accurate and scientifically correct as far as we understand it to this moment."

"Write me two-thousand words and send them to me at this address," he said, handing me his business card. "I like how you know how to make it flow."

We were delayed another four hours or so, into the deep, dark night where gritty eyelids of exhaustion fray nerves. Endless airport noise and movement, Swahili on the crackly Tannoy, zizzing mosquitoes. I wrote long pages then later found my companion at the holding gate where I handed over my first essay. He invited me to write an article every fortnight until he said to stop.

"He gave me five-hun-der-ed U.S. dollars and he hasn't said stop yet," I told Philomena and Biddy, sometime after my parents moved to Cork. "I write from history with a human story."

"Hisman stories," says Biddy.

"Or humstory?" says Philomena.

"Yes," I agree, "and there is no end to them. So I keep travelling and writing. I am a traveller and a writer." The thought made me pause. Without choosing direction, my life seems to crisscross the planet, another reason following the one before, insisting that I journey. In every place I have absorbed the earth; the fibres of my being are my travels, my blood flows with my stories, my breath their every tale.

"Am I in your stories, Jesus?" Biddy asks.

"You are my living inspiration in all Cork-based tales, Bridget," I respond solemnly.

"Oh Jesus wept," she laughs. "Shur what kinda nonsense could you write abou' me in Blackrock? Yer Boston friend will be tellin' you to stop soon."

"Bridget, in some way, I have written all about your extraordinary ability to retain information, I have written your colourful scarf stories, your bingo-calling at the hall. I have told the world about your prowess in crosswords and sudoku and all the mind-puzzles of the daily newspapers. I believe you are a dab hand at bridge. I also believe you own and use every electrical gadget ever invented on a daisy chain of extension leads. And of course I make sure everyone knows your kindness towards your cousin."

I had to stop there. The incredulity on Philomena's face was disconcerting. I was struck by my own honesty insofar as I had written all these things, in the embroidery of Cork based tales. Her truly unique nature was somehow a cause for awe. Philomena retained a stoic silence.

"Oh dear, Jesus. Are you serious? I mean are you really serious? Have you really wrihhen things about me? About Scratchy 'n' all?" Biddy seemed to be in the throes of such a mixture of emotions, she knew not what to do.

"Yes," I had to answer simply. "Yes, Bridget, I have. You are a very important character in my tales from the Two Spoons."

The leg-jigging ceased. She sat straight and tall on her stool. Philomena was paused somewhere between laughter and tears with no knowledge of how to proceed. She began a discourse behind me, with Kathleen, relating to café matters. I carefully watched

Bridget, unsure myself of what came next. I am certain I saw her grow taller.

"Why thank you, Jesus. Tha' is so very nice to hear. I have no desire to read about myself you know but it's comforting tha' others migh' derive enjoymen' from my very ordinary life. Now I shall leave you in peace." She slipped off her stool and gave what could only be described as a satisfied curtsey in my direction before wafting out the door.

"Oh dear, Jesus. Are you serious? I mean are you really serious?" Philomena's head poked around the kitchen door.

"I'm afraid so, Philomena. She has featured strongly in my narrative. Not always recognisable as Bridget but the colourful kaleidoscope of her tales is irresistible."

"Y'know she can't do crosswords or sudoku?" Philomena had bravely ventured from behind the safety of the counter.

"I guessed not. It's just a whole series of letters and numbers isn't it? Whatever she chooses?"

"Yes. She sits up there on the high stool all knowingly with the paper and just fills in squares. She has no idea that a crossword clue is related to an answer. If they ask for a five-letter word, she chooses whatever she thinks of first. Sudoku is too easy to bother with. 'Shur anyone can fill in nine numbers in a square. Ih isn' very helpful to give you a few to star' with.'" Philomena did an accurate Biddy impression.

"I suppose she is amazed at what takes anyone else so long to complete one?"

There was a loud snort from Philomena. "Whuh, whuh, whuh, whuh." She had a wonderful deep belly laugh that shook her from tummy to tip. She rested her large frame on the edge of a table. But the flow had only just begun. "Whuh, whuh, whuh, whuh."

"Oh dear Jesus in heaven," she wheezed between guffaws. "Oh dear Jesus. She often tells me that Marguerite Foley must not know very many words." Philomena was struggling for breath now. "That, that, that it takes her so long to do the crossword, that, that," she wheezed and exploded in mirth, "that she must be PRETENDING she knows what she is doing. 'Shur I have them done in half the time it takes her,' says she."

Kathleen came through to query the noise. "What has you in such a state, Mrs. S?" she asks of her boss.

"Biddy's gold star award for crossword completion. Whuh, whuh, whuh."

Kathleen caught the infectious laughter. "Ah! Did you not know, Jesus?"

"I guessed."

"And the sudoku? Just a string of numbers?"

"Yes, I guessed that too."

"But d'you know what, Jesus? Mind poor Mrs. S there, before she has an accident." Kathleen said with a grin.

"Oh dear God, Kathleen, it might be too late." Philomena mopped her tears and brow.

"What, Kathleen?" Although the laughter was infectious, I was ill at ease with the cause. I had no desire to belittle the poor woman, entertaining as she was. The situation had unintentionally been initiated by my word foolery. I was contrite.

"In every Biddy crossword I have seen, she always gets in the words mammy and dad. Every single one. And if they ask for a ten-letter word, she writes ballylicky."

We were silenced by this. The absolute pathos. "Ballylickey?"

"Yes, where she came from. She spells it wrong mind you. B-a-l-l-y-l-i-c-k-y. She leaves out the e."

"So it fits in ten squares? I am astonished at her brilliance."

"Yes." Kathleen grinned impishly.

Philomena lifted her tear-stained face from the table. "Oh dear God forgive me, I have been lookin' out for that woman since she was six years old. I think he would spare me a laugh at her expense. Here's the last bit, Jesus."

Philomena loudly blew her nose on her apron, straightening herself into an upright speaking position. "Whuh, whuh, whuh," she collapsed again into a heap of mirth. "She once, very solemnly told Ambrose over his shoulder, that if he couldn't think of a six-letter word that she knew a good trick."

Kathleen smiled brightly as she remembered. "Oh that's right."

"You tell it, Kathleen, for I fear I shall succumb."

"If you just want to write in a shorter word, all you have to do is use your pen to colour in the squares you don't need."

I had to laugh. "That is ingenious! Maybe she is right and everyone else is wrong?"

"Well she gets her money's worth from her newspaper, that's for sure. And who's to say what's right or wrong, eh Jesus?" With a wink, Kathleen disappeared off to her duties.

"Who's to say indeed."

∞

The same Bridget McCarthy clattered through the door of the Two Spoons late one Saturday afternoon. I had just recently landed at Cork airport, loosening my legs while walking the six or so kilometres to Blackrock. We sat in the café over tea and a scone, catching up, and I was pondering whether to travel onwards to East Cork or remain in the city to see Ambrose.

"Oh Philomena, I'm so hungry I could devour the Lam' o' God off the floor." Bridget tittered. "A nun's arse through a conven' gate even."

"Biddy!" Philomena shot me a look. When she saw me laughing, she visibly relaxed, remembering perhaps that I am not the real Jesus, or at least the one they were taught to be afraid of.

"Tea 'n' a biscuit is all you're getting I'm afraid," she quipped. " It's the end of the week for me."

"What date would your birthday be, Jesus?" Kathleen came through from the kitchen. "Oh hello, Mrs. McCarthy, can I get you something before I go home?"

"I hear it's jus' a lonely lihhle biscuit for me, Kackleen. Is there enough tea?" She peered into the pot. "Geh me me mug."

Philomena tapped Bridget on the arm. "May I have my mug, please, and her name is Kathleen, not Kackleen. Everyone deserves courtesy, Biddy."

"Please may I have my mug, Kathleen," Bridget sing-songed like a bold child, with a side-long glance at Philomena. "And in answer to your question, it would have to be December twenty-fifth of course, Kackleen," she continued with a gleeful squeal, before I myself, could draw breath.

"Ah for the love of God, don't be so silly all of the time, Biddy," Philomena remonstrated, dunking a Rich Tea into her cup.

It was a quiet time, near the end of the last day's work for the week, slowly cleaning up. Kathleen was always busy, Biddy dropping by for the last of the news. Robert was tending to the fire before closing up for the night. I liked Robert, a bright and cheerful young man and devoted to Philomena. He was attending college, doing his trade certificate in plumbing and had been in the back yard of the Two Spoons doing jobs since he was old enough to work.

"Well?" Biddy pressed me, eager for a new story, but reluctant to give others their story space.

"I was due," I stressed, "on December 25th, but I did not grace the world until December 27th. And of course there is a tale."

"Well shur we've nothin' else to be thinkin' of, so we may as well hear ih." Bridget sniffed and examined her bright pink nails.

"My mother tells of how my father attended an Officer's Dress Dance at the Naval Base where he worked, on the night of what we called Día de San Esteban, St. Stephen's Day. The Americans at the Base had taken to referring to it as Boxing Day. It was a Base Day Off."

"I always wondered where that came from?" Philomena interjected. "The English say Boxing Day as well."

"That's where the Americans in Spain picked it up. I'll tell you why in a moment, Philomena. He was never good with alcohol, my father, and imbibed just a little too much of the Yankee liquor. Papá rolled in home in the early hours of December 27th, singing at the top of his voice, proudly telling Mamá in a most drunken manner how he had got into a terrible argument with one of the officers. He argued that St. Stephen was a Grecian Jew who converted to Christianity and the day was nothing at all to do with opening presents from your relatives. In turn the officer had argued that Boxing Day was thus named due to a nautical tradition. Sailing ships when setting sail would have a sealed box containing money on board for good luck. If the voyage was a success, the box was given to the priest, opened at Christmas, and the contents distributed to the poor."

"Ah!" cried Philomena. "I'm all me life waiting to hear that bit of information."

"Oh never mind any of tha' stuff," Biddy interrupted crossly, impatient for a story.

"Anyway, my father thought it would be just the business, as you say here, if I started to make some moves and he could take my mother to the hospital in his dress suit. Oh wouldn't that be fun?"

"Oh! I can just imagine." Philomena smiled. "Dashing Daniel. They're full of good ideas when it comes to birth, but nowhere to be seen when needed."

"Well he was all for that, Mamá told me, until she suggested he sit down while she got her things together and they could set off in ten minutes. Of course in ten minutes he was a snoring pile of bow tie and tails in the kitchen and she was in her bed. I made no moves for some six or eight hours more. She called Abuelita Rosa and Sean, who took her to the Naval Base in his truck. And my father snored on."

"So December 27th was the day?" asked Kathleen.

"Yes. And, by the way, the Real Jesus was born possibly in September, possibly in the seventh century b.c. and not a.d. at all."

"Now THAT'S sacrilegious!" exclaimed Biddy. "Wha' about Christmas? Wha' about the stable and the donkey and the Star?" Biddy was fraught. "And wha' about my 'Hark the Herald'? That's my all-time favourite?" she demanded.

I shrugged. "None of it really meant anything until the early Christian church began to gain a foothold in the popularity stakes back in the fourth century. And numbering the years from the birth of Christ only started in the sixth century. They needed to respect the pagan or non-Christian beliefs of many civilisations if they were to convince them to convert to the Roman version of Christianity, Biddy. They were busy reorganising the world after all, and they couldn't just ride roughshod over what the collective populous believed."

"Our ancestors were pagan," Robert added. "They placed the birth of Jesus near to the Winter Solstice, which was far more important as a pre-Christian time of celebration. All of their beliefs and rituals were natural, following the seasons, or the sun, or the moon." He reddened. Robert never said very much and occasionally surprised himself.

"Exactly, Robert! The things they could observe and understand every day or every cycle, every year. The shortest days were celebrated as the sun would go no lower, signifying a change in season and meaning new growth would begin again. The curtain of darkness would rise with the sap."

"Oh I like tha'!" Biddy's humour changed instantly, her eyes opened wide with childish delight. "The curtain of darkness," she screeched excitedly, bored with our now otherwise dull discussion.

She jumped off her stool, dramatically feigning a swoon, her hand to her brow in mock suffering.

"Wha' do you think, Philomena? The curtain of darkness descended upon me an' I was blinded. There was no ligh'. Oh I think I could be on the stage. Wha' d'you think, Jesus? Am I good ah this?"

"I think you had too much sugar in your tea, Mrs. McCarthy," intoned Robert wryly.

"Arra shu' up you, Rober'. Tell your birthday story, Philomena, ah go on, go on, tell ih." Bridget climbed back on her stool.

"Ah will you whisht up, Biddy, 'tis only a nonsense."

"No, what is it, Philomena? Have I heard it?" I asked her curiously, for I was and certain I had not.

"Well maybe you have and maybe you haven't."

"Oh, I have heard this," exclaimed Kathleen, leaning across the counter. "This is so weird!"

"Is it Kathleen? Do you think I should tell them?" Philomena eyes twinkled.

"Arra, go on Mrs. S. It's definitely worth a hearing."

"Well, we were married on December 31st and my eldest boy, Con, was born a year later on January 1st."

"All marital laws intact," said Robert. He reddened quickly again, realising he was possibly just a little out of line with his peers and employer. Philomena ignored the interruption.

"Stan was next, thirteen months later, on February 1st. Two years later Dan was born on the 1st of March. Peg was born three years after that on … ."

"April firs'," screeched Bridget. "My birthday! 'Tis bad enough to be Fool's Day withou' sharing ih with one of her children."

Philomena paused, started to say something, then stopped. After a breath she continued.

"And then five years later, when I thought I was long done, and Ambrose said he was definitely done, Michael was born on the 1st of … ."

"May?" I suggested.

"Correct!" She laughed. "I have little to single me from the crowd, but I suppose it's a good story."

"An' the *Guinness Book of Records* wanted her story," chimed in Bridget, "buh faith and wasn' there a wan in the Philippines or off forren somewhere like tha' who had one more on June firs'. Pipped at the pos', Philly!"

Philomena frowned; Biddy was crowing and she was most certainly not a Philly. The English words I learned in the Two Spoons were nothing short of a miracle.

"That's quite extraordinary, Philomena, and so unexpected in anyone's life. But I think much more of your self singles you out from the crowd."

"Why thank you, Jesus. You are too kind."

"And what of the Fibonacci Sequence?" I enquired. They both looked at me blankly.

"The wha'?" asked Bridget.

Robert left his fire-tending to join us, so he knew. "Oh of course! Zero, one, one, two, three, five … ." He waved his poker excitedly, "the gaps between the years of their births. It is the start of the Fibonacci Sequence of Numbers, a.k.a.: $Xn + 2 = Xn + 1 + Xn$."

"Oh aren't you some clever clogs?" Biddy nearly sneered, but she couldn't really, for Robert was the most lovable boy you could meet and certainly part of the furniture at the Two Spoons.

"We did it in Maths at school but also in Biology," added Kathleen. "Nature's Secret Code or what was it, Jesus? Nature's Universal Rule. My biology teacher pooh-poohed it, said it was all a load of nonsense?" She looked at me.

"Oh it's been around forever," I replied, "and there are a lot of popular myths, but it's definitely there as a natural rule. It is connected to common concepts such as Divine Proportion, The Golden Ratio, Phi, mathematical sequences, and visual patterns observed in nature and music. But all of nature will adhere to some mathematical principles."

"Leonardo was a great fan, wasn't he?" asked Robert.

"Di Caprio?" asked Biddy, eyes widening. "Oh I love him. I'da hung off the fron' of the Titanic for him any day."

"DaVinci," said Robert, rolling his eyes at Kathleen. She laughed.

"Now she'll think it's Tom Hanks racing around Paris with Audrey Tautou." Biddy was still imagining the Titanic.

"And tell me, Jesus," Philomena interjected, "If I had had a child after Michael to fit your, whatever, your … Fibber Sequence, how long would I have had to wait?"

"Three plus five. Eight years, Philomena."

"Oh thank the Divine Lord." She blessed herself. "I got away with that then."

∞

What Philomena didn't tell in her story she told me another time, in a quiet moment in their little house on Church Lane. We were most probably waiting for Ambrose and my father to return from God knows where, doing goodness knows what.

"In between Peg and Michael, I lost a child. Gosh I hadn't even said anything to Ambrose, y'know, about it. I was unsettled one night and was up outta bed foothering about at that bewitching hour of four in the morning. I was often up at that time—dogs, cats, children, Ambrose's mother, my mother. I did it all at four a.m. 'Twas often the quietest part of my day. Anyways, I made tea, made toast, buttered the toast, felt, well, odd is the only word for it. I used the bathroom, met my blood there."

I reached across and squeezed her hand gently so she knew she didn't have to continue.

"I must've been awhile, for Ambrose was awake when I got back to my bed. He asked if I was all right, in his own way, 'Oh you've been gone for a wee while pet?' I was frozen so he put his arm around me and I just said, I miscarried. I passed it out of me and that was that. He said nothing at first, I was thankful for that I remember, and then he just kept me close to him and said, 'We have four lovely children, Philomena my love. If the good Lord gives us another we will have five. And we have each other.' "

She felt her cheek with her fingertips, searching out the stray hair for plucking.

"I cried for a bit, for I didn't know then that life has its ways. Then it wasn't very long before I was giving birth to Michael, a real dose I can tell you, and upon my soul he took his time about it. He had no desire in the world to come out and would have waited until he was six years old if he could."

I smiled at the vision of Michael in his school uniform ready to be born.

"And I lay there in the hospital at four in the morning, thinking of my new boy—it took us a week to name him—and I thought of my miscarried soul and d'you know, Jesus, I knew it was him. Michael. Like he had come to us once, then got cold feet and went back to God then thought ah okay, I'll do it this time. Is that nonsense to your ears, Jesus?"

"No," I replied, "not at all, Philomena. It makes perfect sense to my ears. And you are his mother, he was carried within you. If this is the thought that intuitively comes to you, then that's your truth."

"The Gospel according to Jesus?" she looked at me quizzically then laughed.

"Amen to that cousin."

∞

"Why is it the Two Spoons, Philomena?"

"Two Spoons? Oh wait 'til I tell you that one. When my lads were young they always heard me saying oh two spoons of sugar or two spoons of honey or two spoons of custard—everything they tell me had a measure of two spoons."

"I like that story."

"Oh it wasn't difficult. 'Twas Tom O'Toole's Tools when we bought it, back when Michael was ready for school and I was well ready for something that wasn't children, or minding something for someone. Ambrose and the older boys got at it that summer and stripped everything back to what you see now, fireplace, wooden floor, timber beams. Tom says they're there since his grandfather built the place so that's a few year, years ago."

I smiled at her self-correction. Bridget's habits were contagious, although Philomena had explained they were acceptable. Two years in the Gaelic language would have directly translated as dhá bhliain, a bhliain being a year.

"Off outta the blocks we went that September. Michael went off to primary school with the nuns and I haven't stopped since, Jesus. Maureen Doherty is with me since the start and just covers me if I want a day off now. Kathleen came along when she was only thirteen or so looking for summer work, so that's eight, or possibly nine or ten years now. Robert turned up the same way a year or so after Kathleen. I think they were in primary school together. His mam is Ruth Ryan over in the McSweeney's Villas. She had a tough run with her man; thankfully he took off and left her alone and she's made a fine job of that boy since." She heaved a bucket of autumn red apples between her feet.

"Tell me one of your own travelling stories, Jesus, 'til we see if we can shorten the apple peeling." We had cleared the trees of fruit in Ambrose's field and a huge old pot simmered on the Rayburn in Church Lane kitchen, stewing apples for the freezer.

"Give me a country and I'll sing you a song."

"I remember not long after I started the café, you were in Canada. What did you do in Canada?"

"Hmmm. Let me see. Yes, west to east, Seattle City in northwestern U S of A, across the border to Vancouver City and Victoria Island. Then we drove across the country. Vancouver to the mountains, to Calgary, to Montreal. Fabulous. It was late August and September. The hugest machines you ever saw, gobbling up wheat fields against blue skies. And they worked all through the night too. They have railway tunnels winding in the hills and goods trains so long, the engine is coming out one end of the tunnel and the last carriages haven't gone in the first. Van Horne's Road they call it, the railway and Canada itself got built along it, east to west to the Rockies."

Philomena deftly sliced an apple into quarters dropping it into a pot of cold water with a resounding shlop. "We went to the American side of Niagara Falls back in 2000. Our millennium trip to see the boys in Boston. Oh Lord God, five hundred miles with Con and Stan in this huge big station-wagon thing. Dan flew up at the weekend to join us there. Where would he have flown to? 'Twas a funny name, like cows I used to think, to try to remember it."

I laughed. "Buffalo."

"That's it! Buffalo. But the colours Jesus! This was October. It was majestic is all I can say."

"Ah, the New England fall colours, yes, I drove through them after Canada." I watched the apple peeler lay the fruit bare in my hands, the storyline forming in my head.

"On an earlier trip en route to Australia and New Zealand, I had met a Canadian, Mark, in Malacca. Malaysia you know, the far east, in my early days of travel. We shared a hostel dorm room for several hot days, we shared food in the kitchen and talked and drank some beers. We visited temples and shrines, learned how Buddhism, Islam, and Hinduism all happily co-existed in this corner and crossroad of civilisations. Extraordinarily peacefully co-existed you know, and that was the '90s. I wonder if it lasted? Anyway, 'Come and see me when you are in Canada,' Mark said, so I did. As you do."

"As you do," repeated Philomena.

"I looked him up in Calgary and we shook hands and talked and ate and drank some more beers and laughed at the differing circumstances, not to mention the polar opposite climatic conditions. Even though it was only autumn, it was very different to the wet season in Malaysia. He took me driving from their cabin in Canmore, Icefields Parkway, off road in the Rockies. Fabulous scenery and a fabulous experience. Travelling is never dull."

"Oh! The Rockies. We watched them on Discovery one wet Sunday, myself and Ambrose. We once talked of travelling again but that's as far as it got."

"They are stunning. Most mountain ranges are, Philomena, including the ones you know here. And these too are majestic. Often we shared the driving and in one of my turns, a kind of grey overcast day, there was a car coming straight at me, dead centre of the road."

Philomena gasped. "Oh no!"

"Oh yes! I swerved to the right and came to a slithering halt on the shoulder of the road, the car at a forty-five-degree angle pointing down into a ditch. I'm on the upside now remember, it's a left-hand drive and we're driving on the right."

"Oh no!"

"Oh yes! So we looked at each other, established that neither of us was injured—this was in the days before air-bags—gingerly clambered out of the vehicle, knowing that any shift of weight might send it slithering even farther, or over onto the roof.

" 'Walk away,' Mark whispered to me. Quite calmly, I have to add, as if even raising his voice might have sent the car toppling over. 'Take the key and walk away.' So we walked from the back of the vehicle, back along the road, the way we had just driven."

"What did the other car do? Did he stop to help you?"

"No, Philomena. He probably never even saw us. 'Native American,' Mark said, 'stoned or drunk or both, off the reservation.' No life for them, Philomena, no hope, misplaced, displaced, lost."

We peeled apples in a safe place in Cork.

"Native? What we call Indian like? Do they live on reservations?"

"Government land, re-settlement programmes, anything to keep them out of life with the rest of the folk."

"Bit like our itinerant Travellers here?"

"Yes, just different, a different ethnic background. Just like me in Ireland."

Philomena paused. "Yes, but your ethnicity isn't so different?"

"Because I'm largely perceived as Caucasian, mostly white, settled European. Maybe middle-class? That's how I get about unquestioned or uncorralled into a reservation."

We peeled some more, dropping quarters into the pot, the Rayburn drubbing and drumming its hum.

"We walked back along the road, enough yards to keep our feet moving, to a chapel. A simple white cruciform timber chapel. Plain wooden benches, dedications, plaques to all the deceased benefactors long gone, mostly of European descent, I imagine. You know the type of place?"

"Yes, I can imagine."

"We sat on a bench in the stillness and then without warning, I began to shake. An uncontrollable, limbic brain reaction to an adrenaline situation. Then I began to cry, there in the quiet, thousands of miles from my family, my roots, my familiar, in the company of a good man the Universe had sent my way. I had looked at death coming at me, on a Canadian highway."

"And you escaped it."

"Yes. Mark said to me 'Hey Jesus,' and he held my shaking hand. 'It's okay, it will be okay.' And guess what he said next, Philomena?"

"Ah shur how could I? What could anyone say?"

"He said, 'That crazy driver just gave you life. By not taking it away, it is all the more precious than it was.' Isn't that something? Isn't that the most amazing way to turn a situation around? When we went outside again, the cloud had gone, the sunlight was startling, the mountains were crisp, the air clear, the sky bright. The adrenaline heightened my senses. I heard the hawk screech, the glacier melting. I felt the life around me."

"How did ye get out of there?"

"Mark lay sprawled across the hood of the car on the topside, and I very slowly and carefully reversed onto the tar road. And on we journeyed."

We were silent save for the scrunching of a peeler across an apple.

"It never ever occurred to me, Jesus, that you may have been close to your death. In all our tales and times, that has never occurred to me." She looked at me directly. "I cherish our every moment."

"As with every moment we live and breathe, Philomena. I am sure I am not the only bright spot in your day."

∞

Cadíz 1986

I have taken some time to recall Mama Tia; the stories of Abuelo Sean and Abuelita Rosa seem to crowd out the other memories of my early life, in the same way as my connection to Cork and Ireland is so much stronger than my connection to Cyprus. I am sure a person can be drawn to one thing and not another, coupled with my father leaving Cyprus at ten years of age. I never met my grandfather Samuel Hadrian, leaving Mama Tia to fill in the blanks, which she chose not to. My father also chose not to, or more truthfully, he was unable to.

By the time of my childhood, she had made herself old and worn and bitter; long days of Casa des Angeles, long hours on her feet in the half-light. Twice as many years of life in Spain had not erased her Grecian fervour, although she only ever returned to Cyprus once. My father took her on a trip for her sixtieth birthday and came home lamenting the waste of his savings. There was nothing to be seen of her family, little to be recognised of her village and, if truth be told, the trip salted the seeping wounds of bitterness. Cyprus was wracked by its own wars, its own fight, Turks and Greeks, caught in the maelstrom of international waters.

Mama Tia had deep-set, dark eyes, as stern as Abuelita Rosa's were soft. Her short grey hair, flecked with black, was usually pulled back tightly in a bun. She had pudgy, doughy skin, a hard line of mouth not helped in any fashion by a quick tongue, often constantly in motion as she rolled an olive pit around her teeth, or a boiled sweet that smelled of aniseed; even that was distasteful to my childhood self. I realise of course that this was my childish perspective, for close familial ties often blur the true picture. I would have overheard parental discussions about things she said or did, or how a customer reacted to a particular situation. It would have been impossible for this not to have coloured my own sketch.

She took snuff, a sequence of actions I followed closely, for initiation of this procedure meant a short interlude from her lamentations. The ochre coloured powder in a glass jar, a measured amount on the rear of her left hand, the quick action to her nostril and the following long inhalations, nasal twitching, sniffing and snorting was simultaneously fascinating and disgusting. There were the yellowing tissues peeking out of her housecoat pockets or thrown on her kitchen chair along with a head scarf, yellowing thumb pads from blocking a nostril to snuff through the other. I drank it all in.

She was an icon of course, in Cadiz, for Casa des Angeles was a popular taberna, and the parents of my classmates and friends would have known her and her hostelry. Many of the Naval Base residents would have chosen the taberna when they visited the city, so within the cross cultures of Irish musicians, Naval personnel, Rosa's medical colleagues, and locals, there was always an interesting atmosphere.

We children would often hang out around the taberna, on bikes or skates, with the football, eating ice-creams, or occasionally Mama Tia would furnish us with a jug of sticky, syrupy lemonade and bowls of potato crisps. I was a favoured friend; for my family was small in number, I had no rivalling siblings and two generations of adults mostly good-humoured, generous, and fun to be around.

For a period in the mid-'70s, we would watch pop videos in the house of Pedro and Ana, for no one else had a television—maybe with Isabel, maybe Margarita too. The British rock band Queen played "Bohemian Rhapsody," and we would colloquially sing Mamma Tia, Mamma Tia, Bee-el-ze-bub put the devil inside of you, of yoo-oo-oo, of YOU-OO-OO—dancing wild with screaming air guitars. Childish fun, that makes me smile as an adult but wince at the hurt it would have caused her.

Her redemption, "Always present in an unpleasant place," Mamá's life lesson for me, came in the form of her stories which she would recount to me in every detail, speaking a combination of Greek, Spanish, and my father's English. These were childhood stories of Cyprus and her brothers, the taberna her mother owned, her father's fishing boats, for they were not of poor means. Stories of the goats in the mountains, the rose-tinted memories of a childhood in the sun far away. Stories of the endless footfall of customers through the taberna. I liked the taberna, I liked to help there and business was always brisk. I rather believe she saved all her ill humour for the family, as if it was somehow all our fault. She never turned it on me when I was with her and her customers. My father largely ignored her complaining, which possibly helped nothing or no one except himself. She did get on well, even regularly sharing laughter, with Abuelita Rosa, but then that couldn't have been any other way. Everyone easily loved Rosa.

Coming to what was to be nearly her end, she was intolerant of everyone and everything to the point that my father employed a couple to take care of her and the taberna. Abuelita Rosa would visit and croon and make sure she was clean and dressed, Mamá would ignore her lamentations and caress her hand and read to her in Spanish or English. Mamá never took to Greek and obviously never felt the need to converse too deeply with her mother-in-law. What she already spoke would suffice. She would play softly on her violin. Sean Seamus always called it a fiddle; he used to laugh and say, " 'Tis a fiddle if ye're buyin' and a violin if ye're selling.' "

Sometimes after studies or training classes, I would sit with Mama Tia and make some shape of her ramblings, fitting them into the stories I had heard as a younger child. She would place her hand on my arm, not sure whether I was a stranger or not, and whisper, "What's it all about pet?"—at least that's how I translated it from Greek. "Calma, Abuelita, respira suavemente," I would try and soothe her. "Jesús te espera." Breathe gently. Jesus is waiting for you. From the kitchen I heard the music of ABBA on the radio. I can but smile and pick up the refrain, "Mamma Tia, here you go again."

She wasn't decrepit or infirm but something inside her was giving in. She would mutter indiscernibly, sometimes cheerfully, sometimes darkly, and fiddle with her prayer ring. And always the snuff. I warmed to her then, for she now was the child. I was older, wiser, and had cultivated a patience with the world. That Redemption, always present in an unpleasant place stayed in my mind. My own wisdom could now ground me.

The doctor who attended after her final collapse pronounced it to have been most likely a brain aneurysm, which may have also accounted for her declining behaviour. She was in the taberna yard getting air with Micha and Eva, her caring couple, sharing stories with my father in Greek and Spanish when her face changed. She whispered to my father that she felt ill, then without warning, vomited violently into Sean's cut-stone drain. She never regained consciousness and passed on after some six quiet hours.

It was several months later, sitting in my parent's kitchen in Cadiz, as they were moulding and shaping their plan for the future with Abuelita Rosa, that I heard a small noise arise in my left ear. A soft hum, then a more persistent ringing, so I paused in their conversation to listen, to attune to this disturbance in my body which rose in pitch to a constant wave. I breathed my yoga breaths, focussed on the sound and was instantly conscious of a memory forming into a scene in my still mind. In this picture, I was in the great cathedral of Bristol, drinking coffee in the community café, when a small dart of sunlight settled on my cup causing the surface to shimmer. As I lifted the cup to drink, the light rose to my eyes, forcing them closed, and I was warmed both by the light and the liquid.

There, sitting with my parents and Abuelita Rosa in Cadiz, the noise in my ear diminished and I knew my Bristol memory was the moment that Mama Tia had passed on. She had shared with me on her final journey, in the city of her husband's birth.

∞

Cadíz 1988

Within two years, my father had retired from the Navy, for Rota Base was downsizing, the Americans were largely moving out. Mamá was still teaching; Abuelita Rosa had retired from the Naval Hospital, she was nearly seventy, sprightly and well. I was nearing the end of my studies with Dr. Zhao and planning a long overseas trip for the forthcoming year.

My father was tense, anxious, unwell. He would uncharacteristically complain of headaches, nausea, ghost pains in his ankle. Retirement was proving problematic for him. I would hear him argue with my mother, "It is your bloody music, not mine," his impatience and anger bursting forth in a rabid torrent. Or I would overhear, "What about Jesús? Where will home be for Jesús?" It was not my place to interfere; I was no longer a child in their marriage so I would hug them both and stay out of the way. Sometimes I would stay overnight at Dr. Zhao's to give them space for their growing, or sleep in Abuelita Rosa's casa de jardín.

One evening in May, my father was outside Dr. Zhao's house as I left to return home from my studies.

"Ah there you are, Jesús, I am taking a walk. Have you time to walk with me?"

I hid my surprise. This was not the father I knew, in any shape or form.

"Sure Papá. It's hot eh? Let's walk to the harbour and get a beer."

"Oh splendid! Just what I thought too."

We ambled through the small streets and lanes of old Cadiz. After all the years here, I realised my father had spent an inordinate amount of time on the Naval Base and not so much on the city paths. We passed the time well, noticing this and that. Sometimes I would say, "Abuelo Sean built that, or fixed that." He seemed surprised that I would remember.

"I am not sure I would remember anything that I might have seen in Cyprus before I was ten."

"Ah, but that's so much longer ago, Papá."

We laughed together and he put his arm around my shoulders.

"I'm not a Spaniard, you know, Jesús?"

I was perplexed by this curious comment and did not respond.

"You know. You know what I mean. I'm, I am, am not from here. Then I am not from England either, despite how I sound. In fact, what I miss most is the sea. Getting off the land and onto the sea. Being on it."

I nodded, walking in step with him, waiting for him to continue. We paused at Calle Ahumada, where a taxi driver was berating an errant cyclist in good Spanish style.

"I know this is Spain and it is where I have lived and I have never really lived anywhere Greek, you know, Greek that it mattered."

I took his hand in mine. "Papá, you have so much on your mind and so much to say and I am going to listen to everything. I am here only for you, for as long as you need me. Let's get those beers first."

We made our way to Calle Méjico, dodging evening traffic, thankful to feel the cool sea breeze, to hear the slapping halyards on masts, familiar dock sounds, the groan of a cruiser pulling off its berth.

When we were settled in our seats I turned to him. "Okay, Papá, you have my ears."

"Well, well, oh, I just don't know, Jesús. It's all such a confused muddle for me. I'm not even a middle-aged man at all and yet I already feel like a retired old fool. I do not know what to do next."

I took his hand again. Abuelita Rosa came to mind so I did nothing, except stroke the deep tendon lines to his fingers.

"I just don't know, Jesús. Mamá seems intent on moving to Ireland, to Cork. She says, 'Sólo para ver,' just to see, but I think that's just to get me to agree. But this means something to her, it is important for her, she loves her music and Rosa will be wherever, with your Mamá. She says we are young enough for change so we should seize the opportunity. And to be quite frank with you now, Jesús, I am bloody terrified."

I nodded my understanding. "I know this, Papá. I can see why." Somehow, his hand was still in mine.

"Well you'll be off doing something fantastic with your life and what will I do next? Hmm? What's fantastically next for me? Hmm? Oh I am pleased to no longer be serving but in truth it is all I have ever done."

We sat for a while, listening, watching. I felt he wasn't finished. He took his hand away and, taking off his sunglasses, leant on his elbows, wiping his eyes with his forefingers, massaging the bridge of his nose. The third-eye chakra was my thought. Clear sight. We sipped at the beers, for there truly was no hurry.

"You know, back in 1945, I was just eight, eight years old. We lived on the south-western part of the island, south of Paphos, Episkopi Bay, near enough to the RAF base. I was going to a sort of school near there that one of the older RAF officers had started. Just too many children running wild. Feral you know, like the goats."

We laughed together. Laughter and beer and evening sunshine, the perfect stage. His-tory began to flow.

"Two of the uncles had volunteered to fight with the Allies. They were back, one pretty well shook up, the other physically intact but never too sound in the head. The war was still at large in mainland Europe and the East, my father was still out there somewhere on the seas. So this chap from Cambridge is teaching us all in English, the three R's. He's happy, we're happy, happily singing along with him in this big, demountable air shed he had borrowed off the base. He lived in a hut beside it. But the political stuff from before the war hadn't gone away. Enosis, they called it. That is, out with the English and we'll become part of Greece thank you. So the pre-war anti-English sentiment was creeping back into the locality. I wasn't the only half-British weanling I can tell you. And my mother was more fortunate than many, in that she was actually married to the man who fathered her child."

My father's tale was paused by the waiter coming with more beers.

"Y un plato de bocadillos por favor." I called to him as he left us. I was wise enough in my early adulthood to know that the wonderful combination of sun and beer in the early evening, might be regretted the next morning.

"My father turned up one day in late '46. I thought it was a usual period of leave, but it was sick leave. Turns out he was working on the Jewish evacuation programme. Straight from being chased around the Med and Aegean by guns and bombs and now this. Millions of Jews with nowhere to go, trying to get to Palestine. Fifty-three-thousand displaced Jews moving into internment camps on the other side of our island. Fifty-three-and-a-half-thousand. Six-thousand-two-hundred-and-something orphans, mostly young children like me. My father and his lot had to patrol the seas, intercepting boats trying to get to Palestine, the Holy Land. They desperately needed somewhere safe after the horrors of the war. The Holocaust. The Navy had to hold them back and bring them to Cyprus, slowly drip-feeding them to the Holy Land over the next three years."

Our beers sat untouched, condensation trickling down the glasses, forming droplets on the table. I gently touched one and it ran along to join another and another. Fifty-three-and-a-half-thousand human beings in tents and huts wondering where their lives were going next. The waiter brought us our tapas.

Papá continued quietly. "My father stayed with us for a few weeks. I think it was the longest period of time he ever spent with me. He would walk with me to Captain Jack's for school, spend the day working with the uncles, or in the taberna drinking beer. By the time I came home, he would be snoring in the garden, or on the porch. I would do my chores and wait for him to wake, then we would eat and walk to the beach, or up to the mountain. I couldn't then fathom the enormity of what he had experienced, both during his war service and now in its incredible aftermath. The damage it had done to him. I remember a softness then in my mother. Her dashing young sailor of course had changed. War had changed him. One drunken night he shouted at me after some misdemeanour. I am, after all, a nine-year-old boy. He shook me until I rattled then he shouted that he would take me across the island the next day to see how the little Jewish children lived in the camp. He would leave me there and see how I liked that!"

The silence was longer this time. I didn't break it. My father's jaw worked incessantly on a peanut.

"We survived it. The following year, he positively leapt at the chance to transfer to Cadiz. It took them until 1949 you know, to move all those interred in the Cyprus camps to Palestine, and by that time the powers had created the State of Israel. Statements of statesmen. Declarations of what was deemed best for a body of persons, humans. I saw the camp myself, near Larnaca, before we left for Cadiz. I have never forgotten the nausea I felt, all those human beings, many having survived the awful bloody war, waiting for someone else at a desk, bloody miles away, to decide their next fate. Seeing that, you know, we are not really human, Jesús. The animals are kinder to each other."

I inhaled deeply. Papá drank some beer, ate tapas and sardines. I broke bread and handed it to him.

"I am sorry. I don't know where all that came from. I suppose retirement has given me time for thinking, reflecting. That, and the death of my mother of course."

My father: Cypriot war child, Cadiz naval teen, Royal or American Naval adult, son, father, husband, son-in-law, all the roles he had fulfilled and no idea of him-self.

"Papá."

He finished chewing and sipped his beer. "Well then, Jesús, what comes next?"

"Just you, Papá. Whatever you would like next. No more Naval Base, no more taberna?"

"Oh no! No taberna, Abso-bloody-not!"

Ah! The sun and the beer had found each other.

"You love Mamá?"

He looked at me quickly, surprised by the question. "Of course!"

"No. Not of course, Papá." I shook my head. "People don't always love each other forever. Maybe it is also time for a change in this?"

"Oh no, no, no. No! I love your mother. There is no question of a future for me without her."

"Bueno! So now you have a good starting point. No navy, no taberna, yes María, so that's yes Rosa also. What else?"

He sat thoughtfully chewing, popping salted nuts into his mouth. I could not see his eyes behind his sunglasses; I could see frown lines softening his forehead, smile lines slowly deepening at his temples. He swallowed a mouthful of his beer, resoundingly thumping the glass on the table.

"Roses!" he declared.

"Roses?" I was intrigued.

"Yes, roses. Oh yes! I had a commander at the base who kept an envelope full of articles and clippings from newspapers or magazines, as to how to best tend to and grow roses. He worked much too hard, never took a wife, never had a garden, then had a heart attack and died. Just there, on the base. When we cleared his office I found this envelope and I thought, I will do this. I will keep roses."

"Wonderful. That is so wonderful Papá. Now you can do just that."

"And vegetables. I will grow my own food. No more canteen mush for me."

I laughed and he too laughed at his own absurdity. "Papá, you have spent thirty years telling everyone how the navy food was just splendid."

"Oh pure crap, Jesús! I was lucky enough to have a home in Cadiz and not have to take all my meals there. They got very fond of quick meals, fries, pizzas, all that easy 'n' cheap food. Oh dreadful rubbish. It was much better out at sea though," he mused.

"And now you can choose for yourself. De la semilla al plato. From seed to plate."

"Very good yes. I can do that. Where though, Jesús? Where? This is the question. Spain, where I am? Or Ireland for your mother?"

I munched an olive together with a honeyed almond, relishing the savoury and the sweet. "I love Ireland, Papá. I loved it when I was ten, I loved it again when I was eighteen. I loved it with Mamá last year. Most certainly there is no reason not to sólo para ver. Just go to see. At the very worst you can come back to Cadiz."

He sat thoughtfully. "Yes, I realised walking here with you, I hardly know Cadiz. I have spent so many years ferrying across, or driving in and out of the Naval Base, I have missed the city growing and changing. Then between weekend trips away with you and Mamá, or helping my own mother in the taberna, I never made the time."

We finished our beers. "Another?" I asked.

"Hmm, I think not, thank you. We might see what that lovely Rioja is like at home eh? And your mother will be wondering what has become of us."

"Perfect, Papá."

He pulled his wallet from his shirt pocket but I stopped his hand. "Papá, I would like to buy these beers. I would like this to be the first step of your new journey in life, whatever you decide. And I am honoured to be with you, making it or taking it."

"Oh nonsense, Jesús!" he cried. "You can't pay for my beers. You had to do all the listening. I never once even asked you how you are getting on with Dr. Zhao?"

"We have time now as we walk for my turn to tell, Papá. Please let me do this. For you."

"We may never sup in Spain again you know?"

"You're hardly departing on the next tide?"

"Your mother would be."

∞

They sold everything—Rosa's house and contents, our own house and fittings. The taberna went to an English officer and his wife who had come from Huddersfield and were now retiring from the Naval Base. All the innards and outers and chattels of our lives. I kept my grandfather's tools in the painted black toolbox he had made, carefully storing away the little wooden creatures he had carved on our ramblings through my first ten years of life. I wanted to be there, sorting and packing, calming my father's anxiety, sharing and stoking my mother's excitement. My parents and Rosa boxed what they thought they might need in Ireland and together we watched it craned onto a freight vessel in Cadiz. I chose to depart some time before them, to walk the north-west coast of Spain in September sunshine. Soon after, my family would finally leave Cadiz to drive through Spain to northern France in their VW camper, before catching a ferry from Le Harve to Cork.

"Hey, Jesús," my mother called to me, one of the days before I left them.

"Mamá?"

She leaned against a stack of cardboard boxes, taped and labelled, ready to go. She held up a large white well-used envelope that had the Royal Navy insignia in the top corner.

"Roses?" she enquired of me.

"Roses, Mamá? Commander Abbott, I believe."

"Sí, Jesús. Roses for Cork." She smiled. "I thank you."

"No es nada, Mamá. Una nueva vida para ustedes dos. What could be better? A new life! What an adventure. I love you."

"Not as much as I love you, Jesús."

After a week or more of walking, reflecting, unravelling the Cadiz ties, I was stopped in my tracks outside Mirador de Monteferro by a deep desire to be with them. I arrived unannounced two weeks later and I was there as they disembarked at Ringaskiddy Port, outside the city of Cork in southern Ireland. Suddenly, there were here my dearest family, swept amongst a sea of smiling faces of my mother's relatives, cheering and waving Irish and red-and-white Cork flags. My Great-Uncle Jerry, the pony whisperer—a younger, taller version of Abuelo Sean. His daughter and sons, Great-Aunts Frances and Mary, and Mary's daughter Philomena and her husband, Ambrose, and several of her own family. Her brother Frankie and his wife Dympna were also present. I could not have ever imagined this, for it was not a greeting but a home-coming. All this at seven in the morning.

"Rosa, María, Daniel, family of John James, welcome to Cork!" The accents were broad, loud and sing-songy. My great-aunts clasped my mother to them, tears flowing freely down their cheeks.

"Welcome, welcome, welcome."

∞

Rostellan, East Cork 1989

They bought a cottage in Cork, after a period of deliberation while renting a small seaside house. Abuelita Rosa walked and walked, the stones of Sean's ancestors guided her way and she would smile and talk to strangers on the path in her Cork English-Spanish. But it was a harbour place, a place of accents and colours where patience was the norm, acceptance a priority. Rosa quickly felt at ease, at home. She was bright and energetic and her nursing skills played a deciding role in where they settled.

The local doctor or GP, general practitioner, made her acquaintance. In those days he offered every hours attendance from the surgery at his home and he had never had the help of a nurse. Rosa became "the Spanish lady who took my bloods," or "Mrs. O who changed my dressing." In time she became known as Rosa O. We would hear her hailed on the path, in the local shop or Post Office, "Rosa O! How are you?" "Rosa, lovely to see you." In six months, Rosa ingrained herself to Sean's folk and, agreeably, my father admitted that as she was the sole earner in the household, they could live only in proximity to her employment. They bought the Cottage by the Water, as it was locally known. And my father bought a boat.

It was a small cabin fishing boat, the Lily Kathleen, enough to pootle around the harbour with a few trailing lines. In truth, it was enough to poke, to explore, to follow charts and currents. He pressed and pressed but neither my mother nor I were the sea-pootling kind. I would walk the world and happily never step on the sea. I used to laugh and say to my father, "Abuelo Sean told me not to," then Mamá would laugh and say he told her not to too. Abuelita Rosa came to the rescue, lining up Cornish Dave, whom she had met on a surgery visit, as first-mate for my father's fishing trips.

Pretty soon, things took off in every direction. Before I could turn my head, I was charged with house-sitting the cottage by the water, a newly acquired pair of young Springer Spaniels, a few rooms to paint, a hedge to clear, and a series of articles to complete in order to earn a few dollars. Dollars made just about as much worth in Irish pounds as Spanish pesetas in 1989.

Abuelita Rosa and Mamá, a mother-daughter cacophony of excitable chatter in Spanish, set off in the VW to explore the Beara Peninsula in south-west Cork. It had been twelve years since our Great Trip and my mother was fuelled with the possibility of sharing this adventure with her own mother.

My father packed a kit bag and, with a visible leap in his stride, hitched a ride with the ladies in the VW to the other side of the harbour, to where Cornish Dave and he were to crew on a lovely Looe Lugger motor-ketch berthed at Monkstown. I had once driven them over to Monkstown and, although not a seafarer, I was impressed. She was a classy eye-catcher, a 1935, 45-footer plus bowsprit, a black hull with startling white gunwales. The MK Voyageur was a beauty of polished teak, brass portholes, and flapping sails that promptly turned two grown men into yabbering school boys. She too had come from Spain, where her skipper, Tony, had spotted her and instantly coveted another man's goods. He struck a deal and sailed her to Cork for a full repaint and clean-up on the hard. They were now to set sail for the Scilly Isles to visit Dave's daughter and then up the south-west coast of England to Bristol.

There was a mid-afternoon quiet once they had all departed, that silence that descends when other beings withdraw their presence. A palpable absence. Watching for the evening ebb tide, I hopped on a bicycle and biked the six kilometres to the gates of the old fort overlooking the vista of Cork Harbour, just so I could jump and wave and shout as the four sailors set forth on their adventure. My face was one huge smile for my father, my heart brimming with love for the Universe that sent him this opportunity, my eyes salty with tears.

Later I pulled an old deck chair out of the shed, for the cottage had come with an assortment of pre-owned possessions. The Springers snuffed and snorted through the dewy grass. A silence enveloped the harbour in the late July setting sun, except for the phot phot of summertime tennis balls from the club at the old Air Force base. The full moon arose over the lake. In the stillness, a curlew called and on a nor'-westerly breeze I caught the strains of music from the town of Cobh. An accordion played "The Parting Glass." I heard my steady heart, louder, the music louder, my hair prickled and lifted, and out of nowhere a soft sighing wind.

"Here I am, Abuelo."

"Indeed y'are, Jesus. Shur can't I see you myself."

∞

On their return some three or so weeks later, my mother and hers were quietly relieved to be at home in their new home. "Tierra," Abuelita Rosa said as she sat at the kitchen table. There had been plenty of activity on their arrival, oohs and aahs at my paint-work, reuniting with the Spaniels, ferrying bits of this and bits of that from the VW, last scrapings of butter, empty bread wrappings, smoked fish from Passage East—for they had looped their way west then north and east on a Fine Tour of Munster.

Over a busy meal of salad and new potatoes I had prepared for them, amidst the collected ramblings of anachronistic snippets, my mother began the tale of discovery.

"Oh precious Jesús," she began, sweeping cutlery and plates away from her, to clear some space in the confusion of stories and create a clean canvas for the next sketch. "Please," she gestured to the chair, "please sit and write for me, for I cannot trust myself to recall it all. What a journey! For more, fantástico, estupendo than being right here in Cork where my father was born, is the story Rosa has. Estrafalario!"

"Rosa?" I asked quizzically, "Abuelita?"

Abuelita Rosa smiled and took my hand. "Jesús," she whispered, her head bowed over my hand, then suddenly jumped out of her sitting to her little feet, clapped her hands together, and shouted to the ceiling, "I'm from Cork, boy!"

I was astounded. The simplicity of the connections, the wondrous weaving of the worldly web. Notwithstanding Abuelita's instant attraction to Abuelo Sean, his music, his language, his ways, back there in Cadiz. And a story unfolded, that for some reason not one of us had ever considered or questioned, of the lineage of Rosa's own family. Perhaps Sean with his tales and tunes, his engaging easy-going way, had permitted her to slip into the shadowy wings? She could now make her way to her own centre stage.

In the first days of their Fine Tour, having idled from Monkstown to Blackrock and drank copious quantities of tea with a spider's web of relatives, they had meandered down to Kinsale for their first Tour Stop. In conversation with a local historian in the old Town Hall museum, Rosa's family birth name was queried, as Kinsale is a town of immense connection to Spain. Upon hearing it, the historian immediately brightened and cheerfully announced, "Ah! The Terry's of Cork!"

And there it was in dusty documents: Rosa's grandmother, one Ana María Herrera y Terry, of Amalia Terry Vienne, descendants of one of three Terry merchant families from Cork. Pre-empting, and then escaping expulsion from Cork in the late 17th-century Reformation, they followed their existing trading links to Cadiz.

There they were, Rosa's ancestors, Domingo and Guillermo Terry, Dominic and William, persecuted by Cromwell for their Catholicism in Ireland, granted privilege and nobility for the same beliefs, and their commercial success, in Spain. They married into other Irish families, and Rosa's maternal line was to a McNamara merchant family from Waterford.

Abuelita Rosa fished through her handbag, extracting items to the table—book, reading glasses, assorted lotions, maps and tourist leaflets, before retrieving a many-folded sheet of paper with handwritten notes scribbled in every direction and shape. This was my task, to decode all the information they had received into a narrative. My eye was drawn to a list, a table of companies in the Terry family name: cotton, steamboats, savings bank, insurance, mining, railways, timber, and, of course, politics and military. How had we not known of this before now? How had I not questioned it myself? Upon his return to Cork, my father exaggerated the business claims, presenting Rosa with a carefully wrapped Terry's Chocolate Orange. It remained unopened on top of the fridge for quite some time as a testament to the ancestral success.

"This was so long ago, Jesús," Abuelita Rosa started. "So long before my mother and me. Hace demasiado tiempo. My Mamá says of a fire when I was a child and muchos registros se perdieron. Many?"

"Records, registers," Mamá replied.

"Sí, records were lost. She and my aunt lost la herencia. Inheritance. Sí. She returned from Madrid to Cadiz and never spoke much of them again. Afligida. Grieving. My father fought in the Republican Army; I knew so leetle about him too. Always talking, talking, dashing about full of politics." She threw her eyes heaven-wards. "Discurso político y argumento. Means nada, nothing to a young girl. I was also but a young girl when I met Sean Seamus. Ah! He was so exciting, in the middle of civil war and all that político. He

came off a boat from another country, with his stories and music."
She smiled, idly running her thumb along the spine of her book.

"It was a new country with Franco. My Mamá did not live much
longer, my life goes a different direction. I loved my studies of
nursing and helping others, I loved your Abuelo Sean and soon I
had lovely María to take care of. There was war everywhere. Even
in Rota Base we were busy, you know; hospital ships would be
coming with wounded soldiers. We were not with Hitler, we were
not with America, but we had soldiers to help, whoever they were.
What was I to think about my ancestors? Nothing. Nada. Men in
frock coats making business deals. Pfff."

That was Abuelita's summation of her dusty history. But if she was
from Cork, then I was even more so now. Into my international
pot was another spoonful of Irishness. The historical Catholicism
in our genes had paved a golden path for my ancestors—persecuted
in their homeland, revered in their new land. His-tory unfolding
its path.

∞

It took us some time to poke a little more in the parchment
records of Rosa's forebears. After her discovery on their Fine Tour
of Munster, we had again travelled to Kinsale, west of the city
of Cork. A most beautiful location, wedged between the wide
harbour and the river estuary, three-storey merchant houses clad
in the slates of Spanish influence. My father was always at ease
in a marine setting and we moseyed for an hour or so along the
pontoons of every manner of berthed craft. He would point out
this or that, features of each style of vessel, weighting, lines, keel
types. I loved their look, their shapes; so I happily moseyed with
him, smiling at, or cheerfully hailing crew busy in their chores,
the rocking marina enough momentum for my non-sea pootling

self. The clinking halyards a rhyming metre, the flapping flags mesmerising, the shafts of sunlight sparkling on the sea riveting.

We found the back streets of the town—always the back streets, poking along lanes, peering around doorways. It seemed to be our way anywhere in the world. Abuelita Rosa and Mamá drifted to the tourist shops, crafty things, woolly sweaters, and "tat from China," Papá would tease. We climbed narrow foot-worn steps to the Bowling Green, narrower steps to the Ramparts, fished along a one-car street that allowed two to pass. We found fun because we are foreigners, and somehow can laugh at the peculiar ways, the Irishness of a one-car street that has two-way traffic. In a short walk we were surveying the breadth of the harbour, the meandering river to the New Bridge. Cruisers of all sizes were in varying stages of setting forth from the marina for an evening sail. "Racing, I would suspect," Papá ventured. "There," he pointed. "That is what I have to see." Across the harbour, the star-shape Charles Fort, immense, impressive, a magnet to a military man.

As we descended an uneven winding stair of stone, from our viewing point, I asked of him, "Well, Papá, how is the going and seeing in Cork working for you?"

He stopped and turned back uphill to face me. I was a head and shoulders above him as he leaned back against the limestone wall, pink and white valerian brushing his hair, penny-wort stalks growing from his shoulders. I could but smile and say, "It looks as if it might be suiting you, sir?"

He grinned at me before pushing himself off the wall and straight into my arms, his head buried in my chest. "I think it just might be, Jesús. Yes, I do."

Kissing his greying head, I told him, "I love you, Papá."

"And that is what makes all the difference, my child."

∞

A quiet period followed as they settled into life in East Cork. I came and went a number of times, marvelling each time at their progress, their undertakings in making the cottage their own. Between the kneading of the dough and the shaping of the bread, I would help my mother shift some six barrow-loads of field stones to where my father was bounding their field. At another time, on the instructions of Mamá, he formed a circular path through a wildflower meadow. "A caim," he told me. "A Celtic Christian tradition, an invisible circle drawn around a person, aware of the all encompassing love of God within, encircling, unfolding and protecting."

> *May You be a bright flame before me,*
> *May You be a guiding star above me,*
> *May You be a smooth path below me,*
> *And a loving Guide behind me,*
> *Today, tonight and forever.*

I liked it. I liked my mother's embracing the Celtic past. We talked about this across the kitchen table, the detritus of another meal pushed aside. Having just spent nearly a month camping on the Dingle Peninsula with Seán Ó Ceallaigh's book, *Ireland: Elements of Her Early Story*, I pored over the *Reader's Digest Atlas of Europe* and drew pencil lines for Mamá on a clean sheet of paper.

"Here, Mamá. The early human stories have movements like this."

I fanned lines on the blank page from Germany to Spain, Spain to France, across the Mediterranean to North Africa, to the Middle East, back across the Med to Spain, up through Iberia and across the Atlantic to the south of Ireland. Back again to the continent, back to Ireland. Ten-thousand years of footprints across our corner of the globe.

"There are books from the 5th century, there are fables and tales, there are stories along the Biblical lines, but it seems there were definitely visitors in Ireland from Spain as far back as six-thousand years ago. Not necessarily yet called Spaniards, but they had broken their endless journey on these shores, built settlements, stayed for a few generations. It was only in recent times that humans needed to name everything, draw borders. Remembering of course it was the winners wrote the stories. The anecdotal or oral evidence was unluckily not always recorded."

She nodded, lips pursed. "So everyone is no one, no one is everyone?"

I looked at her quizzically. "Yes," I hesitated. "Meaning no one is from anywhere particularly?"

"Sí," she nodded, "that is what I mean. We say Spaniard, French, Greek, Cypriot, Irish, English, blah, blah, but it just depends which ancestor you have? Where they were able to travel to? Or if they travelled at all."

"Or got ship-wrecked, or blown off course, or taken hostage or prisoner."

"Sí. Or thrown out like my ancestral Terry family because they did not like the new English queen? Everyone's story is just a story, no?"

"Yes, Mamá. A story, a storyline that joins us to our forebears, ancestors, wherever they came from, whoever they were."

"So the story of my mamá, the Terry family story, is not so surprising? Although we lived in Cadiz thinking Cork was so far away—and why did she fall in love with a Corkman?" She laughed.

"And the other man she chose was Chinese-American," I reminded her. "And why did she not fall in love with a nice man from Cadiz? And then you have to ask why did you not fall in love with a nice man from Cadiz? Or what was his name from Nerja?"

"Antonio," Mamá sighed. "He had the most beautiful eyes, Jesús. And a very nice culo." She patted her bottom. "Hmm, I remember it!"

"Oh Mamá! Please!" I laughed, then shrugged. "But it wasn't to be Nerja. You chose differently and now your story and Papá's story is back in Cork. Such is the way of the world."

I liked my parent's resettlement programme. No one talked fondly about Cadiz other than in recalling stories, no one lamented. Occasionally Abuelita Rosa would berate the weather, missing the hot sun, but the life she made amongst the Irish more than compensated. She was revered in her position, every day brought a new tale of new patients she had met at the surgery, new stories of half-English words or phrases. In a small community of course, everyone knew who she was and why she was here. Everyone knew Abuelo Sean's ancestry.

∞

Wales 1990

When our new lives gave us the space, we took a trip to Wales, to walk about in the southern area of the Gower, Pen Rhys, and Oxwich Bay. Just us three—Mamá, Abuelita Rosa, and me in the VW camper. We took a ferry from Rosslare, the south-east Wexford corner of Ireland from where Abuelo Sean had retched and reached across the Irish Sea. My father was happily rebuilding walls around the cottage and equally happy to be relieved of his immediate women folk. My tenacious mother had gathered all the knowledge from her aunts and cousins, which didn't amount to much, for Sean Seamus was the only family member who had ever been to Pen Rhys and Oxwich Bay.

Snaking along off the ferry, with thundering trucks heading to cross the Severn to the rest of England, we were small and we were strangers. I followed the map in my mind across the back of Swansea town to where the cattle-gridded road welcomed us to The Gower. To where there was stone everywhere; a two-thousand-year-old hill fort, a pile of white stones, moss-covered and draped across rocky edges and hillsides. Cliffs dropping away to an expanse of beach, and rising ledges lifting again to wooded glades, clinging to the coastline. The moors were high and heathery, the sheep indifferent to our breathless presence.

It was just as Sean had recalled for me and, as I then realised, my mother had heard the same precise details from him in her early life. The VW wound steeply uphill and downhill, along impossibly narrow lanes through swooping beech trees, tidy farmyards nestling into their hedges, as if the land had formed around them in some ancient earthen lift. We would sit and wait in the smallest gateway as a couple of dogs herded a tight flock of woolly sheep along the lane, brushing and bumping the side of the van. A friendly "hullo" and a wave of a stick and a "Well now, what a day," from a following farmer.

We didn't know the car-penter's name, but Mamá asked the right questions in the right places—until she unearthed a hamlet and his house and an old lady with yellowed teeth who somehow remembered the Irish mason, all those years ago.

"He was my grandfather," my mother told her, her voice catching in joy. As in so many places and cases I have witnessed, Spanish-Irish-English is to be understood by something as diverse as hillside Welsh, possibly only through divine intervention.

"Oh what a fine singer he was and all his lovely stone work. I see it every day."

I didn't get that immediately but the old lady repeated it twice more for Rosa and Mamá. Our ears quickly tuned in, for she had much to say.

"I remember listening to his voice in our kitchen. We were in the Gardener's house across the green from the Master Carpenter. They had a little platform in behind and a wee beer-house where the men gathered after work, or after a celebration, and told stories and sang their songs. Your grandfather was a baritone, a fine booming sound with that lovely Irish lilt. Pen Rhys has been my home for every day of my life and I think I am somewhere near middling-ninety years. Oh yes my child, I have seen so much."

I looked on at this exchange. My grandmother, probably two decades younger than this Welsh miracle. My mother and I, two generations hence, in the very place my great-grandfather spent twelve years of his life before my grandfather was born, where they spent a week together on the only holiday Sean Seamus ever had as a child. Here we were, weaving threads of life together over tea and buttery Welsh cakes.

Stepping outside, I crossed a neat green square to where the squat grey church had, in its antiquity, become the landscape. My hands opened the forged gate their hands had opened. Circling rooks and jackdaws called their constant cry around the tower my great-grandfather had helped to repair. The storm of "oh nine" Abuelo Sean had told me. The tower bell rang the hour. Baritone, harmoniously, from the Greek barytonos—deep-sounding.

"Is that you who is related to the mason?" An old man stood against the graveyard wall opposite the gated entrance.

"Yes sir. Yes, he was my great-grandfather."

"And Dilys below yonder with the ladies, she would be my sister. I barely remember him from that time, for I am younger than she but I remember his visit with your grandfather, the boy. Would he have been eight or nine years old?"

"Yes," I nodded. "Just about that." I was even more taken aback at the thought that someone could remember Abuelo Sean as a visiting child.

"Aye, a lovely wee lad. We had no idea what he was saying for the early part but we got used to him. And he was mighty with the football." He smiled. "I am David."

"I shook his outstretched hand. "It is lovely to meet you, David. I am Jesus or Jesús we say in Spain."

He raised an eyebrow. "So how did the Cork boy get himself to Spain? Or is that a very long story indeed?"

"Indeed!" I laughed.

"I have been here most of my life, except for war-time. He swung his stick outwards and to the south. "I could walk you through every inch of that estate you know, 900 acres and every tree that grows there. I have been walking Pen Rhys all of my days, since my father first handed me an axe. The Master Carpenter was my uncle, my father was the Head Gardener." He poked at the loose gravel-path with his stick, quiet for a moment, as old men often are in recalling their tales. "If you like, I can take you to the walled gardens when the ladies have supped? I remember your great-grandfather telling me they were similar to the gardens he would have known, local to where he lived. Would you know of them?"

"Oh I do! But they are all ruins. There is nothing left but the high walls, ruined store-houses and cottages. The story is that my grandfathers seemed to have built many of the garden walls, indeed many of the demesne walls."

"Ah! You will be interested then, in seeing how they are laid out to work. We have vegetables all year, and they have just recently picked and filled the trays in the apple-house. 'Tis all a bit much for my creaking bones but I help where I can." He was quiet again. "The old boiler for the vent system finally gave it in, a few years now I suppose, so they have gone over to the gas now." He nodded, idly picking at wizened lichen on the white wall. He straightened up. "Well you poke about here then. Look for my lot, the Taylors, you'll see their graves that way to your right. I'll go see if the ladies are supped. Then we can stroll down to the gardens."

"That would be wonderful, David, thank you."

As he moved towards the gate, he whistled for a sheep dog I had not noticed, lying low outside the wall. Forged steel clanged as he laid down the closing hasp. I leant my back against the sun-warmed stones, looked up at blue skies through bright green beech leaves and breathed deep breaths of air that was not Welsh or Irish or Spanish or Greek but air of mankind, without names or borders. Humankind. I am your kind, your kin, your family. We are one. A deep sigh escaped me for the ancestors I could feel, their hands I could touch through stone and soil. In the guestbook of my life, they are the founding signatories.

∞

I like the odd hours, the hours outside mainstream living; taking the dogs from my parent's cottage by the sea, along the shoreline at twenty past ten on a July night. A strip of pink and orange settling on Great Island, curlews crying in the half tide. We startle a heron who hastily takes off and would probably be croaking "Jaysus lads, wha' time o' de nigh' is dis to be gaddin' abou'?" Kathleen and Robert in the Two Spoons had introduced me to the comedy sketch the "Lough Birds" by The People's Republic of Cork. Thanks to it, herons always have a Dublin accent. The same heron squawks and mutters, muhhers, to himself, gliding a wide arc in the stillness until I am not sure if I see him or his reflection. "Woul' yez feck off an' leave me ah-low-en."

My parents had kept these same hours. They had once woken me at two in the morning to see Halley's Comet, or we would go for a picnic at Pinar de la Algaida when all the other cars were heading home. My mother would cook sausage and potato, resting the oven dish on hot clay bricks, wrapped in layers of newspaper to keep it warm for our supper, with a large thermos flask of homemade soup or coffee. Sometimes Abuelo Sean was there, often Abuelita Rosa, after he had passed on.

Or there was nothing out of the ordinary in setting off at eleven at night to see the new moon, or the old moon setting, or Jupiter aligning with Saturn, or five in the morning to see Venus and the first sign of the sun. We would drive up to Grazalema in the mountains to the Sendero de Charcones trail. My father would talk of planet conjunction, my mother nod knowingly then wink at me and say. "Es simplemente hermoso ver; it is just beautiful to see." Or sometimes she would say, "Look for the rainbow, Jesús; there is the Archangel Michael protecting you under his arc."

They both were particularly excited when we first made a midnight foray to see the International Space Station pass over, my father in deep awe, saying, "There are men in there." We watched the steady reflected light form a long arc across the stars before becoming invisible to the eye. There was silence from them both. It was both unnatural yet fitted to the natural.

Years later my father would sit wrapped in a blanket outside my tent in West Kerry, watching the satellites travelling their own course amongst the stars, although the world had changed too much for him to be amazed. Now it was something dark and sinister, constant watching, constant communication. He did not like it so much and would say, "I must not let them draw my eye." But it was impossible not to watch. It was still an incredible feat to any engineering mind that they were there at all.

In Cadiz, we would go camping, not far away and always leaving late in the evening in my father's old van, spreading a groundsheet on a grassy field or dunes or forest clearing, warm Mediterranean nights, listening to the sounds of the world around us. Sometimes we would drive north to Doñana, before it all became national reserve. "Under here," he would whisper, "is an ancient place, a lost city. I feel the earth pull me when I am here, like a door to another world."

He told me of Darwin and the theory of survival of the fittest, he told me of Doñana's José Valverde and the survival of the one to make the most use of their energy.

My father would name the stars and constellations, the visible planets, telling the Greek myths of Cassiopaeia or Andromeda, the Gemini Twins, Orion the Hunter with his dog Sirius. He would have us watch for lynx, or eagles, or the squacco heron. Many years later in Cork, he earned my mother 194 points in Scrabble with squaccos, by connecting the word across two triple-word squares. Abuelita Rosa and the doctor argued, unsuccessfully I believe, that squacco could not be pluralised.

Often I would fall asleep listening, knowing that even when I slept he would continue telling the night creatures their names and place. In English, in Spanish, in Greek, softly calling the world to him. "Know these things," he would tell me, tying a hook to a line on a river bank. "Know their habits and place, if not always their names. We busy ourselves in our important lives, Jesús, but the whole world is important and we were just another part of it once, not its master. We just think we are in charge."

I am a coastal person and everywhere I travel I seem to somehow end up at the sea or near a large body of water. It's the sound, the smell, the vastness that reminds me how small we are. I am of it, I am the Universe. God is in everything Mamá told me always. I am the rock, the sea, the sky, the squirrel, and the rose, the Buddhists taught me. I am them and they are me, until there is only us. We are one.

I like to surf. It's not really surfing but throwing myself prone on a board and catching a wave. I own only half a yellow surf board. *BM Australia The Minimal* is written on it, in flashy black script, which is oddly specific, for I found only half of it washed up on a beach. My father straightened the crooked break across the centre, sanded and fibre-glassed the raw edge to shape it as a body board. It has done a fine job for many years. He says when he passes on I am to burn him, carry his ashes out to sea on my board and deposit him to the elements. "Hither and thither, in wind and weather."

I like to walk. Anywhere, any distance. I am not at all fond of running. Anywhere, any distance, even for a bus or to get to the store before it closes. At Stansted Airport in London, I was once surprised when someone clapped me on the back saying, "Hey, the London Marathon, '92. What kind of time did you have?" I looked wide-eyed and rather surprised at a lanky long-haired young man, then quickly replied, "Oh I don't mind the time; I just like being part of the excitement." He grinned and said something about a time of four-fifty-two, agreeing that the buzz was "unreal." With that he gave me a high five and moved on.

My London Marathon tee-shirt had come from Oxfam, free to me after days of volunteering. It was perfect; large, clean, relatively unused. Perhaps the wearer had done four-fifty-two in their marathon run or perhaps four-thirty-something, or maybe broke the three hour barrier? Who could ever say? Maybe it was a joke tee-shirt for some big bloke going away on his stag weekend? It didn't matter but it was nice that it brought a connection. The young man didn't need to know that I don't run, that I abhor running. I just do not pound my joints on a man-made surface and expect a good result. Dr. Zhao used to cast his eyes to heaven and say, "Always walk, Jesús. The fluid of the brain likes three to four kilometres an hour, this is the speed at which the brain works best, the senses are best attuned, the joints move freely without undue stress. The heart gets plenty of condition without forcing it. Just walk. Eat well, sleep well, and walk. And laugh. Laugh lots. You will live to be a hundred."

"D'you hear that?" a man asked of me once, somewhere on a cliff-top overlooking the brightest blue sea. I had greeted him cordially as I passed on the path, then made to continue on my way. "D'you hear that?" he repeated. Stopping still, I heard the alarm cry of the skylark that perceived we were too close. Farther away a herring gull screeched and landed on a cliff edge, farther still the plummeting sound of a gannet breaking the waves as it dived to fish. I looked at him in the sunshine, his face beaming and bright.

"That's the sound of my life, right now, in Dolby stereo at full volume. Isn't it just fine?"

And with that, he raised his hat and went on his way.

"Isn't that just fine?" I asked of the skylark.

The Buddhist teaching in Plum Village suggested that walking meditation is to fully enjoy walking–walking not in order to arrive, just for walking. We walk all the time, but usually it is more like running. Our hurried steps print anxiety and sorrow on the Earth. If we can take one step in peace, we can take two, three, four, and then five steps for the peace and happiness of humankind. When we shed the mantle of this world, lose the cloak of material protection, we stand naked with our brethren, our kith, our kind. humankind. Nothing but our selves. Nothing to shield or protect us, pauper or Pope.

I think of another day: waking with a real head-full of nothing in particular, but everything. Sneezing, nearly coughing, tired in myself, I took the dogs out. Too warm for wellies, I found myself in the wrong footwear, meandering into scrubby bushland where I had never ventured before. Chiff-chaffs called from the alder scrub. Seeing openings and clear spaces, I pressed on, knowing I wasn't far from anywhere known, yet entirely unknown. Tangles of young blackberry briar and gorse picked at me, wet nettles burned me, straggly grass caught my sandals, but I needed to keep to the non-path. Other words of Thay or teacher, Thich Nhat Hanh formed a mantra in my fuddled head. "Every footstep kisses the earth, mindful breathing is my anchor. I am breathing in, I am breathing out."

It took only fifteen or twenty minutes, maybe half an hour of life, before I circled back to the clear foot-worn track. Why? I wondered, yet I found I was smiling, not sneezing. My heart was light, my head not so full. There is no one who could have taken that path with me, or for me. It was an entirely lone journey and, although brief, I found myself again.

∞

Two Spoons Café, Blackrock, Cork.

On a Tuesday morning, the large table in the window of the Two Spoons is occupied by the Four Anns. I had observed them and then their regularity, their immediacy of engagement in any manner of any subject. I observed the slight stiffness in Philomena's greeting, Biddy's conversation that would edge up one decibel and a turn or two of the speed dial, as if she had inhaled an espresso shot before they arrived. It was a curious reaction to four middle-aged women at their gatherings, although I also learned they had other regular meetings—bridge, a book club, films and fringe theatre outings—the occupations of retired professionals.

Anne Small was referred to as Anne with an E and headed up the Historical and Archaeological Society of Cork. Ann Dolan was the retired county librarian; Ann Nolan, a retired civil servant who taught computing classes at night school. Ann Clarke, a retired maths teacher who looked over her glasses and said, "Good morning, Bridget," just refraining from adding and have you all your homework done?

The ladies were regular in every sense; two teabags in the large yellow pot kept just for them. Two small pots of hot water on the side. Eight slices of brown toast, four jam portions, all with Flora spread, not butter. Every second Tuesday at nine o'clock and every first Friday after eight o'clock Mass. Nine to eleven. Occasionally they would have the small breakfast, generous enough, with toast. This order on occurrence would be phoned in the day before by Anne with an E. Small, so Philomena would know it wasn't just a toast day.

For some reason, which I was curious to explore, the small, generous-enough breakfast with toast order really set Philomena on a pot-banging parade. I looked at her once quizzically.

"Why so cross about four small breakfasts, cousin?"

"Ha? What? Oh, oh, am I?"

"Four-Ann pot-banging? Yes, you are."

"Oh, oh I don't know, I know. I just can't explain. They climb right up my nose those four."

"Yes, even Bridget seems to get flustered by them. She often escapes?"

Philomena laughed. "Ya, outta here like a hot snot. Oops, sorry, Jesus, that's a bit rude! I heard it from Ambrose. It didn't sound so rude in a Scottish accent."

Kathleen was making the tea and collecting the necessary tableware for the ladies. "Nothing like the Four Anns to set Mrs. S off," she threw over her shoulder.

"Why so, do you think, Kathleen?"

She paused, idly polishing the yellow tea pot, the fascinating use of motion to assist clear thinking. Repetitive actions; polishing, stroking, pulling, fiddling. All the actions we humans use to clear the passage of our thoughts from mind to vocal cords.

"They have a special tea pot. They talk all high-falutin' stuff as you'd expect from retired big brains. They are a fairly formidable foursome, but d'you know what upsets her most, Jesus?"

"I am waiting to hear, Kathleen … ."

"So am I!" laughed Philomena.

"The Something for Nothing Equation."

"Generous portions and then more?"

"Yep!"

There was a strangled snort from the other side of the kitchen. "AND the bloody pots of hot water on the side. AND the Philomena would you be so kind and Philomena could I just have and Oh, I do apologise, Philomena, would you please and on and on and on and on 'til they get to the till and 'tis like it's their very last penny they have to extract for two hours at the biggest table and a mountain of washing up and Philomena, did you see the French film at the Triskel? and Philomena, how are all your brood? AARGH! They make me SCREAM!"

We were silenced by this outburst. Then Kathleen laughed.

"There y'are, Mrs. S. I bet you're glad you got all that off your chest. That's been bursting in there for some time it seems? Arra, they're just a bunch of smart but bored old ladies. And probably jealous that you have it all."

"I have it all, Kathleen?" Pure Philomena incredulity. "I have it all? I'm the idiot runnin' after them and cleaning it all up."

"No, that's MY job, Mrs. S. And I like it. And you pay me to do it and they pay you. And you go home to your lovely cottage and Ambrose and children and grandchildren and what do they do? All four of them? Big old empty houses, children gone away, no warmth, no love. Oh I'd be you any day, Mrs. S." Kathleen swished out.

"And they are being served," I added, somewhat cautiously to the heaving rear view of a troubled Philomena Sowersby.

"What?" Philomena was stopped speechless in her four rashers of bacon. "What? Served?"

"Yes, you are serving them. They pay for service. That gives them status. This is true of all of your customers Philomena, so perhaps there is more to the tale? Do you know them outside of this setting? In everyday life?"

"N-no, not so much. Our paths wouldn't really cross." Philomena paused, still a bit flabbergasted both at her own outburst and our combined reactions to same.

"And another thing. Anne Small once asked for two more pots of hot water, oh this is years ago, Jesus, and THEN on the sly she slipped in two of her OWN tea bags and pretended nothing, but I saw her. When she got to the till I said, no extra charge for hot water, Anne. I suppose you paid for your own teabags? She didn't like that one bit."

"Hmmm. So you perform a function in their lives. And they very nicely can extract what they like from you for a small price. That makes them powerful. Although I would doubt it is all four of them?"

Philomena was plating a sausage, rasher of bacon, and beans on each plate, ready to add an egg which was spitting and bubbling in a pan.

"Do you ever get one of them on their own?" I sliced toast into triangles and carefully arranged them into two baskets.

"Well, yes, Anne Dolan would sometimes come in the afternoon for tea and cake, sometimes with a grandchild. She smiles at me, or reads her book or the paper, or actually now that I think of it, I often hear her conversing with Kathleen or Robert or Marguerite Foley. Often times I miss her as I'd take a nap upstairs." Philomena reddened slightly at this admission, although it was perfectly acceptable for someone of her years, it was her own business and, of course, it was one of those unspoken facts, known to all.

"And Ann Nolan has been in with her family, Mrs. S?" Kathleen breezed through collecting plates of breakfast. "They're all very nice really, y'know. There's just something different when they're in their gang." She laughed. "Power Rangers on Barry's Tea and Toast."

"Human dynamics, Philomena. The Power of Four. What if you went out there and eyeballed just one of them with a perfectly ordinary *And how are you today, Ann?* Then only she can answer. Deflate their power with smiles, not scowls."

"Oh I don't scowl, Jesus, do I?"

"Well, it's not a smile, my dear. And it is especially for those four."

"Oh Lordie! Now you have me bothered. I never meant to be rude."

"Oh stop it! They are handing over cash one way or another. You give them space to be together. You are creating and they are creating. Why let the negative outweigh the positive? It is so unlike you."

"Two more, Kathleen. Have you everything?"

"Yes, thanks. I'll come back for the toast basket, Jesus."

"I was at school with Anne Small." Philomena was clearing away the cooking detritus. "She was mean to Biddy. Regularly and unnecessarily. Biddy was just a tiny, skinny little thing from West Cork. She clung to this raggedy little dolly she carried everywhere, hmm, let's see, yes, Anne-Marie she called it. She used to say, 'Two names were better than one.' Lord if she was bright enough to know what a hyphen was, she woulda been over the moon. Anne Small once took the dolly and hid it in another classroom for three days. She doesn't seem to remember any of that. She was awful."

"Ah! The kernel of truth behind all our emotions. Your instinctive care for Bridget colours everything, my dear."

"Oh whisht up, Jesus! This is silly. We are all big grown women now."

I smiled. "Parts of us never grow up, Philomena. So let it go. Forgive her, Philomena, for she knows not what she did. Does that sound familiar? I think I have said that somewhere before?"

Philomena chuckled as Kathleen called another order.

"Shouldn't one of those eggs have been poached, Philomena, not fried?"

I ducked as she flung a bread roll at me. "Ah, Jesus, you're always so bloody right!"

"It is my job, cousin. It is just my job."

∞

Rostellan, East Cork

A voice called, a loud Hie, stopping me in my tracks one day as I strode the road through Rostellan. "Hie!"

It wasn't too long, perhaps just some months, since my parents and Abuelita Rosa had moved here; I had been here and away on several occasions in the intervening time. My father retired to a low-key life in Cork while Abuelita Rosa filled her days with nursing and socialising locally. Mamá went to teaching a little in the locality, covering sick days, maternity leave, staff shortages in six small schools. So much so, that the primary-age children of the parish had a smattering of Spanish to add to their colour. In return, she was picking up a Cork twang and new songs and stories from her students.

"Hie!" An old man hailed me. I crossed to his doorway in a neat terrace of two-storey cottages.

"John James O'Sullivan was your grandfather?"

"Yes, that's me. Very pleased to meet you. I am Jesus Josephus"

"Oh that's not an easy one to carry around," he laughed. "I'm Timmy. Here, here now, let me fetch you something." He was a tall man in his time but now bent and stooped, with red braces and a check shirt. He turned into the cottage, returning quite quickly with photographs in his hand, so they must have been to the ready.

"I was born the same year as your grandfather in this parish but not this village, closer to the sea. But I would have known him here through the music, see? We played all the time, Ash Tree Cross, Ballinrostig, Guileen Pier, sometimes even across the water there at the Ferry Inn. Sometimes here on our own pier too. He was a fine musician. Oh and I tell you we had the craic. Here now,

I have these for your grandmother. I met her at the doctor's this last week and said I would root them out."

I had seen perhaps only one photograph of Abuelo Sean in his Irish youth, before he departed for Cadiz, and I was not quite ready for what he handed me. He proffered an old and grainy picture, ten or twelve children with a lady. "That's Miss Murphy with her sixth-class children on their Confirmation Day, outside the old church in Aghada. 1927. See here, that's John, and next to him Finbarr Kennedy, my cousin. He was of the blacksmith's family at the old forge. That's why I have the photo."

Looking proud and upright and straight at me with a fresh haircut, my twelve-year-old grandfather. And before I could pull myself together, Timmy proffering another photo, said, "And here, that's four of us playing music at the village green, the Harvest Fair, 1936."

My twenty-one-year-old grandfather, his head thrown back in a soundless laugh, a cigarette burning his left fingers as he pulled the concertina wide across his knees.

"That's myself with the box."

I could not speak to this old soul. No words would form.

"He was a grand lad John. He was grand. Great fun."

"Yes," I managed to whisper in reply. "I thought so too. I was only ten when he passed on, but we had great fun together."

"I have one more for you here." Four young adults, smiling, on the edge of a pier or pier wall, under bunting and a portion of a hand-painted sign, ' 'ate Regatta 1937.'

"That's me and my girl, my missus she became. I lost her there four year ago. That's John and young Hazel Ward. Whitegate Regatta."

"Hazel Ward?" I queried.

"Yes, God love the poor lass." He crossed himself slowly.

I looked at the monochrome image, unmistakably Abuelo Sean and this man I stood with now, in a younger frame. Beside each of them, two fine girls on their arms and one of them, strange as it sounds, I had never heard a mention of. "Hazel." I said again. The photo shook slightly in my hand, disguised as a sea breeze, then I felt that familiar warm air around my neck. If I listened closely, there probably was a faint concertina chord somewhere in the wind.

Timmy frowned, a small crease in his weathered face. "You have heard the story then?"

"Only partially I believe. Will you tell me?"

"Sure I can. Well, yes I suppose, if you like to hear it." He looked at me through old blue eyes. "Remember now, I was very fond of your grandfather. We walked or biked many miles and played many more together."

"Yes, I understand."

"So I have no axe to grind with the man at all at all. We never knew the full story until months after he was gone."

"Yes, okay." I could not recognise my own voice. The story of Abuelo Sean, before he left for Cadiz. There was a fogginess around me, and the photo I clenched was held by someone else's hand.

"We first met Hazel at the old Corkbeg Hotel, your grandfather and me and a couple of others were playing at a gathering there. A fine girl, Ellen Walsh, was the fiddler, and Hazel was known to her, so she introduced us and oh boy, oh boy." He paused to laugh lightly. "You could feel the heat in John James! Oh boy! He didn't turn his head again!"

Timmy scratched his bristly throat. " 'Oh boy,' I said to him, 'you keep your eyes down and yer mind on your squeeze box,' for she was the daughter of one of the officers at the fort y'know. They lived at the fort. But a right friendly lass she was."

My eyes went from Timmy to the photo and from parsing of the opening lines, I knew the story could not end well.

"So it was a summer of playing music and meeting the girls at the old pier by the Corkbeg Coastguard. Old Battersby was the man in charge and we'd play him some music, the girls would gather perries and crab, he'd smoke a pipe and tell us sea stories."

"Perries?"

"Periwinkles, little shellfish. Grand altogether."

Timmy paused to recollect. "Grand days. Swimming or picnics when we weren't working, which was hardly ever." He laughed. "Always working. But in summertime it could be nine, or even ten or eleven o'clock before we were heading home. Long evenings of walking out. That's what we called it. Walking out. But never alone. I'm full sure Hazel wasn't telling anyone in the fort with whom she was spending her time. My good girl and she became fast friends, so the girls were often together without the men, which is how the grown-ups would have liked it too."

His tale paused as he shifted his stance off the half-door. "I'll have to sit for a bit now if you don't mind, my legs will not stay up for long." He swung his stick outwards and we moved off the doorway to the wall across the road, watching the gulls feeding under the causeway, the egret sharp in the ebb tide. He pointed his stick towards the shaly spit where cormorants and shags were drying their wings.

"My father used to tell me they're directly descended from prehistoric creatures and they have no proper glands, that's why they have to hang out their wings to dry. I watch them every day, the longest link to prehistory around here. Back before man or cow existed."

"Phalacrocorax," I told him, "bald raven. One of the species is even called Aristotle. My father was born in Greece."

"Is that so? You're a mixed up bunch then." He laughed. "I did my time with the Merchant Navy, Jesus. There's no country I haven't met, haven't seen or heard."

We watched the life around us. The oystercatchers cried pip, pip, pibbit. He looked at me directly. "I can see by you, young Jesus, that you have not heard Hazel's tale."

"No," I admitted. "I haven't. Although my great-aunts have told my mother, some time ago. I was not present and did not wish to hear it at the time, nor did she wish to tell me. And I am almost certain my lovely grandmother does not know."

"Well we can keep it like that if you prefer?" He was empathetic in his question. "There's not many around now that would have the story."

"No, please continue, if you can take the time? I am ready to hear this."

"Ah! Time is all I have now," he laughed. "There's nothing else calling me, except the man above." He raised his stick to the sky, smiling at the thought.

"In '38, John knew it was all hopeless, smitten as he was. He had two chances of Hazel, little or none. Things went a bit rocky, so he kept his way away. My missus told me of how heartbroken she was, the poor mite, but shur she probably knew full well that this was the only path. Then she came to him in the spring, while he was working on the estate in the gardens. She was in the pony and trap on the way to visiting the lady of the house at Jamesbrook. It seemed quite a way for a young girl to be travelling alone, although John did not question her. There was no one in the big house at Rostellan. Old Mr. Engledow was gone nearly a decade. He was the last to live there." Timmy stopped to look towards the causeway, memories quietly screening behind his eyes.

" 'Twas a fine, fine place." He shook his head. "Grand, but it was nearly all finished by then. They were mining for clay up the creek, so the bosses used the house as offices and some rooms. Bits were slowly going missing. They still worked the old gardens and the farm estate, so John kept busy fixin' and building. The army blew it up in '44." He kicked at his stick, cleared his throat, his chin moved left and right across the ball of his thumb.

"Now I'll never know what passed between them on that day, so I cannot say, but it rose John mightily into a dither. Couldn't play a tune straight, couldn't think of his work. Eventually wouldn't even try the squeeze box. Some days or weeks later, I was fitting shoes to a horse in the farmyard, that's over Saleen way, and there was this mighty hiatus and John was havin' a clatter off a poor young fella, one of the Walsh boys who made a bad mortar mix. Ah!"

Timmy stopped his story and leant on his stick. He pointed across the causeway.

"I waited for him there that evening and said, 'c'mon man, we'll have some porter' and he had calmed a bit, so after a few bottles I said, 'you're eatin' up over that girl, what's to happen?' And his answer was something I have never forgot and that largely framed what came next. John said, 'She's but a girl and there'll be others, but a life of lies I cannot lead.' And d'you know, Jesus, he seemed better for saying it out loud. Lighter like. And it wasn't the porter. 'Twas like a weight lifted off him."

I nodded. Whatever was to be revealed, Abuelo Sean was an honest man.

"We had a big outing the next day, Saturday. We went to Cork city early, in Tommy Mac's lorry."

"The Grand Prix!" I exclaimed, entering the tale on knowing ground. "He told me about that trip."

"He did?" Timmy seemed surprised that I could recall.

"Finn drove, so there was no porter."

Timmy laughed. "Aha! The real truth comes out. Indeed, Finn was a bit of a … "

"Dry oul shite," I interjected.

"That'd be it," he laughed. "That's exactly it. Just as John would have said it too."

And then I remembered how Abuelo Sean in the telling had ended that tale, back in Rostellan, full of burning fuel and tyre smoke.

"That's right. Back to Rostellan for porter, as mad as any young bloods could be, mad for drink." He pointed up the hill. "Up to the Pump, hootin' and hollerin', and goin' on. John had forgotten his woes."

"But something happened there, at the Pump. He never told me anymore about that day because he was so upset. I had never seen my grandfather cry."

Timmy looked at me sympathetically. "Aye. I'm not surprised. Old Mary says it, probably not knowing that it would mean owt to any of us, although she would have known through the gossip that my missus and the girl were on friendly terms."

"Out?"

"Aye, owt. Any bit at all. She had no knowing of John's affections for the lass."

I hardly hear myself asking. "And what was the news?"

Timmy paused, swallowing, his ancient throat dry with the memory. He shook his head. "She had thrun herself off the middle ground of the fort, by the old invisible gun battery. Way from up high, down to the sea below. She slipped away from it all."

The sea birds were quiet on the water. The memory was given due silence.

"Oh the pain. Oh, he must have been distraught. And her too?"

"Aye, aye. Even after all these years, the war 'n' all, 'tis one of the saddest things I have witnessed. The demise of a young spirit. 'Tis just not right sometimes."

We watched the carousing feeding birds again, squawking furiously at their own and any other. A pair of mute swans glided through the mêlée.

"Did no one see her? Was there no one watching, or on guard at the fort?"

"Well as you'd have it, in near one hunder-ed and fifty years, no, no there wasn't. Y'see the very next Monday, the agreement was signed for the British Government to hand the forts of Ireland over to the new Free State. Hazel's lot were the last to be in there, and they were hardly functioning as a garrison at all. They were only waiting for the orders and were all moved on by the summer." Timmy straightened in his seat. "And then the commotion let loose. Her parents and family are quite obviously distressed at her passing. John is silently dying of a broken heart, although I think he must have known that this wasn't the end of it as far as he was concerned. The word gets out that she had been with child. Before you could spit there into the sea, John with a big shove from his father, was on a boat to Spain."

"But it wasn't his child?" I was perplexed.

"No, no it wasn't, I think we all knew that, but the truth took a bit longer to come forth."

"Do you think she told him? That day in Rostellan?"

"Yes, I think she did. Me and the missus could only surmise after, that she had suggested to him that they elope. Run away."

"But Abuelo Sean wouldn't lie that it was his child?"

"Yes, that's what we thought too." Timmy paused, then frowned. "What did you call him?"

"Abuelo Sean. Grandfather Sean."

"Sean? Is that what he became down there in Spain?"

"He used to laugh and say it was easier for the Spanish to say— Sean, Say moose, o sool i vawn."

"Yes. That could be true," Timmy mused, "although it may have kept him away from prying eyes also."

"So why did he leave if it wasn't his child?"

Timmy looked at me. "The young stone mason of the village against the might of the fort? He would have rotted in prison over there for the rest of his natural days." Timmy's stick pointed directly at Spike Island. "They'd have had him before anyone else."

Tears unbidden again. My whole life was built on an injustice, on the pain and suffering of a man I had loved and cherished. Yet strangely, without it, he may have remained a Corkman in Cork.

"John took the boat, then holy war erupted here for a while, and remember, they were also preparing to take down the Union Jack up there and fly the new Tricolour. It was all an awful mess. She had thrun herself off the King's own fort, that needed an inquiry. Then it all went quiet about. No one chased John down. So our guessing and some of the local chinwagging, embroidered of course with the girl's own tales she had recounted to my missus and the friends, led to the near truth that the girl was being, em … ." He dropped his gaze and crossed himself again. "She was being seen to maybe. Or interfered with, by someone at the singles barracks at the fort or if not, in the social scene they kept about. We didn't ever know no more about it."

The swans circled, pausing below us to preen, working beaks through to feather roots, dipping heads under to carry water drops to wing pits.

"It was Patcheen Mike had found her floating in the tide, early on the Saturday morning, when he was out at his pots. He shouldn't have been in the area of the fort waters, so he made up some story of seeing the shape of her on the surface, knowing 'twas no sea creature. He raised the alarm at the Coast Guard in Corkbeg and that set it all off. Once the fort knew, all the local lads slipped away, outta the way. Patcheen told me it was because she had bruises, black and blue about her face, down her arms and her back. Someone had taken heavily to her. Someone was very angry." An oystercatcher ruckus erupted, then took flight in unison, swooping past our view. Pipit, pipit, pip.

"That's about it. Poor young Hazel Ward." He wagged his finger at me. "There's no mistaking the genuine affection they had for each other, Jesus. Not at all. There was no turning that tide. He was smote as any man can be. His heart was broke."

I fingered the photo, unsure of what to say, unsure of myself, my grandfather's silence of this tale. "You two had a good life together?" I ventured finally.

He laughed. "Oh up and down like any other. But she was a good lass. We made a good team together and we left a few players to carry on after us."

"It must have been strange for you to meet my grandmother? She and Sean met reasonably soon after he landed in Cadiz."

"Yes," he mused. "I didn't think of it at first. I hadn't expected her at the docs, so I didn't put it all together in my own mind until afterwards. But yes. She got him and Hazel didn't. The roundabouts of life." He kicked his stick. "I haven't told that tale in near fifty years. 'Twas buried way down. I lost my friend, my musical companion, an' we all lost Hazel. It took a long time to heal." He looked at the swans. "They mate for life you know? It sounds great but it isn't all that enjoys it. Mind you, might be easier when there's no speaking!"

Droplets of sea-water ran off the startling whiteness of the birds below us, distracting my attention back to a memory, an airline bestowed neighbour, travelling from London to Dubai. In the course of our long and varied conversation, he had queried our Western laws of monogamy and marriage, declaring the practice to be wholly unnatural in any species. "This cannot be right?" When I told him my parents had been together all their lives, he said. "Yes, yes, exceptions." Ex-c-ep-c-ons his Eastern tongue had pronounced the word. "Some animals, some birds, largely exceptions. Ask yourself where this habit came from. The Romans? The Christians? Putting kingdoms together, dynastic lines, evading tax laws. Why for two thousand years do you follow this? I don't understand. Have you stopped the thinking? The thinking for yourselves? You do it because somebody says do this, this is the thing to do. I cannot believe this. You in the West have so much to learn from the East." I could inform him that for the Celts in Ireland it had been all about cows. They married for cattle. The more cattle, the better the wife.

The swans fluffed and flapped enormous wings, settling gracefully into mute arcs of bright light.

"I think, Timmy, I might not show this photo to Abuelita Rosa or Mamá. It might be best?" I handed him the regatta picture, Abuelo Sean smiling and in love with a tragic girl.

"Aye, you are right there. Y'know, Jesus, there are some that are wise and there are some that are otherwise. You'll think different now, knowing the tale. Come to me anytime to hear more about him and I welcome hearing his life abroad. I missed him often in the years since."

I stood to walk him across the road, but he waved me away. "Arra, I can do that on my own steam. On, away with you." He proffered his hand for me to shake and, on an impulse, I put my arms around his neck and kissed his head.

"Thank you, Timmy. I probably needed to know that story."

"On away with you now, I'll be seeing you again."

This time I knew, with the ball of his thumb it was a tear he was wiping from stubbled cheeks.

∞

I met old Timmy many more times on my wanderings. Mamá had looked lovingly at Timmy's old photos with Abuelita Rosa, commenting on Abuelo Sean's hairline or the way he held the concertina. Abuelita Rosa laughed at the school photo, shuffled about in her bedroom to return with a photo of Mamá on her confirmation day, to compare the likeness between them.

"Ah, María," she sighed, "you always have more of him than me."

We all laughed, somehow all of us knowing, we were not laughing at what she had really meant.

My mother accompanied me to return the photographs and meet with Timmy. She brought her concertina under her arm and neither Timmy nor I mentioned that we had exchanged Hazel's tale.

"Sit down there now, missus, and let me hear a bit of your sound." Timmy pulled a chair from his kitchen table, wiping the seat with a tea towel. Mamá sat and undid clips to remove the concertina from its black leather case.

"Bien entonces, Timmy, what would you like to hear?" She leaned across the concertina, threading her hands through the straps, flicking her hair over her shoulder, and pulled an opening chord.

Timmy stopped and stared at the instrument in her hands. "Is that … is that your father's box?" he whispered.

"Sí, yes, Timmy," Mamá replied, somewhat surprised. "This is it."

"Oh dear Jesus in heaven. I never thought … ." He leaned forward to touch the bellows, placed a long finger on the fretwork by Mamá's right hand. His shoulders lifted, his eyes shone as a sob escaped his lips. "Dear Jesus and all the saints. It never crossed my ould mind." He wiped his cheek. "Oh Lordie, Lord. I haven't lain eyes on that since your father took off in '38. I can't tell you the number of tunes I have seen him play on that, there … ." He shook his head in wonder. "Oh God how he loved that box. We carried them miles." He stood up and moved to an alcove to the side of the fireplace. Reaching down, he lifted an old leather case and, laying it on the fireside chair, unclasped the lid, lifting out a red Hohner accordion.

"He built me a bracket arrangement outta scrap metal from the forge for the crossbar of me bike, so I could carry this." Through eyes bright with tears he smiled a huge wide smile at Mamá.

"When we were but laddeens, we were mitching school in the spring and summertime to take any bit of work that was goin'— pickin' stones and praties, saving pennies in jars for sweets 'n' stickies. My father played the fiddle and when I could get me hand on it, I would copy what I saw him do. It felt right to me, the music. So I gave up the sweeties and saved me pennies under the floorboard." Timmy hauled the accordion strap to his shoulder and, sitting back at the table, pulled a chord. The instrument wheezed and belched as he shifted his long frame to a comfortable position.

"By the time I was a young boy, teen-age like, and finished with schooling, I was good on the fiddle. But my eye had been drawn to John Wall's accordion. They played music in our house, or in the ould shebeen in Guileen. He'd give it to me for a go, gave me the first instruction and, sitting amongst them, if you have the ear, you find you learn it quick." He pulled a series of notes and broke into a tune.

Mamá smiled at him and let him play a few bars before joining in.

" 'The Lark in the Morning,' that's the girl, you have your father's style. Oh ho! There'll be no stoppin' us now." Timmy's eyes shone brightly and his smile was from heaven. They played through the tune together and, as he pulled up the final chord, he beamed at Mamá.

"Just lovely. Good girl you!" He leant on his elbows and took his hands from the straps. "This is John Wall's father's accordion. I bought it for three ould pounds in 1930. That there concertina came from the same family a year or so later. I had met your father at a music session in Whitegate. He had been learning too but beggin' or borrowin' an instrument to play. He was good, you know. John Wall spotted him a few times and said to me, 'He's alrigh' that O'Sullivan lad. I have my aunt's concertina, he can have it for two pound.' "

He pulled another series of notes, his long old fingers nimble across the keys. "One Sunday mornin' after Mass, I got on me bike to Rostellan to tell him, an' faith, he disappeared into their house and came back with a tobacco box of coins and said 'let's go.' He too had been savin' anything he could find and he had two summers of stone work with his father on the estate under his belt. We biked to Ballynoo to the old farm and found John."

I closed my eyes and, in my mind, I was nine years old in Cadiz, playing football with a man I revered, yet in my ears I was twenty-something and Timmy's voice was recalling that man as a teenager in rural Cork. I steadied my pounding heart as the faintest of whispers stirred at the nape of my neck. When I returned my attention to the old man's kitchen, he was grinning and nodded to my mother's hands.

"Outta the hay loft above the cow shed it came. John said it was the driest place to keep it. That's your concertina now, María, from

Eily Wall's hands. 1930 …'31 or early '32, I'd say."

They played on together. In this old man's kitchen in Cork, I watched my mother. I watched the concertina and tried to recall all the places I had seen this instrument played in the hands of my grandfather or mother since I was a child. How many times had I read: C. Jeffries Maker, and wondered who that was? I wondered where all those who had listened to the music had gone on their ways. I wondered whether it knew that it was back with the accompanying accordion with which it had already played on its musical journey. The hair rose on my neck and whisperings in my left ear, "Now for you, Jesus, isn't that something?" If I were truly mad, I would swear I could smell a cigarillo.

Timmy's daughter Julia had let herself in the front door and nodded to me from the hall, smiling at the music. She disappeared to the rear, and muffled sounds of a kettle being boiled soon followed, plates being laid on a tray, Julia soon returning quietly with a pot of tea and thick slices of fruit cake. Mamá winked her thanks, never losing sight of Timmy's hands on his keyboard. At the end of the reel, Mamá turned to see Julia leaning on the door frame.

"Hello. I am María O'Sullivan. From Cadiz. Very pleased to meet you." She leant across the concertina to shake hands with Julia.

"Oh, I know exactly who you are," Julia answered laughing, taking her hand. "I'm Julia. You would not believe an ould man could be so excited at the news of newcomers moving into the parish."

We all joined her laughter.

"Look, Julia, look," Timmy whispered, "it's John's concertina. The very one." Timmy was still smiling.

"So you've met this box before, Dad? You sounded well together."

"Oh I have, lass, oh that I have." Timmy's smile faded a little, sadness creeping into his eyes. Right there, we all knew a story, one we had all somehow heard in our own separate ways.

Mamá broke the silence. "Eily Wall, she would have bought this concertina, Timmy?" She paused to drink tea.

"Well, now that you ask, that had its own story of course." Timmy also stopped to sup and chew his cake. "It's a lovely thing, English made. An Anglo, and I can't say rightly who it was brought it here to Cork; but the old man Francis Wall won it playing cards in Cove. Some young sailor had a bad run of luck in the game, but shur that fella coulda stolen it or found it, or it coulda found him in no-knowing-what ways. Francis felt sorry for the sailor and gave him a couple of extra quid, which he probably couldn't spare at the time, but he knew a good instrument when he saw one. All the Walls were musicians way back. There wasn't much of the concertina in Cork then. Lots of it in Clare, not so much here; it had all gone west or south after the famine days. So his sister Eily Wall put herself to the learnin'. She would travel to Cove by boat of a time, pick up tunes from sailors or other musicians. Being a port town, she'd find all kinds there, including Clare men. Fond of them too I hear." His eyes twinkled and we laughed.

"Arra I'm only pullin' yer leg," he laughed with us. "She was a fine musician by all accounts and married a guard and moved away. So John Wall only came by the box after she passed on and 'twas he threw it into the hay loft."

"So it has had several hands before my grandfather?" I asked.

"Ah yes. Well I suppose Eily would have got it somewhere in the early part of the century. I'm guessing it was made latish in the one before, so other than the sailor who played a bad hand at cards, one or two more perhaps? And shur then it was just John and yerself?" he nodded to Mamá.

"Sí. Just us two."

"And what about yerself, Jesus?" Julia asked of me.

I smiled at the inquiry. "I have never, ever even held it, Julia. I have touched it, yes. As a child I was fascinated by it, by the sound Abuelo Sean made, the colours, the sun dancing on the keys. I loved the hexagonal shape. But I have the memory of him shaking his finger at me saying 'not for your little hands, Jesus,' and I took him at his word."

"For the next twenty years." Mamá smiled.

"No desire at all to play, Jesus?" asked Timmy.

"Truly, Timmy, this is what I love best, to watch. To watch my grandfather, or my mother, or now to watch you play. To feel in my heart that you are 'makin' music up to God' as John himself would have said. I watch every time my mother, or my grandfather, played until they are finished, then put it away in the case."

Mamá smiled at me. "For the first ten years of life, Jesús spent more time with my father than anyone. ¿No es así? Name a tune, Jesús?"

"Ah Mamá! Please! You will make me the fool."

Timmy pulled a sequence of chords and notes, Mamá's eyes brightened and she looked at me. "Oye, you cannot mistake this one, Jesús?" she smiled.

"Now that is most certainly 'The Maid Behind the Bar.'"

∞

As we walked the path home, my mother linked me, pulling me close to her, smiled up at me, the concertina in its case tucked under her left arm. "Truly Jesús? No desire to hold the instrument or play?"

I returned her smile, my wonderful black-haired mother, flecks of grey at her temples and ears, the fine morning mist settling on the collar of her suede coat. "Truly, Mamá. It is for you. It was for Abuelo Sean."

She squeezed me to her. "I never asked you. I always thought, it's okay. If Jesús wants to play, Jesús will ask."

"Truly, Mamá."

We stopped to watch a feeding frenzy amongst the gulls, as a neighbour threw stale bread-ends into the receding tide.

"At nighttime, I used to lie in bed in Cadiz, Mamá, when I was small, when Abuelo Sean was still with us. I used to think of you and Papá in the next room, Rosa and Sean in the next house, Mama Tia asleep above the taberna. Rodriguez, Pedro, Ana, Isabel, Margarita, Sr. Dolores, all asleep in Cadiz. My mind would picture them in their beds, in their houses, Sr. Dolores in the convent. I would think of Lola in the market, asleep somewhere. Miguel on his boat. Everyone I knew, where they might be sleeping, where they would be safe. I would go through the list and always at the end before I would fall asleep, I would imagine the concertina, dark and snug and warm in the velvet house with the black lid closed, safe from anyone's hands, other than Abuelo Sean or you. I would think of C. Jeffries. Maker. El fabricante. Fabricante del sonido. Maker of the Sound. I would hope C. Jeffries was also asleep in a bed, somewhere safe too."

Mamá smiled again. "Jesús. Te quiero mucho. I love you so much."

∞

Two Spoons Café, Blackrock, Cork.

"Have you ever been married, Je-sus?" Biddy just couldn't refrain from inclining her head between the Je- and the -sus.

Before I could inhale to answer, I realised an answer was not required. Bridget's conversation opening was for her own story- my input was only to listen.

"I was married for a while myself, Jesus. He was a nice fella. We meh at a dance here in Blackrock, so tha' was easy. Philomena was there so tha' was probably before the baby factory started. Tee hee hee," she tittered. Tihhered I guess.

I raised my eyebrows. "Baby factory? This is what, Bridget?"

"Ah spittin' out babies, y'know, like they did." She wrinkled her nose, then shuddered.

I didn't comment. I remembered this was a facet of Irish life more so than anywhere else I had travelled. Babies or no babies, a kind of national fascination. I am guessing it stemmed from the code of Catholic regulations governing the laws of marriage. It had never been a feature of our Spanish Catholicism.

"He was in insurance, countin' the monies," Bridget continued. "Came from Wes' Cork to the South Mall so we had something in common. Y'know our common background in Wes' Cork. Although he didn't come from anywhere near Ballylickey. Couldn't dance ah all either." She raised her eyes to heaven in a beseeching way. I was reminded of the fact that Bridget had spent seven rather miserable years in Ballylickey, so commonality between them was a 'figary.' I had liked that word when I first heard it in Beara. I was also intently concentrating on listening, for her words were achingly missing their closing tees.

"Buh he was good fun. Ah leas', I used to laugh ah mos' everything he said."

She paused, perched on her high stool, her idle foot swinging to her time, her shoe slipping farther and farther along a stockinged foot. Seated below her at a café table, I chose to focus on that, rather than the constant movement of her upper body as she surveyed the reasonably busy café. It wasn't my favourite time to be at the Two Spoons; I preferred it when Philomena was not busy. But I was awaiting my father and Ambrose.

"Anyways, we meh a few times, courted a bih and Philomena's mother seemed to like him, so when he axed me I said yes."

"To marry him?"

"Well, noh so much to marry him buh I though' that's whah he meanh and after a while he seemed to think tha's wha' he meanh so tha's why I said yes." This came in a breathless rush.

"Ah, of course." It was a lame reply, but there was little else to say.

"He, well we, because I had a bih of money from the aunts, bough' the lihhle bungalow at the top of Barrack Streeh. He loved greyhounds."

"Greyhounds?"

"Yes. Yes, the skinny dog things for racing."

"Ah, yes, carreras de galgos, we say in Spanish." It wasn't anything I knew much about but could guess that it would encompass a whole industry—like Ambrose and his horses. There would be characters, stories, tales of super-dogs and tales of woe.

"Galgos, that's a greyhound. Hmm." Bridget sniffed derisively.

"Horrible things in any language if you axe me. He called them all after me."

I must have looked perplexed, even to Bridget.

"I mean, Bridgeh, Bid, Breege, Bee, Bridie, Bidelia. I was pleased at firs' buh ih goh tiresome then I have to say. Then we had Bridgeh Two, Bid Two, Breege Two. Oh 'twas grindin', wasn't ih, Philomena?"

Philomena came through from the kitchen looking harassed and hot. "What? What now, Biddy?"

"Himself and the greyhounds."

"Oh all called after you. Derivatives of Bridget?" She nodded then threw her eyes skyward. "Hmph!" Once again Philomena walked directly into the heart of a Bridget story.

"We never did ih', y'know."

Philomena was busy with a customer, the café was abuzz with background noise and, despite my immediate reaction of thinking I had not heard her correctly, I knew I had heard her correctly and I intuitively knew exactly what she meant. In order to create a pause, I ventured to ask.

"Did what, Bridget?"

"Did ih'. Y'know, the thing. The marriage thing. Marriage 'n' all tha'."

"But you did actually get married?"

"Oh we goh married. We had the Mass and the breakfas' and we lived in the same house for fifteen years, actually fifteen years, five months, and twenty-two days. He moved ouh on March thirty-firs' so he wouldn' have to geh me a birthday card. I never axed him to move ouh either, jus' so's you know."

"Ah!" The pathos of the story was crucifying. Bridget herself seemed to register no emotion whatsoever. I idly stirred my coffee, which needed no stirring at all. She stepped down off the stool to retrieve her shoe and, bending closer towards me, she lowered her voice.

"No, we never did the 'thing'. We took a few days in Skibbereen for our honeymoon and we sah down over a cup of tea and he muhhered somethin' about doin' somethin' about tha' thing and he said he wouldn' be doin' ih and I said well I wouldn' be doin' ih, so we agreed tha' was tha' and we would never do ih. We had heard so much from our mothers and my aunts tha' ih was wrong and sinful. Ih was bes' jus' to leave ih alone." She returned to her high stool.

"So you never did it?"

"No. Never."

I broke a biscuit and dipped it into the half cup of now cold coffee, for occupation more than anything. I am nearly fully sure we were both talking about the same thing but I was afraid to say the words; consummation, intercourse, sex, making love. It was best left alone, just as she said.

"I don't know why I told you all tha', Jesus. I never told anyone else, noh another soul, noh even Philomena." She sniffed and studied her nails. "Philomena always says you are good to tell things to."

"I am flattered, Bridget. And honoured. Thank you."

"You won' be writin' any of tha' now to yer man in Boston will you?" She crinkled her nose in distaste then laughed, somewhat nervously I thought, as if it hadn't occurred to her before she told the tale.

I murmured my assent, "No, of course not, Bridget. Your story is only for me."

"He wen' off with Shlap anyways," she sniffed.

"Shlap?"

"Ya, Shlap we called her. She wore much too much make-up and badly too, leh me tell ya."

I averted my eyes from her bright pink lips and an uneven scattering of powder.

"Oh she though' she was ih. I mean she really did think she was ih. The best thing since the sliced pan."

I didn't like to break her flow but none of that made any sense at all to me. I guessed it wasn't the same ih we had just conversed about.

"We called her tha' long before they were doin' ih. I suppose he did ih with her?" She paused for the briefest of moments. "Ih never crossed me mind before now though, about tha'. Buh I suppose they did. She wouldna have stayed with him otherwise, would she, Philomena?"

"What? What? Oh not now, Biddy. I have an awful feelin' that I never... ."Philomena trailed off, turning back in through the kitchen door.

I was slightly uneasy. I have had many conversations with many persons of many countries, cultures, and creeds. In the moment, I did not understand my disturbing reaction to the personal details of Bridget's married life. I carefully examined the square basket on the counter, where Philomena displayed a colourful array of chocolate snacks—yellow shortcake, pink wafer, purple biscuit, surrounded by bags of Tayto crisps. I breathed slowly and focussed on these. She kept no other confectionery. I knew she had a jar of sweets under the counter and would surprise an especially good child with one. I knew for certain there were no lollipops. No lollipops ever, since Michael had fallen on his one when he was six and damaged his palate.

"Oh I can see now I'm behher off withou' him," Biddy was saying, "buh fifteen years is fifteen years, ih's nearly sixteen, as I said. All that time makin' dinners and washing underpants and socks and ironing shirts." She grimaced. I remained silent, the metronome swing of her stockinged foot maintaining my focus now.

"Oh, we had good times, did a few trips away. He looked after me in tha' way. But ih was still a surprise when ih happened, old Shlap. I just never though'. Oh hello, Mrs. Murphy, you're lookin' grea', so much behher. Has ih all cleared up now?"

It took me a moment to realise the conversation had changed, her attention moving to a new vista. I caught Maureen Doherty's eye as she ching-changed at the cash register. She smiled enquiringly, half-apologetically, as if it was her fault that I was the audience for Bridget's Marital Tale of Woe. I returned her smile, nodding to confirm my understanding.

"Where was I? Oh ya. Well he never hih me or did any of those terrible things they write abou' in *Woman's Weekly* or *Hello*, y'know. I read the mose terrible things, Jesus, when I'm at Tracy's gehhing me hair done. Ih was all, well, jus' dull, really. I loved me outings with the parish groups, oh ih was grea' to geh away for a day or over the nigh' if we wen' to Knock or Lough Derg. Then I'd sometimes take a lihhle trip with Philomena if she wasn' up to her eyeballs in babbies. Then I took to the bingo-callin' because they were stuck, buh I can see now it was good to geh ouhha the house. And shur he could be racing those cursed dogs two nigh's a week anyways in Cork and Youghal. Then he had a couple of good dogs so he'd go away overnigh' to Waherford or Limerick. An' all the walkin' he had to do with them. I never though' a thing of it. Isn't tha' the kinda thing men do? So I suppose all in all, we hardly saw each other, certainly for the last five or eigh' year."

I was nodding my attention and understanding. Her story was probably indicative of many marriages, although it was definitely the first confidence of its kind for me. It took all of my effort to stay with her.

"Oh hi, Michelle, ya, ya, oh I see, thanks so much, ya fine thanks, I'll give you a call on Friday." Bridget was half-standing on her foot-rest, widely mouthing these words, waving towards a departing customer. I could hear this exchange, but I'm certain the gesticulating woman at the café door would have had no understanding of what Bridget had just said to her; it was a non-conversation.

"So there they were on a Saturday morning in me kitchen. Me very own kitchen." She shook her head at the memory. "He though' I was gone with Fr. Downey to the Novena in Limerick buh ih turns ou' tha' when Fr. Downey had said to me 'will you come with me to the Novena,' I though' he meant jus' me. Y'know, on me own. When I goh to the Parish office at eigh' o'clock, there was a bus and fifty other parishioners. I was more than a lihhle bih disappointed and then there were no seats lef' on the bus, so myself and Gina Mac and Paudie Keeffe goh lef' behind. I even had a lihhle flask and had made a sandwich for Father. I called here to Philomena buh she was too busy making scones to have the tea with me. I was so upseh noh to go, isn' tha' righ', Philomena?"

"Oh the Limerick Novena is it?" Philomena shot me a look which meant she knew exactly where Bridget was in the story of her marital exposé.

"An' she was so busy here, there was nothing for it buh to go home and I found them, there they were in me own kitchen."

I warily looked to see if perhaps Bridget was upset at this disclosure. She had certainly stopped in her flow. But no, she had engaged eye contact with a couple who were preparing to depart over a sea of tables and bobbing heads.

"Coo-ee, coo-ee Patsy, Patsy," she called, waving so frantically I thought she would dislodge herself off the foot-rest. I glanced at Philomena who, with a raised eyebrow, queried my state of mind. I reassured her with a mouthed "It's okay."

"Kissin'."

"Kissing?"

"Oh the filthy Jezebel. The filthy thing, Jesus." She tut-tutted disapprovingly. Tuh-tuhhed, of course.

"Unmistakably kissin'. All over each other like a rash." She reddened slightly under the shlap, well, make-up. She inclined her head in a reverential bow. "I am very sorry, Jesus. I read tha' once under the hair-dryer at Tracy's, an' I thought ih very descriptive. I have never had the chance to use ih."

This is the story of the moment of revelation when a woman discovers the infidelity of her husband of nearly sixteen years and all I could do was nod, silently.

"So he seemed a bih embarrassed; she was brazen ouh. Wanted to know wha' I was goin' to do about ih. Do about wha'? I said.

'Abou' ih. He and I are together.' Oh work away, I told her, but move ouhha me way, me throat's like the floor of a budgie's cage and I'm dyin' for a cuppa tea."

I continued nodding like a solar-powered dashboard toy. I had no words.

"So tha' was tha'."

After several moments, that seemed to be that conclusively. I gave her due pause. "I am so sorry, Bridget. That can't have been very pleasant for you to witness. And there is grief in everything we lose."

"Oh noh another word about ih, Jesus. God forgive me I cursed them righ' enough." She speed-blessed herself, Formula One style. "I goh over meself righ' quick though. He packed his bags and moved to hers and good luck to them I though'. Ih was quite nice really, havin' the place to meself. He took the smelly dogs too. And shur I was never much of a cook. The nuns taugh' me all the polishin' 'n' dustin' but they never goh me cookin'. Philomena has mostly fed me since."

∞

"Well?"

"Well, Philomena?"

"Well, you got it. The story of Himself.

"Indeed. About Himself."

We were above the Two Spoons in Philomena's apartment. Ambrose had refitted the first floor, thinking it would be a good rental property and great security for the café, but Philomena never took to the idea. He made a separate entrance from the backyard so she could slip away when things were quiet, snooze in the afternoon if that worked with the staff. She overnights there if Ambrose is away racing, or at horse fairs. "Or when the sinus blockage makes him sound like his own trombone." Her father's old Robert Roberts radio sits on the windowsill—the wireless, she calls it. Two easy chairs, no television, handy kitchenette. Bridget stays with her on occasion. "Sometimes she calls to me late, hoping I might ask her to stay. She has that thin tap-tap on the window below. Sometimes she even brings tea in her hot water bottle. If I make tea she doesn't say anything. If I don't, then she will pour it herself from the bottle. All those living alone seem to have their odd ways. She's good company and she's always so pleased to be asked. Ax-ed she says."

"Himself?"

"Xavier."

"Ah! Nearly as popular in Cork in the 1970s as Jesus, I would imagine?"

"Xavier. Ex-av-ee-er, she used to say. He's been Himself since the, well, since Shlap. But at the time she thought he was just that, her Saviour."

"Made the decision easier for her. Although, there seems to have been no decision to be made?" I queried Philomena.

"Yes, that's right. That, and when she was in the convent, she had dreamed of being Sr. Bernadette Aloysius Xavier Ignatius. Baxi for short. She would be polishing the chapel floor and everyone would be friendly and call her Baxi. Course she never got that far in her religious career."

"Ah!" I am thoroughly dumbstruck by the logic of Bridget's life.

"So Xavier. It must have been a sign."

I nodded. "Yes, it must have."

"Xavier McCarthy. She was all agog when they met y'know. Nice enough fella, bit too old for her I thought but beggars can't be choosers. I was already with Ambrose and the thought had occurred to me as to what would become of her when we got married. So I let things happen at their own pace. He seemed keen enough." Philomena tapped her fingers on the arm of the chair to the sound in her own head.

I nodded again. Philomena was possibly recalling exactly what she thought might have happened to Bridget, should she not have found a husband. Through the floorboards Bryan Adam's "Summer of Sixty-Nine" reverberated from the kitchen below. Maureen had obviously forgotten we were upstairs and I smiled at the thought of her with her air-guitar or using a soup-ladle microphone, alone in her own rock 'n' roll space. She shrilled below us—'The Best Days of my Life'.

Philomena picked up her tale. "We did the weddin' here in Blackrock church, she had the aunts and their men and that was the sum total of her relations. I filled up a few more seats with my lot. He had a handful of work colleagues, no parents, a brother came from Dublin to be his best man, another brother and sister off the farm in Kealfincheonbeg. It was all over by one o'clock."

"Wait now, Philomena." I interjected quickly. "Kale what?"

"Kealfincheonbeg. Why?"

"And you can't pronounce Ambrose's Scottish estate? Dear God, Philomena, it doesn't sound too dissimilar a task to my uneducated Spanish ear."

We laughed together. I paused and thought, I so love to laugh with Philomena. So I told her. "Talking with you reminds me all the time of my grandfather. I loved to listen to him and laugh with him too, Philomena. Thank you."

"Oh, Jesus!" She smiled. "How lovely! The pleasure is also mine."

We were silent awhile. Muffled sounds from the café below drifted through the floor. I could hear Maureen turn the key in the lock. Closing time. 96FM went to time-pips for the six-o'clock news.

"Y'know, Xavier had a spell with the Presentation Brothers. I suppose that's why he was older and still unmarried. He had done a few year, years, in the seminary but preferred the learning and books, so gave it up to do accountancy. He told Ambrose one night at a dance. If Ambrose wasn't playing with a band, he and Xavier used to have a beer together. Xavier played the flute sometimes. Ambrose liked him. And shur I suppose what Ambrose felt for horses, Himself felt for the dogs. When our dancing days were done, we used to meet them in McCarthy's No Relation on a Saturday night for a drink. Arra, there was no harm in the man at all. He was a smart enough fella. I could see how they were mismatched. 'Tis a wonder it went on as long as it did. It was no surprise really that he took up with Pauline O'Neill."

"Shlap?"

"Yes. That's my fault actually." Philomena reddened, shifted in her chair, fiddled with her wrist watch. "She became Shlap when we were in our twenties. She appeared one night in McCarthy's No Relation with Martin Dullane. She had more make-up on her than any of us ever even owned. I never drink much but I had had a couple of BabyChams and thought Shlap was a great nickname for her." Philomena reddened again. She fished about her cheek for the stray hair to fiddle with. "It seems so childish now."

"But you were young, Philomena? Nights out in McCarthy's No Relation were probably not terribly exciting?"

"No," she agreed, "and I really missed my dancing. I had three small children then I suppose, maybe four, and life was moving on. I don't know why I ever stopped the dancing. I shouldn't have. Babies, then later Michael and the café. Life just whooshes by, Jesus."

"It does indeed. Whooshes."

"She worked in Cash's, the big department store in the city, Pauline, so make-up was her thing. We knew her in a small way back then and shur I would never have guessed when it happened, that it could be she. It seemed so unlike Xavier. So in the telling of the story, it has always been Shlap and Himself. Biddy rarely refers to it now. I'd say many have forgotten she was ever married to him."

The old alarm clock with two top-mounted bells ticked loudly.

"She stayed in the bungalow. God knows she even tried a bit of B&B there, took a notion one year. Started as Green Acers 'cos she spelt it incorrectly on the sign. Not that there was a bit of green anywhere up there after those greyhounds, not to mind any fraction of an acre. But that's Biddy for you. Then someone graffitied the sign and made it Green Achers. Biddy kept that. Like a metaphor for life she decided. It wasn't all that successful; she hasn't the scantiest level of commitment, and she had no intention of supplying a breakfast. They were to come to me for that. I humoured her for a while, then something else took her fancy, can't remember what, and that was it for paying guests. So she decided to sell the bungalow and move when Barrett Homes finished building at Mrs. Farquharson's old place. A fabulous new apartment complex, The Friendly Companions, 'tis called, top of Duchess Hill. She was taken by the lovely plush red carpet and the en suite bathroom. N-sweetie she calls it. Thinks it's called this to make the night sweeter so a person doesn't have to go freezing down the hall."

The conjured image of Bridget McCarthy in a nightgown tip-toeing along the tiles was nearly more than I could bear.

"I said to her, there's no bath tub, and would she mind, and she said, that's okay she never used the bath since Himself used to wash the dogs in it. The last time she used it was when she spilled Lucozade on her Aran cardigan and needed somewhere to soak it." Philomena laughed heartily at this, "whuh, whuh, whuh," the easy chair creaking beneath her. I had to apologise and say I did not know what an Aran cardigan was.

"I'm sorry, Jesus. I always seem to be laughing at ould Biddy, but she's such a poor little waif, even now, after the better part of our lifetime on this earth. The Friendlies was built for older persons who live alone or in a couple but don't need nursing care. Sorta like a retirement community. So the first people she meets when she gets to The Friendlies are Johnny and Jenny Salter, the resident caretakers. They're from off Bandon way, west of the city. Jenny's father gets the first apartment because they are minding him. Johnny does all the jobs, light bulbs, gutters, cuts the grass, all that kinda thing. Jenny keeps an eye on everything else, all the comings and goings, does teas and coffees in the day room of a Thursday for all the residents, so they can all get together and chat. Shur Biddy is made up."

I must have looked puzzled, for I was guessing made up had nothing to do with make-up.

"Made up, happy out, in her element. Absolutely the best thing she did, she never looked back. She can lock the door and trip away off wherever and whenever she likes. She had this ancient old car, Impy, a Hillman Imp. Bright blue. She was a picture I can tell you. It died a death there only a while ago." Philomena nodded to herself then chuckled. "But of course, she always seems to be getting on the wrong side of Jenny. She gave them all three biscuits instead of two one day when she asked, ax-ed, Jenny if she could help and do the teas. Then she never took their money. The Salters only get a stipend for staying there, the accommodation is free, so the teas money is pocket money for Jenny. You couldn't tell that to Biddy though."

"Bridget seems to manage without an income?" I had been curious about this for some time.

"Oh, the aunts. Every one of them seems to have done well, through marriage or business, and none of them had families either. So as they one by one popped off, they all left her their estates. Estates, meaning inheritance. 'Guilt,' Ambrose says. They never really looked after her, just pushed her from pillar to post."

"Ah!"

"Yes. Our Biddy has quite a substantial cushion behind her skinny little bottom."

I immediately visualised this, Bridget lounging on a couch of cash.

"And shur she can live on air. Wafer thin ham and thin-sliced bread wouldn't break a bank. That and she automatically gets the state pension at sixty-five, which is, as I said, whooshing towards us. But of course I have to keep an eye on the banking for her as well. She really isn't bright enough for the magic card."

"Debit card?"

"Debit, credit, any card at all. We have an agreement, Mr. Tunney at the bank and myself. I get regular phone calls about her account activity, depending on what company she has attracted to her.

There has been a certain amount of straightening out her fan club, all who have a good nose for her wealth." She looked at the alarm clock. "What time are you expecting them? I haven't had a word from Ambrose."

I glanced at the ornate luminous hands. "He said about six or six-thirty. Please, do go up home if you would like to?"

"No shur, I can take a lift with Ambrose when they get here. Are you sure you won't stay? The beds are made and I can get a bit of dinner for your dad downstairs?"

"No, really, thank you, Philomena. He likes to get home if he has been away all day."

"Unless they stopped at the Thady Inn for a plate. He often does coming from the Kerry side. Ambrose likes that place. 'Best ever steak 'n' chips,' he says. Although I think he and old Peter O'Flaherty used to do a bit of post-race money-counting, something like that between them."

She nodded to herself, idly curling her cheek hair. "In the days when you could drink and drive, he would stop for steak and Guinness. Isn't it funny when there's something about a place that keeps drawing a person back to it? It must be the ambience, or the character of the proprietor, or something like that. Do you think?"

"Well, I suppose you could ask Jimmy Jack or Marguerite or any one of your regulars, Philomena."

She laughed, "It's the roasties and extra slice of beef keeps Jimmy Jack at the door. Here I'll tell you about Aysha while we're waiting and while Biddy is fresh in your mind."

"Aysha? This is a place? Or a person?"

"Oh yes! A most definite person." Philomena nodded seriously. "Oh yes, a.k.a., or should I say, formerly known as Maureen Noonan of St. Gerard's Villas on the Ballyann Road. Her mother Hannah and I would have been at the Ursulines together. Maureen was the youngest of a long lot by quite a stretch and what a rake she was growing up. They couldn't keep a leash on her. I couldn't say that she ever finished her schooling or anything like it. Anyway she went off foreign for a while and came back in trailing gowns and head gear, renouncing all that was Noonan and now to be known as 'Aysha Diamond Sky'."

It sat there flatly between us.

"Aysha what?"

"Diamond Sky. Y'know, a bit like the Beatles had it."

"Ah! She went to a monastery or maybe a hippie commune or some such?"

"Yes, I suppose so. Not a bob to her name of course. So she had to sell her wares somehow. Massage, reading cards, hot stones, bit of fortune-telling, all those things that would make me nervous, for one. She lived in a caravan at the back of her granny's field." Philomena began to laugh again, the chair creaking with every guffaw. "What's this thing they do in your ear?"

I was puzzled and could not answer.

"With a candle? 'Tis an Indian thing if I am not mistaken?"

"Ah! Exactly that, ear candling. I have no experience of this though, Philomena, so I can only imagine what it is."

Philomena guffawed with silent mirth, a handkerchief pressed to her mouth. The easy chair creaked a gleeful rhythm. "Oh dear, Jesus, dearest Jesus."

"Is that one for me or for the real Jesus?" I queried between her gasps.

She nodded through her laughter, "Ear candling. Shur she could hardly find a candle to fit Biddy's little lug-hole. Then there was tickle therapy. You can just imagine THAT!"

"Bridget McCarthy. I could just write a book on her alone."

Philomena nodded again. After a few more minutes, she finally regained some composure.

"Anyway, Biddy was sorta, what would I say, kinda went mad for seeing her."

"Drawn to her, attracted to her?"

"Yes, that's a good way of putting it. Drawn to her. For what seemed like an age she would natter on and on about Aysha said this and Aysha said that. Aysha this, Aysha that. Aysha blessed this, lit a fire under that, blah, blah. There was always money involved of course, in receiving spiritual advice from the same wan. Oh a hundred more stories but the one that still makes me laugh most is the HAT."

I could only smile at the thought of what was to come. If it made Philomena laugh again, then I was ready.

"She arrived below here one morning sporting this big colourful woolly hat, like a South American rancher in the mountains. Least that's what I thought anyways, havin' seen them on Discovery. Turns out, I was on the wrong continent, for it was all the way from Tibet." A smile tickled the corners of her mouth again. "You wouldn't mind, only it was the most beautiful day, not woolly hat weather at all, at all. She says 'I goh a new hah.' I see that, I says to her, trying not to laugh. 'I goh it from Aysha Diamond Sky.' Oh, says I, that must be a hundred euro I suppose. So she was delighted then 'cos it was less than that. It was only ninety."

We chuckled a bit, warming to the story.

"But here y'are, Jesus. Listen to this, it was real wool and came with a special blessing she said, 'for peace and serenity from the Dial-a-Llama'." Philomena began to "whuh, whuh, whuh," the chair creaking with each guffaw.

"Wait for this, Jesus. She was afraid to ask Aysha too many questions 'cos she felt a bit foolish for not knowing," Philomena paused, "but she wondered if she could get a number for the Dial-a-Llama to thank it." Philomena threw her head back and roared with laughter. "Poor Biddy. She was sure that the wool had come from the llamas on Horan's Farm and she could give them a call to thank them for their blessing."

"Of course she has no idea who the Dalai Lama is?"

Philomena couldn't speak. Just shook her head in mirth. "If ya saw her, Jesus. The waif in the knitted hat. Could you call the Dalai Lama for me please and release me from this cross of misfortune that I bear?"

∞

The years passed, a decade of our lives; coming, going, nursing, teaching, boating, writing, creating our home. My father grew roses, my mother grew shrubs and flowers, and they both grew edible foods. Abuelita Rosa would pot seedlings in the shed for the greenhouse, dead-head pansies, weed the potato row, pick slugs off the lettuce bed. From seed to plate, as I had suggested might happen. They pickled and bottled and froze fruit, berries, vegetables; dried and packaged seeds for the coming spring. Their lives were simple and busy in a beautiful place by the sea.

In far away places I would sit with an aerogramme, composing my life onto the blue ultra-thin page, imagining the excitement in the cottage by the water when it arrived with Pat the Postman. I would write the address first, draw a box around space for the postage frank, then cover every possible millimetre with my story.

My mother kept all these letters carefully, chronologically, in a Clark's shoe box, black, size 4, EUR 36. Rosa's walking shoes, nursing shoes. These were my diaries, my travelling tales. I would try to give them an idea of where I could receive mail and catch up with their lives, then I would sit in the same faraway places, eagerly retrieving mail from Poste Restante.

In Cork they continued to do what they had begun on arrival, my mother teaching in the local schools, my grandmother nursing at the doctor's surgery, my fathering tipping about pots in the harbour, in his own way.

My mother's musical learning took a different direction now that she was in Cork. No more awaiting tunes off a boat, visitors idling by in Cadiz, searching out a dusky taberna. She joined the local traditional group, playing in halls and barns and kitchens, or a quiet Monday night in the local pubs, watching, learning, much as she had always done in Cadiz. She cultivated friendships through her work and her music. Her stack of copybooks grew, also carefully filed chronologically, each book marked with the start and finish date and an abbreviated list of the contents. She would bind five books together with a rubber band. At the very rear of the pile was 'Papá 1, 2, 3'. Sometimes I would open the bureau drawer just to see my mother's neat, teacher's handwriting, occasional notes in Spanish, doodled drawings of items that caught her interest.

I would choose one book, see chords and music notes, the names of the musicians, maybe the venue in which they were playing: Murphy's Bar, John's Barn, Cooper's, Eliza's Garden, Jacko's, Ballin Arms. Neat notes on tempo, tone, witticisms a player might have uttered, stories they told, nuances—such as "Ten-Penny Bit" by Martin's cousin from Kilrush. Hurried notes in Spanish, something Rosa told her, a note taken perhaps after a phone call: Jesús, Malaga, June 10; or a bed-and-breakfast to remember—"Mrs. Ita Walsh, Rockyview House, Fanore, May weekend." I loved my mother's life. I found this gem cut out from some or other publication and stuck inside a copybook cover:

The school children were drawing pictures of Bible stories. Maggie's picture showed four people in a plane, so the teacher asked which story they were from. "The flight to Egypt." said Maggie. "That must be Mary, Joseph, and Baby Jesus. But who's the fourth person?" asked the teacher. "That's Pontius the Pilot."

Great-Uncle Jerry had musicians in his family, David a champion accordion player, Ken a master of stringed-instruments of any shape. In their home, they have a workshop producing many types of wooden sound-box with strings attached. It was the craft Jerry had grown to, having retired from his working life and returned to Rostellan. He would make, shape, whittle and carve, his bottom resting on a repurposed barstool, yellowed stuffing escaping from cracked and torn leather, manuals and pamphlets, handwritten sketches pinned to sawdusty walls. He wasn't a player but knew what it needed. Ken would laugh and say, "He'd tie four strings to the top of a tissue box just to see what sound it would make."

I would watch Jerry as I watched Abuelo Sean all those years ago, working and talking, spinning tales of his career in law enforcement, tales of his first years in Rostellan growing up with my grandfather. I would see his expressions, his movement in the same way my grandfather moved, smiled, spat in the dust, scratched his hairline, closed one eye to see the measure of a piece of his work. I remembered Dr. Zhao, "We are all waves of energy Jesús, just waves of resonating sound. Some things we hear. Some things we do not hear, but it all vibrates within us, and we too are vibrating. Frequency, tone, harmony, this is resonance with our souls."

I visited many times with Mamá for music, for tea and talk with Jerry and his wife, Tish. And regularly my grandfather would sit on my shoulder, breathing across my neck, whispering in my ear, "Look at that, Jesus? Isn't that grand?" or "Faith and I'd love a go off that." I am certain I heard him cry.

After some discussion, and with permission from my mother and Abuelita Rosa, I took my grandfather's toolbox to Jerry. It sat on the work bench between us whilst he shook his head sadly.

"I missed him so much, Jesus, I used to cry myself to sleep. I never saw him before he left. He was just gone from us. All my father would say was that 'tis best. Even Father didn't think he would never come back again. And shur the girls were just heart-broken. Mam would say, 'C'mon now, we'll do a decade of the Rosary,' an' have us all on our knees praying as if that might fix things. And shur then they'd all be sobbin' thro' the prayers. My father got tired of it all, I s'pose he knew we all blamed him for sending John away. It must've been for the best. But my father never recovered either."

Jerry fiddled the catch on the box, lifting the lid slowly. The wood was worn and shiny around the hasp and handle and, even as he opened it wide, I could smell the cigarillo smoke, the oily scent of rag for minding the concertina, Abuelo's lovely sound. At a glance I could see the tobacco tin of oddities, the next tin marked screws, another marked box, which contained concertina buttons, tweezers, and old reeds. The folding wooden ruler, a blackened pliers, his whittling knife. Jerry lifted the top tray and beneath was the tidy array of chisels, tapping hammer, the old round wooden-handled screwdriver that was produced at every job, the heavy hammer, its ash handle worn smooth with JJOS carved on the butt end. Jerry lifted the hammer out of the box.

"This is the hammer he left with," he whispered, a tear forging a clear path through his dusty cheek, along the shape of his nose. "1938. More than fifty years ago?" He turned the hammer in his hands, feeling the weight, stroking the handle, imagining all the Irish and Spanish stone it had helped to work and shape.

"Dear Jesus, I was so lonely those first years knowing he was gone away. Lonelier than even being in Dublin when I was first in the guards." He smiled, the tears undisturbed. "Even the missus couldn't make up for it." He wiped the tip of his nose with a craftsman's thumb. "Shur we had no words for it. No one talked ever about loving your brother. But I did. Oh yes sir, I did. We were great mates."

∞

Great-Aunt Frances, whilst not a musician nor the mother of a musician, was the mother-in-law to two of the local group of players. She had lived her life in East Cork, an integral part of all parish activities, inheriting the task from her mother to be a carrier of community knowledge, a keeper of the family genealogies. Frances was the cartographer of local life, mapping the connections, joining the dots of a neighbourhood history. Her six offspring are a book unto themselves.

On regular afternoons Mamá and one of her cousins, or one of the traditional players, would convene in the school hall and teach the parish children new tunes. An assortment of instruments would appear—much like the story of Eily Wall's concertina—fished out of chimney nooks, fiddles lifted carefully off the picture-rails where they hung, awaiting hands to bring them life. The room would fill with the sounds of scraping bows, tuning accordions of all sizes, guitars, harmonicas, banjos. Excitable youthful chatter awaiting instruction. One line also of tin-whistles, flutes, low-whistles. Instruments of sound tempered by generations of musicians, the woven thread of tradition pulled together harmoniously by a common tune.

On other days Mamá might relieve the old school tape-deck machine and play basic tunes while Mrs. Keniry or Mr. Cahill would teach youngsters to dance reels and jigs. The music took on a different life, a physical expression of handmade chords, punctuated by the calls of "Left, left, slide, one, two, three, LEFT! Not that left, Claire Doyle." Mamá adored this time, meeting her primary school pupils under the tutelage of another, her only task to provide the sound.

On Saturday nights she would sit in the kitchen of the cottage by the water, the weekday tasks complete, tea at her elbow and the Robert Roberts radio tuned to RTE for "Céilí House." When I was in Cork, I would sit with her awhile, then move to my father watching The "Late Late Show" on television. Or I might choose to listen to them both through the floorboards of my attic room, weaving the tapestry of our lives.

In Abuelita Rosa's world of general practice, the local doctor was an old-school practitioner; the surgery was the front room of his house, there were no timed appointments, the practice was not yet computerised, so he kept a hand-written book for his records. The telephone would ring loudly in the hall and, in the absence of his wife, Morna Doc, it would remain unanswered. His patients knew this, knew his ways. In attendance, he would nod and listen for what was left unsaid, knowing that possibly what was spoken was not all that was amiss. He and Rosa understood each other.

I clearly hear her say, "Look at the colour, listen to the voice. Smell them. Simpatía, empatía, these heal as much as medicine." I remember her doing this, saying this. But mostly I remember this day, as she sat by me in our garden, "I take the pulse with my fingers, no machine. I take the bloods pressures. I sit by them. I see their ages, see their colours, smell them, listen to their sees-tems working, speaking their truths, or not. Look into the mouth, more smells, tongue, teeth. See the hair. See the skins. But, Jesús, always, always see the eyes. And always let the eyes see yours."

My father and she became a pair in the locality; she would ask him to take her out in the VW to see someone who might have difficulty in travelling into the surgery. She would change a dressing, take a blood sample, check on the needy. Sometimes, he would say, she would do nothing but hold their hand. This was not strange for me; I was there in Cadiz with Abuelita Rosa and Dr. Zhao. I knew what she knew about dis-ease. She knew the value of touch. She knew pressure points, knew how Dr. Zhao relieved many situations.

This is what she did in East Cork. My father would stand in farmyards chatting, or walking the lanes with a spotting-scope, finding a yellow-hammer's nest in Finure, photographing starlings bathing in puddles in Roches Point, as he waited around the parish for Rosa O to perform her tasks. He continued his listening and learning, deciphering a new tongue.

She was aging though; already nearing seventy when they had travelled from Cadiz, there was only a short interval to share her wisdom.

They would take trips, the three of them in the VW, back to Beara to show Papá the sandstone hills, the copper mines, the folding, rolling landscape. He drank beer in Denis' Bar on Bere Island, climbed high onto Ballaghboy to marvel at the cable-car construction to Dursey Island. He took his women here, a new adventure for them to the tip of Beara, to the tip of Dursey Island by pony and cart. To the edge of the same Atlantic waters they had shared farther south, off the Cadiz coast.

On one trip they pressed on down to the Mizen and I received a postcard from Ireland's southernmost point while I was as far south on the globe as I have ever been, in Invercargill, New Zealand. Sometimes the intervening miles were long and wearying. My mother filled her school copybooks with their adventures, homely bed and breakfasts in every nook and cranny, down every lane. "Fed the lambs, Catherine Morris, Failte Farmhouse, near Caherciveen with Rosa, April."

Their choice was to never stay in a town or city; if a village had one street, this was enough. Here were the stories, the characters, the histories. I laughed many years later reading of this in her copybook account, for I was always mirroring their habits, half a world away.

Our paths would cross of course. Often we would sit in Cork and exchange our letters and copybooks and regale tales in greater detail, our lives lived alive in each other's hearts. I was often lonely or homesick while tripping around the world. I met many travellers who did not keep contact with their families. I could but nod and accept different paths, the complexity of familial relationships. My path was never thus. If the hourglass ran accordingly, I would join them on trips, sometimes travelling with them, sometimes meeting them en route. The VW was a tight fit for three adults and a pint-size grandmother and often two Springer dogs, so I would throw a bicycle and my tent on the roof to be able to ride sections and meet with them later in a day. Or walk long paths through farms, hillside contours and Mass paths, village to village. On days my father or mother would ride the bike, one other of us would drive, taking the slow road until we all met again.

My progressive, widening vision of a travelling world allowed me to reflect on this dynamic: it is not usual for three adults to cohabit seamlessly in this way. The more stories I listened to, the more her- and his-story I learned, the more I understood the balance my parents and Abuelita Rosa had achieved in their lives. Even to her mid-eighties, my grandmother quietly pursued her own interests, collected her own thoughts and experiences, graciously accepted her place as a part of their marriage. Equally my parents had found the same balance in their relationship, their individual lives flowing and ebbing over the steady fulcrum of their love. My father was not a traditional musician, my mother was not a seapootler. Allowing each other the heartfelt freedom to follow their own course gave a calm to their shared experiences.

I recall arriving to Rostellan late one evening, a blustery April, the chill falling early as May Day approached. They were at the picnic table, the brazier blazing warmth. Julia O'Brien played her fiddle and Mamá had the concertina on her lap, Papá was singing and playing his guitar, and he smiled as I walked down the avenue. Abuelita Rosa took my hand and pulled me to sitting beside her.

"Heaven Knows no Frontiers." Papá said as he stopped strumming and smiled again.

"Jesus, 'tis yourself," Julia remarks cheerily.

"Philomena Sowersby must have copyright on that greeting," and I kiss both Julia and Mamá on the cheek.

"Your dad is keen on a Corkman."

Mamá explained. "We are singing the songs of Jimmy MacCarthy. He is good for all of us to learn. Julia has them all on that round thing, what you say, Julia?"

"Compact disc."

"Oh come, Mamá! You know what a CD is? You can play them on the music system?"

She waved her hand at me, "Yes, yes, but I never know which hole to stick them into." They all laughed.

"It sounded great, Papá. Let's hear some more."

He cleared his throat and, raising his eyes to Julia, said, "Last verse?"

She nodded and smiled, raising her eyes from the fiddle, crimped cheek to shoulder, and she sang as she played.

My father rests his guitar, "The man is pure genius."

Mamá claps her hands, the music-light blazing in her eyes, "Okay, Jesús, wait until you hear one called 'Ancient Rain.' You will love this," she says.

"No, no, no, please favor for me," cried Abuelita Rosa. "The lovely blue rose one again. Then I can go to my bed singing, ready to dream the lovely dreams and all of you can sing all night like little cheel-dren."

∞

Blackrock, Cork

"My parents owned this house here, Jesus, downtown Blackrock."

We were ambling in spring sunshine, as it seemed Philomena was in no great rush to return to the café, which was in the capable hands of Maureen. This was definitely in the earlier years of our return to Cork, for I was certainly still learning the ways, the language, the turns of phrase.

"My father, Kit, Christopher Flaherty, was a trader; he'd buy and sell anything and was one of the first to own a motor-van and travel his goods about. He used to travel east to Cobh, Carrigtwohill, and Midleton and all the small stops along the way, for every village had at least a couple of shops, public houses, bakeries, everything anyone could want, but no one had transport. He sold shop to shop, buttons and bolts of cloth, all sorts of anything that would turn a pound. He was a clever man and a great wit; folk liked him. My mother's family had a shop in Rostellan and that's where they met."

Philomena lowered her large frame onto the low stone wall across the road.

"He used to travel that way once a month and my grandmother suspected something was afoot when he appeared again after three weeks and the next time in just past a fortnight. Then he turned up one Sunday in his Mass coat and tie. He walked out with my mother and Frances—this in the 1950s—there's no unchaperoned outings I can tell you. They'd take the Green Boat Steamship to East Ferry for the tea dance. Oh! How I loved her stories. They were married at the end of the summer after six months courting and she moved with him to his family home here." Philomena jerked her thumb in the direction of the house across the street.

"They honeymooned in Killarney for a week, the Arbutus Hotel. I remember her telling me how they went out for a stroll in the town one evening while waiting for her bath to be drawn."

She saw my puzzled look. "Filled like. The phrase must've come from drawing the water from the well in buckets. Anyways, this young fella came cycling up the street callin' 'Mrs. Flaherty, Mrs. Flaherty, yer bath is hot!' Mary Flaherty she was now. Oh she loved my father but she did pine for her mother and sister Frances."

"Pine for?" I asked. Pine is a tree.

"Longed for, grieved to be with them. Your John James was in Spain, Jerry was gone with the Guards and ended up in Waterford. Frances was still at home. My mother had never lived anywhere other than Rostellan. My father's parents moved out, as was the way at the time, to a smaller house towards Rochestown. They had come in from the west side, Kinsale way, and he worked at City Hall so they were comfortable, y'know, had enough money. This is the house in which I was born. Wilhelmina first and I was the big surprise ten minutes later, for my mother didn't know she was bearing twins. Frankie was four years after that."

She paused as if to add more but carried on. "This is where we were living, when you and your mother came on the Great Trip. You didn't come here because my mother went to Rostellan to Frances to see you there. We had no spare room for you, for Josephine, my father's mother, had moved back in with us after Grandaddy Flaherty died. I was in the college doing Home Economics and Business for two years."

Philomena paused again, selecting which memories to convey. There was no need for me to speak, for she knew I would listen to every word.

"And it was here I was living when I first met Ambrose. I was nineteen years old. I have to tell you, Jesus, something that always makes me laugh when I look at that house, even now so many years on. Y'see the top window on the right side and the crack in the bottom pane of glass? Well," she paused again, reddened slightly then laughed quietly, her big belly laugh, covering her mouth with her hand.

"Where's Biddy McCarthy? Because if she ever heard this, it would be the end of me. I'm only tellin' you because you are about the only person who would laugh and wouldn't tell a soul."

She paused again, finding the threads to start weaving her tale.

"About a year and a half after we met, we were going out and not going out because Ambrose kept going off to Scotland to his father, who was a gamekeeper on some huge place in the highlands. Anyway he appeared outta the blue one Sunday morning, my father and mother were at Mass and going to East Cork straight afterwards. Wilhelmina was away doing her nursing and was about to be married to the draper in Milltown Malbay, so for some reason I was at home alone. Up turned Ambrose off the Innisfallen boat most unexpected, no letter or telephone call. He could be like that. Well, I was thrilled to see him! All a'flutter and flustered and when he heard there was no one at home, there was no stopping him at all but he picked me up and said, 'Enough of this Catholic nonsense now girl, this is our time.' And up the stairs as quick as you like, into my bedroom he took me and kicked the door closed behind him."

She paused, a long pause this time, remembering.

"That's okay, Philomena," I said, taking her hand, "I don't need to know."

"Oh no! It's quite all right, Jesus," she reassured me. "It was just extraordinary, quite unexpected, and such, well, just such lovely love. So vastly different to anything I could ever have imagined without going straight to Hell of course. And oh so different to the fire and damnation the nuns said would pour upon my head, or the silly snickering of the girls at college who mighta kissed a fella once. But wait for this bit, Jesus, this'll make you laugh. We were lying there musing about life and all the possibilities that lay ahead of us and what we could do with it and all of a sudden there was this caterwauling noise from the street. Ambrose bolts upright, 'Holy God it's our retribution. Already! The Lord has spotted our sin. What on earth is it?' "

She paused, smiling, and chuckled a bit. "Well, he leapt outta my bed and y'know Ambrose, all six-feet-four of him, starkers as the day he was born, straight to the window to see the parish priest swinging the thurible, strutting down the street at the head of the Corpus Christi procession. And whatever turn of the head he gave, he looked straight up at Ambrose and he is sure to this day the priest must have seen him, although I can't see how it's possible. But apparently he did falter a step or two in his proceedings and Ambrose swung the shutter so hard the bolt cracked that little pane. And here I am, married a thousand years with five grown children and that house has changed hands twice since and no one has ever fixed the glass. So I have my little reminder as I walk past, of my first encounter with love."

∞

"So how did Ambrose come to be in Blackrock?" I asked Philomena.

We were sitting in their little house on Church Lane and she had piled wood on the fire. The kettle was sighing before singing on the Rayburn in the kitchen next door. Philomena's old armchair seemed to expand to comfortably absorb her, as she rolled a stray chin hair between her finger and thumb. This aberrant feature of solace and comfort, has never been near an electrolysis needle or a beauty therapist's hand. From underneath her elbow on the arm of the chair, Queenie the cat eyed me, a sniffy cat-look. I was the intruder here. This night, I was awaiting the return of Ambrose and my father from the racing in Listowel. "Y'know, he could be coming anytime at all?" Philomena enquired of me.

"His mother is from here and went to Liverpool in the early '50s to train as a nurse. Ah shur she was part of the eternal flow, to and fro, across the Irish Sea. Her mother's brother had landed on his feet there, in the building trade, y'know, government contracts in post-war England, so he kept his head down and his nose clean and the work was steady. So Eileen was there for four years training and working in the hospital as they did then. One night Ambrose's father, Stanley Wilton Sowersby, was carted into the hospital, ranting and raving in his loud Scottish voice, blood all over him. He had been at the racing at Aintree with good results, he had backed the winner of the National, an Irish horse if I remember correctly. I do recall Ambrose telling me that it was a bad day at Aintree, for four horses died in that race alone."

She paused, closing her eyes to draw the memories "Anyways, his full-of-drink and worse-for-wear companion had turned the car into a low wall and then into a river, trying to find their digs for the night. So having been carted hollering into the hospital, somehow Eileen's calm voice took the noise outta the ould Scot and he lay placidly while they stitched him and set his bones. She saw him every day then for four days until she had a day off and then he was gone when she got back. She thought that was it. Then faith and didn't he turn up at her uncle's house a day or so later with a corned beef."

"A corned beef?" If it was what I thought, I was astonished. "That doesn't sound so romantic?"

"He remembered her saying it was her favourite dinner at home in Ireland. It got him right in favour with the uncle of course. He lived in the back of nowhere in Scotland and invited her up for the May bank holiday, so she took the train and a cousin with her on the uncle's insistence. 'I can't be tellin' yer mam I left you off alone,' he said. Faith and they hit it off big time, she loved Scotland, loved the big open skies after four or more years in Liverpool. She sent the cousin back telling her to pack her things and send them up second class. She got a job in the local hospital; shur nurses were like hen's teeth after the war."

"Hen's teeth?" I inquired.

"Yes," chuckled Philomena, "my mother used to say that. Apparently hens don't have very many. Anyways, the romance blossomed through the summer, the date was set for the weddin' in the local church, but Eileen of course was Catholic, so the rumpus started there. She didn't particularly care, nor did Stanley of course but her family were appalled at her marrying a Presbyterian. So they eloped."

"Ran away?"

"Yes, not too far I believe. Far enough to let the heat out."

"The heat out?"

"Yes, y'know. Wait 'til the fuss had died down and eventually went back to Bray Nap, Stanley's estate. D'you know, I could never, ever say the name of that place? I only ever call it the estate and that's been some near fifty years now. Sure enough she's pregnant with Ambrose in ten seconds."

"They hardly drew breath," I laughed. "That's the phrase my father used about his conception."

"Indeed they didn't, but she was sickly in her time and low-spirited in a Scottish winter. Stanley was a rascal of course and often away working on the far reaches of the estate, or off with the horses, so she was lonely too. She had nice girls at the hospital but no real new faces, so was a lone outsider. God love her, it must've been hard. She came home to her mother the first time when Ambrose was still a babe. Eventually she was sick for home and left for good when he was twelve. She put him into the Brothers school here in Cork. I can tell you that was an awakening for him. There were twenty-two in his whole school in Scotland. But he was taller than most of them here, so he didn't fare too badly. He went to Scotland every Easter and summer to Stanley and that's about all of it. I first met him when he was nineteen or twenty, at a dance. He never danced but he spent the entire night watching me and Cecil Fitzmaurice."

"Cecil? Was he your novio, your boyfriend?"

She laughed heartily, reddened a little in a memory, then added hastily. "Good God not at all." She pulled idly at the chin hair. I raised an eyebrow, for there was obviously more to the tale.

"We danced together like milk and honey."

"Oh Lord! What does that mean, Philomena?"

"Y'know, milk and honey, tea and toast, brandy and port, all the good things that go together well. We danced beautifully together. Always did. Cecil lived with his mam and, when she died, he sold up and moved in with his friend Kevin Healy in the old cottages. They're still there, they keep roses and those yappy little dogs. We had no word for it at the time, gosh not for many more years, but there they are, still to this day. Lovely men. They come to the Two Spoons regularly."

"Why was he called Ambrose?" I asked. "That's not a Scottish name? St. Ambrose was 4th-century Italian and the patron of domestic animals?"

"Oh Stanley's doing. Full of drink no doubt. It apparently also means immortal and, yes, is rather religious too by all accounts. St. Ambrose was one of the founding fathers of the church. He must've done all the holy work, for Stanley and Ambrose never did partake."

Queenie mewled as the bulk of Philomena shifted over her while poking the fire.

"Wilhelmina married Tommy Walsh from Milltown Malbay, Frankie married Dympna Laverty from Crookstown, and I got Ambrose Stanley Sowersby Esquire. I couldn't have found anyone more different."

"Yes, but of course it broadens the gene pool?" I suggested. "Broadens the minds."

Philomena laughed heartily, "Yes indeed! We broadened the Cork gene pool all right." She paused again, shifting Queenie from her expansive armpit to the crook of her elbow. "It's funny, Jesus, Ambrose was an only child. I think she lost one when he was two or three; she said she just couldn't get warm."

"Neither of my parents had siblings. My grandmother neither and I have none," I reminded her.

"Yes, you are an only child, your mother, your father, Biddy, all only children. I was one of three. I had five, Biddy had none—although I doubt that that marriage was ever even consummated. I don't think they ever even turned off the light."

"The light?" I am sure I sounded slightly exasperated. "What does that mean?" Even now after some years, there were Irish phrases in English phrases that made no sense to my Spanish self. I was also reminded to keep Bridget's marital secret safe.

"Oh it was common knowledge that you only got pregnant in the dark at nighttime. It was the only time IT happened here in Catholic Ireland. IT couldn't happen if you didn't turn off the light." Philomena laughed, possibly at the absurdity of the notion.

IT of course, was the same as Biddy's ih, which she had never known, never experienced.

"And if it was dark, you never saw the husband in the flesh, for that was a mortal sin. And oh my word! If he wasn't your husband, the fiery gates of Hell were awaiting you."

"Dear God, Philomena. I don't think the Catholic nuns in Spain ever taught that kind of thing? In fact, for sure Sean thought some of them were quite hot for him and not at all shy. Except of course for the Irish nun, Sr. Dolores. She was all about fire and fury."

"We had our own version of everything here in Ireland, Jesus. The nuns were great teachers and nurses, but, oh goodness, they had some strange ideas about love and marriage. And I couldn't tell you how any of us ever learned a thing about *ih*, as Biddy says, you know, love, or sex or any of it. I remember old Mrs. Callaghan from Castle Road coming into the café one day and she overheard some of us discussing this very subject, how we never knew, what husbands expected, an' all that jazz. She sniffed and announced to us all in her very grand English accent, 'I had nine children, I was forever pregnant and no one had less sex than me.' We laughed and laughed."

"And you were happy with five children?" I asked her.

"Good Lord, Jesus, what can you do?! It was the '70s and '80s in Holy Catholic Ireland." She stopped with a heavy sigh. "It is hard to explain how, well, oppressed we were. Yes, oppressed. Put down, by the clergy, the church at large. And shur, they were advising the lawmakers. Edna O'Brien wrote a trilogy *The Country Girls* in the '60s, and she was sent running to the hills by the Catholic hierarchy, through the powers that be of course. Her parish priest actually burned the book. Called it 'filth'. Too much sexual imagery for the hypocritical purists. But y'know, Jesus, she had her finger on the pulse of Ireland when the rest of us had no pulse at all." She pursed her lips. "Edna O'Brien. I read that book when I was in my twenties and even then I was a bit surprised by the, well, honesty of her writing, you would have to say. We had no words for our feelings, who we were. Like I said, we had no words for the love Cecil and Kevin Healy have."

"And Love was always love."

"You can sing that one, Jesus. So we had love, Ambrose and me. That's how I learned about it." She nodded, scratching Queenie's ears. "And to boot, Ambrose wasn't even Catholic, or of any religious persuasion. He was just Ambrose Sowersby and that was enough for him. He was happy to learn love with me." Queenie pushed upwards, her contented purring filling the warm silence.

"There's five years between Peg and Michael—and old Reggie Sutton the gynie—well he should have been retired. Michael was a big, awkward lad, not an easy birth, and Reggie heard me cry out 'Oh Lord, let that be the last of them.' I was past thirty and had done nothing except raise one generation and care for the previous one. I wanted a life, something for me. Anyways, ould Reggie went out and found Ambrose and told him about the new baby and added the caveat that this should be the last. God bless him. Reggie I mean."

Philomena paused to stroke Queenie again. I attended to the persistent singing in the kitchen, lifting the kettle to the side and closing the stove lid. As I settled back into my seat, Philomena continued her story.

"Well then, later that summer he went off to Stanley in Scotland for a few weeks, as was his wont. His time there was a bit less during the child-rearing years. When he returned, we took a small house on the Dingle Peninsula for the August fortnight, plenty of room for four children to run about and Michael a babe in arms. My mother was with us then. So Ambrose is up to his knees in the sea with children running an' shouting, and he says to me, 'I met ould McCracken in Brae Nap.' Oh, yes, I says, old Rory. He says, 'We had a few whiskies one night and he got out a bit of local anaesthetic and his tool-bag.' His what? I was not with him at all. And standing there in the sea off Dingle in his swimming togs, in front of everyone he says, 'Y'know,' and points to his genitals and makes a big cutting movement with his hand. 'Out of action now!' he says. McCracken did it? I tell you, Jesus, I was shocked outta me standing. Rory McCracken was the estate vet. 'Oh yes and a fine tidy job he did too and we finished the whisky bottle an' I haven't thought about it since.'"

I laughed at the thought of the gangly Ambrose losing his manhood to the estate vet.

Philomena laughed with me, "And guess what, Jesus? What I hadn't told him was that Reggie had put ME to rights after Michael and tied my tubes. His precarious shenanigans with ould McCracken was all unnecessary."

"But will forever make for a good whisky story," I agreed.

"Oh yes indeed. You can't beat a good story, eh?" We were silent for a while, firelight licking the room. "Stanley used to come here at Christmas though, after Eileen left Scotland. But always back to Scotland for that New Year thing they do."

"Hogmanay?"

"Yes, that's it. I can't imagine it can be hugely different to New Year anywhere. Can't stand it myself, I'm usually in bed by ten. They both seemed happy enough with the arrangement, Ambrose says, and if they were happy, he was too young to know anything else. Eileen had a few positions in the city for the first two years but then she got in with Mrs. Farquharson on Duchess Hill. Moira Farquharson."

"Where Biddy lives?" I enquired, "And what, pray tell, is a 'position'?"

"Yes, where Biddy's place is now. A position is usually employment in a household. Young girls often got a start in a big house as a scullery maid or kitchen hand, older girls might be a handmaid to the lady of the house. In this case, Ambrose's mother would have got a position as a nurse or companion to an elderly lady. Mrs. Farquharson was quite elderly by then and she took a liking to Eileen, who by all accounts, and my own mother attested to this, was an excellent and well-trained nurse. So Eileen took care of her really, until Mrs. F passed on, which was many years later. They were very good for each other. Mrs. Farquharson insisted that Ambrose come out of the Brothers, and she sent him to board at the Abbey school in Tipperary. She paid for that."

"Bored?"

"Boarding school. Live-in like. He stayed up at the school all through the term. Otherwise he was up there with the lady and his mother, so they did well. Between school and Scotland and the two ladies on the hill, he was well occupied. He was always fixing and making and doing."

Philomena reached again for the stray hair along her chin line, a stroking, plucking motion until she had it in her grasp, where she rolled it between thumb and forefinger. I knew this was unconscious and recollective and that she would continue in her own time. Queenie snored; I mean that, snored loudly.

"Funny she never took up with anyone else, Eileen. She seemed happy with the old lady and Ambrose, quite content. She still had her own mother here down in the village and a streel of Donovans scattered about. But Ambrose stayed Scottish—loved going there, loved the estate, the long daylight in the summer. The huntin', shootin', fishin' world of Stanley. And of course the horses. Always the horses. He would go for as long as he could during the longer school holidays. Stanley would send Eileen a postal order every month for ten pounds sterling." She shifted her weight, crossing her legs, pulling at her bra strap. "Oh Saints preserve us, this must be the most inconvenient garment ever invented."

I did not comment, for there was a large amount of Philomena on the other side of her bra straps.

"When old Mrs. Farquharson died, she left a large sum of money to Eileen and Ambrose separately. Oh she knew what she was doing. The old hall was fairly dilapidated by then, so she divvied that amongst her own, stretched far and wide and not much bothered with her. The old colonel had been in India; he was from Lancashire, I think, then took a government post here in Ireland, customs, Ambrose said. Threw the old pith helmet on the hall stand when he moved in and there it stayed 'til they sold to the council, a year or so after she passed away. 'Twas abandoned up there for a long time, then they built the new flats that Biddy's in. So thanks to Eileen and Mrs. F, we had a bit of a head start on us. We could buy this place and the field behind and Ambrose bought the old cottages below and started by cleaning them up and reselling them." She paused, remembering, nodding, smiling.

"It wasn't easy, mind you. We worked very hard. Always working, Jesus. His first two mares were in the field by the time Stan was born and, if truth be known, life has rolled along like that for all the years since. Houses and horses and always a job on. For all of Stanley's mischievous ways, he taught Ambrose well. He was, is, well, resourceful I would have to put it. Can make anything outta nothing."

"Just like my father. It's no wonder they get on so well together."

"Indeed," said Philomena, "your father is about the closest thing to a friend Ambrose has really had."

"Must be the similarity in the backgrounds that draws them together?" I suggested.

"And the same similarities that keeps them apart from all the rest." Philomena nodded. "Good men, liked by everyone but only really known by a mere few."

Queenie stirred, stopped the snoring, and started purring like a small engine.

"You've heard what they say to each other?"

I inclined my head in a puzzled way.

"I heard them here, one day in the yard, oh ages ago now. Your father was holding the ladder while Ambrose was securing something on the roof rack of the van. He called out 'That's her now, Dan Sam Joe.' And your father responded saying, 'Stepping away now, Am Sam Sow.' "

I must have looked incredulous, for Philomena started to laugh, "whuh, whuh, whuh." She snorted and wheezed a bit, the armchair creaking rhythmically under her, until Queenie mewled strongly in complaint.

"I am stunned! I have never, ever heard my father be familiar with anyone, Philomena. I think it must be the naval training. He has never so much as attempted to shorten my name, or say Hey or Zoos or anything vaguely familiar. And my mother is María and not very often 'pet' or 'darling' or such endearments. I am astonished!"

"I can see that, Jesus. I can assure you Ambrose is not so familiar with pet names either. Then all our lot are one syllable, probably for that reason. Except for Michael of course," she sighed, "but he was always the exception."

Queenie settled again, one eye open for more disturbance.

"He bought a small van, oh somewhere about when Peg was a year or two or thereafter, and there were long discussions as to what should be put on the side of the van, y'know, 'Ambrose Sowersby, Builder, Horse-Trader, Fixer, Plumber, Mover of Things.' The list was endless, so it was our Con, or perhaps Stan, no must've been Con the eldest, who tore a page from his copybook and wrote 'I. SHURLEY GENERAL CONTRACTOR' And that's what it was. It was Ambrose's answer to everything, 'aye, surely.' "

The old clock ticked, in the kitchen the Rayburn hummed and caroused its own song. I thought of Sean Seamus and his ear for musical sounds, how he would have broken into a tune as he sat there. A sadness welled through my heart remembering his ways, his manner, remembering his-story, how he would have liked Ambrose and Philomena, here in a different place and time, yet connected to him in so many ways.

"They shouldn't be much longer," Philomena said to the silence, "and tomorrow's a work day. I could use getting to my bed. And you have a bit of drive home. Why don't you stay in the apartment with your father?"

"Thank you but no. He will be eager to get to his own bed. And will need the half-hour drive to tell me the things he doesn't tell Mamá after a day racing with Ambrose."

The Rayburn sang. Philomena followed shortly with, "Did I ever tell you how he arrived home with Patch?"

∞

Ambrose put me to rights with his account of the Scottish estate. "Braecnap Tri Lairigdruim."

"Ah!" was all I could reply. There was nothing in any of my mothering tongues to match that. "I can see why Philomena never got it."

Ambrose smiled as he lit his pipe.

"Even Bridget McCarthy made a better hand of it than Philomena. Wait 'til I see if I can remember the little birdie, hmm, yes, she says 'Break neck three lorry drums.'"

"In her best Wicklow drawl. Luckily no tees or aitches."

"Indeed! Och 'tis aisy enough like all things when you take it in small bites y' ken. Brae is upland, cnap is lump, tri is three, lairig is pass, druim is ridge. It more or less describes perfectly where it is. No postman could go wrong. Philomena came with me just the once, before Con was born. It may be wild and beautiful, but och it's a long journey no matter how ye do it. It got easier with the 'planes from Cork."

"And your father, Stanley, is he still there?"

"Aye, the ould coot is heading to ninety now, still riding every day, not much in the way of hard work but he did that in his time. He worked the estate, you see, it isn't his. But he was well looked after." Ambrose watched the firelight quietly, sucking softly on his pipe. I was reminded of Sean and his cigarillos, wafting blue smoke circling slowly in an upward draft.

"The neighbours are on Trí Tor O Cloch Bán. Philomena tried that more often than Brae Nap as she calls it."

"And that translates as?"

"Three, Tor is hilltop, cloch is stone, bawn is white. Three tops of white stone. Aisy eh?!" He laughed heartily, spluttering and coughing on his pipe smoke. "Och, couldn't be simpler. I'm afraid us Celts or Gaels were quite good at calling a spade a spade."

"Keltoi. It's a Greek word, Ambrose. Kelten, the Germans said, and with a C the French said Celtes. The hidden ones. The Celts shared orally, so their secrets or wisdom or knowledge were hidden from other cultures. They never called themselves anything, so the word Keltoi was applied to those people much later on. And because they were only oral or verbal, their stories were written by the Romans or Greeks, so we only get what the writer thought, not the Celt. Like your own 'kilt,' hiding what might be underneath."

Ambrose chuckled again. "That's a Biddy McCarthy word, with a tee of course. 'I was kilt from the climb up your hill!'"

We laughed together, Scotsman and Spaniard by a fireside in Cork.

"Gall," Ambrose spoke and a cloud of smoke came with the word, as he gesticulated with the pipe. "That's said like howl. That's a 'foreigner' in Scots Gaelic and also in Irish Gaelic. Donegal, doon-na-nowl, translates as the 'fort of the foreigner.' I'm not sure who was fortunate enough to be that new arrival."

"Isn't everyone a foreigner?" I asked of him. "Where are we all from at one same point? Before there were borders and divisions and nations? Some roots are deeper than others but we all arrived from somewhere to somewhere else. Surely it is time to stop differentiating and to just be human. All of us are the same blood once and we all breathe the same air."

"Daonna. Person. Belonging to the race homo sapiens. I think that is far back enough, eh, Jesus?"

" 'Nil me ach aon duine,' Sean once said to me. I am but one man."

"Aye." Ambrose sucked his pipe thoughtfully. "And I am a man divided, Jesus. I lived here, I lived there. My wife and children all come from here, my work, my horses, my mother's roots and her wider family. My father is everything Brae Nap suggests. It is a part of my, well, I dinna ken what to say really."

"Soul?" I suggested. "Something deep in here?" I pressed my fist to my heart.

"Aye, aye. That's about it. The smell, the air, the peaks and troughs go on forever. I could ride all day without encountering another being. I just love the place. I suppose it was my childhood playground." He tapped his pipe on the hearth and laid it on its side.

"My father doesn't often make forays south across the border y'ken? His trip to Aintree back then was only his second, and I doubt that he has had as many again. It was like he was, what would I say … ."

"Destined?" I offered.

"Aye," he enthused, "aye, destined, that's the word, destined to meet my mother. Like a magnet drew them together. Och, she loved it up there too but it's a tad remote for a wee girl. An' she had four years in Liverpool, so Brae Nap must have seemed like heaven in 1950-something. She could get to the hospital for her work and we had a wee house close to the road for her to travel along, but we were still five or six miles from the town, which wasn't easy in the winter time. She did well to do as many as she did. But I was sick when we left there for Cork. Sick to my very core. I dinna say a word to her, I couldna let her go alone y'ken? And I was still a tad young to be left behind, especially when old Stanley wasn't the most reliable of fathers. Ach he could ride away and not be seen for days." He poked at the glowing coals on the fire.

"Anyways, I got there every year, often for school Easter holidays and always for summer holidays. He would come here then for Christmas, so it wasn't so bad really." Ambrose reached behind him and lifted a trombone off the stair. He blew the first three notes of a scale and laid it on his knee.

"You have your own wanderings in your family, eh, Jesus?"

I could only sigh. "Indeed. My father grew up in a small village in Greek Cyprus, then moved to Spain. My grandfather was born a Corkman and then he took a boat to Spain, never to return. My other grandfather was born and raised in England and hardly ever went there as an adult either. In every story, Ambrose, there is shifting of people and places. Cultures crossing and dividing. My grandmother remained fervently Grecian, despite living twice the years in Cadiz. My grandfather was by all accounts quintessentially English. And Abuelo Sean was eternally Irish."

"Aye, my own sons are in America. Although I can see Dan coming back to his mother soonish." He lifted the trombone to his lips and began to play. A lovely long, slow tune.

"Barbara Streisand, early 1960s. 'Happy Days are Here Again.' She's a cracker."

The kitchen door creaked softly and opened a little. Queenie the cat strolled through, nonchalantly surveying the scene.

"Dan was a softie after the other two lads, y'ken. A real quiet sensitive lad. He was a bed-wetter, no matter what his mother tried to fix him. An' an ould doctor at the races in Gowran said to me, 'stop yer tryin', he'll give it up at fifteen.' An' he did. Like that!" Ambrose snapped his fingers. "It just stopped."

I nodded. I remembered Rodriguez in Cadiz and how his brother ran every morning before school around the back streets near our house, with a bag on his back. We were beer-drinking teens before he told me that it was the wet bed sheets, taking them to his aunt's house, where they had an electric washing machine for their laundry business.

"I remember a year or so after we moved here, my mother started working with Mrs. Farquharson on Duchess Hill. Pretty soon the old lady sent me off to boarding school, which I didn'a mind at all y'ken? The ould Christian Brothers and I weren't ever really going to get on. We had a couple of bed-wetters there, an' I can assure you they had a hard time. The dorm master was a great guy though and he would often bale them outta trouble and do the laundry himself if they had class time. An' there were a few of us boys who helped them out. We'd take it in turns to call them in the middle of the night to go for a pee. Little Pat O'Shea from Abbeyleix never even woke up when ye called him. We devised this system in winter, when it was too cold to get out of the bed. We stole the empty milk bottles from the kitchen and had them use them like an ould fella, what's this they call them?"

"Bedpan?" I suggested.

Ambrose shook his head in the memory. "Aye, that's the thing. They were the shier boys too, like Dan. My Dan is gay y'ken?"

"Yes, I know that. I have met him a couple of times."

He laughed loudly. "He went to Boston to find that out. He shoulda asked me, I coulda told him myself!" He lifted the trombone and blew a few quick blasts and a quick riff, his long leg bouncing and swaying to the beat.

" 'Don't tell your Mother.' Downchild Blues Band, Canadian, 1975. Denis loves this one, bangin' away at the piano." He blew again for a few minutes, before laying the instrument across his lap.

"Ach, I just love it. One of the prerequisites at the new school in Tipperary was that you had to play an instrument. Well I can tell you, all I ever blew was a hunting horn, but och there was no despairing with Mr. Maguire there, he clapped his hands and said, 'You, the tall Scots boy, get up to the back and take this.' And he handed me a trombone. So I blew long and hard and the room stopped and I'm sure I rattled the ould winda panes. 'Yes, yes,' he says, 'that'll do nicely thank you.' And that was it, I was off on my trombone career." Ambrose lovingly shifted the instrument that sat idle.

"Maguire gave me my first lessons. He allowed me to stay in the music room after homework and I did my best to skip the phys ed 'n' all those classes I dinna want. And the ould Gaelic, which actually I understood more of than I let on. I rode the horses, an' because I was new from Scotland, I dinna have to do all the football and the other stick thing. Which was fortunate for all the other boys. I woulda been quite lethal with a long ash stick at the end of my arm length." He grinned.

If I am the exact six feet, then Ambrose carries another four to five inches on me; long, lean, willowy, with a long ponderous face and bright twinkling humorous eyes behind black-rimmed glasses, his head topped with a full shock of white hair. The trombone is a natural extension of the man.

He played again, pausing to throw in lyrics. " 'Comin' Home Baby Now,' Mel Tormé, 1962. Harry Bett was the trombonist. Oliver Two Hands likes to do all the finger clickin' instead of playin' the drums." He wiped the mouthpiece and lay the trombone aside.

"My mother was terrified of the thing, an' the first Christmas I was home from school, ould Mrs. Farquharson was quite delighted. I could play as much as I liked in the ould house, no one could be disturbed, so she set me up in the drawing room, big high ceiling and long windows, and I played along to all the gramophone records they had. I'd play anything, anything except classical. Loved jazz. Loved jazz. And then her son had left a pile of Southern American Blues. Och!"

He picked up the trombone and blew a sequence of long pendulous notes. "Och. Just loved it. Ould Maguire was fallin' all over me when I got back to the school. He produced another stack of records an' he had a new player, so we moved to vinyl, ould 45s. He had Al Jolson in 'The Jazz Singer' so I played all of them, 'Waitin' for the Robert E. Lee,' 'Blue Skies,' then Peggy Lee and Benny Goodman. I loved it, the swingy jazz style."

Speaking music from his heart, my fingers resting on the arm of the old armchair began to prickle and tingle. My mind focussed a little less on the sound of Ambrose and his trombone and heard in the distance of my ethereal self, the sound of a concertina pulling chords as Ambrose fingered trombone notes. A warm shift of air crossed the nape of my neck and drifted around my head. A smile touched the corners of my lips. I am not a musician but I knew one was calling.

"When I met Philomena," Ambrose had changed tack when I came back to him in his sitting room, "she was a dancer. She was everything else too—a student, a sister, daughter, but oh my word was she a dancer. She loved it. Herself and the sissy, och I must na say that!" he chided himself. "Cecil. She loved to dance with Cecil. It was a bit awkward of course for I dinna dance. I just dinna, so I would have a pint of beer and watch and try to understand what them lads were sayin' to me over the din. Then we went on a bus one evening to Ballycotton, the Cliff Palace, the Cleft Palate, Bridget called it, 'cos it seems the owner or someone had one. Turns out the trombone player was ill from eating shellfish and probably a bit much of the ould Harp."

I raised an eyebrow in query. "Harp? A musical instrument?"

"Harp. An Irish lager version of Guinness. Frightful stuff to my taste buds. But I got to play the trombone, thanks to it. So then she could dance and I could play. We were all right after that. We went to dances all the way to oh, probably when Michael was due. As long as Philomena's mother got to play cards in McCarthy's on a Friday night, she babysat on a Saturday."

He paused to stroke Queenie the cat, who yowled in a discontented manner when the trombone slide tripped her on her passage to a comfortable chair. Ambrose had not the cosy frame of his wife for a feline squatter.

"I used to throw in the 'Rocks of Brae.' Your grandaddy would ken that one on the concertina, I think. Not much of yer usual dance tune, but I got Philomena and Cecil to put together a waltz of sorts to it and d'you ken the whole of Cork followed them and learned their steps. Ambrose Sowersby, Trombone Master of the Dance Floor." He blew an off-chord note as he laughed. Queenie was disdainful.

"Oh wait 'til I tell you about Cecil, Jesus. I can bet you herself hasn't told you this story."

"Go on," I prompted. "I knew she was keen on him but she says she knew he was gay but they didn't really know what that was at the time. She just loved to dance with him. I also assume he loved to dance with her?"

"Och aye rightly! She said that? Well she dinna ken he was a gay boy at the time. They were dancing together awhile before I met her, a good year or two anyways. And sailing from Blackrock Boat Club. They started that crack before they finished school, I think she said. You gotta remember, there wasn't a lot of room for a fella and a young girl to be together doing anything much in Blackrock in the early '70s. Och the frowns! So they're doin' this sailing small dinghies and then the dancing and I suppose they must have been close in school age as well. She told me this herself now, with her sister present, so I'm not breaking any confidences or being disloyal y'ken? I know she wouldn't mind YOU knowing, but don't tell Bridget eh?"

The ultimate secret-keeping watershed could only be Bridget McCarthy.

"Well I think maybe it was when they had finished their final schooling and Cecil says to herself, 'We can take my uncle's boat away for the weekend, let's sail down the coast.' So she's beside herself with excitement for the week, never stopping to think why it is her ould parents aren't too put out at the idea. Maybe they think the uncle is going along, which still would be a bit odd eh? Her sister thinks that perhaps ould Kit had the nouce about young Cecil already and perhaps his dear daughter was in no danger at all. 'Oh you'll be fine and safe with Cecil,' he said to her, with a wink."

I could see perhaps where the story was heading, coupled with a few earlier references to Cecil himself.

"Y'see Philomena was waiting and waiting for an age, for Cecil to make his move. It seemed obvious enough to her that he was keen. Perhaps just a tad too chivalrous, which she mistook for the ultimate in decorum. Cecil was a well-brought-up boy so knew his manners. And another curious thing, Jesus—no one once mentioned the dangers of sailing the south Irish coastline in a boat they weren't used to. That's how blind they all were to anything but the hot blood of youth. So she gets to the boat club on Saturday morning, wild with excitement about the impending trip, absolutely thrilled to hear the uncle would not be accompanying them, and equally crestfallen at the news that young Roger O'Shea would be. 'A right couple of birds y'have there my love,' her father said when he carted her down to the club. She was a bit surprised at him and not sure what he meant. But she was determined she was going anyway. Oh what an adventure! So Cecil instantly allocates bunks—Philomena in one cabin, he and Roger in the other. How else could it be of course in 1970-something?" He squeezed himself back into the chair, throwing his head back to laugh at the conjured memory of three teens on a boat on the big blue sea.

I had rarely been transported back to Philomena in her youth, having shared many hours and tales with her in every other aspect of life.

"Anyway, I won't bore you with sailing details of which I wasn't informed of a great deal. They shot away along down the coast, missed Kinsale, and ended up in that lovely wee spot with the ould hotel, long narrow bay to it, Court … ?"

"Courtmacsherry?"

"Aye, aye that's the place. Courtmac. We took the kiddies there several times afterwards. Con and Stan did that wind-surfing lark for a wee while there. What a palaver that was? Four children and dog and all that gear. And I thought a trombone was an awkward piece of kit."

"Go on," I prompted again. "How did the Mills & Boon adventure unfold in Courtmacsherry?"

He laughed. "Ooh not to her liking I'm afraid. They went ashore for fish 'n' chips and the boys went for a feed of pints, which neither of them would have been much used to. She got tired of their twittering and sitting around waiting, so said she was taking the dinghy back to the mooring, so they had to go with her or be stuck ashore. They nearly capsized the dinghy and Philomena is no lightweight now and she was no lightweight then I assure you, Jesus, so there must've been some amount of boyos awash in beer. She was sick and tired now, the ould girl, of the carry on, so she took to her bunk in a wee huff. But the salt air knocked her out and when she awoke all was silent except for Cecil snoring away in his cabin. The other fella was passed out on the floor of the main cabin, a half empty bottle of Paddy Powers rollin' beside him."

"Paddy Powers?"

"Good Irish whiskey, Jesus. Cecil plied the poor wee sod with alcohol, hoping to loosen him up to a bit of how's yer mother, or perhaps to work up his own courage to chance a bit of how's yer mother, and luckily for all three on board, the alcohol won."

It was far enough away in time and space in everyone's life to laugh at someone else's foolish youth.

"Her fury and confusion evaporates at the sight of the poor lad and the mature maternal instincts kick in, so she covers him with a blanket, goes for a quick dip in the bay off the back of the boat, then my lovely Philomena does what she does best. She cooks the boyos the full Irish breakfast, makes them drink pints of cold water, then sets sail for Blackrock."

"And that was it for Cecil?"

"Och aye, for Cecil and Philomena was all in her head. In his head it was all sailing and dancing and good fun. So that's the bit they kept going with. And d'you ken, Jesus? She admitted that their dancing improved hugely when she stopped waiting for the romantic dish to make his smooth move. He was a gay boy who could dance. They did some of the competitions then for a year or so and left the floor standing."

Now that meant absolutely nothing to me in English or Scottish, or Spanish.

"Standing?"

"Aye, standing. They couldn't keep up with them. By then I had smooth-moved my way to her, so Cecil was relegated to strictly dancing." Ambrose harrumphed to himself at the memories, picked up his pipe and re-lit it, puffing thoughtfully. He crossed and uncrossed his long legs.

"Yes, indeed, all a long time ago now."

I smiled inwardly, for he didn't know that I knew, he thought no one knew his Corpus Christi story, other than himself and Philomena. And, of course, perhaps the parish priest.

∞

"I played once with one of the pop stars y'ken? Oh not long ago, much to the thrill of the grandies. Peg's eldest fella Aidan woulda heard of her, Leddra something, lovely wee girl. Lovely song too. Just your kind of thing, Jesus, called oh something like 'Story,' I think it was. The deal was all Irish musicians and Denis Carthy got the piano job thro' Cork Boys. He carried me and me trombone along for the crack. 'Twas the U2 studios 'n' all. I wasn't fussed about all the stardom but oh I loved the fun of the recording, being allowed to improvise with the trombone. It was just like a regular session with all the boys. There were eighteen pizzas for lunch and we came home full of Coca-Cola. I have it there on a CD if you'd like to take it."

I knew this wasn't Ambrose's only brush with fame, but it was the story he chose to tell me. He played all the Cork Jazz Festivals with some big name or another or someone missing a trombone player, or someone short in a quartet or quintet. He was quite the popular figure in the Cork circuit, and he spent the rest of the year with Denis and three others playing live in bars or clubs or in each others' houses.

"It's a good thing ould Mrs. Shortt next door is deaf as a post, so I have never had a problem with practicing. I go in there," he gestured to the door behind me, "across the hall to the front room and play along to the LPs. Sometimes I improvise a few Scottish airs to get Herself riled up. Neil Diamond in the new *Jazz Singer,* the platinum album. Oh what a ripper that was! Philomena likes that and sometimes would come and sing along. Otherwise she stomps off to bed with ear plugs and lets me at it."

Queenie had another attempt at crossing the room unhindered.

"My boys in Boston sent me a headset, those big ear-muff things, back a few years ago, so Philomena dinna have to hear the records playing, just the trombone. And y'ken I think she missed it. For years now I tell her I'm goin' 'jommin at Denis', and I dinna think she knows what I mean."

I smiled, for there wasn't often a joke made at Philomena's expense. It was unusual to hear someone talk of her from this close proximity. She had told me herself how Ambrose plays carols with 'the Salvo's' or Salvation Army at Christmas. Biddy loves 'Hark the Herald' and no one ever stops to think that perhaps Philomena has heard it a zillion times since the Jazz Festival at Hallowe'en.

"Straight from honky tonk to carols. Every year. 'Tis a wonder he's not dead before the turkey."

I loved Philomena's stories. Cork was familiar to me as a young child through Abuelo Sean, but his own stories were much more localised to East Cork, for the twenty-three years he had lived there. There was only the occasional foray farther afield. It was the rhythm, I believe, the sing-songy flow like a babbling river, the tone, the turn of phrase, the hint of intimacies as their lives unfolded. This was story telling; his story, her story.

∞

There was a longer tale of Biddy's infatuation with the Christmas carol 'Hark the Herald', embroidered into a greater understanding of her place in the Blackrock community and life at the Two Spoons. Her deceased father had a cousin living in Birmingham, England, a place I have never been. Bridget and Philomena refer to this woman as 'Scratchy,' due to a skin condition that results in "snowflakes." I have heard Bridget laugh uproariously at the thought of making porridge from the kitchen floor sweepings. My Spanish linguistic brain missed that on the first passing and Philomena later translated it for me. It is not something I would ever choose to imagine.

That Bridget spent long weeks on end at various intervals looking after Scratchy, or indeed on any number of travels, didn't cause concern to anyone. Biddy was known for her flightiness, her short attention, her butterfly-like ability to flit. An inability perhaps to be still or present. Her apartment, her life really, was such, that she could turn a key and depart. I would see Philomena sometimes with blue Basildon Bond notepaper and a pot of tea, saying, "I'll just bring Biddy up to date on life in Blackrock." Or, "Oh wait until I write that one for Biddy." Or, "Oh, Biddy'll be so disappointed she missed so-and-so."

Then Bridget would reappear, breeze back through life in Blackrock as if the elapsed time were nothing at all. It was many years before I realised that, in fact, that was the greater truth. There was no time in Bridget's life. Every moment followed the previous one with no thought for the next one. It was a concept I had learned many years earlier from Dr. Zhao, one most mortals struggle all their lives to experience. When I brought this notion to life over tea with Philomena, she seemed surprised by the revelation.

"What do you mean? She doesn't know the time?"

"She has no appreciation of time in the long view. Let me explain it this way. In the Greek language, chronos time is the measure of time as we know it: in an hour, yesterday, tomorrow, linear, chronological time. But kairos time is different altogether. Kairos time is the moment we are in." I snapped my fingers. "Now." Snap. "Now." Snap. "Now. The Greeks thought of it as the space between the arrow leaving the drawn bow with enough force to hit its target. An exact moment. Or like the shuttle passing through the open weave in the loom." Snap. "Now. A definite opportune moment."

"Quality of time versus quantity?"

I looked at her in surprise. "Well, yes, I guess that's one way of putting it."

"I would think like that when I am baking. If I only think of the task at hand then I am present in the kneading, or mixing, or shaping. Sometimes it is like there is nothing else in the world but that action. Sometimes I bake just to find that place."

"Space."

"Yes," she agreed. "Yes, space. If I get it right, it's my meditation, or yoga, or whatever it is you do."

"Kairos is the word used to denote time nearly twice as often as chronos in the New Testament. It is about being present."

Philomena's eyes brightened, "Here listen to this, Jesus, this is what you mean." She straightened herself in the chair, cleared her throat and began to sing, her shoulders and hands swinging to keep time, as she peeled off a full verse. She laughed as she slapped a hand on the table, making the cups jump. "That's our own Donegal legend, Enya. 'Anywhere Is.' I remember Peg playing it on some CD and I was always intrigued by the lyrics, so she printed them off for me somehow. I'm sure they are in there somewhere by the phone."

"I really like that, Philomena."

"Yes, it stuck in here." She tapped the side of her head, pushing her glasses up to rub her eyes. "Yes indeed. Anyways, space, it doesn't always work with the baking. Kathleen will attest to that."

"What's that, Mrs. S? I heard ya singing. Things must be good." Kathleen came through from the kitchen.

"Baking isn't always a calming activity."

Kathleen pulled a chair towards herself and sat on the edge of the seat, redoing her pony tail. "She would say to me, Jesus, 'hould on there, Kathleen, I'm doing the bread now.' And the pounding and kneading would be relieving the latest annoyance or the possible irritation of Biddy McCarthy."

We laughed together at Kathleen mimicking Philomena pulverising a sticky ball of dough.

" 'Cos you need energy and vigour to make the dough move."

"And when the old arthritis kicks in, she makes scones or tarts, lovely light, soft movements. Like she's letting the pain go with it."

Kathleen's hands gently plied the air, as if she were fingering piano keys. Philomena looked askance at her young employee.

"Is that right?"

"It is right, isn't it? It's what I always thought anyway." Kathleen stood to go. Philomena looked up at her.

"You're such a lovely girl, Kathleen. I am so lucky to have you here with me."

Kathleen stopped in her tracks. "Aw, thanks Mrs. S. Shur I wouldn't be here if you weren't just as lovely." She kissed the top of Philomena's head, grinned, and disappeared through the kitchen door.

Philomena looked at me. "Well, speaking of same, that was a moment." She shook her head, smiling broadly. "Where were we? Yes, Biddy and time. I know what you're saying. Let me tell you something though. There's things she just wouldn't miss, where chronos time is of the utmost importance. Let's see," Philomena counted on her fingers, "Tuesday night Bingo calling. Friday night cards in McCarthy's No Relation, Sunday Mass, June weekend Parish trip to Knock. That kinda thing."

"Yes, but she would depart to, where was it? Birmingham? And miss all those things without noticing. She isn't in Birmingham wondering about calling bingo numbers in Blackrock?"

"No, no, I guess she isn't. Yes. I always feel it's like she has whooshed off the planet."

I laughed. "It's probably not something you could ask her."

Philomena laughed with me, "whuh, whuh, whuh," her tea sloshed onto the table. "Ah, Jesus, will you stop! Wait 'til I tell you about the time she nearly didn't make it home for Christmas. She was off with Scratchy. I suppose she was gone five or six weeks into early December and whatever she did, she would always get back to Cork for the Christmas. In fact, she would always be back for the carols here on the Saturday before Christmas. Y'know, Ambrose and the Salvations. She sings so off-key, it embarrasses Ambrose, but the lads in the band just laugh, and Ambrose used to apologise for her. He'd say things like, 'Och, she's a good friend of my wife' or 'Apologies lads for the screeching sound of Christmas fever.' But shur it wouldn't be the same without her. And absolutely 'Hark the Herald' is her Number One, Top of the Charts favourite."

There was something irresistibly hilarious about Philomena's imitation of Ambrose's Scottish accent. I laughed enough to bring Kathleen back from the kitchen. "What are you two at now?"

"Whuh, whuh, whuh, Bridget's 'Hark the Herald'."

"Oh that," Kathleen shook her head somewhat sadly. "God love her, she's so tone deaf it could only be funny. And no matter what Ambrose and the lads would play, Biddy would be at the front of the crowd screeching, 'Play 'Hark the Herald,' Ambrose!' "

"So eventually he'd say, 'Lovely Bridget, thank you, yes now, thank you, that's quite enough now,' and he'd be catching my eye and jerking his head saying 'Get her outta here!' So I'd have to call her and ask her to bring out the mince pies or jugs of punch."

Laughing at the antics of Bridget McCarthy never seemed cruel or unkind. It was like she was a Divine Gift of Comedic Moments. Had she appeared at that moment, she too would have joined with us.

"Anyway, there about, oh, fifteen year, years ago, I got this phone call about a fortnight before the Christmas. 'Twas herself, sobbing, and beside herself so much so, that I had no idea in the world what could be wrong. That and the fact that it was lunchtime on a Thursday."

"Carvery day!" Kathleen interjected. "Oh what fun! This was before my time here, Jesus."

"So I'm up to my eyes and Maureen Doherty is runnin' around like a blue-arsed fly and all I can get is this wailing and blubbering from across the Irish Sea. I had myself nearly strangled on the phone cord, so thankfully Peg came in, I threw her an apron and put her in behind the counter. Well, to cut a long story short, Biddy had been shopping in Marks and Sparks ... ."

My quizzical look stopped her.

"Marks and Spencer's Department Store."

"Ah! I understand now."

"There was a kerfuffle with a store detective arresting someone for shoplifting, and our Bridget was so agog following the unfolding drama that she got beside herself with excitement and left the store with all her Christmas goodies unpaid for. So then SHE found HERSELF in the locked-up room with the security chaps. And she just went to pieces. So they have this 'Shoplifters Will Be Prosecuted' policy, and when they eventually got some sense outta her, they took all her details and told her to go home to Scratchy. In the heel of the hunt, you can imagine the consternation, not to mention the commotion, when she was told not to leave the country until they had sorted out the paperwork. They weren't overly bothered if she missed her carols at the Two Spoons, although that was of paramount importance to our Bridget. So she rings me, sobbing."

We drank silently, the humour drained at the pitiful thought of Bridget grounded in Birmingham.

"Well? What happened?" asked Kathleen.

Philomena threw back her head and laughed. "Oh we got Georgie McNulty onto the Brits."

I looked from one to the other, awaiting the explanation.

"Garda Georgie from the local station."

"Ah! And he could help her?"

"Well, he surely did. He called them up and sure enough the sergeant in charge there was Billy Thompson's son, Billy from Passage. So Georgie wrote them a letter and faxed it through to them, vouching for Biddy's innocence. And what's more, he had a plan for extracting her back to Cork in Garda escort."

"Oh! I can't wait to hear this," Kathleen exclaimed.

Philomena laughed again. "Georgie was going over himself a day or two after, to pick up a couple of ponies for Christmas presents for some mates. So he informed the bobbies that he'd be escorting Mrs. McCarthy off the island. That was good enough for them."

"She made it back for the carols?" Kathleen enquired.

"Oh she did indeed. A bit quieter in herself after the experience I have to say."

"Well, she's here herself now to tell us." I gestured towards the door, as a scarlet headscarf flicked through the air with a flourish and in the same movement she seemed to have removed her coat, hung it on a chair, and perched herself on the high stool. Seamless integration.

"Coo-ee, 'tis me, oh you're having tea, I though' it migh' be tha' time of the day alrigh'. Kackleen, you're looking well, would you geh me my mug please, oh how'ya Jesus, you're back in town, how was your trip? Well, Philomena, you just won't guess who I meh?" Biddy paused briefly, inhaling softly, sniffing the air for change. "Is everything alrigh' here? I haven't disturbed anything?"

"Oh not at all, Biddy. I was just telling them about the time you nearly got left in Birmingham for Christmas. Do you have Georgie's letter?"

After all these years and all the stories, I was still a little surprised at the immediacy of their communication. The poignant directness, how between them they knew exactly what moment each was in. There was genuine warmth and affection between them.

"Georgie's lehher Philomena? Leh me look, yes, shur 'tis here all these years since." Biddy made a show of rummaging in her handbag, knowing exactly where to look, in a zipped compartment at the rear. She pulled out a worn envelope with a crest of the West Midlands Police on the back and unfolded the sheet of facsimile paper, waving it towards Philomena who gestured to me. I took it from her hand.

"Be careful now, Jesus, there's only one copy of THA' lehher."

In the pixellated facsimile script of pre-Internet days I read:

> *To Whom it May Concern:*
>
> *My name is Gerard William McNulty. I have been a guard in the County of Cork since 1974. I believe that you have a Mrs Bridget McCarthy due to appear in your courthouse on Christmas Eve, appearing on the charge of shoplifting.*
>
> *My reason for writing is that I wish to vouch for Mrs McCarthy as an honourable and fine upstanding member*

*of our small community of Blackrock in the County of Cork,
Ireland. I have known her since my training began. She has
no previous record of shoplifting, in fact she has absolutely
no criminal record at all. She is, what you might say, easily
distracted. By all accounts she saw that the security guard at
the store had apprehended a person withdrawing goods from
the store whilst actually walking out the door. You will find,
if you check your security cameras, that it is highly likely that
Mrs McCarthy may have been a little "wide-eyed" at the
commotion and completely forgot to pay for her own items.
You will also find that Mrs McCarthy has a fine substantial
bank account; and herewith is enclosed a note from Mr
Aiden Tunney her bank manager.*

*On Friday next I intend to visit the UK on a matter of personal
business. My vehicle will accommodate Mrs McCarthy and
I am of the optimistic opinion that you will release her from
the restriction she is under at present; that is, that she has
been advised not to leave the jurisdiction. If necessary, she
can be fined in a manner suited to her small misdemeanour,
within the boundaries and council of Blackrock.*

Yours
G W McNulty
Garda Sergeant
Cork

"Well now, Jesus, isn't tha' a fine personal commendation from a member of our Garda forces?"

"Indeed, Bridget. I trust you made the carol service?"

"Oh Jesus, I did, I did. Oh I would have been so heart sore to miss them. Ih is my favourite time of the year. I love every momen'."

I smiled at her and looked at Philomena. "What else do we have if not the moment?"

Philomena snapped her fingers. "Kairos time is tea time."

"Carols time? Is that wha' you said, Philomena? I didn't hear tha'. Did you say carols time? Wha' do you mean? Are there carols today? Are you finished the tea or wha'? Will we have another? Kackleen did you geh me my cup?"

Kathleen raised her eyes to heaven. "Bread-making time, Mrs. S."

∞

"D'you know, Jesus," Philomena stood by the kitchen sink, "all those years ago the things we put up with, y'know, Irish Catholic, Scottish Presbyterian, Protestant, unmarried mother, Dublin jackeen, Cork culchie, all those ... what would you say ... ?"

"Labels?" I suggested.

"Yes, labels. Ways we say things and call people. Pigeon holes to put them in."

"Identify them perhaps? Identity?"

"Yes. Yes. It's not right is it?"

"No, Philomena," I agreed with her. "It is not right. I lived with Greek and Spanish and Irish and Queen's English, English Naval officers, Yankee sailors. No one was just them self. Just an ordinary human being. It is helpful to us though to create a picture, a story."

"Every day in the café, I look them all in the eye and say good morning, good afternoon, hello, how are you—and I try to just see the person. I no longer try and work out who or what they might be from the look of them. I have so often been wrong, misjudged them, and if I have learned anything from the Two Spoons in all the years, it's that everyone has a story. Oh we laugh and say the piggy smell of Jimmy Jack, the Four Anns of Bridge, Marguerite of the Crosswords, and all of those means of identifying a customer. But every one of them has a story, don't they?"

"Her-story, his-story."

"Hum-stories." Philomena paused as she dried a pot, pushed up her glasses on her nose, fiddled her bra strap from under her bosom. "We should be in charge, Jesus. We have it sussed."

"I would have to laugh at the thought of being in charge of anything. I think we're doing best when we just manage the little bit we have been given, Philomena."

We carried on with kitchen tasks silently. I paused in my chopping. "Sometimes I get tired you know, tired of the sound of my own voice, the thoughts in my own head."

"Why's that, Jesus?"

"Well, ah! I stop and think who am I to be telling anyone anything? Who am I to be telling anyone about their life? What if I am wrong, or misleading, or misunderstood?"

She placed her hand on mine. "That's what being a mother is like, Jesus. In every word we say to our children."

"Abuelita Rosa would always say, 'Words are important, Jesús. Words we use in any language. They construct or destruct. Use them sparingly and wisely.' "

"Oh that's good advice for working with the public, I can tell you."

I gestured to the corner inside the back door, where the landline phone hung on the wall, its cord twisted and wound untidily amidst a plethora of sticky notes, yellowed, Sellotaped wisps of phone numbers and a jam jar of pencils, pens, broken knives, and an orange screwdriver. This sagging shelf and square metre of countertop was as much an office as Philomena had, the small corner of a busy kitchen.

"Tell me, Philomena," I asked, "the 1993 calendar there, you keep the birthdays on. How did that come to be?"

"The what? Oh, the calendar!" She glanced towards the semblance of an office. "We were open a few years and I had made the habit of jotting down, making a note if you like, if I heard it was someone's birthday, y'know, a customer, the usuals like. I'd be here then in the New Year writing from one calendar to the next, when my Peg said, 'There's no need to do that, Mam, just leave it all on one calendar. You only need to know the date, not the day.' Wise girl she was. I wonder where she got that from?" Philomena smiled, her bright eyes twinkling behind floury glasses.

"So you just write down birth dates?"

"Yes. Yes, I got a second calendar from Sue's News for 1993, and started there. Then I know each month, or each week really, who has a birthday, so if they come in, they get their order for free. Within reason of course. And they always get a slice of cake with a candle. Everyone sings 'Happy Birthday.' Shur it's the one thing we all can call our own, so why not make it special?"

"It is a wonderful thing, Philomena. A wonderful thing to do."

"D'you think so? It would have just seemed ordinary to me to think of it? Aren't I here all day looking at them all, it's not that hard to note their birthday? They're my customers after all."

"I think it is a very special thing you do."

"Well, we have had some fabulous moments. Jimmy Jack had never ever had a birthday candle in his life. Isn't that something? And when we first sang for him he must've been nearing fifty years. I know it is especially special for those who live alone or don't have a family nearby. Mick, Dick, an' Trick Fitzgerald from Douglas Road came in one day to TELL me their birthday was coming up."

I raised an eyebrow quizzically.

"Michael, Richard, and Patrick. Triplets. They lived at home with their mam, and after she passed away someone told them I would do a birthday cake for them. Shur they must've been a good age then. Even Marguerite Foley enjoys it for everyone else but she just would not say what her birth date was. Didn't want the fuss on her, I suppose?"

"Yes, I can see how that would be so." Marguerite Foley, I liked her a lot. We often conversed in Spanish, for she had lived awhile in Madrid with her diplomat husband. She drank Earl Grey tea from a china cup and saucer and ate Philomena's cake or tart with a dessert fork. She would carefully dab her lipsticked lips with a napkin, and conversation would flow around cryptic crossword clues, root sources of English words and pronunciation, articles in the lesser-seen column inches, always engaging. She was an avid fan of my Mr. Onions dictionary of etymology.

Philomena shared an interesting dynamic with Marguerite, a mutual respect, a common likability. She also often displayed a breathless nervousness, arising from uncontrollable factors, in Marguerite's company; a fearfulness of the state of the public toilet should Marguerite wish to use it. Fearful of what Bridget might blurt out unknowingly, or that a random child might be rude to her. Although I admit, I did once witness Bridget race from the rear breathlessly calling, "Philomena, Philomena, come quickly!

Jimmy Jack has shattered the bowl again!" before dissolving into high-pitched tee-hee-hee giggles. This was most definitely not what Philomena would wish upon her customers. A protectiveness of her establishment, a protectiveness of her customer from lesser-known frailties of Blackrock.

Philomena seemed not to notice that Marguerite chose the Two Spoons for her tea and—as a long-time resident of the village—was probably well aware of the lesser-known elements of her home place. Indeed, she knew Jimmy Jack by name and reputation; had he used the public convenience prior to her visit to the Two Spoons was not entirely Philomena's responsibility. However, it was enough to cause some bustling bosom-shifting and a swish of polishing, as Marguerite would settle into her table by the front window, a table Philomena would often mark as reserved, anticipating her arrival.

"Maybe this is why she chooses the Two Spoons as her café? Your natural touch as the hostess of the mostess?"

"Mother of God, Jesus. The hostess of the mostess. Now where did you hear that one?"

"Oh that has a long story back to my tripping around Australia. By the way, I can tell you Marguerite's birth date. But of course you will have to use it discreetly and wisely."

"And how in God's name would you have heard that?"

"Just the date, not the year. Oh a long discussion on numerology and coincidences of mathematics. My date is 27–12 and hers is 26–11. November 26."

"Well good onya, Jesus Josephus! I shall be sure to keep an eye on that one." Philomena heaved herself off the countertop, pushed her glasses onto her head and licking the lead point of a pencil stub, she flipped the calendar pages to November. Leaning her left elbow against the wall and above her head, she carefully wrote into November 26: Marguerite Foley.

"She shares the date with Peaceful Princess." Philomena commented. "I'll somehow have to convey that news to her."

"Peaceful Princess? Ambrose's horse?"

"Oh not just a horse, Jesus. THE horse. The start of a line of Phillies, as he likes to say. A line of racers he bred with Tommy Snap. The Princess wasn't born in our own field, but I can tell you once Tommy had a good gander at her, Ambrose was soon on his way to Tipp."
"Gander? Tipp?"

"Tipperary. Tommy had a share in a stud there and the full might of the training squad. A gander is a good look. Don't ask me why, or in what language."

"There's something special in his horses," I mused. "I am always amazed how my father is captivated by the whole affair, for he was not at all a horse man in Spain. A nature-lover, yes, but never do I remember horses. He took me a few times to Jerez, quite close to Cadiz, to the School of Andalusian Dancing Horses. We would go on a weekday, to see them practice, see the display of carriages, then he and Abuelo Sean would retire to the bodega to try the sherries. That's where it got dull for a small child. But I did like watching the horses."

"Oh I would think it is the whole shebang that he likes."

"Shebang?"

"Yes, as you say, the whole affair: horse, training, racing, the natural way of things, early starts, smells, sounds, y'know, the moving trailers, carrying feed, taping the joints, oiling the tack. It's a whole, well, shebang. A whole way of life. It is a part of Ambrose that I don't share. The highs and lows, yes, I hear about them all. I know more than I think but I wouldn't know one end of a good horse from the bad end of a jinnet."

"Jinnet? I think you mean a jennet, it's a small Spanish horse."

Philomena laughed. "A jinnet in Ireland is a useless cross between a female donkey and a stallion. We have a few of them in here regularly." She laughed heartily, "whuh, whuh, whuh."

I addressed her in a corrective manner. "Now, Philomena, is that a derogatory label you are using to identify your customers?"

I ducked as she flung the stubby pencil in my direction. "I thought I was the hostess of the mostess? Did you forget already? C'mon now, another half-hour an' we'll be done. I've had enough of this place for this week. Give me that Australia story to get us moving."

"Okay, okay, hmm, where should I start? Right, I have it. On my first Australia trip back in '88 or '89, I landed in Alice Springs, off a long overnight bus ride on a hot morning that turned out to be a public holiday, I might add. My travelling companion was Irish, a girl I had met in Sydney, and we had followed the same path for a while. We were gathering our wits about us and were staring at a town map, figuring how to get to a campsite. This big tall Aussie heard our conversation and the Irish accent and just started talking. 'Top of the mornin' to ya both and a hundred thousand welcomes to Alice. And shur how're ya both gettin' on on dis fine day?' "

I stopped my story at Philomena's reaction. My Irish accent was never much to write home about.

"Oh Saints preserve us, I've heard it all! A half-Spaniard in Cork, mimicking an Aussie doin' the Oirish. Wherever your story goes, Jesus, thank you for the comedic moment."

"Anyway," I laughed on, "we're in full blown conversation with this guy, Kevin—where we've been, what our plans are, what we need. Next thing, we're in the back of his Toyota four-wheel-drive, en route to a campsite and, camped in it, his wife Noela. We're putting up the tent, she's cooking us breakfast, and I am in my bus-travelling exhaustion—wide-eyed at the speed in which my life has just evolved without very much participation by me, at all. All on the strength of Deirdre's Irish accent and Kevin's chance passing by."

"Isn't that the way?" Philomena snapped her fingers. Snap. "Life does something else."

"Oh isn't it indeed! Kevin's a retired school principal, they're on the big trip in the trailer-tent, all around central Oz. We spent the next five days in the back of said Toyota, out to the Olgas, Ayers Rock, the MacDonnell Ranges, Chamber's Pillar. Just extraordinary countryside. He was a home-video enthusiast, so there was method in his madness. I lugged a lot of camera gear up those hot tracks."

"Oh it sounds amazing, Jesus. My lads were in Oz before they ended up in Boston. I said to Ambrose we should go, while they were there like, but between one thing and another, it never happened."

"We eventually parted company, and in the intervening years they have been to stay with Deirdre's family here in Ireland. They have visited my parents, they went to Bristol. He was a fan of Welsh Male Voice Choirs so would always catch a performance somewhere en route. I have met them in Cadiz, but we did not live there, so we stayed in Dr. Zhao's. Two of Deirdre's brothers and my friends stayed with them in Australia, for they live near Brisbane on the East coast."

We swapped sides of the counter, Philomena to be near the sink for peeling, me to be chopping.

"Five years later, I was on my first visit to Perth and the west of the country, with a different travelling companion. We visited and stayed with the mother of someone, someone else I had accommodated on their travels in Europe, in the way that young backpackers without a lot of money do. Down south of Perth, Busselton."

"Yes, I have had a few of those here myself after my lot went a wandering."

"This lovely lady was the local librarian. I was whiling away some hot afternoon hours looking at mostly the old pioneering books and stories. She came to me and said, 'Here, you wanna read this one.' It was a statement not a question. She handed me a book called 'Kings in Grass Castles', the story of an Irishman who sailed with his family after or during the Famine. His father died en route, so the young Irish boy became responsible for the family at fifteen or so years old. I can't fully recall."

"What part of Ireland? Do you remember?"

"Yes, he was from Co. Clare, overlooking Lough Derg. Patrick Durack." I laughed at the next memory. "The next day she handed me her car keys and said, 'Why don't you go and have a little walkabout while I am working and don't go and do anything silly like put fuel into my car.' Such kindness. She truly was a beautiful woman. Her husband was Irish, hmm, I think one of the L counties up north of Dublin."

"Louth, Longford, Leitrim."

"Leitrim. Tom, a mining engineer. Nice man, very quiet though. His lovely wife, Anne, was left to do the talking. So I have the book and off I go—walkabout, as she suggested—and had a day exploring, eventually settling into a shady coffee shop with the book. What a read! What this boy Patrick went through. In a nutshell, he was finally responsible for mapping a quarter of a million square miles of western Queensland and he finished up owning a cattle station and a couple of homesteads. The next adventure was to work out how to get the cattle through the mountain ranges to the north-west of the country. The biggest challenge everywhere was the climate and getting water."

"Oh! 'Tis a long way from Blackrock."

"Sí, a very long way. She said, 'Keep the book until you are done and post it back to me.' I took a red-eye flight to the east, to Sydney. My companion stayed in Perth to work in banking. Perth is like being in a different country—it is so far from the eastern states of Australia."

"Red-eye?"

"Cheap, last minute, overnight."

"Ah! Not easy this travelling, writing business."

I had to smile. "Oh it got easier when I could give up the late-night, money-saving transport options. I suppose some wisdom comes with age and disposable income."

There was a silence except for kitchen sounds, a simmering pot, scraping a chopping board into the soup, the low hum of the cold-room motor. I sorted through the memories to continue my tale.

"I went to Canberra, worked with an adventure organisation called Outward Bound. Through someone I met there I spent time on a sheep station in New South Wales and soon several months had passed. My travelling companion finished her banking job in Perth, flew to Sydney, we met up again, bought a car, and set off on a road trip. All this time I am also writing and sending things to Boston by mail, as this is just before the Internet. Actually, I had no idea how my life would change in a couple of years when e-mail and Internet came to the world. I suppose it was the same for everyone. We drove the interior of New South Wales, camping, sometimes sleeping in the car to avoid the mosquitoes. It was a very memorable trip."

"A lot depends on the company. Will you start mixing fruit for the cakes, please?"

"Indeed. We worked well together, 'got on,' you say here. She was a fantastic camp cook; she liked to light barbecue fires with a helpful squirt from a bottle of baby oil. A little hazardous I thought! We lived cheaply and well. I had picked up a trucker's map, so all the roadside stops and truck camps were marked. We would ask the gas stations to keep our ice-packs in the ice-cream freezer overnight, so the cool box would stay cool all day. If you went to the supermarket in the late evening you could get a cooked chicken for a couple of dollars. Those kind of tricks. We took two months to get to the coast south of Brisbane, worked our way north, to what is called the Sunshine Coast, to visit with Kevin and Noela."

"From the last trip?"

"Yes, and they were at home and preparing to travel again, this time to the south-east corner of Victoria state, in a new camper van. We met their daughter, Michelle, there; she was also visiting, from western Queensland. She says, 'Don't go north, come west, we will be shearing eleven thousand sheep next week on our 150,000-acre station.' And that's how travelling happens, Philomena. Carpe Diem, as Mamá says. Seize the day."

"Here, pass me that pot, please. Go on."

"So we head west instead of north, long days driving and looking and seeing." I was stopped in my tale by an odd thought; recalling the straight lines and grids that form so many of the new countries, new towns and cities, newly settled in the last three or two hundred years. Canada, Australia, the U.S.A. Lines and grids of vast wide-open new space, so unlike the early settlements along watercourses or shorelines of the old world.

"I remember having to stop the car one evening as we were nearing Quilpie, for the road ran due west and the sun was setting over the road, reflecting right along the tar surface so it was impossible to see anything. We pulled over, lit a road fire, boiled the billy, and made afternoon tea."

"Oh, Jesus. It sounds like heaven. What have I missed in life?" Philomena stared at the window. "I have spent far too many years in this kitchen." The pot hissed and spluttered as she lit the big gas ring.

"But this was just one experience for me, Philomena. And you are hearing the short, happy version. There were plenty of anxious or homesick moments. A broken prop-shaft in some small town in New South Wales on a holiday weekend. A shredded tyre. Having to be wherever you are going before dusk, so as not to hit a kangaroo on the road and destroy the car. A storm of big yellow insects that splatted all over and stuck to the windscreen so you could not see to drive."

I paused, not sure what was coming next, knowing my voice was somehow not from my head.

"You have had different experiences, different stories. I have, nor ever had a partner, no children. I have shared my familial love. I leave nothing to the world but written words. My indent on the world is just different, no less, no more, just different."

Philomena nodded, somewhat sadly. "Yes, but sometimes you'd wonder why? What's it all for? What else should I have done?"

"But listen! Everyone's experiences, other lives show us something else. They colour in our own story. We arrived to their sheep station, another hour west of Quilpie, which is the last substantial town. This is absolutely real Outback. And it is this whole community— mother, father, aunts, Michelle and Bruce, two young girls, ranch hands, a postal truck delivery once a week. The neighbours are also relations and their homestead is thirty kilometres away. The children are taught by school on the radio. Their hot water comes from deep in the ground, at near boiling point, from an artesian well. They fly a two-seater Cessna aeroplane above the sheep, to herd them from the air, assisted on the ground by trail motor-bikes, or a quad bike. It is a whole world in the world, Philomena. The shearing team are on the station for as long as it takes to shear the flock. There must be twelve or fourteen of them to shear the sheep and as many again to bale the wool and keep the whole operation moving quickly. They feed themselves though and travel in their own vans and campers. Bruce's mother remembers when she and her mother used to feed them all, three meals a day. She said the truck of food supplies arrived before the caravan of shearers. It was phenomenal, Philomena."

"Feeding the masses, hah! I think I have had enough of that. I hope I'll get something easier in the next life." She poked me with her wooden spoon. "D'you hear me? Tell that to the man up there when you're sitting beside Him!"

"When I am the REAL Jesus." I laughed. "But oh! It was so much hard work for them. Always battling the elements, the climate, flock disease, predators. A machine breaks down and only ingenuity can fix it, or a week waiting for a part to come with the postal truck. Bruce's father, Cameron, says, 'I have given my life to this. Work, flies, dust in my eyes and throat, sun cancers on my arms. It is all I have known.' So think of that before you think the kitchen of the Two Spoons is not paradise."

"Hmmm … I wouldn't go as far as paradise, Jesus, I can tell you that for sure."

"Oh, it is life and in every strand of life there is happiness and pleasure and achievement and, of course, so much love. There we are, watching the shearing process in these huge sheds, huge bales of smelly wool, watching an activity I had never previously witnessed, lives lived in a new way. In between exploring and taking in life on the station, we painted the shepherd's hut, we painted the decking and porch, jobs like this to pay for our keep. We talked about many things. Michelle grew up on the coast, of course, in suburbia. This was such a different life. But here is the strangest thing, Philomena." I paused, remembering clearly the moment, my own disbelief.

"We had been there two, maybe three days when I unearthed the book that I had been given by Librarian Anne, now curling and battered a bit, but carefully put away in a plastic bag. I showed it to Michelle, who nonchalantly said with a wave of her hand, 'Oh Auntie Sarah's book. She is Bruce's grand-aunt.' I was dumbstruck. I had no idea. I did not know Bruce's surname, but it was them, the family of the sister of Patrick Durack from Co Clare. I was, by the unfolding of life, standing in the story I had just read."

"Go away? That is incredible, Jesus." Philomena paused her stirring, steam fogging her eye glasses. "How on earth did that happen?"

"How does anything happen? It happens. Like the Two Spoons. Like the sheep station. Like the librarian. Like one life, then the next life, then the ancestors leave a little for the next generation.

It unfolds like a staircase. One step, one step. We are swimming in their pool with water that comes from inside the earth at 90 degrees and cools in a big open pipe so it is 30 degrees by the time it reaches the pool. Who found that? Then I am looking at these two little girls in Western Queensland in pink swim costumes and orange, hmm, what are these," I made a ring around my upper arm, "bandas de brazo, we say in Spain … ?"

"Armbands?"

"Sí, sí, yes, armbands, in their pool, like any happy girls anywhere in the world, having fun. And their great-great-uncle walked here with his horse and a few cattle, one hundred years or so ago. They have fashioned a whole life out of the dust. How does anything happen? Why does anything happen? What is the world but a big storybook?"

"My father travelling around east Cork, sees my mother. Your grandfather chances a change in life and goes to Spain."

"His grandfather got moved off his land in Beara. My other grandfather was moved by service and wars."

"My mother's family were landowners in east Cork but they got that by what would now be considered a sleight of hand. Not commendable, but probably a necessity for them at the time."

"Stories. His-stories, her-stories."

"Life." She paused over her pot, scratching at a spot of dried flour on her elbow. The cold room refrigeration motor chugged to a stop with a final wheeze.

"Fruit-cakes?"

"Ah yes, the real world. Kairos time."

∞

"My brother Frankie was a few year, grrr—how could I pick up the sound of someone else? A few years younger than us twins, four, I believe." Philomena shifted her weight awkwardly out of a café chair. "Oh, that was a long week. I'm getting much too old for this game."

Frankie had just left the Two Spoons and I was clearing away el detrito of the afternoon tea. It was a Saturday, so no great rush, but it was also a bank holiday weekend, a peculiarity I never understood, as to why banking institutions calendared a holiday weekend. I have endlessly forgotten to investigate and no Irish person has ever offered an explanation other than the banks remain closed on a Monday.

On Sundays of these holiday weekends, the Two Spoons became the Sunday lunch venue for Philomena and Ambrose's family. Everyone helped out and as the years passed more attended— Bridget McCarthy; Maureen Doherty; Michael's girlfriend, Sheila, when she became a constant in his life; myself or my immediates if the chance arose; plus Kathleen, Robert and his mother, Rita, once they were part of the staff. These were gay, lively gatherings, an eclectic mix of family and friends, personalities, and ages. Abuelita Rosa for sure just loved the warmth, the noise, the mingling with the younger generation, the incessant flow of wit and chat and tasty food.

Sheila Barry became Michael's long-time girlfriend. She is Shy Sheila in conversation with Philomena and anyone other than Michael. "Indispensable," says Philomena, "is the only word for her. Keeps Michael outta me hair." Sheila works as an auditor for Burke, Johnston & Payne, which Philomena satirises to Beurre, Jamon et Pain in her own head, as the source of Shy Sheila's substantial income. "Painfully shy and retiring," Philomena told me. "I hear she says nothing at the meetings, lets the suits churn away without her. Then they defer to her near the finish and she tells them what they missed. Has them shifting their briefs and feet. She has a sharp eye for the monies."

As an observer and writer of lives, within the dynamic of family and friends resides my own microcosm of the world at large. I am a weaver and a writer, I write while I weave. In many quiet moments with a pot of coffee in the corner of Two Spoons, I found I need never take leave of the premises; writing material flowed constantly through the doors. I would see the painfully shy competent auditor along with the large frame of Michael and his guttural sounds. Their communication was exquisite, exceptionally nonverbal with a repertoire of glances, gestures, inclinations, and touch. In the mêlée of family and friends, Sheila shared her beloved with those who knew and understood him in other ways. She never competed for his attention. I would see her sit with my own mother or Abuelita Rosa, where conversation was quieter or slower, English not being their mother tongue. She didn't hide there, merely escaped.

There were familial sharp moments in the gatherings of course. Con's wife, Majella, was not particularly fond of Bridget and allowed her irritation to surface. That wasn't helped by Bridget mispronouncing her forename, her fundamental right to life. "My-jelly," she would say solemnly, "could you pass me the gravy?" I don't think her carelessness was intentional but you couldn't be sure.

Philomena's only daughter, Peg, was "a leetle mandón," Abuelita Rosa would say. Bossy, or opinionated would be the correct term. I recalled the four Cs I had once read about behaviour that bordered on controlling: critical, challenging, contradicting, correcting. Peg displayed some portion of this in every interaction with her family. "Oh Mam, do you have to wear that jacket?" "Mam, take that scarf off, will ya." "What would you know about cooking potatoes, Michael?" She was not at all shy of her own opinion. Her father would shake his head and gravely say, "My princess after the three princes, a difficult role y'ken?"

Her husband, Gerard, is a Kerryman, of slight build and stature, a computer-programming genius with a "network" Ambrose calls it, as a result of his prowess on the Irish football field. "He did well for himself, has all the medals for playing for his county but I am afraid to say, he did nowt to dispel the princess's prerogatives."

Peg and Gerard have four children. Aidan, the eldest, is his grandad's favourite. They fist bump or high five and Ambrose smiles broadly saying, "Aidan, me lad." There's a tug of war between riding out on grandad's horses or attending the sports field, for Gerard's steely insistence is on playing Irish football, even if it is in the rival County Cork. Aidan inherited his father's stature and agility, entirely suited to Gaelic Football, but also fitting neatly and happily on an Ambrose horse. This is undoubtedly enough to create a certain amount of familial tension.

I was particularly attracted to these exchanges, for I could see the deep affection between grandfather and grandchild. Abuelo Sean, of course, had no competition for his affection in Cadiz, my being the lone flag-bearer for my generation. Aidan was the eldest of six grandchildren in Cork, three siblings and two of Con's. Stan had three more in Boston. I often pictured Abuelo Sean at these gatherings, for he would have been right in there amongst his own. I would smile at my mother and she would wink and say, "Hey, Jesús, pass the box and I will play a jig for the girls to dance."

"Shur we loved him like a little dolly," Philomena's voice drew me back to her recollection of her brother, Frankie, "and it seemed like Mam wasn't so thrilled anyway. We were so small you'd think we'd hardly notice, but she was always crying like she wasn't happy with her new baby. My father of course, was delighted with his little boy. We know now about the post-natal depression and the hormonal roundabout that women ride after childbirth. She was also possibly menopausal."

She straightened herself up from the dishwasher and took the last few plates from me. "She used to visit my grandparents' grave a lot. She was very religious, 'twas what they grew up with. Endless Mass and Benediction and Rosary and First Fridays, the whole shebang but faith an' she never forced it on us. We did the Mass on Sundays with my father but we weren't asked to attend much more than that."

A memory floated into her mind's eye, for she began to laugh heartily, "whuh, whuh whuh," her belly shaking inside her apron, the tea remains sloshing over the side of the mug.

"I remember her going mad once at Wilhelmina, really furious! In a way you wouldn't often have seen her. She came up the stairs without us hearing, into our bedroom, and there I was, kneeling by the end of the bed and Wilhelmina had the sheet draped around her shoulders like a cassock, a tea cosy perched on her crown like the bishop's hat and was flapping a pair of knickers around my head, very solemnly, saying, 'Benedictus, Benedictus, Amen.' Well! I thought she'd kill us! Yet another mortal sin, making fun of the priest's work."

I laughed, "Sr. Dolores in Cadiz had a list as long as your arm of such sins. We were convinced you could really never get into heaven, for there wasn't a chance you hadn't committed one of them."

"Yes, but that was the sole purpose of weekly confession, to cleanse your soul for the week coming, in case you were heading heavenly bound. God forbid, of course, they would always add. Shur we spent our days in the Ursulines either in a state of consternation about the sins we had committed, or a state of terror that God would call us with stains on our soul. I'm surprised there's a sane Irish person alive."

"Is there? I haven't met one yet."

She flapped at me with the tea towel, laughing, "I'll Benedictus you, you Spanish loo-la! Shur you're as daft as a brush."

Despite her laughter, I did stop and think, What on earth does that mean? It is a miracle anyone learns to speak English. When we had recollected ourselves, I continued the menopausal vein of thought. "You know, Philomena, I meet women of that age group all the time. Mid-forties to fifties, unsure of themselves, unsure of their direction. All of the seven-year cycles."

Philomena raised her eyebrows. "The what?"

"Seven-year cycles. I first heard of it from an old Chinese doctor in Cadiz. I won't spell it out now because this is your story. I memorised a short version like this:

> *Seven years old, teeth, hair, kidney energy*
> *Fourteen, fertility and menstruation*
> *Twenty-one, strong kidney, wisdom teeth, body vitals*
> *Twenty-eight, bones, hair and sex. Qi high*
> *Thirty-five, muscles deplete, wrinkles, thin hair, qi descends*
> *Forty-two, grey hair, qi exhausting, wrinkles*
> *Forty-nine, empty qi channels, menses ceases*

So this brings change, mid-life, and the What Next?"

"Oh, I have never heard it so succinctly put." She mused briefly, leaning on the counter, unconsciously stroking her cheek for the idle hair. "Qi, I take it is like your energy."

"Yes, your life force. Qi with a q, or c-h-i; or in karate it was with a k, k-i."

"It seems to fit. Lord save us, where am I now then, I wonder?"

"The Chinese believe that the energy of the kidney is the root of health, the power of the body. Boys have eight-year cycles, that's why they can be in the same class as girls yet seem more immature. Often boys gathering together revert to schoolyard mentality."

"And the men!" she exclaimed. "I see that with my own lads when they're together. I could have a houseful of teenagers again yet there are all these big men loafing about." She hit the go button on the dishwasher which started with a aahhaa-rring, aahhaa-rring noise and the sound of a cascading whoosh. She idly wiped the countertop with the tea towel.

"Frankie used to have an imaginary friend, Tommy. Mind you, that wasn't too hard, 'cos old Mrs. Quinlan's cat, three doors down, was called Tommy. He used to ask Mam, 'Why haven't I a twin like Wilhelmina and Philomena?' And she'd shoo him away and tell him to get on with himself and not be asking silly questions."

I heaved a bag of potatoes onto the counter for peeling.

"C'mon now," she says, "we'll fly through these for tomorrow." She mutters names and counts across her fingertips. "Con and Majella are almost certain. Michael and Sheila, Peg not Gerard, plus three. I have you and Daniel, and your Mamá and Rosa?"

"Papá and I will stay in your apartment when he gets back tonight with Ambrose, yes? Mamá and Rosa will come tomorrow."

"Biddy, Robert and Rita, not Maureen, so that's fifteen adults and the children." She glanced at the clock as she pulled up her sleeves and handed me a peeler.

"Crispy said he'd be here about five with the pork joint."

"Crispy? Like toast? Or chips?"

She laughed again. "Chris P. Christopher Pomfrett, Purveyor of Meats. 'Twas Biddy of course started it, but we call him Crispy 'cos he brings the bacon."

Over the mountain of potatoes for fifteen plus, Philomena picked up her tale. "So anyways, Mam told me her secret a couple of days before she died, not that I knew she was dying at the time of course."

"Oh? Was she not unwell or showing any signs?"

"Divil-the-bit. Happy out. Heartily well if I can use that expression. I was right here," she gestured to the front of the Two Spoons, "just doing the last bits and bobs when she came in with Michael. She used to collect him from the school gate of an evening until he was big and bold enough to walk home himself. This evening she had walked to meet him and said, 'Let's see your mam at the café for a drink.' I made her tea, Biddy called in and chatted a bit; and as Bid was leaving, Mam called her and said, 'Bridget, you take care of yourself and keep yourself well. Don't put up with no nonsense.' She was still married to Himself at that time, but Mam knew it was no good for her."

Philomena paused, her peeling knife scratched at her cheek. She shifted her not unsubstantial weight on the kitchen stool.

"Pass me your spectacles, Philomena."

"What? Oh! Oh, thank you, Jesus."

I ran the hot tap with a squirt of liquid soap and cleaned potato starch residue and goodness-knows-what other foodstuff off the lenses, before polishing them and handing them back.

"That's better, thank you. I can see the bloomin' spud now.

Anyway, Michael got bored and left Mam here with me, so I sat with her and the tea pot. If I had a pound for every cup of tea we have sat over, I'd be a rich woman, Jesus, but I kinda knew inside somewhere, that this was a bit different. An' then, out it came from nowhere."

I could only but wonder what could be next in the her-story of Philomena's life. The dishwasher trundled, water cheese-cheese-cheesing inside its heavy door.

"Frankie's twin died at birth. Luke. He's buried in my grandparents' grave. The little fella was laid to rest there before Mam came outta the Erinville Hospital with Francis."

The only sound between us was the peeler, scraping away the scantiest skin that lies between the outside world and the bare flesh.

"There's a notation marked on my grandparents' headstone: Luke 24:5. Wilhelmina and I commented on it one Easter Sunday, oh about a hundred years ago or what feels like it anyways, when we were there with Mam, and she shrugged and said, 'Well do you know what verse 24:5 of Luke's gospel is?' So we looked it up when we got home."

She looked at me and paused her task. " 'Frightened, the women bowed their faces to the ground but the men said to them, why do you look for the living among the dead?' We thought that was apt enough for a headstone but of course it was nothing to do with the Gospel, it was our brother Luke, May 24. That was his birthday. This was his headstone."

The peeler came back to life, the potato slowly rotating in her hand. She stopped to push a stray hair behind her ear, her glasses back up her nose.

"She told me also that day in there," the peeler jerked towards the front of the café, "that she hadn't wanted anyone to know. Didn't want to hear the neighbours whispering or sympathising or indeed take away from Frankie. So she buried her grief with Luke. She knew, my father knew, and she asked the Erinville staff and funeral director not to make it public, that she wished for her living son not to bear the sadness, only to live in the joy of God's presence."

"Oh dear me, the pains of life."

"Yes, you'd be so worn, so you would."

We worked in silence.

"Thus the imaginary friend?"

"Yes, I think so."

I ran cold water through the peeled potatoes to soak overnight as Philomena returned with a bunch of carrots from the cold store.

"So we're sitting out there, the two of us, and Mam says, 'I just thought you should know.' And I'm thinking Oh Lord I wish I DIDN'T know. What am I going to do with this?"

"Not easy for you at all, I can see that. So you know, your mother knows, and no one else knows?"

"That's about it, Jesus. So I asked her if she wanted Francis to know and she shrugged and said she hadn't wanted to tell him in the forty odd years, so maybe he didn't need to know now. And with that she says, 'Let's go home now, please, not even clear up the tea things.' So she carried them to the counter and said, 'Maureen will get them in the morning.' We walked away up the hill, 'twas the most gorgeous evening in early summer, swallows about the wire, children in the street, people out and about calling

'Evening, Mrs. Flaherty, lovely day.' They all thought well of her y'know. She was very well respected."

I murmured something in agreement or possibly in understanding that she herself, Philomena, would be the same. "La manzana nunca cae lejos del árbol. The apple never falls far from the tree."

"I brought her tea and toast, oh about a week or so later, before I left for the café. Then in the middle of an ordinary day of life, Ambrose calls me and says, 'Come up home now pet for a wee while, I need you here.' So I think it's Michael, God knows why I always think it's Michael, but 'twasn't this time."

The peeler flew up and down in her hand as the carrot lay bare its inner radiant colour. I was reminded of Abuelo Sean's flashing knife blade as he whittled sticks. Philomena pushed her glasses up her nose and relieved her bosom from her bra strap.

"No, 'twas Mam. Ambrose found her in her bed when he came in for lunch and said the light was on the way out of her. When I got there, she opened her eyes and gave me a big smile and said, 'Oh, you're here at last, my darling. I was waiting for you. I'm going to go now to Kit and Luke.' She squeezed my hand and y'know, Jesus, she was gone in a couple of breaths. My lovely mother."

I stretched across the carrots to squeeze the same hand and saw a tear roll from under her spectacles. Reaching for a hand towel, I stood to bring it to her and in the taking, she laid her head against my shoulder and heaved a deep sigh.

"Dear, Jesus, it was such a shock. I had never thought of losing her. She was never sick a day in her life. Always just getting on with every day." Her breath caught, her body shook, white hair against my cheek. "She had moved in with us after Dad died and we just rolled along all those years, day by day by day."

I crooned the soothing sounds of Abuelita Rosa who always seemed to know when no words were required. Philomena lifted herself away from me, wiping her eyes, straightening her glasses.

"Oh shur, 'twas an age ago but she was still me mam. I don't think you ever get past losing your mother. Then in the days after the funeral, I told Wilhelmina about the twin and in the ensuing discussion we thought Frankie should be told. But I needn't tell you Wilhelmina wasn't volunteering to do the telling. She may have been a bit miffed that Mam had told me but shur, there was no changing that."

Philomena straightened herself up, blew her tears away noisily, and pulled the chopping wedge from the rack. In silence we peeled and chopped carrots into batons.

"Well, of course there was Dympna in the way of telling Frankie anything."

I looked at her curiously. "Why so?"

"Well she's very protective of him, likes to shield him from the big sisters. A bit ... ."

"Controlling?"

"That's the very word. He's Francis, not Frankie. She's Dympna Laverty-Flaherty and she likes the world to run to her tempo. Frankie is the head bobs man." She must have seen my frown, for she immediately clarified, "Bobs, money, Chief of Finance at Tait's Freight. They have the oh painfully perfect house that gives me the willies. I'm always certain I'll leave a blob of jam on the white carpet, or a smudge of chocolate on the cream walls. Oh! I'll tell you sometime about the dinners. Ambrose and I go there once a year when Frankie has done my accounts. It's worse than having a tooth pulled, I can tell you." She chuckled, the moment of grief and sadness passing. Brevity into levity.

"So off she goes a few months later, away on a yoga weekend. Ambrose says, 'Whisht an' int it eatin' at you woman, so spit it out.' "

I laughed. I don't often hear Philomena mimicking the Scotsman. She looked at me in surprise.

"Go on, Philomena, while you are speaking the Scottish. Give me the name of the estate."

She roared with laughter, "whuh, whuh, whuh," her ample bosom shaking over the bowl of carrots. "Oh! Jesus in thy mercy, I can't."

"I can, and I am truly Spanish."

"Oh aren't you the clever one then! Anyways, off goes Dympna. Off goes Ambrose racing with Michael who's only a young fella and I'm at home in Church Lane with hot flushes and a dose of haemorrhoids. Oops! Sorry, Jesus. That's probably a little too much personal information."

"But it's the truth! I can't imagine that it is pleasant, so the truth sets the tale."

"It certainly does, Jesus, all that and this burning thing inside me, so I picked up the phone and said, 'Frankie, come for a bit of dinner this evening.' And he did. I was putting down the apple tart and cream when it just came out in a burst, 'twas nearly like watching myself on the stage you know, in a play. 'I've something to tell you,' I says and he says, 'I know.' 'Know what?' 'I know what you're going to say.' 'How can you?' 'Because I was never told by Mam or Dad but I knew inside all the time.' And then he told me how a couple of times after a few whiskies Dad would look at him odd and say, 'Here's me boys.' And when he was nine it was Dad's birthday and he came back from McCarthys No Relation and Frankie was going to the bathroom when Dad opened his arms and said, 'Come here to me, boys.' Frankie thought perhaps he was seeing double but it just wasn't right."

"McCarthy's No Relation? That's a funny name for a pub and I always forget to ask you about it."

Philomena cast her eyes to heaven. "Oh Biddy McCarthy again. She's been calling it that for years, to somehow differentiate her family name from theirs. Or disassociate herself from a den of iniquity." She laughed. "I said that phrase to her once and she came back to me about a week later and said, 'I just need to axe you Philomena, is McCarthy's No Relation a den of liquidity because they sell drinks?'" She shook her head. "The strange thing was, Jesus, I wondered where she had got the word liquidity. It wouldn't exactly be her vocabulary."

We laughed together, as we finished tidying up the peelings.

"And that was it. Another chapter of our lives—Luke 24:5. Frankie didn't know that bit."

"Do you think he told Dympna?"

She paused in the folding of a tea towel. "No. No, I don't think he would. She's just not the type to want to know. But we know, and Ambrose knows, and now you know."

I nodded. "Sit there for a minute, Philomena. Don't move anywhere now, okay?"

I went out to the backyard, to Robert's shed, and found the candles they kept ready for power cuts. Coming back to the kitchen, she was sitting just as I had asked, leaning on her elbows. She cocked her head sideways and watched my hands as I lit a tall church candle stuck unceremoniously in an empty whiskey bottle.

"Frankie was just recently here, so his energy remains. Your mother was here in the telling of her tale. The old walls keep the stories, the floor boards keep the feelings. We'll give Luke a moment to himself, knowing that we all know. Maybe he came back to your Mama and Dad and Frankie in a different way."

We sat in silence for quite a few minutes as the candle flickered and sputtered, the flame staying steady and strong. Philomena crossed herself, the Sign of the Cross through wordless but moving lips. I watched the flame and, as the tingling in the nape of my neck lifted, I looked at Philomena.

"The cat."

"What? What cat?"

"The cat, Tommy."

She frowned and stopped, puzzled. "What do you mean the cat?"

"I mean the cat wasn't just any old cat, was he?"

She looked momentarily puzzled, confused, as her logic mind sifted through memories of long ago. Her hand flew to her mouth.

"Oh! Saint's preserve us. The cat! Mrs. Quinlan's cat. He came after Frankie was born. Mam was terrified the kitten would climb into the cot. Us girls were either cooing over Frankie, or in Mrs. Quinlan's for the kitten. He used to hide in her hedge in the backyard."

"There you go. And I bet you the kitten was always with Frankie?"

"Oh holy Jesus! Sorry, that's not you."

"Ah, Philomena. I was doing so well."

"Oh dear God, that cat. Mam gave up trying to keep him out in the end. Dad told her it would do no harm and he was right. The only thing he told her was not to feed him, to let him go home for food. And that's what happened."

The flame flickered quietly, then suddenly blazed high on a surge of wax.

"God be with Luke and Frankie. That cat was still there when I left to marry Ambrose, Frankie was still at school."

"And probably stayed around until Frankie was sixteen or so?"

She looked at me strangely. "Why would you say that?"

"Sixteen. Twice eight. About the time Frankie was coming into his own as an adolescent, young adult."

"I can't rightly say how long Tommy lived."

Silence again, eyes fixed on following the mesmerising flame. The dishwasher spat and hissed its last dying breath with a determined crunch.

"Does it feel right in your bones?"

She turned the whiskey bottle around gently to let the wax run a new path. The flame glittered and danced on her glasses.

"Yes, Jesus. Yes, it does." She paused, moulding wax under her thumb. "Although I probably won't tell Ambrose or Wilhelmina."

"Try Dympna. Maybe she will get the story from the yogic end."

"Oh I doubt it. I might tell Frankie sometime. He might be pleased to know."

"Tell Biddy. She will tell everyone."

"And once again, you and I will be carted off on a trolley to St. Ann's Home by the boys in white coats. Shush now, there's Crispy at the gate. Blow out that candle before he's thinking we've gone mad. He woulda been at school with Frankie."

"The walls know, Philomena. We can wait until they start talking."

"Well," came a loud voice from the kitchen door, followed by a huge man in a white butcher's coat. "Is there a power cut with ye?"

∞

One quiet Monday morning, I met with Marguerite Foley, sharing a table with a lady unknown to me, clad in a vivacious lilac jogging suit. An equally vivid multi-patterned carpet bag with wooden ring handles hung from the chair behind her.

"Ah! Jesús," Marguerite beckoned to me to join them. Calling me by the Spanish pronunciation, I overheard her remark, "Jesús Josephus, you remember me telling you? Come and meet my friend here, Mrs. Callaghan from Castle Road."

"I am pleased to meet you," I said, extending my hand.

She smiled and reached towards me, "Likewise I'm sure." She sniffed and scrutinised me. "I can hear you are not from Cork?" Her accent was English, or Anglo-Irish, I could not be sure.

"No, you have that right," I laughed. "I was born in Cadiz, in Spain. And I can hear that you too are not from Cork?"

"Indeed not! Although I have been here three times longer than I was ever in England. I visited Cadiz with my parents in 1930 or so, I suppose, on a cruise."

I must have looked surprised, for she quickly clarified.

"We sailed from Southampton. We lived in England. My father's family is Irish but my father is London born. I was a teenager, but I remember the beautiful old city."

"That is where I lived, in the heart of the old city. My grandfather arrived there from Cork in 1938."

"Just as I arrived here to Cork," she exclaimed. "Maybe our ships passed in the night."

Marguerite interjected. "Jesús is a travel writer. Mrs. Sowersby is a close relation, so we have met here many times." She squeezed my hand. "Jesús is my crossword completer."

"You do yourself an injustice, Marguerite. I have rarely met you without the crossword all neatly done."

"Do sit with us, Jesús." Mrs. Callaghan also used my Spanish name.

Philomena came from the kitchen, a broad smile of greeting. "Well, Jesus, 'tis yerself. I thought I heard you. Are you joining the ladies?" She fussed and flapped a bit about, accidentally setting an adjacent chair rocking with her ample posterior. I took her hand, rising to my feet to kiss her cheek.

"Great to see you, Philomena. I can't wait to catch up with you."

She reddened and smiled, nodding. "You too, sweetheart. Coffee?"

"We were just comparing our father's stories, Jesús," Marguerite is saying. "Isn't it extraordinary how we all got here?"

"It seems to infiltrate every article I write. Every history story comes with a human tale."

"My father was Estonian." Marguerite continued.

"Not to be confused with an Etonian," quipped Mrs Callaghan and they both laughed. I knew enough about England to appreciate the joke.

"Yes. He was only nineteen and his father and brother had already been taken between the wars by the Russians. There was a slave labour trade, you know. It was truly a terrible time."

"Slave labour?" I am sure I sounded as surprised as I was.

"Oh absolutely, Jesús. Any able-bodied man the Russians could use in the mines, or oil-fields, collective farming. There were endlessly divided loyalties, you see. Estonia was once part of Prussia, part of Finland, then Danish, Swede, Poles, Russian again, then independent. My father's family came from the eastern part of the country, so nearer to Russia than anywhere."

I was silent. A whole new topic to explore, Eastern Europe between the wars and many millions more stories of life.

"The Russians and Germany divvied up Eastern Europe between them in their nonaggression pact in '39, and Estonia went under the Red Army. I do not know and my father never said how he ended up fighting for the Germans. The German army came to rout the Rooskies in the middle of '41. What does a child ever remember of their parent's lives?" she mused. "Although we walked miles together, every Sunday. I remember riding on his shoulders through fields, just swaying along."

"In Estonia?" I was puzzled, for I had thought Marguerite's background was also English.

"Oh no, no. He was taken by the Allies as a prisoner of war when it was all over in '45. He was in Berlin, and luckily where the Americans and British were tidying up and not in the Russian sector. Had he been there, he would most likely have never been seen again. The ragtag remnants of the Great Nazi Army, rousted by the Allies and Russians." She shook her head. "Pointless, wasn't it all?"

"Absolutely," agreed Mrs. Callaghan. "There was no good came of it for anyone. You have a very good recollection of the history though?" she queried Marguerite.

"Yes." Marguerite answered shortly. "I should have!" she then laughed. "I married a British Home Office secretary and we had successive terms in Eastern European countries. I have been fascinated by the machinations ever since. The powers that be had tried in '39 to keep the country neutral, but there wasn't a chance of that, for it was right there in the middle of the Hitler Stalin ding-dong. The country lost twenty-five percent of the adult population, then a large swathe of land and freedom back to the Russians afterwards. It was abysmal for any Estonian."

We paused, far away in time and geographical space, for the ladies to sip their tea.

"My father was shipped to Northampton as a prisoner of war, to a field camp across the road from my grandparent's house. The prisoners were hired out as labourers locally so they could earn some money. I think perhaps no one really knew what to do. What do you do? The war is over, none of these prisoners were true Nazis or Reichstag officials but in fact just the rounded up remains of soldiers in German uniform. My father of course hadn't any English. Some of the local ladies were knitting socks and handing out care parcels at the camps. My aunt was going to the camp one evening and asked my mother to walk with her. My father answered the knock on the hut door. When Mother refused to enter after her sister, my father gestured to indicate that everything was okay. She said she somehow knew instantly that everything was going to be okay. He began their nearly fifty years of marriage there, sifting through a box of his own possessions, photographs, and whatnot. She began by teaching him English."

Silence fell at our table. There are so many moments of recollection in the lives of others that remain painful, despite the passage of years. The visualisation of men drawn into a conflict that was not theirs; behaviours, commands forced upon them. Their ordinary lives made extraordinary in the process, the lives of their families railroaded onto an unknown track.

Philomena came to us again with a French-press of coffee. Kathleen had inscribed JESUS and a cross on the side of the pot with a Tipp-Ex. Philomena bowed her head to her hands clasped in prayer, saying to the two ladies, "You are in esteemed company here. Jesus has a blessed coffee pot."

They chuckled good-naturedly. "And I believe you keep a china teapot, cup, and saucer for me, Philomena?" Marguerite replied. "You can hardly have a shelf full of crockery especially for individual customers in there?"

It was my turn to laugh, taking Philomena's hand and kissing it.

"At a quick count, cousin, I estimate there are eight customers with special cups or crockery parts that I have seen as of yet."

Philomena swiped playfully at me with her tea towel as she took her leave of us. "Arra, get on away with yer nonsense."

"What a joyful lady," said Mrs Callaghan. "I shall make it my business to come here more often."

"The crockery with the Two Spoons logo, was a present to Philomena from Ambrose, when she had been in business for ten years. They are quite the pair," I mused, as Philomena returned with three portions of raspberry coconut tart, plated with dessert forks.

"God! I'll be worn out if I have to trip over to this corner again. Try this ladies, I know for sure this is a favourite of Jesús." We exchanged smiles, for she doesn't often use my Spanish name.

"She is a pure treasure," Marguerite agreed as Philomena moved away again. "I am exceptionally fond of her."

I smiled inwardly at the unfolding of my own history, my familial connection, my listening to Philomena's stories that resulted in my own honourable position in the Two Spoons Café.

Marguerite continued. "My father could have been shipped to Canada or Australia, but he chose England, thinking it would be the closest to any chance he might have to see his mother or family again. I don't think anyone really knew what to do anywhere. In any part of Europe or the wider world, touched by the war, I mean."

"I can imagine the chaos." I ventured.

Mrs. Callaghan smiled. "I was already here, in Cork, with five babies. I was having my own war."

I had my aah! moment, recalling Philomena's remark about Mrs. Callaghan on Castle Road.

"We were affected only by rationing here in Cork," she continued. "Everyone seemed to need tea and sugar. Petrol and travel were luxuries. I think of it every time I sit with a pot of tea. I remember my children bringing me a caddy full of seeds from the dock leaf plants, happily telling me they had found tea growing in Dick O'Neill's garden."

We laughed. She leant forward over her tea cup and said quietly, "But I never saw my mother again. I could not travel back to England after 1945. She died alone."

Marguerite nodded. "My father never saw his family again either. We grew up with an entirely blank canvas on my father's side."

Abuelo Sean, in different circumstances, came to mind, gone from Cork in an instant, never to see his family again. Yet in his new Spanish life, he escaped the war.

"My father eventually left farm work and went to the shoe factory. He could never return to Eastern Europe, even when he became a British citizen in the early '80s. They told him, you can go there on a British passport, but if anything goes wrong, because of course it was then Communist USSR, we will not be able to get you back. So he stayed at home."

In later years I read *A Woman in Berlin*, a diary of some eight weeks of life in Berlin between April and June 1945 as the war drew to a close, epitomising the very chaos Marguerite referred to–the daily struggle of life, for water and food, sheltering as best they could in a place that was battered and broken. I have recommended it to so many as essential literature, if for no other reason than to demonstrate the fragility of life, of living conditions, of those who survived.

Marguerite laid down her fork and patted her lips. "What I very clearly remember, though, is my father's contentment. He was the steadiest, most even-tempered man I have ever met. I could dance the tango naked with the milk-man and he would not bat an eyelid. He would have something to say afterwards, but I would have to wait to hear it." Her eyes twinkled mischievously.

"My father was the opposite," said Mrs. Callaghan. "Always dashing about, dying to travel or travelling, coming up with new harebrained schemes. And yet completely useless without my assistance, or my mother's assistance. You know? Off to a dinner in London without his shirt studs or wallet. That kind of useless. I absolutely loved him. He bought me a car for my twenty-first birthday saying, 'On away with you now, Pop, find the world.' And he promptly had a heart attack and died, leaving me absolutely bereft. He was already gone when the war started. I have missed him most dreadfully all of my life."

Sitting safely in a café in Cork, with the memories of two ladies and of how war touched and changed their lives, is just one of the precious moments in which I try to reside every day. My Plum Village practice of Touching the Earth comes to my mind. I close my eyes to the sounds of the ladies and see Thich Nhat Hanh sitting in the garden with us at Plum Village as I began my life's journey, his fingertips in the grass. I hear him clearly say:

> *Touching the earth every day, return to the earth, to our roots, to our ancestors. We recognise we are not alone but we are connected to a whole stream of spiritual and blood ancestors. We are their continuation and with them continue into future*
> *generations. We touch the earth and let go the idea that we are separate, we are earth and part of all life.*

Opening my eyes I see both ladies looking at me curiously. Marguerite touches my hand. "You seemed to disappear. Are you okay, Jesús?"

I smile at her, "Thank you, Marguerite, I am just fine. I had a moment there just remembering, just processing all that you have told me. Thank you both for sharing your stories with me. I am humbled every time I hear the fabric of the lives of others." I raise my coffee cup. "Here's to those who have passed and left us richer for their presence."

Mrs Callaghan wrinkled her nose with some measured disagreement, pursed her lips, and replied, "Indeed."

I wasn't quite ready to explore that one.

∞

Cluain Alainn, Tipperary

"Och the horses? I dinna ken where to start, Daniel?"

Papá and Ambrose had found firm friendship, cast together primarily by the ancestry of their wives but also from many common threads of personality. On this particular trip, we were in Tipperary at the stud farm, with Michael and Tommy Snap, where the Ambrose line of *Phillies* were bred. I had accepted the invitation to travel with them, somehow certain there would be good writing material in the offing.

"Tommy an' I were lucky way back along, hmm, back where, Tommy? 1980?"

"That's about right, Ambrose." Tommy was a shorter man, not a difficult thing to be beside Ambrose, but still shorter than many. His shortness was accentuated even further by my father, myself, and Michael, for we each carried at least a head and a half in height above him. Tommy had a wide round face, balding forehead, and a rim of ginger hair. His face was lined and creased with the stories of hours of outdoor work in all weathers. He scratched under his collar, squeezing his eyes shut behind rimless glasses in the remembering and to a one, we all seemed to shift our stances wider or longer to come at least somewhat closer to eye level with the man.

" '80 or early '81, I s'pose?"

I imagined myself as a fourteen-year-old in Cadiz, far away south in sunshine, growing up in another world. I looked at my nodding father, possibly also recalling faraway climes, the white starched Naval uniform, the briskness of authority, the sea, the sun.

"Aye, aye, Tommy spotted this cracker," Ambrose was recounting the tale. "Peaceful Princess. Well, we dinna ken tha' right then. The naming took another bit o' time, but we knew we had a winner. She jus' looked good, aye, good, you'd have to say?"

"Oh she just was," agreed Tommy. "She was the kind of foal that looked right at you and said, 'Here I am for you, Tommy!' So I gave me ould Scotsman here a call and said get in your truck and drive to me. An' he did."

Ambrose laughed. "Abandoned the poor wife with three boys and the mother-in-law and raced off to Tipperary."

"So we bought her right then and I minded her like my own babe." Tommy stopped and laughed as well at the memory. "And I also had four at home with the missus."

Ambrose picked up the tale. "She ran all over the south, jump racing, point-to-points, fabulous creature she was too. I'd take her for a wee while as she got older, stronger, and we'd run her in the sea at Fountainstown. Aye." Ambrose nodded and pursed his lips.

"What a fine sight, out before the lark, not a sinner about, knee-deep in the tide. Just magic."

"We saw she was goin' to be big, so we got the other two boyos onto the ticket." Tommy nodded satisfyingly.

There are always moments in Irish discourse where my Spanish brain halts and I think Dios santo, ¿qué significa eso? Good God. What does that mean? What it means of course always unfolds.

"Kevin and Bernard, the other syndicate members," Ambrose clarified. "There's four of us, equal shares in the project. Great fun really, eh, Tommy?"

"Oh Lord! Yes, yes. It certainly has kept life interesting, Ambrose, good sir."

"We have bred from the lovely Princess and her line ever since, some stunners, some disappointments of course, but, oh, never dull."

"Peaceful Princess, Phine Philly, Paddy's Parade, Pint o' Porter," Tommy scratched his forehead.

"Peg's Parody, that was Peg's choice. Peter's Phortune, that was your lad's, Tommy?" Michael was a very quiet soul, his speech impediment holding him back shyly from anyone but the closest company. He had grown up with the horse story.

"Are they all spelt with a P?" my father enquired.

"Aye. It just happened." Ambrose smiled. "I was in charge the night the Princess was to first give birth; Tommy here was gone for some shut-eye. An' myself and Bernard, the vet, had the easiest-ever birth a horse could give a man. 'That's one fine filly,' he said to me after a clean-up and a wee dram o' the good stuff. I was tellin' Philomena when I eventually got to m'bed and she laughed and said, 'That's a grand name for a good horse,' but she spelled it the next day with Ph instead of F. Philly, the nickname she hates for herself, y'ken?"

We all laughed.

"And that, as the man says, was that, really," agreed Tommy. "We started on P's and stayed on P's.

Tommy said dat. And dis. I smiled at the thought of Tommy from Tipperary with D's instead of T's, in conversation with Bridget without any T's at all.

Michael nodded. "I loved her." He reddened at his own admission. His father smiled at him and put a friendly arm around his shoulders.

"Michael, m'boy, she loved you."

Michael blushed harder, pushing his father aside. "Arra, get away with your nonsense, Dad."

"Aye 'tis true! Michael here was just a wee lad when the Princess had finished her racing and was breeding. Sometimes we would take her to Cork to our field for a change of scenery, get her away from the five-star pastures of Tipp, show her a bit of rough livin'."

Tommy and Ambrose laughed together.

"And she would eat out of your hand, boy." Tommy smiled up at Michael. "Nothin' she liked more. You were a bit shorter then, son."

Michael the adult beamed. He had the height of his father and the girth of his mother, and in his smile he was Philomena all over.

"So you have her lineage, here on the stud farm?" my father asked.

"Aye, pull on yer boots and we'll go for a ramble."

We spent the following two hours on foot, through majestic spring green beech-lined lanes, lush pastures dotted with primroses and daisies, bright yellows of lesser celandine, nodding daffodils. Endless miles of wooden gates and fences, meeting another and yet another protégé from the Princess stable. I stopped trying to keep the hierarchy in my head, breathing in the mixture of voices and accents, trilling birdlife, whinnies and neighing from the herd. Patch, the Jack Russell, tripped along at Ambrose's feet, snuffling the hedgerows, poking into holes in hedges, wary of the longer four-legged creatures in his radius. Michael's shyness deserts him in trusted company; my father and I seemed to fit that category, and Tommy has been a life-long presence. It was wonderful to meet his true jovial, witty self, and he was a natural amongst the horses.

We met young enthusiastic grooms and would-be jockeys and, in truth, the vastness of the enterprise was awe-inspiring. I watched my seaman father joke and laugh with land men, rooted in their place and purpose. I listened as the stories flowed.

Our circuitous route brought us to the stable yard, to a tack room of gleaming shining parts. Bits and bridles, stirrups and reins, saddles of all sizes, martingales, girths, hoof boots, a spotless cobbled floor where grooms sorted tack after the morning's ride. A stable hand came through pushing a trolley laden with scones and cakes, pots of tea and coffee.

"If my mother needed a day off," Michael suggested, "we could send her here, Tommy."

A long oiled bench served as a work space for tack repairs. I ran my hand along its surface, breathing the scent of linseed oil, and across the warmth of my back a breeze stirred. Through a shaft of sunlight on the cobbled floor, behind my eyelids I see an old man squinting in the strong Mediterranean sun as he oils the bellows of his concertina. "A mazurka, Jesus, three-four time. Polish, I believe, not unlike our polka—swingy, dancey, da-de-dada, da-de-dada, dah-de-da-da-da-da. This one is 'Shoe the Donkey.' "

I smile to myself, that's real Abuelo Sean humour in a pedigree stable. 'Shoe the Donkey' indeed!

On our journey south to Cork, my father and I are quiet in the rear of Michael's big jeep. Up front, the conversation roams from fillies to foals, from building to Boston, father and son without intervention. The long frame of Ambrose fills the passenger seat to the roof line. In the thrum of fast travel, I try to recall whether I have ever been seated behind Ambrose, beside my father, in a vehicle driven by Michael and I find it is a new dynamic, where all roles are jumbled into a different shape. I glance at my father, who is watching the countryside move at seventy miles an hour, the Greek seaman with a head full of Tipperary horses. After the scones, there had been stallions, and then the pedigree wall, the map of lineage that rivalled any monarchy, followed by another wander through the outlying farm.

"We'll get grub," Michael is saying, somewhat to the rear, mostly to his father, "at The Horse and Jockey, I suppose?"

I make no effort to translate this in my head, for it becomes apparent in the next five minutes what he meant. Grub, however, I have continued to fail to understand, other than it has four letters like food.

The bar is busy and fast, serving many of the horsing world in some passing way. Ambrose nods and smiles, raises his glass across the room, tips his hat. My father surveys the unfolding scene and smiles to me, leaning across his steak of gigantic proportions.

"Dear Lord, Jesús," he whispers, "I cannot possibly eat this much cow."

"Just sneak half of it into a napkin, Papá, and into your pocket. The Springers will love you."

"Patch will have climbed into my pocket long before we get to the Springers," he laughs. We gingerly tackle two food mountains.

"There is a world outside us all, Jesús, which we are fortunate to witness but will never be part of. Much and all as I love a good day out at the races with Ambrose, if I ever fancy purchasing a Burberry jacket or itching tweed cap, please do smack me to regain my senses. I, for one day, am all horsed out."

∞

"Tommy Snap? Ambrose?" I leaned forward to hear. The jeep was quiet, Michael's face lit by the orange and red tones of the dashboard, his eyes blinking at oncoming lights.

"The Snap bit, is it, Jesus?"

"Yes, please."

"Y'ken, you'd think Tommy there is the great racing magnate, the stud, all the gear and millions of pounds of horse flesh in the fields? Well, in his head he's still the little fella who got lucky—small house, four grown children, missus still works for the council, nothing much else changed in Tommy's life, other than the stud got bigger an' bigger. His missus is just under six foot herself and he tells me he was quite drunk the night he tried to court her affections, d'ya ken? He told her she was too tall, that he was hoping to breed a line of jockeys; and quick as a flash she told him he was unsuitable, that she was looking for basketball players."

Ambrose and Michael laughed. Having spent the day with Tommy and meeting the essence of the man, both my father and I could join them.

"So they agreed to meet again with no drink involved to see if they could get past their spatial differences and perhaps they might just get along. He never drinks now, isn't much of a party animal, and if you were to ask him to play a hand of cards, guess what he likes best?"

A momentary silence from the rear is soon filled by Michael thumping on the steering wheel.

"Snap!" he shouts.

The jeep fills with laughter on the road home.

∞

Blackrock, Cork

"Maybe Peggy Thurston's demented head knew what she was doing when she ran into the traffic?"

The question came from nowhere, as conversations often do. We were by the river in Blackrock, coffee in hand, a dull but warm day. Philomena perched on the low wall watching a couple of mallards fighting each other, a spectacle for the waiting hens.

"What brings that to mind, cousin?"

"What? Oh sorry, Jesus, I sometimes don't notice that I have spoken my thoughts out loud. Oh, it would be my friend Jack's anniversary about now. He was caring for her at the time and shur he was nearing eighty-five. He told me afterwards how he was getting dressed after his shower and was about to tie his shoelaces when he thought he heard the front door. By the time he got down the stairs, she was gone, off down the street. He had to find his glasses before he got himself out and out the gate. She somehow had stepped into the two lanes of traffic outside the library. Maybe she was crossing the road? Maybe she thought she could? Maybe she just didn't know or see anything? Or maybe she had a clear moment and decided to end it all? He was her carer, and he was the kinda fella who was always in charge. I mighta run away myself. Who will ever know?"

"Hmm. That would still have been very difficult for him to witness."

"Oh it was, it was. There was not a mark on her. By the time he arrived, she was dead. The poor young fella driving the van was stupefied with shock. Then there was the ensuing hullabaloo. Anyways, Jack lived on after, until he was ninety-two, I think."

"Oh a long life indeed. I am sure he would have had some stories."

"Indeed. I can tell you a couple. He was a decorated war hero, Second World War, an Englishman. Straight into the planes from school, what's that again in England?"

"RAF, Royal Air Force."

"Yes, that's the one. Straight in at sixteen, somewhere in northern England." She paused as the mallards cackled and pushed each other through the grey water. "He trained as an aircraft fitter, couldn't be a pilot because he was short-sighted. He showed me his log books, meticulous they were. His first flight in 1935 and every flight he took all the way through the war, all the way after the war, Malta I think he was, then east Africa. All the way to 1975 when he had his last flight. A lovely neat row of little green notebooks on his book shelf." She gestured with her hands forming a tidy square, and then laughed a little.

"But the rest of his place was a pure mess. Saints preserve us! I used to take him a bit of dinner after Peggy's accident. He was all right lookin' after her with some home-help, but he let himself go after that. Elizabeth Byrne was his daily and she called to me one day to see if I could get him to eat. I'd call with a sandwich and tell him to eat it while I was there. So faith an' he did and talked a bit too. We started like that. So myself or Maureen or sometimes Kathleen or Robert would drop up a plate of dinner every two days or so. And a bit o' apple tart, sponge cake, something like that. He was fond of proper egg custard, just like my own mother. Nothing wrong with his health at all otherwise. He was still out and about, getting the paper from Sue's News, lottery ticket, pension of a Thursday. Sometimes he would call in to the café, but that grew less and less."

"Did I meet him? I don't think so?"

"No, no, you'd remember him. You would have been stuck in a corner with him all day if I know you." She laughed then looked at her watch. "Still okay for a while yet. Kathleen wants to go today at four, so I'll get back for then."

The mallards flashed their green-and-blue heads in a shaft of sunshine that pierced the clouds. I heard the far away hum of a container ship as it nosed its way to the port across the river, a stray yacht without sails motored past the castle.

"Well, his first ever wartime outing was on board a vessel, can't remember why he was on a ship? Being transported somewhere, I suppose? His first posting I think he said. He was sick the whole time and stayed on the deck because he was too ill to go down to his bunk. The very first night he felt well enough to go below, well they were torpedoed by a U-boat, weren't they? Somewhere in the mid-Atlantic. He was able to help get some of the lifeboats launched and then had to jump ship himself, wearing his greatcoat and boots. I remember him saying that he was only twenty feet from this torpedoed ship when it tipped straight up and just slid to the bottom. What a waste! He was rescued sometime after from that adventure by a lifeboat, and I think they were shipped onto another boat. Would that make sense?"

"Yes, I suppose. My war history wouldn't be terribly accurate, Philomena. Papá would know more."

"However it was, imagine that as your first outing in the war? Then later on, they were on bombing raids over the continent, Germany and Italy. Would that sound right?"

"Yes, that probably would be right. Mussolini sided with Hitler."

"They were new planes he said, not too many problems for an engineer, and it was his job to sit beside the pilot and keep an eye on things. Once you strapped in, that was it and it was always freezing up there. On a bombing mission, his job was to go back into the rear to make sure the big bomb was dropped properly. They were bombing Milan. I remember him saying that. He said 'what did Milan do to deserve this?' They dropped their load and before they knew it, they were hit by a dropping bomb from one of their own planes above."

"Oh! My good Lord."

Philomena nodded. "That's it. He was in the back of the plane already and the pilot told the crew to jump, but Jack just couldn't open the back door. Just would not open. Now I know nothing at all about planes or physics, Jesus, but the plane went into a spin, so he stuck himself somewhere, trying to stay safe. All of a sudden the spin stopped and he saw that the door had opened. He says to me, 'If that weren't the hand of God, nothing was.' " She paused and we gave this thought due attention. The hens paddled away nonchalantly from the squabbling mallards.

"The next fellow was pulling at his parachute and making his way to jump. Jack was doing up his own parachute and making his way to the door when he looked at the gunner man. He gave him the thumbs up and was going backwards out the door, when he noticed the gunner had no parachute. His last sight was the man blessing himself and waving to Jack."

Philomena stopped in her story, shifted her weight, crossing and uncrossing her legs. "All he said to me was 'I wish I had known. I wish I had noticed sooner, I don't know, he could maybe have clung himself to me and we would have taken the chance and jumped together.' " Philomena drew herself up straight, folding her hands across her bosom. "He gave himself terrible grief over this. Terrible. Said he dreamed of this man a lot." The ducks drifted away, idly paddling the currents.

"Jack lost his boots in the fall, strained his groin when he landed with his parachute in Italy, and ended up in a prisoner camp for a few months. Survived all that, escaped, walked across Italy to the Allied lines, with lots of help from the Italian locals he said. Gave them his rank and number at the front and they shipped him home. Straight back to his squadron when he got there. They gave him the weekend off and a train pass to go see his mother. Back to work on Monday, his pay backdated to the day of the raid, nine months earlier. Lived to ninety-two."

We were silent. Life drifted along the river. Gulls fought over something inconsequential. Children shouted behind us, a bicycle bell rang shrilly—all sounds of every day.

"I was amazed every time he told me stories, Jesus. We wouldn't have had too many war vets in Cork. Lots of them fought for the Allies somewhere, but none who I knew of. Ambrose would have come across them in Scotland all right. I was fascinated by Jack's stories. He could recall all these tales of death, destruction, bombs, guns, engines, young lives. He had no ceremony about him at all, none of that Veteran's Day stuff for him, he was doin' his job. He got paid, dealt with whatever came next and thought himself lucky to survive. Thought himself lucky to have served his country. Thought himself lucky to be bombed over Italy and not on one of the German missions. He didn't think he could have walked out of Germany. The Italians were a much different matter." She inhaled deeply, pushing her glasses onto her forehead, massaging her eyes.

" 'Tis a quiet life I have lived really in comparison," she laughed. "Poor old Jack. Faded away in the end. Her family was from here so they retired to here after all the RAF travelling. Said he owed her that. I am glad to have known him. Fed him."

"But much more than that, Philomena, you were there to listen. That's just as important as the doing of any heroic acts. Being. Listening enough to be able to recount the tale to me so this is the memory, the sharing of the story, the life of the man. It is not everyone can do it."

"God knows where I found time for that. I suppose it must be only five or so years that he's gone." She blessed herself, up and down, three or four taps to the middle of the bosom. I am fascinated; it must be uniquely Irish but undoubtedly still recognisable to heavenly or angelic beings as a ritual blessing.

"It's the why, Jesus. Why? I heard one man's story. There were what, six, seven other fellas on that plane? And there were how many planes that night? And how many Italians fightin' on the ground? And how many other wartime activities all over Europe that night? Why? 'Cos one little fella in Germany was too big for his boots? And there were a dose more egging him on, pushing him along the path? Is that just too simple an answer?"

She stopped. She breathed deeply, stroking her cheek and chin to find the stray hair. "I mustn't get angry. Mustn't let it rile me. I could never stand one person taking advantage of another. I suppose that's all it is really, on a far bigger scale."

"Oh lovely Philomena!" I moved beside her to give her a hug. "You are a treasure."

"I can't think about these things too much, Jesus. I don't listen to so much news anymore. I think my time is better spent reading good books or listening to music. There's nothing better than a dance around my kitchen, even to one of those ould pop songs Kathleen plays. I hear millions, billions, million pounds for this or that, all those kind of figures and I try not to think of all the waste. The wasted resources. Energy. Lives. All the things thrown away. I try to look after my own corner, my own family, the ones God sends through my doors. So help me, that's all a body can do, isn't it?"

"Yes it is. That's it. That's all it is, Philomena. And you are doing that right."

She harrumphed, crossing her arms again, pulling herself tighter to her self.

"And God? He thought it was the hand of God. What do you think?" I ventured.

"Oh I still call him God like I have known Him all my life, although I have this half-cracked cousin that trips around the world and tells me it's not just a bearded white fella, it's everything, mother and father, light and dark, what is it? Yin and Yang?"

She smiled at me and I could only laugh. "So you ARE listening to me?"

"Oh! Every word, I can assure you."

"NOT a long-haired bearded man in the sky. God is our word for an energy. Balance, duality, male and female, light and dark."

"That's it. That's what I said."

> *Mother Father God, I am your child*
> *I am a child of this Universe*
> *Fill me with your love*
> *May I be a beacon of light and love*
> *To all whom you send my way*
> *In my words, thoughts, deeds and actions*
> *This is my prayer.*

"Yes, that's the kind of thing I mean, Jesus."

"I'll expand that for you now, Philomena, and think about this. It's probably not a universe. It's probably a multiverse. Universe is too simple, I think. I think perhaps we are the tiniest dot in a much more complicated system that we only know a fraction of. That maybe even the astronomers only know a fraction of. I am guessing there is more unseen than seen."

"I hate to say it, Jesus, because it means I'm understanding everything you tell me. But I get that. Your father told me that once before too, quite some time ago. I asked him, 'How are things in your world?' meaning East Cork, of course, and he said, 'My world is but a sliver of what we know, Philomena, just barely one of those.' He was pointing to a grain of sugar on the table."

"Yes, I have heard him say this."

"Then he laughed and gave me a squeeze and said, but of course East Cork is a golden honey pot."

She looked at her wristwatch and levered herself slowly off the wall. "Now then, Jesus, back to the real world of the Two Spoons. At least I can be fairly certain of my world inside those four walls."

∞

On one particular Bank Holiday Sunday lunch in the Two Spoons, I recall Ambrose and Aidan nodding and winking together, planning the Holiday Trip to Tipp to the stud—so perhaps we were at Easter holidays. Rosa was conversing with Shy Sheila and Mamá. Peg's middle child, Roisín, was plaiting my hair, while the twins, Callum and Eileen, swung off my legs. The meal had been cleared, there were pots of tea and coffee, the last of apple-cinnamon sponge cake being scraped out of bowls. The windows were open to the quiet Sunday street and Philomena glowed with pleasure and contentment in her little enclave.

"Do you get sisters, brothers?" Abuelita Rosa asked Sheila.

Sheila shook her head with a smile.

"No? Me not too."

I could see Rosa looking along the table. "Gerard? Brothers, sisters?"

Gerard nodded and shouted back over the noise. "Two of each, Rosa."

"Hmm. May-ella? Sisters? Brothers?"

Majella smiled. "One brother, one sister, one sister died."

Rosa continued her scan. "Maureen? You have them too?

Maureen nodded and held up two fingers.

"Ree-ta?

"None, Rosa. Just me."

Rosa worked around the table to Philomena. "Hah, hmm, Philomena?"

"Yes, Rosa?" Philomena smiled at my grandmother, curious as to where this was going.

"You have," she counted on her fingertips, "uno, dos, treis, cuatro, cinco, seis, siete, ¿Qué son los hermanos, Jesús?" she turned to me to translate.

"Siblings."

"Sí, sí, no siblings, only child. Hijo único, cuento siete. María, Daniel, Jesús, Ambrose, Sheila, Ree-ta, Bree-geed. Siete. Seven. Hmm."

"And you also, Abuelita?" I reminded her.

"Oh sí! Sí! Mí mismo. Ocho. Eight. And together here we are, dos, cuatro, seis … ." Rosa swept the room counting under her breath.

"Quince. Y los niños? Y siete. Twenty-two." She nodded, satisfied with her result.

"Qué fracción, Jesús? Percentage?"

"Abuelita Rosa! Gusta escribir, pero simplemente no tengo cabeza para las matemáticas. Writing is for me, not maths!"

All around the table laughed.

"C'mon, Sheila, that's your department," Michael gently jostled his girlfriend.

"Gerard's!" called Sheila, deflecting the spotlight.

"Eight outta twenty-two, that's just more than a third, say thirty six percent." Philomena didn't pause. "Shur 'tis my job all day. How do you all think I'm still in business?"

A great roar of laughter arose.

"Och, no flies on you, my sweet. You tell them girl," Ambrose kissed his wife on the cheek.

Rosa smiled, a smile of true happiness. "Just one, just one, just one, eight of us. And you are the numero uno, Philomena. You are the one who brings us together, to family. All family. Gracias." Abuelita Rosa joined her hands under her chin and, closing her eyes, bowed her head towards Philomena. "Digo de corazón gracias. From my heart. Gracias."

∞

Cottage by the Water, Rostellan, East Cork

The arrival of Patch was Ambrose's story. He was in East Cork with us for a few days, helping my father re-roof a section of the cottage and install another roof light over the eastern end of the attic. Cottage is a loose word, for there was ample room for my parents and Abuelita Rosa, and I had an attic room for when I was home with them. The other half of the attic space was given to books and the essential paperwork of living: tax forms, car registration documents, insurance certificates, files and folders of stored information pertaining to their lives. And of course the manuals and instructions of every implement or gadget they had ever purchased. "The hole upstairs," my father called it. My mother misunderstood him to mean the whole upstairs and would chide him saying, "Some of that is space for Jesús, Daniel."

Patch had travelled with Ambrose, abandoning his post in the backyard of the Two Spoons, where he was primary resident. Mamá sat in a deck-chair at the garden table, chatting with the men after their lunch break, the Jack Russell beside her, gently nuzzling her hand.

"Oh Patchy, Patchy, lovely thing, where do you come from?"

Ambrose lit his pipe, enjoying his leisurely break from tripping up and down a scaffold with slates. "Och, Patch, the wee pup."

Without leaving Mamá, the dog turned to hear his master's voice and, to my eyes, I do believe Patch smiled and possibly even winked.

"He's coming for twelve or thirteen years now. We were racing at Listowel and, if I'm right, I think it might have been Perfect Pony won the two-thirty. It was a bit of surprise to me and Tommy. The horse was a good racer but not the quickest at the three-quarter mark, where ye need to get up some speed. Bernard was driving that night, so I actually consumed three pints of beer instead of two and, to my utter regret, without anything to eat except a very expensive ham sandwich."

My father groaned, "Oh! I certainly know those beers. Did absolutely nothing for my guitar-playing but my singing improved immensely."

"And a cigar, Daniel. All a cigar ever did was make me sick."

"Oh! Good Lord, I know it." My father shook his head and pointed to the roses climbing profusely behind Mamá. " Do you remember, María? It wasn't just growing roses in Ireland old Commander Abbott had a hand in. He doled out Cuban cigars after one particular Naval gathering, in which I felt compelled to partake. I don't think I have ever been so ill."

Mamá smiled at him. "Lucky for me we had a nurse in the family who took charge. I stuck to my day job."

Ambrose picked up his tale. "Unfortunately I had let a wee Traveller boy catch my eye and I knew right away that I was snookered. One of them was onto me like a shot. 'Mister, are ya lookin' for a pup? G'wan mister it's the last one, the runt an' no one wants him. I tell ya, ya won't be sorry sir. Ah I'm sure you could use a good pup. He'll be a great ratter. This is your pup sir, I have it here for you.' "

We to a one laughed uproariously. Ambrose looked surprised, "What? Have ye never heard a long Scotsman impersonate a Kerry Traveller boy?"

My father clapped his hands. "Dear God in heaven, that was a tonic Ambrose. I do hope there's more."

"Well, I had been away for a few days so I was a little anxious about bringing something back to herself. I thought it woulda been quite nice to bring her something she dinna have to stick in a vase, or eat, or pretend she liked. So we bargained a bit more, me and the little Traveller boy. 'Ah go-on now, go-on now you can do behher than dat, gimme fifty smacks an' he's yours, kind sir. You look like a daycent fella and you won't miss fifty, fifty's good for me, good for you, and look now, look now, at the lihhle doggie, shur yer missus will love him as soon as she claps eyes on his lihhle face. Go on sir, go on sir, you can do me for fifty.' Or some such plámásing." Ambrose had taken off his glasses, crouched forward in his chair, and scrunched up his face mimicking the Traveller boy making a sale. My father laughed at his antics.

"Plámásing, Ambrose?" I asked.

"Aye, Jesus, sweet-talking or flattering. I pulled out forty euro and said be off with you now and put the 'lihhle fella' in my pocket. Luckily the horse an' gear was already loaded, so I hadna to contend with tha' after pints and pup." Ambrose paused to relight his pipe. "Well, I am full sure I snored all the way from Listowel to Cork and I am full sure the little pup slept too. When we arrived to Church Lane, Philomena was about, as is her wont when I'm on my return. She frets about towing the horse-box; having never of course done it herself, it always seems like it's going to be a disaster for everyone else. She was fussin' about as she does, pretending she was busy and NOT worrying—och, y'ken, endless cakes on the go, tea towels in the drier, that kinda thing."

Papá nodded seriously. "Yes, I know exactly."

"So we chatted away about this an' that, how the day went. An' of course I've slept off me pints and am now starving with the hunger but could na' ask her to go to any trouble. So she does it easy y'ken, plate of sandwiches, tea already made, cake a mile high. I'm a lucky fella that I was never prone to the heavy side. I'd be bigger than me own house if I was."

"So she liked the pup?" Mamá queried.

"Och, I was waltzing all around her, tryin' to get her to see him in ma pocket but she was too busy being busy, so in the end I had to say, 'Ah here, woman, will ya look.' She thought I had torn me coat and needed a repair, so in the end I had to fish the beggar out. 'Oh what's that?' I had to stop myself from saying, well it's not a two-year-old filly."

"Not something you could say to a wife!" Papá ventured.

"Indeed not! So once she had him in her hands, he of course peed everywhere. 'Is it for the grandchildren?' she asked a bit cross like. No, of course not, it's for you. I don't think right then she was too pleased with me and right then I was not too pleased with myself, and my head was now hurting from pints of beer and the cigar and none of it seemed such a good idea in the harsh light of my own kitchen. I thought perhaps I shoulda just raised me arms into a big scary boo and sent the little Traveller boy a runnin'."

"Oh sense you have left me, a poor oaf in your wake." Papá smiled broadly and looked at me.

I quickly found a refrain. "Take speed goodly fellow, your chance I will take."

"Rightly so. We're there, her with puppy-pee running off her elbow, I'm inhaling sandwiches and tea and wishing to lay me head down, when I notice she has this tiny wee smile on her and she says to me, 'He has a lovely brown spot there on his cheek. I'll call him Patch.' Then the cat gets involved, hisses an' spits like a pea-shooter, so herself lets a roar at the cat and puts the doggie on a towel in the old enamel bread bin. You'll probably have to let him out in the night for a pee, y'know, my love, I tell her, wondering if this could be my fatal blow; but she's doin' that motherly thing where they no longer hear you and it's just puppy, puppy, puppy."

Papá nodded, "Yes, I know that one too."

"So she puts newspaper on the floor and leaves him in the utility room, telling me that she's been up in the night for so many years I must never have missed her. I'm sensing this could be dangerous territory for a late-night discussion, so I say to her I think she is the most wonderful woman in the world and do call me if you need any help. That must have diffused things, for I remember nothing more about it."

"And that was the arrival of Patch?" Mamá tickled his ears, "What a sweetie you are all the way from Kerry."

"Aye, Patch. Another thread in the tale of life in Church Lane. But, och, wait. There's more. Pretty soon I got what I did not reckon on at all."

"Oh? What was that, Ambrose?" I asked him.

He puffed hard to keep his pipe lit, tamping the bowl with his long finger. Pulling the pipe out of his mouth, he laughed and pointed it at me. "Have you not heard from Philomena? Can you guess, Jesus?"

I had to say no. This was not anything I had met yet in Philomena's stories.

"Och, the daft beggar. He's terrified of the trombone. Detests the sound of it. Tha's why he lives at the Two Spoons."

∞

Two Spoons Café, Blackrock, Cork

"Philomena, I meh Marjorie Crowley up from Cobh, y'know." Biddy had arrived in a breathless rush, casting her scarf and coat onto an empty chair, nearly overtaking herself as she turned to slide onto her stool.

"Yes, I remember Marjorie. Gosh I haven't laid eyes on her in years." Philomena paused in whatever our conversation had been before the clattering arrival. "He died I think? Is she still at the back of the island?"

"Yes," Biddy gushed, "and you'll never guess wha'?"

"I'm sure I won't." Philomena eyed her patiently. "What?"

Biddy had ignored my presence completely; my input was not required in this instance.

"Well, y'know Francis passed away about two year ago?"

I heard Philomena mutter years, before she could bite her correcting tongue.

"She says she came ou' one morning and there was this lovely smell of bakin' bread and she hasn't a neighbour in quarter a mile of her and she jus' couldn't help wondering where the smell came from and she followed ih around to the back end of the cohhage and the old coach house and she goh such a frigh'." Biddy actually had to stop to inhale. "There was the smell and with ih this man and wha' looked like all his worldly possessions around him and wasn't he livin' in her coach house?"

"Living there? Permanently?"

"Well, two and a half year as it happens, since jus' after Francis' funeral."

"And how did she not KNOW someone was livin', living," Philomena corrected herself, "in her coach house?"

Even I was curious about that one.

"Well, she lives in one side of the cohhage and her bedroom looks ouh on the waher and her kitchen looks ouh on the waher and her sihhing room looks ouh on the waher … ."

"Bridget," Philomena spoke sharply, "You left your tee's in Wicklow, Bridget, and there's no need for it," she declared forcefully.

"Wha'? Tee hee hee," Biddy giggled. "Oh I do apologise, Philomena. Wuh-ah-ter."

"See? You can do it if you choose to. It's just a bad habit." Philomena inhaled deeply, closing her eyes, perhaps praying to the real Holy Jesus for respite.

"Anyways, she parks her car on her side and she jus' never had any reason to go back around there, so she didn't. After Francis died, she goh rid of the sheepdogs he was breedin' and never wen' in again. She's away an abou' all the time anyway as y'know, up to her sisters, away on bridge weekends an' the like."

"And who was he?"

"IS he! He's still there y'know. He was a college friend of Francis and finished up in the bank in Castletownbere."

My ears attuned to this, for this was familiar territory to me, although the rest of the story was also the extraordinary mix of Bridget McCarthy drama and the exquisite turn of the phrase of Irish life.

"He was a small loans man in the bank and his marriage fell asunder. She was bored of provincial life after the city, so she took off in the nigh' and lef' him to ih. He liked the quie' life and he took the occasional drink, which took to be the habi' as ih does for some." Biddy paused, for deep in her childhood mind was a similar tale.

"Anyways, he fell to having a drop before work in the morning and a hand of poker at nigh' and prehhy soon los' the job, fell behind in the mortgage and found himself in a sorry place. He los' everything. A neighbour puh him in a caravan on his farm buh the roof on tha' went flyin' in a gale o' wind, so he was homeless. He heard on the stree' about Francis dyin' and the neighbour was goin' to Cork to the airpor' so he bagged a lif' to geh to the funeral in Cobh. And free drink no doub'. An shur didn' he hang abou' in Cobh with some of the other college buddies noh pretending ah all, tha' he was homeless and livin' on welfare. Ih seems then he walked to Francis and Marjorie's place to see ih and jus' wen' to the coach house for a look."

"A look? How did a look turn into squatting?" Philomena was perplexed.

"Well, jus' as ih does, Philomena. Jus' did. He lay low awhile, a farmer came for the sheepdogs, Marjorie wen' off to her sister in Meath so there was no one abou'. He made ih a bih more comfortable, walked the six mile to Supervalu in town early of a morning so no one noticed him too much. Goh his dole transferred and tha' was ih. Castletownbere homeless no more." Biddy looked quite pleased with her unfolding story. "The six-mile walk was the makin' of him apparently. He gave up the drink, took to lookin' after hisself a bih more and is the new man. And Marjorie said to him, 'You never ax-ed, you must've seen me?' And HE said, 'You never ax-ed; you mus've seen ME.' An' she said, 'NO.' An' he said, 'Well then.' And tha' was ih. She said he had done it up lovely, the coach house, table an' chairs and fixed the stove. She never even saw the smoke."

"And how's it now?"

"Oh she's mad abouh him. John Brierly. He makes bread in the big crock poh in the fire and she brings him cake. An' they're all happy ouh."

"Well, I never," said Philomena.

"Well, I never either." I broke my silence. "Incredible."

"Well, I have to geh away now. I though' you'd wan' to hear Marjorie's news." And she was gone.

∞

"Y'know, Jesus, sometimes when I look at herself, Biddy McCarthy, I get this, well, 'tis hard to say, it comes across my mind, like a, hmm, like a vision."

I had no idea where this could be going, and it felt like new territory for Philomena, but I could not stop a smile. "A vision you say? Bridget is a vision all on her own. You just heard her, she doesn't require a supporting cast."

Philomena laughed, that wonderful whuh-whuh-whuh belly laugh that shook her from tummy to tip.

"A vision, like the face of Mother Mary, or a Holy Idol?" I ventured playfully.

"Oh! Lord, no. Not that at all. Maybe vision is not the word I'm needing. But it's still an odd one to me. There are two very definite, hmm, well, how would I say … ."

"Images?" I suggested.

"Yes! Images. That's it. That's the very thing. There's a man in a hat, like a bowler hat, 19th-century kinda thing; black suit, waistcoat, watch fob and chain, an' all that, similar build and shape to Bridget, but a man. A horse and buggy stop on a forest track, not unlike Rostellan woods, y'know, a crossroads, and I see him dismount the carriage with a walking stick. Then he reaches for a child in a white dress, who climbs down into his arms, then he waves the carriage on." Her hands lifted and fell as the scene replayed in her mind's eye.

"There's a big woman in the carriage, in all the garb, y'know, the big flouncy dress, hair tied back with a veil or mantilla, and two or maybe three other girls. But the one who climbed down is the smallest, maybe the youngest, and she then walks with him on the track as the carriage moves on. I can feel the look from the woman, sense they are, well, envious or jealous, those others in the carriage, and the big woman is definitely not pleased. Like he chose the child instead of her. Like he loved the child more."

"Resentful?" I suggest.

"Yes, that would be it. Yes, resentful. For the man, not the child. The man, takes my hand … ." Philomena faltered and coughed a little nervous cough. "Well, it always feels like it is my hand, although I am just the looker-on, and they stroll on, along the path." Her hand lifted from the scone dough she was shaping and waved vaguely in the direction of what she could see.

"That one, that image, has flashed into my mind for some time now. Always much the same. The other image, or I suppose you could call it a scenario, or y'know, like a movie scene." She stopped suddenly. "Oh, dear me, what on earth is wrong with me, what nonsense I am fillin' your head with, dear Jesus?"

"No really, I'd like to hear. It is quite fascinating. It is okay, Philomena. Please go on."

"It sounds such nonsense when I hear it out loud. But it always is so real. The other scene is of a horse, rearing up." Her hand waved upwards again, a trail of flour drifting from her fingers and falling like dust around her as she described what she could quite clearly see.

"Yes, rearing. A big horse, with a woman, in long black skirts. Not the same woman, another smaller one, pinched face, hard, or unhappy looking woman. Her hair is blonde, quite definitely. She's struggling to hold the horse, sometimes the scene is dark, mostly we are in a wide open field by a big old pine tree, the horse rearing, but I never hear a sound of noise from anything. I must be small, for I turn away from it and hide my face in someone's leg, the same man I always think, that's wearing the black suit in the other, em, the other scene I told you." She paused. "Even now, I see it clearly, the big horse rearing so close to me, his hooves high in front of me, as if. As if it reared, well, because of me. Because of me being there. And she is falling off then, backwards to the earth. Then there's just the noise of her hitting the earth and nothing more. It's the strangest thing, Jesus," she finished with a whisper. "It seems so real. But I know it's not a memory, or something I saw on TV or heard anywhere."

There was a moment then, a moment of returning to the reality of the kitchen, of a café in Cork, where there were no horses or trees or fallen women. She shaped the scone dough silently.

"How long have you, no, hmm, ah, okay, when do you remember first visualising these things, Philomena?"

She did not hesitate in her reply. "After my mother died. At her funeral. I looked across the grave as they were lowering her coffin and I saw Bridget, Biddy, there in black with her handbag as she does, clutched in front of her. She was upset, for my mother was very fond of her and had been so kind to her. She was such a poor waif of a thing. My mother always used to say, 'You keep an eye on that young wan, Philomena, for she's in need of us.' "

She paused again, her nose crinkling, pushing up her glasses to leave a floury trail across her cheek. "Y'know, Jesus, now that I think of it, she only said it to me, never to Wilhelmina, as if Wilhelmina needn't bother at all with her. And she didn't much either. Anyways, looking at Biddy there in the graveyard, that was the first time the boyo in black, in his bowler hat popped into my head. I remember just then thinking how odd that was and then thinking no more about it."

She paused, idly dusting flour from her hands onto the pastry board, pushing the dough shapes away, then she leaned across the counter on her elbows and, closing her eyes softly, remarked, "I can actually feel the arm about my shoulders. And the fabric of his trousers against my cheek, you know, how comforting it was. Although the rearing horse and what was happening is just silence. The first time I recall seeing that scene was after Biddy's husband went off with Shlap, Pauline O'Neill. I called up to Biddy, at her house, Green Acres, and she was just sitting there, all alone like the waif my mother said, in the darkening kitchen, with the tears running down her cheek. I had never seen Biddy cry. I didn't know she could. My heart broke for her. 'Twas like she was cryin' for everything that had ever been cast upon her and this was one more thing on the pile. She looked so lost, so alone, so … so small. That's when I first saw the rearing horse."

Philomena suddenly stood upright. "Oh! Saints preserve us. What nonsense! What on earth has come over me? I am so sorry, Jesus, for spouting such loo-la."

She walked briskly from the kitchen to the fridge, returning with a bowl of peeled apples. I knew she had lost the run of herself, this was not what she needed to be doing. The shaped dough was still on the board. She dried the apples on a clean tea towel, then noticed the half-finished scones.

"Oh dearie me, I'm all over the place. 'Tis the carvery tomorrow and I'm only half ready."

Reaching for a baking tray, I dusted it with flour and handed it to her. "Do the scones, Philomena. I'll get you the pastry for the tarts."

"Thanks, Jesus." She laughed. She stopped again and folded her arms.

"I just remembered something else strange. I remember Biddy McCarthy telling me once when we were in the Arcadia that she believed she had been a flamenco dancer. As soon as she hears that ould clickety-clack Spanish music, she knew, she felt somewhere that she knew flamenco dancing, but she also knew that she had done it before, and done it to death. I thought she was off her game and, gosh, y'know, she told me that years and years ago, when we were so young."

She trayed the scones and took them to the oven.

I paused my moment until she had pushed the oven door shut with a clang.

"Do you believe in reincarnation, Philomena?"

She looked at me directly in surprise. "Reincarnation? Like coming back after death to do it all again?"

"Yes. Well, sort of. That is sort of what I mean."

"I can't say I have given it a whole lot of thought, Jesus. In school we were told daily we would die and go straight to God in heaven, which was always up in the sky, and God was always a HE." She threw her eyes to the ceiling. "And that YOU'D be there at his right hand, waiting for me."

We laughed at yet another of Philomena's casual insinuations that I am the real Jesus.

"No, seriously."

"Seriously? Well, I suppose it's possible." She eyed me cautiously. "I can feel you have something to say about it."

"Well, try this for starters. Just say we live many lifetimes. We regenerate time and time and time again as new beings, many different forms over many lifetimes. New beings, yet our soul stays constant. We choose a new storyline, a new stage for that story every time. And sometimes we keep the same players in our story. Or we might change gender. Or species. We might be a dog for a while. Or a Queenie cat."

"Oh!" she exclaimed. "Wouldn't that be the life? I could do that one with me eyes closed."

"We learn each time around from the others in our story, for it is only ever about love. We keep doing it until we learn to accept our self, ourselves as children of the Light and die to what is sometimes called Christ Consciousness. Being one with God, whatever we perceive that to be." I paused, knowing she was still with me, although her busy hands were elsewhere. "I think the scenes you visualise are past-life, and the connection to Bridget, which you feel so clearly, may well be that you have shared previous journeys together. It doesn't have to be male or female, for the soul is neither, just a convenient way of recognising another soul. It is the essence of us that is important, not the shape or size. We wear the physical form."

She laughed, "Whuh, whuh, whuh. Do you think I could give back half of my physical form, please? Oh, dear Jesus, I don't know what to make of all that."

I shrugged. "Don't try to make anything of it. If the roles in a previous incarnation were for argument's sake, Bridget as your man in the suit—say your father, offering comfort and strength and protection to you, say the child—then it kinda makes sense that the roles may be reversed in this incarnation and these are the qualities that you offer to Bridget."

"Thus the divide between my role in looking after her and Wilhelmina not? The connection wasn't with Wilhelmina?"

"Yes, maybe. And you then have a different connection with the Wilhelmina soul, most especially if you were twinned with her at birth."

The kitchen was silent. The oven hummed loudly, wafting heat and scent of baking scones. Philomena rolled pastry thoughtfully.

"Our lives are just learning. Offering love and kindness to others. Nothing matters except love. The rest is just white noise."

"So when I had the feeling with Michael. Y'know, that I felt the child I miscarried was him and then he came back to me again?"

"Yes. He was choosing his new incarnation. You as his mother, Ambrose as his father, his siblings, the youngest by a biggish gap. The place for his soul to start a new journey of learning."

"And then he fell on the lollipop when he was six and damaged his palate, so his speech is affected? These aren't just accidents? This is also his new storyline?"

"Yes. Perhaps he needs to listen more and talk less this time 'round. Perhaps he needs to speak only to those who love him enough and will understand him?"

"Oh Lordie, Jesus. An' he's with Shy Sheila nearly ten years now and she hardly says much. That's a lot to take in of a Wednesday morning."

She pulled the scones out and closed the oven door, wiping beads of sweat from her face with the tea towel. I moved the scones to cooling racks, taking the hot trays to ready for the tarts. Philomena was carefully lifting pastry to cover the apples.

"Lifetimes? How many do we have to do, Jesus?"

"Lifetimes. Until we have learned all the lessons and gathered all the bits of our souls together, then we see the Light."

I paused, knowing the next step was difficult, remembering how long it had taken me to grasp it. And sowing the first seed lightly was important. "Of course, we have a misconception also of time, Philomena. We like to think of it as linear, chronological; whereas, it is probably just like a big spider's web, around and around. You and Bridget and Ambrose and Michael and anyone else, mother, father, aunts, Sean, Franco, the Pope, John F. Kennedy, we might all be doing it in other lifetimes at the same time as this one? It could be all one big huge stage with billions of dramas all the time. Bits of ourselves everywhere, rotating around like a disco ball. One minute a Pope, in the same minute a pauper."

"Oh Jesus! Dear Jesus, that's enough now. If the apples in this tart could talk tomorrow, you and I would be carted off by the men in the white coats."

"Philomena, dear Philomena, you could always count on your soul mate, Biddy McCarthy, to rescue you."

"Maybe it's her turn to ride the big horse?"

With that we heard, "Coo-ee, coo-ee" at the green gate to the back yard. Patch barked, a Jack Russell stream of disturbance. I poked Philomena's arm.

"See? She heard you. She knows you were talking about her."

Philomena laughed, a little flustered, as she righted her persona to a recognisable version of Philomena in charge of her kitchen in Blackrock, instead of Philomena lost in a Discussion on Reincarnation.

"Now for God's sake," she whispered through gritted teeth, "don't be tellin' her a WORD of it."

"Oh Lordie, Philomena, where would I begin?"

"How do you KNOW this, Jesus?"

"I know. I just know, Philomena." I looked at her. "Rosa said I was born knowing." Biddy had been and gone, a whoosh of clatter and chatter en route to the bus stop, the lingering breeze of her perfumed presence still swirling amongst the baking aroma. "I feel God, Divinity, the Universe, whatever it is or you name it, in my every breath. And my job this time around is to help others to know this, too."

"It's like you speak the truth to my soul. I am blessed to share your company."

I laughed. Philomena smiled, lifting the tarts from the oven to the cooling tray. She paused, looking straight at me, a wisp of curl on her cheek, a bead of sweat from baking heat on her brow. She spoke softly and quietly.

"No, Jesus, that wasn't a bit of craic. I meant it as a statement. I am blessed to share my time with you. I KNOW this. I just feel this every moment I am with you this last twenty years."

My eyes filled with tears. Unbidden, right from the river of my heart.

"Jesus?"

"Yes, Philomena?"

"Do you know anything about cooking apple tarts?"

"Not a whole lot. Not as much as you do."

"I forgot the sugar. 'Tis more than prayers we'll need tomorrow."

∞

"Philomena, did I ever tell you what Abuelo Sean told me about the birth of your mother?"

"My own mother? Oh no! No, you have never told me that."

"He was whittling away at a stick telling me about your grandfather Michael living in Wales, before he was married. He took Abuelo Sean there you know, when he was nine or ten years old. The twins had passed on and your grandmother was pregnant with Mary, your mother."

"Yes, the twins only lived 'til they were thirty or so months, my mother said. A boy and a girl, Patrick and Anna."

"Oh! I have never heard them named. Abuelo always just said 'the twins.' They lived to thirty-three months to the day, he said. He and his brother Jerry were so excited to be hmm, he phrased it, em, 'getting' a new baby from their mother. They talked for months whether it would be a boy or a girl and what would they do with a girl? She would be no good for football or marbles or 'the field.' I had to ask him what 'the field' meant, and he laughed and said it was their playground, the big field behind the village to the edge of the woods, with the caves underneath through a small hole in the ground."

"That would be heaven to a couple of young boys. I know my lads lived and breathed in our field like that."

"They worked through a list of names, mostly the ones they knew from school. He told me your grandmother had a story about one of her own aunts, who was the last of a line of nine or ten children, or 'chil-der-en' as Sean used to say. When the aunt was born, the older girls were in a summer school in Switzerland and they received a telegram to say they had a new sister, Noreen. They immediately telegrammed back home to say no one could possibly be called 'Noreen' and that she should be 'Leonora Beatrice' after one of their school friends from London."

Philomena laughed, "And she was! Christened Leonora Beatrice that is, although I can tell you she was only ever known to anyone as Noreen all right."

"Your mother was born in the night hours, or as Sean put it 'the cock's head still in his wing,' so that was before dawn. He remembered running from the room he slept in with Jerry, and your grandfather sitting in the front room eating a boiled egg. 'There'll be no school today. You have a sister,' was what he said to Abuelo Sean. 'You may see her when you have fed the hens and milked Bess. Get Jerry.' That was the birth announcement. With that the man went back to his newspaper and egg."

"Oh!" Philomena was oddly nonverbal. "Oh!" she said again. Then her voice cracked a little as she cleared her throat.

"You don't ever expect to hear such a thing about your own parent. Somehow they were there forever, or their life as an infant or baby is rarely recalled, not to mention the hour of their birth. Oh, that caught me a bit. She was such a dear."

∞

Rostellan 1990s

I wandered many long hours in the east Cork locality, poking down lanes, following old tracks through hedgerows laden with May hawthorn blossom, marshy fields cloaked in June flag iris, frosty mornings in the Rostellan woods, across the fields past the tall pine tree that reminds me of Ambrose—long and straight with an outward facing limb that could just be pointing northward to the back waters of Cork harbour, like a Scotsman gesticulating with his pipe. In the spring, the beech lane is bright with the sap-green young leaves, the flurry and business of nesting birds, sea birds calling to their landward cousins from the oozing and sucking mud-flats. I made this my haunt, my home of content.

Sometimes I walk the old trail that once was the main carriageway from the ruined garden walls to the farm estate at the edge of Saleen village, a distance of two or so kilometres. I allow my wandering mind to conjure up Philomena's black-coated gentleman in the horse and buggy—hie-hieing his pony along the metalled lane, busy on his business, managing a huge house and farm and walled gardens bursting with enviable life. He is checking his watch fob and geeing on his charge—truppety, trup, trup, trup through wildflower meadows. I pause under the aged towering pine I have christened Albert, now standing alone between farm fields, forgotten by travellers yet, I like to think, remembering them all.

There is only silence now, birds and trees and crops in the fields. I see the ruined remains of the corn mill, forlorn at the field edge, the carefully curving stone-walled avenue overgrown in elderflower, burdened in mosses and ferns, no more carts and ponies tripping along the way. Are these more of my ancestors' walls? I chastise myself at the absurdity of thinking my grandfathers could have built every stone wall on the estate. The ruins of the corn mill floats on the sound of a dozen or so beehives shielded within her walls, a million tiny wings replenishing life in minute heartbeats of labour. The spirit messengers of the Celts, between the world we know and the otherworld. The old farmyard has long been converted to a dwelling house and gardens laid over the cobbled yard. In the corner of the field Tobar Lisheen springs and gurgles with constant watery life from the earth below.

I follow the old line that signified the border of the estate lands, to the holed and boggy marsh lapping the waters edge. Walls, walls, walls, I hear Abuelo Sean when I was too young and too Spanish to understand the ways of the Anglo-Irish, "Wallin' in what was theirs, wallin' the rest of us out." Leaning against a fraction of the miles of limestone in eastern Cork, I understand the verb walling—to wall, described by Mr. Onions, to enclose, exclude, protect, defend, guard, keep, shield, shelter, encircle, enfold, encompass, surround. I remember myself once being 'atop' a fifteen-hun-der-ed-year-old stone circle in west Kerry, one-and-a-half metre thick walls in a solid circle of protection. Walling in, walling out.

Along the southern shore, the relentless passage of time and sea have scattered the cut limestone blocks of walls amongst the pink hues of sandstone, leaving a neat metre-wide row of footings in the soil, socketed like "all those perfectly, functionally laid teeth" Dr. Zhao had drawn my attention to, not so long ago.

"Stones are the bones," he had told me. "Bones carry the message of who we are. Trees are moving for us, water is flowing for us, it is in us, in all of nature. The elementals are not inferior to us, they are us, we are them. Our mistake is to think we are better. We are the guests not the keepers."

At the boathouse remains by the football pitch, I imagine my 23-year-old grandfather meeting his lovely Hazel, and the intuitive, heart-breaking knowledge that it could never be between them, the mason and the maid. The pause in the moments of their lives, when they had no knowledge of their blueprint, that I knew now, long after the event.

The lightning wheee of a calling starling is followed by the staccato burst of clicks and whistles.

"I was a radio-operator in the Merchant Navy, Jesus," Timmy tells me. "Dot dot dash dash dot. I try to understand what the starlings might be sayin' to me."

"And does it make any sense, Timmy?" I ask, laughing.

"Ho-ho, as much as anything," he cheers. "More than most."

I am sitting on the low stone wall by the causeway, looking towards the ruined estate remains amongst the trees. I know from the old maps that there was an aviary, the Schoolmaster's Meadow, a boathouse or two, some workers' cottages. "What do you remember of the estate?" I ask him.

"Oh shur, the same as most. The formal gardens, the paths for perambulating. The walled gardens were still in operation, beautiful they were, full of produce. I grew up at the coast, remember, and that's only three or four miles away. Shur that seemed like another planet. My father, Lord rest him," he paused to cross himself and he made a fuller hand of the process than any of the ladies I had witnessed, "was born at a little place called Bun Falla, overhanging the sea there west of Guileen pier. 'Tis all ruins now. I useta walk that way a lot, cut across to the big house, the Roche place at Trabolgan. Miles of cliffs and grass and gorse. Lovely." Timmy stopped to muse, scratching at his stubbled cheek with the top of his stick. "I'd only have been coming over this way when I was older. On me bike, I suppose.

The wheeling gulls filled his pause.

"We'd go to the apple-house and talk with Henry Roche; he'd always slip us a few apples or pears for our pockets. The bigwigs were all gone by the 1930s, 'twas starting to fall asunder, y'know, after the war, the Depression, then all the change that came with Independence. Land Acts took away their acreage and without that, they had no income. They knocked the whole place flat in '44. I was away at that bloody ould war." He clicked his tongue against his teeth, nodding.

"The first fella there cleared away an old graveyard, y'know, over by the football field there, by the shore. Reads 1721 on a marker stone somewhere if I remember right?" Timmy pointed his stick northwards. "He were cursed then by an old lady, local here to Farsid, whose son was buried there. She told him their lineage would die out, no son would be born, the crows would not nest in Rostellan. The same boyo had four sons and four daughters, so he laughed at the old woman's curse. But, faith an' didn't they lose four sons and three daughters before he himself went. He left a deaf mute, Mary, and she had only a daughter, and so it went all the way through the 1800s. No male heir. Heaps of crows now though," he grinned.

I imagined their ghosts, the pomposity, the his-story of their lives, their loves in this place.

" 'Twas the fella in the mid-1800s did a lot of the work, planting, laying gardens, making the shape on it. I suppose that's when all the walls started too. Big three-storey house, y'know. I have a photo somewhere." He chewed on his lip, stroking his chin with long accordion fingers.

"One of his four lassies married the Earl of Bantry, took off to the West. His woman was a big stout old trout by all accounts, and y'know it was John's father told me that. I suppose he got it from his old man. Isn't that the way with stories?"

I had a curious moment, recalling Philomena's recent tale: just that, a large woman and two or three other girls in the buggy, stopped in the woods. What will we ever know?

"It was strange here, you know, after John left." Timmy stood up to straighten his aging joints. "C'mon, I have to move every so often or I'm afraid I'll be stuck in the same spot," he grimaced as he rose. "His brother was gone to the guards but the two girls were here with old Michael and Emily, John's mother."

I must have looked surprised. I had never to that moment asked her name. Abuelo Sean had called her an O'Keefe girl.

"Yes, Emily and Michael, so your great-grandparents, am I right there?"

"Yes, Timmy, my mother's grandparents. She would not have met them. It was '77 when she first came to Ireland, after Abuelo Sean passed away. She met Philomena in Cork and we stayed here with Frances. Philomena's mother, Mary, came from the city to see us here. We were only here a few days and someone took us off to Beara, Castletownbere. All I remember is a constant stream of names and faces that were mostly unpronounceable and English that was nothing like the English I had been taught to speak. I had three weeks of babbling sounds."

Timmy laughed and nodded. "That was where your folks landed in East Cork from, way back when. Walk a few steps with me and I'll loosen meself out." He stretched his torso away from his long legs, pulled a paper bag of bread crusts from his pocket and shared them out across the wall into the orchestra of sea birds. The heron eyed us cagily, the snowy egret cautiously stayed in the shadows.

"My own father was a Munster Fusilier in Gallipoli, Jesus, yes indeed."

"First World War, right?"

"Oh yes, yes, the worst world war. Not that any of them have been kind to anyone except the bomb makers. Heavy industry is the only thing sure to gain from the spoils of war."

From the recesses of my mind I hear The Temptations Vietnam protest song, 'War.' What was it good for, absolutely nothing. Tears for poor mothers, while their sons lose their lives.

He paused his walk, flicking at dog pooh with the end of his stick. "Aren't they just awful leaving their dog's mess behind them? Can't they just flick it into the edge or the hedgerow with a bit o' stick? Leave it to the crawly creatures what loves it."

We ambled onwards. "That's the greenshank there," he pointed to the mudflats. "See how it dashes about like a mad thing getting his food?"

He stopped again and sat on the low wall. "Yes, Gallipoli. He served with Willie Cosgrove from Whitegate, him that got the VC. Went to school with him. Cosgrove joined up before him, my old man stayed home on the farm, then got married an' all that. My ould fella was new to the regiment when they were shipped off to Turkey. Your great-grandfather signed up too, as far as I remember the story?"

"Yes, Abuelo Sean told me he took 'the King's shillin,' is what he said. He never told me where he served, I don't know if he knew? He was only just born. He did say the same man never came back?"

Timmy nodded sagely. "My mother would have said the same thing. She was carrying me when he left and already had three more. 'Twas a fright to God, Jesus. Thirty-four-thousand dead there, Turks an' the Allies and lots of them weren't English at all but Commonwealth lads. Shur a fella couldn't be right in the head after he witnessed that. My father got home 'cos he lost his left eye and a scrape off his skull. Never quite walked right again but it was enough to get him invalided home. He picked up the reins and went off ploughing immediate like. Said he'd never leave again." Timmy laughed. "My mother said she'd have to send him away or swap him for better if he didn't learn how to plough a straight furrow with one eye."

He raised his stick to greet a neighbour passing in a car. "Cosgrove retired home here in '36. We'd have met him regular at the Prendergast's, the old Corkbeg Hotel, playin' music. He an' my ould fella would have drank a beer together and tried not to talk about it all. Cosgrove didn't last long tho', his injuries got to him." Timmy nodded. "Cosgrove used to say, 'They were brave men, the Turks, and should never have been fightin' for dirty tricksters such as the Germans.' "

He stood to walk again. "Then I did my bit too. By '40, I suppose, the war was full on and I joined up with the Merchant Navy. My two brothers were already gone. 'Twas the breaking of my mother's heart that stopped me at home awhile. I was a farrier here, you know? Horses all my life. But the horses dwindled after the first war, machines were starting to do the farm-work, then the Depression. So I signed up. 'Twas aisy when you lived here," he laughed. "There was always action on the harbour." He pointed out towards Haulbowline and Cobh.

"Neutral, my arse! We were smothering in Brits and Yanks movin' about. The nasty U-boats were still the problem in the channel, knocking out the supply lines to the Brits. Same as first war." He nodded, remembering. "The sea didn't suit me at all at all, but I did love the radios. Loved the way of them, the simplicity. The brilliance really, y'know? Just a collection of useless parts that together made an incredible whole."

I was reminded of Dr. Zhao with his gyroscope: Simple, but so much knowledge, so many places to be useful. "Oh I must bring my father to you, Timmy. He is a naval man also."

"Oh aye? Spanish then?" he asked.

I shook my head. "Oh! If it could be so simple. He isn't Spanish, but he did work with the Spanish Navy. He trained with the British Royal Navy in Spain, then also worked with the Americans when they took over the base in Cadiz in the 1950s."

Timmy laughed. "Sounds complicated, eh?" He paused on his perambulation then turned around to make his way back. "But that's the way of stories. How they get legs to carry you through life. One of my mates, a fiddle player from Ballynacorra, was in Haulbowline in Dan Fitzpatrick's boatyard, and he got me over there one Sunday after playing at the East Ferry dance. He wanted to show me what he was working on. He was in this workshop with a whole vessel radio unit disassembled around him and madly excited, tellin' me how he was goin' to put it together again." Timmy smiled, resting on his stick.

"There wasn't a naval service in Ireland then, the Brits had left the forts to the Free State in '38, so anyone still here kinda fell between the stools. There was a real mishmash of goin's-on in the old Naval Base, a bit o' this and a bit o' that, lot of vandalism after the Brits sailed away. They were still talkin' the talk up in Dublin about what they'd do to protect the country now that Dev had declared us neutral. We could hardly be relying on the Brits to mind us now." He laughed again, "No siree! Can't really have our cake and eat it."

He paused, his stick fiddling at a few loose stones in the path, his brilliant old mind running across the spines of his memories, neatly stacked and shelved, selecting what to recall. "There was the harbour authorities, of course, and a coastal watch service operating from Cobh, an' they needed to make decisions right quick 'cos things were really hotting up on the mainland. They needed to sort out our national defence. But that ain't aisy in a new country. So me mate asked if it was okay that I helped him and that was the start of it. I worked with the cleaning up of the dockyard, clearing rubbish, painting an' that kinda thing, and in return I learned the workings of the radio inside out. Dan gave me the runabout on all things marine. He had done his time in the first war. Then there was a Marconi set at the coast guard station in Corkbeg, an' Battersby kept me by his side so I could learn the use of them like, the daily use."

I remained silent while he reminisced.

"You know the road down to the old Coast guard?"

"I'm not sure that I do?"

"You've walked to the fort? Carlisle? Well, Davis it is, as it become, once the English left. Just before the gas-bottling plant, down there to the right, all the way down to the shoreline was the coast guard house. 'Tis in ruins now. An' there must've been a hundred steps up an' down to it," he grinned. "I was a fit young man, I can tell you. All that runnin' about and miles on me bike."

We walked on, both of us raising our hands occasionally to salute passing cars we recognised. We passed the Doc's house and I waved in case Abuelita Rosa might have been looking out.

"Soon enough they were desperate for anyone with radio knowledge to serve, so I went to the Merchant Navy. Did me basic training on the Sharpness Canal in Gloucester. We had quite a time of it, three months on-board training, hell for leather." He stopped again, scratched his head, then straightening his back and throwing his stick upwards, he sang to the sky:

"*Oh they sent me off to join the Vindicatrix,*
And they told me it was … something, something … it.
Hmm, let me see … here, here, I have it!

The Quartermaster shouted to the Boatswain,
And the Boatswain showed us where to store our kit.
And then it goes …
We went into the scuppers and spewed up all our suppers.
And wished to Christ we'd never seen the sea.
Ho ho! Oh Lordie me, where did I dredge that up from? That were
what? Fifty-something years ago?"

"That's your naval school song, Timmy?"

"Oh yes, yes. We used to go across the docks to a Seaman's Mission
and one of the lads played piano and I had me box. It was great
fun. Oh 'twere hard to keep away from the ladies, Jesus. Oh yes."
He smiled a little and hummed the tune to himself. "I carried
Eleanor Lucy's picture in my pocket all the time to remember that
I was a well-spoken-for man. It would not be right to make a mess
of things because I could."

He set forth on the path again, back to the wall where we started,
opposite his little house. The crewing seabirds had moved across
the tidal flat to perch in a regimented row, on the knuckled remains
of the sea wall.

"I got turfed onto an oil tanker carrying fuel down the North
Sea. The Danes and Norwegians minded us a bit and we seemed
to scrape through any real trouble. Then I went from the south
coast, Portsmouth to North Africa, on a supply ship and carrying
some troops. We were hustled and bombed off the Channel but
managed to get south to Gibraltar, into the Med. Bit o' runnin'
about there for a few months. Then more troop-carrying trips,
back to Blighty."

"Blighty?"

He stopped and looked at me, inclining his head. "Blighty? Never
heard that one eh?"

"Can't say I have, Timmy, no."

"Came from the British soldiers in India, I believe. Probably from the first war, fellas always wanting to get home to Blighty. So I suppose it came from one of the Hindu words, perhaps?"

I made a mental note to ask Mr. Onions.

"I loved it, Jesus. I loved the excitement like most of the young bloods, but oh, I could live without the sea."

I smiled at him. "Abuelo Sean was sick all the way from Cork to Cadiz. They tied him to the deck eventually and gave him something to do, splicing rope he said."

"That's right, I remember he wasn't fond of the tide unless he was looking at it. I had an incendiary device land in the doorway of the radio room. We were often the first target, to shut us up, if you like. I tap-tapped away in my headphones with one eye on this thing, thinking that's my lot now, when one of me mates—an' I can't say ever which one—picked it up and hurled it overboard." He shrugged and laughed. "Coulda been a dud, of course."

He waved across the road, where Julia was at the door. "Hie! Here, Julia!" She waved to us and disappeared inside again. "That's me lunchtime, me thinks. Will you sup with us?"

"Thank you, but no, Timmy. I am collecting Mamá from the school at noon and taking her to town."

"Oh, fair enough." He stood watching the birdbath in the muddy channel, wagtails darted from wall to water. "Anyways, I went ashore after that, to the radio station at Portishead. Somerset that is, close enough to Bristol. It was mad there." He stopped. "Full on battleground. Long, long days, catch a nap in the back, back to the chair, always listening. We put up some mess tents in the summer to snooze. 'Twas easier than returning to digs. Real short-staffed we were; most operators had gone to sea or had lost their lives." He shook his head. " 'Twas insane really, Jesus. We were right on the front line of everything—merchant ships, aircraft, anything crossing the Irish Sea or the Channel. We could see it all flying over our heads too." His hand passed above his hairline in an upwards motion. "If I thought life in East Cork was dull, I got my dose of thrills, I can tell you."

"That's what Abuelo Sean said when he landed in Spain," I recalled. "If he thought life was dull in Rostellan, he got what he wished for, but he should have asked that it was not so far away."

"Even Somerset was miles away in wartime, Jesus. I had left me missus here at home, with Julia and one on the way. Her mother moved in with her, I didn't get back on leave 'til '43, then I was gone, back again to Portishead. I eventually came home to the farm in '45, just before it all ended for the Nazis anyway. My father passed away, so I took to the plough. When things settled down after the war, I went to our own coast guard service. Sometimes then I'd go to the radio and wireless school in Tivoli, there near the city, to teach. I liked that. And I'd shoe the occasional horse, if I was asked, for ould Bill Aherne in the forge. So between it all, I was not idle. We were not idle, no siree." He clicked his tongue against his teeth. "No siree, plenty to do stayin' alive and feeding the five. I took the missus back to Somerset on holidays a couple of times. We'd take a house by the coast, Burnham-on-Sea or Highbridge, walk the strand, watch kiddies on donkey rides, eat ice-cream, fish 'n' chips in a packet for twenty pence. That kinda thing." He nodded to himself. "Just getting on the Innisfallen across the Irish Sea was wild enough excitement after the war."

The starlings rose in a chattering flock from the telephone wires, circled and wheeled in an oscillating, shape-shifting pattern of black fleck against pale blue sky. The wind picked up, carrying their sound.

"What are they saying to you, Timmy?" I laughed.

He stood slowly, leaning on his stick, then stretching his left arm skywards, he shouted, "For what, Jesus? For what? What was it all about? For what? All that blood an' bombs."

The starlings rolled over the flooding tide, coming to rest with synchronised military precision on the wires above us, shuffling and clicking to one another. "For what? For what? For what? Oh, oh 'tis hot! Tim says for what?"

Timmy smiled. "They're sayin' We coulda told you, we coulda told you, we know what to do. Idiots, idiots, silly idiots, are all of you." He pulled his jacket close around him and made to cross the road.

I stood up to take my leave, then called to him. "Timmy?" He stopped and turned, smiling.

"They say it's bacon for your lunch now and don't be slow."

He gave a big cheer with a wave of his stick and was gone.

∞

I followed Timmy's directions to the old coast guard station, choosing an overcast Sunday morning, depositing my bicycle in the hedgerow by the sports grounds. The road climbed slowly, devoid of traffic at an early hour. The tree-covered hillside below me sloped to the inner harbour of Whitegate, more nooks and crannies of sea and tide, making individual parts into the whole of Cork harbour. Crossing a bridge over the ugly pipelines of crude oil as they snaked uphill from their storage tanks for refining, even industry had sunk into the landscape, yellow ragwort and rosebay willow herb seeding in every crack in the earth. The woods were dark and dense, thick ivy and blackberry underfoot, unforgiving to the stranger. I drop down to the shoreline mid-tide, startling the picking gulls and turnstones. The low-hanging branches sweep to the muddy residue, testing my agility to crawl or clamber on my journey. It is quiet and strange; yet if I turn around, I am still within distance of the village, the movement of traffic, busyness, business, Sunday newspapers from Day's shop after early morning Mass.

In a moment I am there—the protruding arm of a forgotten slipway, the eroded evidence of a derelict life. Nothing but concrete lumps and twisted metal remains, half a water boiler rusted into the shaly shore. I climb onto the scarred and pitted floor of a has-been home, a place of tap-tapping and wireless listening, a place of uniformed punctuality, military precision, shattered and scattered and gone. Pushing through the laurel bushes and obvious lines of previously well-tended gardens, I kick and scratch at the debris underfoot to find Timmy's steps, moss-covered, leaf-littered, shapely worn limestone flags. Remnants of an era, climbing high to the road.

I sit *atop,* as Abuelo Sean had verbalised, remains of other lives, and remember Thay in Plum Village not so very long ago, touching the earth, reminding ourselves daily of our presence on this soil. "Every footstep kisses the earth, mindful breathing is my anchor."

A herring gull glides idly by, pink legs tucked high, a turn of the head and she nearly asks me: What are you doing there? Above me, in a piney knot, a couple of magpies argue fiercely, noisily exchanging their views. I pick my way uphill through the forest to the refinery access road and thence to the gates of the military fort. The yawning chasm of a man-made moat to separate the people from the soldiers. Hazel's Fort, shaped by the limestone arch and secured behind heavy iron gates. Military buildings of another era, watchtowers, sentry huts, neat rows of barracks. There is no more to be seen by the public eye. Below me, Sunday yachts gather in the harbour, the steward's boat laying the course within my reach, should I care to extend my hand. I lounge against the grassy bank as another day unfolds.

∞

Cork-Swansea Ferry

I was at the deck rail, my preferred place of travel on the Swansea ferry MS Julia, high up by the helipad from where I could see all my home, as much as I could call one place home. The ferry passes Cobh on the left—"port," I hear my father correct me, and swings due south following the flashing green channel markers. From my vantage point, I see the tolling bells of the great cathedral chime the hour before the Great Island drifts away and the farther-most reaches of the eastern harbour are before me, the trampled paths of the Rostellan shoreline, the glint of early light on the Jamesbrook windows, the slapping of halyards on the masts of Aghada pier. We are then passing the long stack of the power generating station, then Whitegate village nestling in the lee shore. This view is quickly obliterated by the storage tanks of crude oil, and I am looking directly where I now know there was a coast guard station, where Timmy watched the workings of a Marconi wireless all those years ago. We pass under the bulk of the fort, the little service pier and barred entrance doors above the shore-line, inaccessible to the ordinary person. I imagine ancient footsteps on the ramp, orders shouted, orders repeated, the hustle and shuffle of men under officers. My grandfather Samuel Hadrian knew it, my father knew it, Timmy knew it, Philomena's friend Jack, countless service men and women of every creed and culture—all knew the voice of command. I imagined that Saturday morning when Patcheen Mike found a shapeless lump floating on the tide under this immense construction, a voice of command overseeing the recovery, and how the world changed around her demise. Suddenly, I am accidentally jostled out of my musings by another passenger.

"Oh, I am terribly sorry. I do apologise." His accent was English and I am not very good at regional differentiations.

"Not at all."

He was holding the rail with one hand and from the other swung a large pair of binoculars. "That was dashed clumsy of me. I was looking at that old fort. I found there is so little to be learned about it anywhere."

"Yes, it belongs to the Department of Defence, so it is probably hard to find information about it. How much do you know?"

"Oh, not very much. I know it's old and British built. I'm not a history buff really. Well, I suppose I am but in a different facet. My work is geology."

"Ah! Yes, British built. I can tell you a little more about it. My parents live nearby, and right now I must concentrate on looking out for them, for they will be standing there by the lighthouse wall and waving me farewell."

I pointed south towards the nestled crescent of coastguard houses giving way to the terrace of pilot houses, leading to the beaming light of Roches Point. The fort had passed us, the beach of White Bay empty, save for a solitary soul throwing sticks for dogs. Then I saw them, dressed for the early chill, outlined against the stark white of the lighthouse boundary wall. More ancient walls—1778, my historian friend Willie told me—ancient walls built to keep out foes, to protect friends. I waved furiously, tears in my eyes. Greeting from a distance had become a regular occurrence of our lives, my leetle family waving and blowing keeses as I sailed by, setting off on yet another journey. I continued until we were past the black rocks, the last anchorage of the Titanic in 1912, the foundering of the Celtic in '28.

"Now," I said, turning to the passenger, "you have my full attention."

"How lovely was that? Splendid! I hope you don't mind but I seemed to find myself waving as well. Do give them my apologies."

"Oh! They will be delighted to have caused such a fuss at this early hour."

"Well, I am on a personal quest, really. We sailed in two weeks ago and I spotted the old fort, then I did manage to get there yesterday, as far as one can."

"Yes, to the locked gates near the gas-bottling plant?" My curiosity was truly piqued. "It's not usually on a holiday bucket list. Are you a fort fanatic? Or a military fan?"

"Good God! Neither. You see my grandmother spent some years there as a girl, until they left in 1938."

My throat did actually go dry. I had always thought this was a novelist's metaphor and not a real sensation, but now I know. The familiar prickling at the nape of my neck and all sound seemed to leave my head, except a faint ringing in my left ear. "Ward?" I barely asked him.

He looked surprised. "Why yes! She was Priscilla Ward. Good God! However did you know that?"

I felt slightly faint, lightheaded; perhaps this is sea-sickness? I looked at him directly. "Her sister was Hazel. She drowned a short time before they left the fort."

He paled slightly. "Ah!"

"Oh! I am sorry." It was my turn to apologise. "I shouldn't have been so abrupt. You didn't know?"

"Well, yes and no. I knew she had died tragically but not that she had drowned. She travelled back to England in a coffin."

I had somewhere wondered about that or whether she had been

buried locally but had failed to query Timmy or anyone who might have remembered. "I truly am sorry. You asked me how I knew? The tragic tale involves my now-deceased Irish grandfather. But you should probably first tell me what you know? By the way," I extended my hand, "I am Jesus Josephus and my grandfather was John James O'Sullivan of Rostellan."

He looked at me in the way many do on hearing Jesus Josephus. I had chosen Jee-sus not Hay-Zoos, for somehow I felt this tale was all Irish and English.

He shook my hand firmly. "I am very pleased to meet you Jesus Josephus. My name is Lawrence. Lawrence Morris."

Oh, dear God! was my thought. Oh, dear God! Where will you take me in the next ten hours? I could only smile at the Universe and I most definitely heard an old Corkman pulling on a concertina. "Look what I found for you now, Jesus."

∞

"I do not know the story, Jesus," Lawrence was saying, "for many years would have passed before my appearance on the scene, although I knew there was something tragic." He paused and I saw that he was recalculating everything he had known around the event. "In the way of many families, it was not spoken of. My grandmother has lived a full and interesting life before me and for as long as I have known her to this day."

"Your grandmother is still alive?" I asked of him with some surprise, for I occasionally forget that Abuelo Sean was still reasonably young when his musical lungs cigarilloed away.

"Oh very much alive! Shall we say hello?"

"Alive and here on this boat?" I was truly astonished. This was certainly an elbowing from the Universe and I hear the opening strains of one of Mamá's double jigs, "Ship in Full Sail."

"Yes, indeed, and probably tucked up in her cabin."

It was not until later years that I would succumb to long hours of travel and reserve a cabin on each journey across the Irish Sea. In this instance I was cabin-less, flapjacks and egg mayonnaise sandwiches furnished by Mamá, along with my laptop, stowed in my daypack. I was completely thrown at this turn of events, having thought myself well-attuned to the nuances of the flow of life. We descended from the lofty heights of the top deck, to continue the unfolding story.

"Granny?" Lawrence paused and knocked at a cabin door before using his key card. "Granny? We have a visitor."

A vision in a pale pink hoodie sat upright in a bunk bed. "Is it the purser or cabin staff? I'm having difficulty with the Internet connection. Surely we should have on-board Wi-Fi the first hour at sea? I wanted to see my Scrabble score." She raised her eyes to look at her grandson, who grinned at me then glanced heavenwards.

"No, Granny, not the purser."

"Oh hello. Who have you met, Lawrence?" Her voice was slow and rich, thoughtful in her every word.

"My name is Jesus Josephus," I answered, stepping into the tidy space in which I felt the extent of my six-foot height.

"Pleased to meet you, Jesus, or is it Jesús? Are you Spanish?" She laid her iPad aside to extend her hand in greeting.

"Yes, absolutely, but I have travelled enough to be either, and am usually Jesus when visiting my parents in Ireland."

"Splendid. I am Priscilla. How did you meet my grandson? He would have been combing the coastline through binoculars for rock striations I might guess?"

I mentally calculated her age, based on the story of Sean and Hazel. She must be near her mid-eighties; and I pause in my wonderment as to how I am to introduce our connection, for it will point to a painful past.

I take her hand in mine and quietly say, "Priscilla, I apologise for the seeming informality. Lawrence introduced his family name as Morris, but I do not know if that is your married name? I would usually address you as Mrs. or Ma'am."

"How fabulously mannerly!" she smiled warmly. "Mrs. Kendal is my married name, and Priscilla is just fine."

"Lawrence was looking at the Fort of Carlisle as we sailed past, and my family live nearby."

She nodded, looked directly at me and, leaving her hand in mine, replied, "I lived there for a while as a young girl. I am sure Lawrence told you this?" I nodded my assent to which she chuckled gaily, saying, "It was nearly a thousand years ago now! Did you know someone locally from that time?"

There was only the truth to be told. "John James O'Sullivan of Rostellan was my grandfather."

Her eyes closed, her hand stayed motionless in mine. I pressed my left hand onto the back of hers to reassure her that there are only stories between us and from them, hopefully, understanding and friendship.

"He went to Spain on a boat, didn't he? After, after it happened." Her eyes fluttered open, her hand remained still.

"Yes, landed in Cadiz and never returned to Cork. My mother, María, was born there and so was I. My parents now live in East Cork, in Rostellan."

Her eyes widened at the mention of Rostellan, gauging my honesty, my intent. "Oh! The lovely big house. It's all gone now, I believe?"

I nodded.

"I drove there only once again, with my husband, you know. We had a holiday in Ireland sometime after the war. We started in Rostellan and East Cork, but I couldn't bear it. I couldn't go back there. We spent most of the time in the Southwest, and I never ventured again."

"We stayed in Ballymaloe the last two nights," Lawrence added from behind me. "It was always something I wanted to do and it suited our early departure this morning. Granny stayed by the fire while I explored yesterday."

"Do you like coffee, Jesus? Maybe we should have some coffee and a chat?"

I nodded and smiled at her. "I do not wish to disturb your morning, Priscilla."

"No, I am certain you did not intend to but that is just what happened." She smiled at me, squeezed my hand, and made a move to leave her bunk. "But that's okay. It is time enough to break the bondage from the family secret, and Lawrence may as well know it all as we talk."

We climbed the stairs to the upper decks and cafeteria, Priscilla leaning lightly on a walking cane, the only indication of her advanced years. Along with the pink hoodie, which had a smiling sun emblazoned on the back, she wore navy leggings and trainers. Her hair was held back by a folded hairband of rainbow colours. She chose seats by pointing her cane to the bow windows that caught the early eastern sunlight, saying, "That'll do nicely, Lawrence. Will you order the coffees, please? I think I'll have a double-latte. I am going to need a boost. What's your poison, Jesus?"

"Americano, please, Lawrence. Just cold milk."

Settled in our seats, she swept the room, saying, "I like to travel in the shoulder season now that I am aging. I have given my time to families and children and their needs. I have sixteen grandchildren and four greats. Lawrence has always had a special place in my heart. I would rather travel with him than anyone. Do you understand that connection?"

"Absolutely. I have no siblings, nor aunts, uncles, nor cousins. I have no children. I had Grandfather John for only ten years; his wife, Rosa, is with us still. She has lived all her life with my mother and father, across the yard while we were in Cadiz, now with them in Cork."

"Lawrence does not know the full story of what happened in Cork because I have chosen that. His mother is my daughter Claire and I never told her either. As far as I was concerned, the story died with my parents, for my other brother and sister were too young to know, or at least remember what passed. I inherited my parents' house, so I have been able to carefully select which items and memories would be family history. I have four children, and all they know is that Hazel passed away before we left Cork. There are two photos of her on display on the piano." She waved her hand vaguely, then greeted Lawrence cheerfully as he returned with the coffees. "I knew you couldn't possibly eat anything after that Ballymaloe breakfast, Lawrence? I thought I would sleep it all off, but young Jesus here has put paid to that!"

Laughing, I replied, "A double-latte will keep you going until next week, Priscilla." It was just there that I realised that I knew nothing at all about them, other than this was the moment that was meant to be.

"Okay, Granny, this is it. This is the time for the Hazel story that I know you have not told me." Placing the coffees tentatively, Lawrence raised his eyebrows questioningly at his grandmother.

I watched her carefully, for grief and loss were paramount in the tale. I gave her pause by adding, "If it helps, Lawrence, my grandfather never spoke to me about it either. It was an old musician friend of his, recounted the story some years ago in East Cork."

"Oh?" enquired Priscilla, "Who was that?"

"Timmy O'Brien."

She nodded. "I remember. He played the accordion and I would have met him in the Corkbeg Hotel. He was courting Eleanor, who was Hazel's friend." Tears rose from long-ago memories, brightened her eyes as she sipped her coffee. "So what did Timmy tell you, Jesus?" she asked me quietly.

I breathed slowly, slowly sipping, allowing space and time to take charge. "I want you both to know that I was a child in Spain, with an Irish grandfather who was fun and happy there and who had many stories for a child's ears. I knew there was a darkness as to why he had come to Spain but that did not colour our connection. He spoke longingly of his home country, eventually smoking himself to his death in 1976, still a reasonably young man. And I loved him as a grandfather." I breathed again, giving time to my coffee, then with that, I summarised Timmy's version of the story.

Priscilla nodded without interrupting, occasionally closing her eyes, spontaneously placing her head in her hands, then returning to sip her latte. I did not speak of the damaged condition of poor Hazel's body. As my story drew to a close, Priscilla looked at her grandson, who also listened intently without interruption, and reached for his hand.

"That would largely be the local version of events, Lawrence," she spoke to him softly and directly. "All of it is true and, I should add, Jesus, my sister was truly smitten with your grandfather. Absolutely no doubting it, even though I was three years younger than she. I too, in my time, experienced first love and recognised all the signs she told me of."

"So what happened that Jesus does not know of, Granny?" Lawrence ventured.

Priscilla sighed deeply, chin in her hands, elbows on the table edge.

"It is exactly as Jesus has recounted, Lawrence. I can fill in some gaps, for of course it was a dreadful experience for my parents and all of us, all too who were stationed at the fort. That it occurred just prior to our departure, our return to Britain, allowed much to be left unsaid, much to end up in paper reports in the Ministry of Defence."

She paused to view circling terns through the bow window, occasional splashes of sea spray carried on the wind. To the port side I could see a couple fishing trawlers, with a gaggle of following gulls.

"As far as I have ever heard or surmised, Hazel went to my parents just as we were due to leave. We were to be taken to Cobh and then by naval service to Pembroke. My father was remaining for several more weeks. There was all the departure protocol, stock-takes, stores, armaments, meetings with War Office Personnel. Not to mention being there to see the flag-changing service through, the ceremonial handing over of the fort to the new Free State. Hazel assumedly told them that she was with child. She had not told me yet, but she did subsequently, as she was immediately told to go to her room and await my father's orders. We spent some rather quiet hours there. She didn't tell me very much, so I just held her hand and we sat on her bed, talking about this and that, about returning to England. I do not know why she chose to tell my parents, perhaps because our departure was imminent and she wished maybe to remain in Ireland? I do not know." She sighed.

"She told you it was not my grandfather's child?"

Priscilla nodded, then put her head in her hands and began to sob. Lawrence immediately rose to comfort her, looking at me with alarm, followed by a trace of annoyance, for it was my appearance that had broken the walls of the dam.

"It's okay, Lawrence," Priscilla said into his shoulder. "It's okay. I needed to end this, for it has been walled into my heart all these long years. Poor lovely Hazel; she was so beautiful and kind. It was just such a terrible tragedy that she thought death was her only option."

She straightened herself, smiling briefly through her grief at Lawrence, whom she squeezed and reassured. "It's okay, darling. I will pull myself together and complete the saga for Jesus. It will allow some things to make more sense for you too, dear."

I sat quietly, sometimes closing my eyes to breathe in the importance of the story, knowing more than anything that this morning would bring relief and healing to this elderly soul. There was elemental energy about and, Lawrence or no, my guiding angels were laying down the path that we were following. In my mind's eye, I created a circle around us three mortal beings, inviting any spirit energy to come to the table to assist. I visualised a golden thread connecting us, weaving a filigree web around us, softly embracing us. I imagined Hazel and Abuelo Sean in their youth, talking and smiling as they strolled together up the Corkbeg Road. With the rolling motion of the vessel, the vibration of shuddering engines as they carved through the waves, we were unthreading the life story of one soul to heal the journey of another.

"We shared a room in that fort and—oh my word!—it was not a comfortable place, you know. Damp, and a mouldy smell everywhere." Priscilla paused briefly, then continued. "I was forty-five years old before I attended a counsellor, what you call a therapist now, who took great pains to tell me that it was not my fault, that I had no blame whatsoever in the events and all I could do was grieve her poor soul."

We remained silent as she gathered her thoughts, dabbing her eyes and nose with a handkerchief.

"I think I had known when it happened. Well, what do I say, her impregnation. There was something different about her that I could not miss, in her mannerisms, her moving about our bedroom, around the fort, attending events we were required to attend. It wasn't the beautiful deflowering of the maiden one might expect. She was quite excitedly different at first but became withdrawn and quiet. Of course, I had no idea why. We had a farewell dance at the hotel, from which she departed early saying she felt unwell. A celebration of sorts for everyone locally. The official evacuation of the Cork Harbour garrisons would be in July, the final British departure from Irish soil. It was not a small thing in so many ways you know. There had been a military presence in Whitegate for a very long time, so this was quite significant. Berehaven, and I think Donegal, did not evacuate until later that year."

A heavy splash of seawater against the glass startled us all. Lawrence reached for his grandmother's coffee cup to steady it on the table.

"She never said, she never told them who it was. That of course made my father even more furious. He beat her badly in his fury. He was always so terribly angry when even minorly provoked. My mother spent the larger part of her time and energy dissipating this anger, that we would not be at the receiving end of it, which of course was only a temporary interlude to the fiery explosions. These were often physical, you know, a sudden slap across the head or shaking of the shoulder—he could be quite vicious. My younger brother grew up terrified of him. Of course he nearly throttled me also in his desire for truth, as if I might have known the perpetrator of this deed." Her lips pursed, she frowned through a dark shadow of memory. "It was long after his death that I realised how twisted all this was, how his military training combined with his personality had somehow given him permission to be terrifying to us and his subordinates. It was very, very wearing." She stopped, sipped her latte, her hand tracing the satisfying curve of her walking cane. "Hazel never said, so there is no point in my surmising, but if I had to choose one man above all others, it would have been the handsome foot soldier in the singles barracks, who was often our driver. Just one of those enigmatic persons. Even I remember his twinkling eyes and mischievous ways. There would have been very little unsupervised contact between them, of course. It was not permitted." She sighed. "But somehow rules have a habit of not getting in the way of things. We are terribly complicated beings, we humans."

Lawrence interjected. "So you think it somehow happened between Hazel and this soldier, however or why ever, and it was just an unfortunate accident?"

Priscilla nodded then shrugged. "Isn't it often? An unfortunate accident. I think perhaps." She looked at me. "Much and all as she loved your grandfather, Jesus, she knew that relationship also would have been forbidden. As it was, we were often chastised for even speaking with the locals at events or in the village. We had some freedom, of course. We had to have some freedom. We had to live, and to do that we had to live outside the barracks, the fort. That would always involve locals. Indeed my mother was quite friendly with many of them, including the Major and Molly at the hotel, Mrs. Hawgoode at the store. And there would have been many of our, well, class for want of a more modern word, in the vicinity. We attended social gatherings at Whitegate House, Hadwell, and Castlemary, and sometimes even into the town. Thus the need for a driver." She sighed deeply.

"So Hazel knew she was with child, knew there was nowhere she could go with this, and rather than further invoke her father's fury, she chose to end her life." I spoke quietly, remembering how Hazel had approached my grandfather suggesting they elope. I had not recounted this, for I felt it was an honourable refusal on my grandfather's part and a desperate measure on Hazel's.

"Yes. Her death could be construed as an accident, which it eventually was, for paperwork purposes. She chose her time to coincide with British withdrawal, the flurry of activity surrounding that, and well," she spread her hands, palms upwards, "gave herself up."

"But my grandfather left in a hurry, as if there was a suspicion that he would be to blame? I don't understand? The local word was that she was with child and the assumption then was that it was my grandfather's. Timmy said if they came for him, or for someone to blame, that he would have been thrown into prison?"

Priscilla nodded again. "My mother intervened. Hazel remained steadfastly silent on the matter but assured her that no local boy was to blame. They could hardly start interrogating every man in the district, so Mummy somehow defused my father's fury and directed his attention to the fact that she had committed this act off the walls of the King's fort. Therefore, if it became an issue, there would be a full enquiry. It was better to keep the matter silent amongst ourselves and, as far as possible, continue with the official programme of evacuation. We carried the story with us, until now of course. My parents rarely spoke of it and, only when asked, referred to Hazel's tragic death by accident. There were never any details forthcoming to my grandma or grandpa or anyone else. Of course everyone respected their necessity to mourn and did not ask questions. Once we left, it was easier to lose it all in the faraway fug of half-truths. The Irish Sea was between us and it."

"But the locals would not have known any of that? So with the village whispers of her pregnancy, my great-grandfather may have acted too hastily by arranging for John James to leave for Spain?"

"Yes, it would seem so." Priscilla rested her chin on the top of her cane. "Oh how the world turns!"

We were silent. The smallest of events, the smallest of sacrifices in a tiny corner of the world, yet the largest of rippling effects through all our lives.

"We were already, in a military sense, preparing for war, although it wasn't declared for another year or so. My father's new posting had not been finalised, so we were largely all adrift. Hazel's death compounded that. We left Cork with Mummy and went to Grandma's house in Tenby for that summer. Hazel was buried there."

"Probably by the time you arrived to Tenby, my grandfather was sailing past on his way eventually to Cadiz. His first stop was in Bristol."

This time the silence lingered, each of us pondering how our familial story, our history, had shaped our lives.

"We stayed in Tenby, went to school there, for my father knew it would not be safe anywhere near London if war were to happen, which of course it did. There were bombs dropped regularly over Cornwall where he was stationed, and he died in '42, seemingly a stroke then a heart attack, following a bombing event. His angry head finally imploded."

Lawrence interjected, "You were in Cardiff? Studying?" He turned to me. "My grandmother has her doctorate degree in pathology from University of Wales."

Priscilla smiled at him. "Yes, threw myself completely into schoolwork and studies. Got myself away from my black-garbed Mummy and all that war." She waved her hand dismissively. "I loved my grandma, she took care of us all, got the other two into school and held us all together. Grandfather was also very supportive, very gruff and detached in that old man kind of way, but they absorbed us into the household. Mummy only really came right after Daddy died, you know, pulled herself out of it, out of the misery, although I am sure Grandfather had a hand in that. Simon was about to start public school and Mabel was still only eight or nine. We had all lost Hazel."

I looked at her, leaning on her cane, lighter perhaps for shedding the story, for verbalising her pain. I reached for her hand. "Those were Timmy's words too, Priscilla. He said to me, 'I lost my friend, my musical companion, and we all lost Hazel. It took a long time to heal.' My grandfather never saw Rostellan or his family again. He was not a sailor and he vowed to never step foot on the ocean, once he landed in Cadiz."

"I liked him, Jesus. He was such good fun. And I was often with them, out at Corkbeg strand, or walking the lanes to White Bay and Roches Point, Whitegate Regatta, all those things. It was usual to accompany your older sister, chaperone them you know. There were often six or eight of us all that summer, just youngsters enjoying life. And they played such terrific music! We couldn't do the Irish dancing but, golly, we gave it a good go! I loved to watch Eleanor and her friends Patricia and Sally. They were splendid. Gosh it seems so long ago. I feel very old now."

"Nothing a double-latte doesn't fix, Granny!" Lawrence broke the gloomy reverie. He too reached for her hand, squeezed it, and said, "I am glad, though, that you have let it all out. It was no sin on anyone's part you know, just a series of tragic events. And we are all lucky to have you."

"Yes, at a table on the Julia many years later." I laughed. "My grandfather would have loved a double-latte!"

Priscilla smiled, dabbing at her eyes with a coffee napkin. "I can just see his fingers racing on those buttons after a dose of caffeine! What is it called again? The instrument?"

"A concertina. My mother plays it now. She used to play with Timmy when they first moved to Cork in '88. He lived to a good age, although I never met Eleanor. They had four children."

She sighed again, more wistfully than with a heavy heart. "There is plenty more to tell, I'm sure, Jesus, and I would love to hear some of his Spanish exploits. He had a way of making everything, well, fun really, and he always included me or Eleanor's younger sisters. We even had Simon and Mabel in tow on occasions and they were, gosh, just small children. He used to say some shocking things to us about the British in Ireland, but it was in good humour. He always said nothing was anyone's fault, it just was."

I nodded, my older adult self remembering his entertaining East Cork stories told in faraway Spain, told without remorse or bitterness or anger but with the acceptance of a story that unfolded, a life that was lived as best one could. "It doesn't make it any the less heart-breaking for everyone, though, no matter how long ago it all was."

"No, none. Our hearts only heal over the pain of loss. The scar remains."

" 'A scar on my ould heart,' that's as close as my grandfather came to describing it to me, but, gosh, I too was only eight or nine. It was the only time I saw him cry."

Priscilla gave a deep exhalation, a release, her eyes closing, her chin resting on her hands. "I might take a nap now, Lawrence, make use of that comfy cabin. We can talk again later, Jesus, perhaps? We still have some time?"

"That would be lovely, Priscilla. I would like to hear of your medical career. I had several years of informal training with a Chinese-American Naval doctor in Cadiz, and my grandmother was a very accomplished nurse." I reached for her hand again. "I am truly glad we met and talked and I am truly sorry that it upset you. Hopefully in time you will feel better for it."

We stood to part, then she smiled and waved us both away. "I am certain I will feel better. You two youngsters stay to talk together. I can find my way back. Stay away from that coffee, though; nasty habit!" She manoeuvred herself from the armchair. As she turned, she leaned on her cane and paused, "It was all such a nonsense you know, Jesus. Nonsensical, the Irish-English thing. Ireland was right to want her forts back, but had no military might, so left herself vulnerable as things escalated with the Germans. Churchill was exceedingly unimpressed with de Valera's call for neutrality and then all those very brave Irish men signed up in droves to fight for the British anyway." She shook her head sadly. "I suppose many of those boys we knew in Whitegate and Aghada were part of the bloody war."

I nodded. "Yes, Timmy too, although he was in the Merchant Navy. My grandfather escaped it all by being in Spain. Wasn't that the hand of fate?"

She pursed her lips in agreement. "Churchill had a right go at de Valera when it was all over, how they wouldn't allow the Allies to use the southern ports, and rightfully Dev defended his actions. Many in Ireland disagreed with his stance of neutrality, felt it brought bad luck to the new state. I was a young intern in Cardiff by the end of the war and I remember the anti-Irish feeling after his speech. Fortunately, I was brave enough to say to them, you have to know the Irish. You have to understand their story to know their actions were not meant to be an obstruction, but were the very understandable actions of a new country freeing themselves from the shackles of foreign rule." She shook her head. "We would all be better off if everyone just minded their own corner and left others alone."

∞

Lawrence and I sat silently, an uncertainty as to how we would proceed from here. We each excused ourselves, one after the other, to use the restroom, our shared story slowly seeping through our beings, our time together incomplete. On his return he brandished his phone and smiled. "Granny is settled into her bed and asks what your plans in the UK might be and whether you'd wish to join us at home?"

"Is that in Tenby?" I queried, slightly puzzled, for, if so, it would have made more sense for them to be on the Pembroke ferry.

"Oh Lord no! One of my aunts has that house now, Simon's daughter and family. My mother and father lived in Oxfordshire and Buckinghamshire. Daddy was a fellow at Oxford, his field was geophysics and Mummy is a classical violinist. Music is her life. Granny married Bob Kendal from Bucks and his father was a big chap in Scotland Yard. I am also an Oxford fellow, pure geology though. So we still live in Bucks, a place called Roughwood Lane."

I looked at him curiously; my recent map-scanning and research had seen this name. "Near Chalfont Saint Giles?"

"Yes, that would be our nearest village. I attended primary school there. However do you know Chalfont?"

"My first stop on this trip is Bristol, where my paternal grandfather hailed from and where I have some friends to catch up with. I am then bound for Chalfont to look into the life of Geraldine Geoghegan, an extraordinary woman, early photographer, and maker of photographic and cinematic filters for Sanger-Shepherd. I stumbled upon that through a series of events in both Ireland and London. I am a writer; I travel and I write."

"How ridiculously coincidental is that? That house was part of the Roughwood estate. The photographer rented the cottage from my grandparents, Priscilla and Bob." He shook then scratched his head confusedly. "You are definitely carrying some strange earth energy with you today, Jesus."

"My mother's life is also music and teaching; she was a primary school teacher. She plays the concertina and the fiddle—mostly Irish tunes, but I have heard her play along to pop songs on the radio. My father was a naval man, primarily engineering, in Spain, but not Spanish, a story that I will share with you over lunch. You will have some of my egg mayonnaise sandwiches and flapjacks, now that you have been within waving distance of my mother and share her life story line?"

We laughed together, the pure joy of finding friendship and common thought, and a bubble of gratitude arose within me. Oh God! How I love my Universe and what it sends me. I see a smiling Thich Nhat Hanh, a picture from 1984 on my bedroom wall, his hands in prayer under his chin, a beaming smile on his face, snapped just as he had uttered to us all: "God has given you all to me and me to you all. Be ever thankful for the smallest grace."

"Your grandmother?" I asked of him during mouthfuls. "It has to be yoga or Tai Chi or something similar that keeps her so spritely and lithe. Is she eighty-three or -four?"

He grinned, wiping homemade mayonnaise from his lips. "These are very good sandwiches! Yes, both, yoga and Tai Chi, and yes, eighty-four in a week or so. She made us all do yoga, which we did because it was such fun watching Granny do Sunny Day exercises as we called them. Then I took classes again in college before committing regularly when I was first married. My wife is now a teacher of yoga and body works, you know, all that kind of thing. I am forever grateful I have not turned into a bent-over-looking-at-rocks permanent position. I owe all that to her. In fact, it seems ludicrously easy to me to clamber along clifftops and ledges, and that is entirely a result of keeping physically fit and well. Three children have helped with the exercise, of course."

"I can see Priscilla is quite the character. I am so glad to have met with her, Lawrence, and thank you for the happy coincidences of the day so far."

"Oh, stop it, for goodness sakes. We both know this had nothing to do with either of us. I can fully see that something had to pry that story from her." He mused silently for a moment. "So maybe it is Hazel and Sean or maybe Grandpa we have to thank. Who are we to know?" He smiled. "But, yes, you are right, she is quite the character and I love her dearly. I always have. We have flowed along forever, in and out of each other's lives; I would seek her, she would seek me. Being good travelling companions has always been, well, the icing on the cake." He stopped suddenly. "Did you say your grandfather hated the sea?"

"Yes, he was sick from Cork to nearly Cadiz and never sailed again. Not so much as a rowing boat on the harbour."

"Funny that. It is exactly how I am, love looking at it but absolutely no desire whatsoever to be anywhere on it. Yet I have hardly noticed this journey thus far. I too, would usually be truly tucked up in my bunk with Sea-Legs, or some such chemical concoction." He lifted his pullover sleeve to show his acupressure wristband for seasickness.

"Me too!" I laughed, lifting my sleeve. "I only come by sea because I love to have the VW camper-van. Then I do not have to think about accommodation or coffee and toiletting stops."

"No! Truly? We too are in a little camper-van! Granny owned it from new in '94 and only recently admitted she may not be the safest driver on the road, so bequeathed me the honour."

"I am going to guess, Lawrence. I am going to call on my Universal Resources and guess that your van is parked two in front of mine on the car deck, in the row to my left. I was admiring it as the stevedore waved me to a halt. It is a C15 Citroen Romahome, dinky little thing." I laughed at his expression.

He slapped his thigh, then the table, causing the flapjacks to dance their own delight. "So fabulous! What a journey this will be!"

"There are definitely fairies about today, Lawrence."

∞

Hags Head, Co Clare, 2011

"Do you remember the Millennium Party, Jesús?" Mamá shielded bright sunlight from her eyes, squinting at me from where she lay on springy sea grass on a clifftop in Co. Clare. I raised my sunglasses to look at her, her question surprising me, and what may have roused that memory.

"Sí, yes, Mamá, of course. I have to poke through the web of years to bring back the details but, yes, yes I do. It was the best fun. What brings that to mind?"

We were travelling together in the next version of the VW, slowly en route to Ennis, to the annual Fleadh Cheoil, a national traditional music competition. This would have been her umpteenth trip to the Fleadh, to which I may have accompanied her three or four times. We were to meet Mamá's cousins Kenneth and David, Jerry's sons, in Doolin and travel together to the town.

I would leave Mamá in her lodgings and travel west to clamber the crags of Burren rock and lie on sun-warmed stone absorbing ancient energy, while she took workshops and lessons with the greatest Irish musicians. Every time afterwards, she smiled widely and brightly and jigged for days and days, describing new players, new sounds, the new generations that brought a different energy, different style to the music. And how she just loved playing with the children, all ages of musicians, sharing workshops and classrooms, sharing, sharing the beautiful sound. As a child, I sometimes watched Abuelo, carefully oiling the bellows of his concertina, cigarillo smoke rising up into his eyes. "Feed the leather well, rub in that oil." he would say. "I have to be careful here in the Spanish sun," he told me, "that the bellows don't dry out in the hot weather, but also that I don't get oil all the way through them, to destroy the sound. My beautiful sound."

I remember the prowess of Sharon Shannon on her button accordion, at full volume in the VW as Mamá played along to 'Sparky,' 'Bungee Jumpers,' or 'The Blackbird,' just tearfully lost in the machinations of that sound. The fingers of traditionalist Liam O'Connor would race across his piano accordion, while Lisa Aherne sang 'Rise Up.' My mother played her heart out to these tunes and—oh, that smile—bursting with musical freedom. She took the sound to Ambrose and said, "Play, Ambrose, play the trombone. Let's see what we can do." They took Planxty, Stockton's Wing, Scullion, Moving Hearts—and played the tunes they liked.

Ambrose would jig and pull chords, jamming with María. One Sunday, they all arrived to the cottage by the sea—Ambrose, Denis, their jazz pals Trumpet Arthur and Oliver Two Hands the drummer, then cousins Kenneth and David, Julia. My mother orchestrated it. She said, "Let's all get together and try some things. It is all music." Philomena arrived in the Two Spoons van with Maureen and Majella, a cargo space full of food from the café, and it became a party.

"Liam O'Connor said this, Jesús," Mamá told me that day, "and I have memorised it forever: 'You don't own the music. You can't own the music, any more than you can own the air, or own the water. The music is lent to us. We only have it for a short time. It's what you do with it, in the time you have it, that counts.' "

Back on the clifftop in Clare, my mother retrieved my attention.

"Oh let me see what drew that memory?" She mused, "I am listening to the birds and all the different sounds below us here between the cliffs and the sea and thinking about getting older and thinking it is so lovely to be able to travel with you, spend time with you, Jesús. Then for some reason, I had a vision of my Mamá. Wasn't she just the most glorious sight in that wonderful cascading purple gown? And her Party Hat as she called it."

"Yes, indeed!" I agreed. "Sharing fruit punch with Morna Doc, equally resplendent in flowing blue. And that fabulous cerise pashmina to keep away the winter chill." I could see the photos in my mind's eye.

"She was eighty, Jesús. Mamá Rosa was eighty. There were so many of us that night, celebrating together the closing of an age."

It seemed so far away as the sun now scorched our bones on the Atlantic edge and my mind drifted slowly to recall. I had returned to Cork after a long trip nearing the end of the millennium. Papá had installed a new DVD player—the old VHS finally gave up with a waft of black smoke. For Christmas I had brought him "The Very Best of Father Ted." Just for my father, for my mother would be aggrieved, offended at the insinuations about her church. Rosa would miss the nuances or declare herself demasiado antiguo, too old. There is nothing anywhere in my world more memorable than laughing with my parent, enjoying the same scene, the same slapstick nonsense. "Is that right, Ted?" became his holiday refrain; or I would catch him unawares with "Would you like a cup of tea, Father?"

Preparations for the Millennium Party had taken some time in that week between Christmas and the New Year. In the centre of 'the Caim,' the Celtic path they had laid in the wildflower meadow that adjoined the cottage by the water, Papá and I prepared the ground for a Millennium bonfire. In order not to leave a residual scar on the earth, we carefully cut away the sod, rolling it back to form a two-metre square fire pit. We placed the cut sods at an angle on each side to form an earthen wall around the pit. The sods would be replaced in first full moon of the New Year, a continuing celebration of burying the remains of the past. Papá had been gathering and saving kindling and driftwood for some months. This would be the bright light of our celebration.

Ambrose and his sons, with Papá's assistance, had constructed a makeshift barn alongside the shed, complete with an industrial heater and work lights, so there was plenty of shelter for the party. My mother procured two long white refectory tables from the sale of contents of a Carmelite convent, perfect for a great gathering. I produced a bag of fireworks, legally acquired in Wales and which had gone unnoticed on my passage across the Irish Sea, to where they are unavailable for purchase in Ireland. My mother and Abuelita Rosa made fruit punch and mulled wine, which they bottled and stored. We cooked churros, Roscón de Reyes, and rollos de pastelería with sweet and savoury fillings. On the day, my father lit the grill-oven he had built into the wall of his shed. Crackling kindling, hissing and popping, smoke and sparks rose through the steel chimney to shower the clear afternoon sky.

"These were our ancients," remembered Mamá, "awakening the new dawn." She stretched her arms to the sky in Co. Clare. "Where does the time fly to?"

I remember the music and laughter, a blazing stack of dry timber illuminating familiar faces. Ambrose and his son Con set the fireworks on prepared posts, ready to launch across the tide where curlews cried. Each of us made our wish for the New Year, the new century, then lit a firework.

"Remember the fireworks, Mamá?" I asked, returning from my recall journey to listen to her. "Remember Bridget McCarthy wishing she could have a firework for every birthday. She had never experienced them so close and she shrieked like a child as each one was lit."

Mamá laughed. "Yes, there were many prayers to the real Jesus."

"Let me tell you about your own lovely Mamá. Remember when the countdown began before midnight and we were all trying to gather in that confused circle of crossed hands? Well, in the mêleé,

I found myself between Philomena and my Abuelita Rosa."

"Oh yes! I think I had the towering Ambrose looking down on me and Michael on my other side. Would he have been, what age, Jesús?"

"Hmm, Philomena started the café in '91 when he went to first school, so I suppose four or five plus nine—thirteen or so?"

"So maybe the youngest there?"

"Probably," I nodded to her. "Anyway, there we all are, noise and crazy and all the voices calling together, 'Ten, nine, eight … .' Rosa is counting beside me, 'Seis, cinco, cuatro …¡Tres! ¡Dos! ¡Uno! ¡Feliz Año Nuevo!' Happy New Year! You know how it went?"

"Sí, yes, yes," she smiled widely.

I paused to be there, remembering. Below me the gannets cry, swooping on thermals of sun-drenched air. I remember the crossed hands giving way to shouts and cheers, embraces of joy and belonging. I held my tiny grandmother tightly to me and she cried into my chest. "Oh, Jesús, Jesús, I am alive to be here now. I am afortunada." Philomena joined our embrace, her eyes also bright with tears. "Oh, what are we like? Sobbing like babies." She is pulled away by Peg, "Mam, Mam, Happy New Year, Mam!"

"She cried, Mamá. She was so happy, so fortunate to be alive and still with us." I say quietly.

My mother is silent. I see her nodding, leaning on her elbows and scanning the blue horizon. I sit up to be on the same level with her, plucking a blade of sweet grass and chewing on one end.

"Yes, yes, she came to me also and said that, how happy she was to be with us there."

"So then I spotted Bridget McCarthy, she was nervous, you know, that high-pitched tee-hee-hee-hee giggle."

My mother smiled at my imitation of Bridget.

"I knew she was terrified, of embracing or being kissed or hugged; she is so unfamiliar with physical affection. She is, well, awkward in herself. I took Abuelita Rosa by the hand and said: Show Bridget how to be relajada y tranquila, Rosa, to enjoy this moment with the only family she has."

Mamá laughed, "No better woman!" she exclaimed, in her best Cork accent.

"Mamá! I forget sometimes that you were ever in Cadiz. You truly have Cork by heart."

"Oh, Jesús! Never mind that. Just tell me about my Mamá."

"I see her, some moments later, wrap her arms around the waist of Bridget McCarthy, cling to her like a child. You know the tiny size of her and there isn't a whole lot of Bridget either. I knew she would be whispering Feliz Año Nuevo, Bree-geed."

I stop in my recall, struck by the strange mix of English-Spanish-Cork that we have become.

"I saw Bridget all tense and anxious." I draw myself inwards as I sit on a cliff in Co. Clare, imagining the sheer terror of a woman unable to emotionally express herself, yet surrounded by love and laughter and joy that was hers for the taking, for the absorbing. "She slowly lets go, Abuelita Rosa still clings to her, so Bridget relaxes enough to return the affection, then even smiles. And, of course, she had to be silent, to hear the murmurings of an old Spanish lady in her embrace, somewhere down by her, well, where she should have a bosom."

"Well, that was a Millennial Moment in itself, to keep Bridget McCarthy silent," declared Mamá.

"Then Rosa took her hand and walked her around all the little groups, you remember? Everyone broke away from the circle, sharing the keeses and hugs."

"Yes, yes. I remember not really believing that this was all our family, all these people, me having grown up in Spain with no one. Not one. Your father, or me, or Rosa. Not one relative."

"Or me."

"Yet here we were, engulfed."

I nodded. "That's what I was thinking also, Mamá." The feeling rose in me just as we spoke: Belonging. We sat quietly, the sky alive around us—wind and scurrying clouds of spectral white. "And you know how Bridget always does the holy Catholic Jesus-thing?"

Mamá raises herself to kneeling on wind-blown sea grass, piously bows her head, and performs the Formula-One-fly-swat, dotting her breast-bone while murmuring fa'her, son, holy spirih, a performance we have witnessed many times.

"So when they reach me for hugs and keeses, I take her hands in mine and say: Bridget, in my mercy I have come to thee tonight."

Mamá laughs wholeheartedly, raising a startled look from a passing fulmar.

"She screeches with joy and throws herself at me, kisses my cheeks. 'Happy New Year, Jee-sus.' And she does exactly the blessing of herself and the head bob as if this were her Millennium Prayer. 'Oh sacred hearh of Jesus, I place all my trus' in thee.' It was a lovely moment to share with her."

We are quiet for a while, enjoying the moments, the blazing sunshine warming our Mediterranean bones. Sea birds cry, sea thunders and crashes, a skylark shrills.

"I loved Rosa, Jesús. I miss her so much. Every day." Mamá is facing the breeze, her eyes closed to the memories. I reach across the salted grass, poked with pink thrift and bright yellow tormentil and cinquefoil.

"I miss my Mamá every day I am not with her too. And I love her so much."

She leans to me and I kiss her cheek, wiping her tear with my thumb. We lie back, adjusting our gazes to the far sea, and I recall the words I spoke as a child to Abuelo Sean, on the pier wall in Cadiz.

"El mar y el cielo se ven del mismo azul. Y en la distancia parecen juntarse." I say to her.

She looked at me in surprise. "Jesús! You remember? You heard that from Sean?"

"No, Mamá, he heard it from me. I said it to him one day at the harbour in Cadiz, he was practising some new Spanish phrases and the sky and the sea were just like that," I told her, gesturing to the horizon. "I have been reminded of it many, many times, in many different places in the world."

She took my hand, smiling and shaking her head. "Oh, Jesús, Jesús. You are the special one. He came to me once, after my school-day in Cadiz, and he was trying to remember it correctly. He asked me to listen, that he thought he was wrong in his sentence structure. I remember saying, 'That's a lovely thought, Papá, the sea and the sky coming together in the same blue.' And he smiled and said, 'Isn't it just, my love? Isn't it just.' I too have remembered it since then and thought of it many times looking from my kitchen window in Rostellan. It is often while you are away travelling and I want you to know I am with you."

I think of Mr. Onions and his Oxford book of etymology. Parents, from the Latin parentum: pere, to produce, bring forth. Family, Latin familiaris, domestic, private, belonging to a family, of a household. A collection of faces by which we recognise others, names by which we call them, each a whole, an individual spirit of the earth. "We choose," Dr. Zhao had told me. "We carefully choose our every existence, to whom we are born, our circle from whom we learn and to whom we give. We are one immense web of souls on their journey of learning." My heart forever fills with love for this diverse collection with whom I am connected.

Mamá smiles at me. "You remember this one, Jesús?" she asks, clearing her throat, looking to the blue sea of the blue horizon broken only by faraway sea birds. She hums and la-le-las the opening bars of "Beautiful Affair."

"Stockton's Wing!" I cry, and find my own voice to join her, music and sunshine and memories binding us as mother and child.

"I always loved it, Mamá. I think it was the first tune I heard after you moved to Cork, when I found that Irish music was much more than Sean's jigs and reels and that there was a whole new movement, a whole momentum that appealed to a twenty-something-year-old."

"Ah, yes. I am glad it was there for you." She paused, nodding, remains of the tune encircling her musical mind. "And The Waterboys? You loved their sound too, Jesús?" She hummed 'I wish I was a Fisherman.' "You remember the singing at the party?" she asks. "The rousing Scottish lilt? Ambrose started with 'Auld Lang Syne.'"

"Julia played the fiddle, you played the concertina, young Stan Sowersby played harmonica."

"And later Frank came with the low whistle."

"We followed that with 'You Take the High Road and I'll Take the Low Road.' "

"Then Ambrose uncased the trombone and played, 'We'll Meet Again,' " Mamá recalled. "I have never played so many tunes on the concertina that were not Irish. It's so lovely for those dance tunes."

" 'I Can See Clearly Now,' 'On the Wings of an Angel,'—just some I can think of. I can also recall a very merry Philomena doing a fabulous waltz around the shed to 'Top of the World.' She has a wonderful '70s swing. Who would she have done her ballroom dancing with, Mamá? Kenneth and David? Not Ambrose for sure!"

"Or your father," Mamá laughed. "Do you remember Papá disappeared and seemed to be away for a very long time? Then after ages, he returned with his guitar?"

I shook my head questioningly.

"Do you know why he was gone so long?"

"No? I had forgotten. Or I never thought to ask."

"He was full of punch! He went to the bathroom and fell asleep on the el váter. He awoke when he fell off, then somehow remembered why he had left the party."

"Oh poor Papá! He never told me. I remember him returning. He told us all, to much amusement, that he was going to play guitar only because Mr. Sowersby and he made a wager. And he feared the rum punch would not assist his efforts. Poor Papá!"

Mamá waved her hand above her head. "Oh, Jesús! I saw it all the time. Some nice young sailor would drive him home from the Rota Base after a party. He has no capacity at all for alcohol. But he never wanted the Yanks to know, so he got good at pretending, or swapping his glass with the next one that had not so much in it, or slipping away home. Then he would stagger across the yard, shushing and stumbling, saying, 'Don't wake Sean, Rosa, sshhh.' Then he would forget himself and break into John Prine, 'Ain't we got Love.' Usually he would collapse on the sofa, with such nonsense as, 'Get some sleep, María. We have an early start tomorrow.' And soon he would be snoring." Mamá was laughing at her own mimicry. "Pure dreen-king drivel."

I hadn't known this side of my father, although it struck a chord with me somewhere—maybe childhood or teen memories I had pushed aside. I had never guessed my father to be drunk. Interestingly, he would have never witnessed my inebriation either. It was not something I would have ever wished upon my parents.

"Do you remember Bridget doing the 'Riverdance' thing with Stan and Con and Peg, I think? I thought right there I would die from all the laughing. Oh dear me! Yes, it was the best party ever."

∞

Cottage by the Water, Rostellan 2009

Abuelita Rosa's first warning came after an afternoon nap. She arose from her bed and appeared to my father in their kitchen, confused and unable to form her words. She carried a water glass in her hands, looked at it as if she could not identify it, looked at my father knowingly, but could not pronounce his name. He knew immediately something was not right, seated her in a fireside chair, then called Mamá.

"I didn't hear at all the phone, Jesús," Mamá told me later that evening by telephone, for I was far away in Scotland.

"I was in the school hall with the dancers and just did not hear it. Then one of the girls came to me between the dances and said, 'Excuse me, Mrs. Joseph, your phone is ringing a lot.' I came straight home, but Daniel had already gone to the hospital."

"She was nearly better by the time we got there," Papá interjected. "So much so, she herself wanted to come home. But I thought it best that she be examined thoroughly."

I held my breath, awaiting the continuation, for it was never easy to have a three-way conversation with two participants sharing the same landline receiver.

"She will be there for a few days and they will do some tests, but she is in good form and happy," Mamá added.

"Is she in a ward? With others?" I asked.

"Yes, tonight. Los signos vitales, hmm, vital signs? Yes, are all fine, so the doctors are happy with her."

"Did the doctors say anything at all, Mamá?"

"Yes, Jesús. From what they can determine by doing ... ," she pressed the receiver to her chest so I like to think I heard her heart beat, while murmuring to Papá, "protein tests, sí, they read the rise in the different proteins in her bloods. They call it ... un momento, por favor, Jesús." She faded to silence, then returned with, "I wrote it here, hmm, yes, yes, takotsubo cardiomyopathy. Broken Heart Syndrome. Her heart, Jesús."

"Oh!" I was taken aback. Her vital organ.

"Yes, it is a Japanese word meaning octopus trap," Mamá read from her notes. "That's where they first discovered it, Japan. The doctor says, hmm, sí, yes here it is, the left ventricle valve flips open in the shape of the octopus trap." She read in the staccato monotone of one repeating exactly what was recorded. "He wanted to know if she had recent emotional problems—stress, death, things like that. I thought not, none I could think of. What do you think?"

Behind her, Papá muttered, "I thought she was fine. She showed no signs of any upset to me."

From the distance of Scotland, I was unsure. I had not physically seen her for six or so weeks. "It has been years since she nursed anyone. Has she been out and about much? Papá? Maybe we can ask her once she has time to recover?" I suggested. "Do you think I should come back to Cork?"

"No, no, no, not at all!" Papá exclaimed. "We will see how the next day or so goes and if there are any changes, we will let you know straightaway."

"Yes," sighed Mamá heavily. "Yes, that is best, Jesús. Continue your work and we will talk again in a day or two. Now I need some sleep."

We bade our farewells and I sat on the only hillside on the island of Iona, western Scotland. The late May twilight was still some time away in these northern latitudes and the remains of the evening sun glistened on Iona Sound. I looked across to the mainland, musing and guesstimating how long it would take me to return to Cork. Most profound of all else that I had heard during the call to my parents was my mother's sigh.

My work, as Mamá had alluded to on this occasion, was compiling a series of articles for my Boston publishing house. I was carving a spiritual arc through Ireland, Scotland, and England, pursuing some early Christian monks of the fifth to seventh centuries. History is unreliable, written by the conquerors, embroidered for their own fame or infamy. Folklore history, more reliably, has proven undoubtedly that the inhabitants of these islands were farming at least 5000 years ago. Early in my research, I realised it would be impossible to leave the green Isle of Hibernia had I taken the time to visit every monastic site or settlement there. So I had to make choices. On a map of the British Isles, I had drawn a connecting arc from southern Ireland to eastern England, endeavouring to visit the most noteworthy of remains. Along my journey thus far, I had visited the church of St. Gobnait of Ballyvourney in Cork, where a remarkable seventh-century woman is revered for her miracles and work. My story had continued with the beehive huts of the Skellig Rock, the very western seaboard of Co. Kerry, from where I wove my way through the Slieve Mish Mountains of the Dingle Peninsula to the Reask Monastic Settlement and St. Brendan's Holy Mountain on the northern coast. My journey continued to Brendan's cathedral remains in North County Kerry at Ardfert. St. Edna had served his people on Inis Mór, of the Aran Islands in Galway Bay; St. Patrick was based in the north of the country in Armagh. I then crossed the Irish Sea to Caledonia. Ninian had built his abbey in Whithorn, and now I was currently at Columba's monastery on the island of Iona. St. Aidan in Lindisfarne would be the next stop, after a visit to Brae Knap to see Stanley, Ambrose's father. When I had told Ambrose my plans before leaving Cork, he had laughed, spluttering on his pipe, and said, "Well, that'll be a spanner in yer works Jesus, for he's no saint, that's for sure." To complete my trip, I planned to cross the Irish Sea back to Ireland to Kildare, near Dublin, and visit the cathedral of St. Brigid.

Meanwhile, on the western side of the Dún Iona hillside I lounged in summer foliage, pondering, then sitting more carefully, straightening my spine, perhaps to meditate. My Abuelita Rosa, broken-hearted for some reason this very day. And why was I miles away on a Scottish hillside, an island of all places? Why Iona? What forces of life were at play?

The softest of winds rustled my hair, a skylark trilled her tune. Just a short way to my left was the Well of Eternal Youth, associated with Ireland's own St. Brigid, or Bridget. I smiled to myself, for until that moment I had not thought of Bridget McCarthy in Blackrock. Eternal Youth, eternally foolish youth. Bridget, eternally Bridget, unwavering in her Bridget-ness. Yet nothing is eternal; and my grandmother had just had a blip in her sinus wave. Her steady heart had flipped.

I looked south to the Hill of the Angels, where sixth-century St. Columba was secretly observed by a fellow brother, as angels of white light rose and descended around the monk during his prayers. A conference of celestial beings. Angels. Oh, where are my angels Lawrence and Leah? What is it that I need to know?

A falcon, floating on the evening breeze, caught my eye. Heather rustled against the leather of my boots, scratched against the fabric of my trousers. Below me, Iona shifted into a summer evening of tourists finding meals, campers settling into tents, residents mowing lawns. A fishing boat gently rocked, reflecting glints of the now low sunlight. I remembered then Abuelita Rosa at Mama Tia's funeral in '86, in the old Cadiz taberna while my mother fiddled funeral tunes. "When a question comes up, up from here, stop, listen for answer," Abuelita had told me. "Trust, trust that this is correcto."

I let my self be still and wait for what I needed to hear. Behind my eyelids I see shapes, I see changing light, I breathe Abuelita Rosa lying in a hospital ward, being cared for. Even being cared for, Rosa will be caring, smiling, holding someone's hand.

My wandering mind sees the sixth century St. Columba leaving Lough Foyle in Derry, Northern Ireland, along with his monks in the frailty of leather coracles. His journey was one of self-inflicted penance for instigating destruction in the Battle of the Book, as he set forth to collect souls for the church. I see Edna on windswept Aran; Gobnait in Dunquin and Ballyvourney; the zealous anchorites high in their cell huts on Skellig Michael; and Patrick, cold and lonely, tending pigs in Antrim. And St. Brendan, atop his Holy Mountain, watching the sun descend into the wide expanse of the yet unnamed ocean to his west, unable to say where it may spend the oncoming night before it reappeared as morning to his east. My mind sees stalwart men and women, carried by their love of their God, fifteen hundred years ago, when nothing was as is, except the mountains and the seas, the stars and the skies.

I find a feeling of safety, of security, here on my journey with the ancient souls. Now through my languid mind filters the variety of words used through the passage of time for a journey, a way, a path to follow: turas, caim, camino, pilgrimage, thudong. Ancient words. My mind ceases its wanderings, the call of the lark becomes faint, the sound of the sea washes gently over me. In the stillness I find peaceful silence.

It is dusk when I rise to pick my way downhill to the east, to the occasional lights of the village, the campsite. There is nothing more to know just now, other than Abuelita Rosa is safe and well and I will see her again soon.

∞

In my parent's garden, sweet peas cascade from the rear wall, curling tendrils climbing a cast-off fishing net, their early scent wafting in morning breeze. Swallows swoop and call, darting under the eave of the stone workshop, tending to mud-nests of young chicks. It is mid summer, the sun is high, the grass is short and showing signs of weariness, awaiting rain from the cloudless sky. In the casa de jardín, the round garden-house my father built by the rowan tree, I find my grandmother watching garden birds through binoculars.

"I am toda la mañana, the whole morning, sitting here, Jesús. Look! See the robin. This one is different, white on his wing. I see him every day." My grandmother is smaller in herself, comfortable in her space yet altered by her experience. A blackbird pokes in the grassy overhang beneath the fuchsia hedge, searching for sustenance from damp roots.

Some years previously Papá had laid out twelve metre-long timbers. 'Dodecahedron,' he wrote, and included in the parcel of Polaroid pictures he sent to me somewhere in western Canada the numbered order of prints—twelve timbers laid out on a timber deck, twelve uprights in place, and a spiral succession of windows to the sea. A 'cantilever roof,' he informed me in red biro on one photo, which meant little to an imprecise person on a travelling journey, but it greatly impressed one of the Zhao engineers in California. The central wheel for this cantilevering feat is the bottom of a beer keg that Papá had begged from Creedon's Bar. I now sit in this roundhouse construction, in awe of his capabilities, how everyday life has given him the chance to explore and extend himself.

"I am pulling myself together, Jesús, in the cloak of my life. You know, nearly ninety is just a number, yes? Just a number. In the hospital, oh, I heard all the time: Oh, you are great for eight-nine," she mimics playfully the well-meaning conveyors of the sentiment. "As if it was a miracle. Ppff," she snorts, lifting the binoculars onto to the table.

"One still feels at eighty-nine. One still laughs, still loves. Todavía ama. I loved your grandfather. I loved Lou Zhao. I love your mamá, papá, you. You are my family. I love the Doc, and Morna Doc; she is my friend. They are my friends. I am safe with them and," she wagged her finger at me, "we understand each other. This stays important in all the years, yes, all the way to these eighty-nine years."

I pour my coffee, she declines at first then adds, "Maybe just a leetle mouthful. There is nothing now for my heart to not like."

The rhythmic tap, tap of a hammer comes from the shed where my father is doing whatever he is doing that day. It is already warm, with only a faint breeze through the open door.

"See here, Jesús," she extends her left hand, "this is where I cut the edge of my nail, see where it is gone, when I was, hmm, cincuenta, sesenta y tantos. Yes, maybe sixty-something. Chopping onions, not thinking of onions, thinking of something else and," snap, the same fingers snap, "the damage is done. It stays with me, this damage. And here?"

The same hand, this time her thumbnail is proffered. "See this, la onda, what is it?"

"Wave? Ripple?"

"Sí, wave, in the nail. Bang, bang, like Daniel there." She jerked the thumb towards the door. "Hammer, building the house in Cadiz with Sean. Bang! Oooh! Oh I screamed."

I was surprised. "I didn't know you helped build it, Abuelita?"

"Oh yes, yes." She nods. "Sean did the heavy things. I did all the inside timber, hammer it to the wall. I had the patience for such things and he did not."

"And our house too? Across the yard? Did you help build that?"

"That one first. That was the one. We were there all the time until María went to Seville, to teaching college. Then Sean built the small house for us and he said María have the bigger house when she is getting the married."

I had not known this until now. Or maybe there were things that I did know, that I did not remember. We were silent for a while.

"I put cream on my feets, Jesús, at night, same feets, same legs for all these years. They have carried me all of the way." She smiled and nodded, reached down and lovingly stroked her left shin. "Imagine if they could tell the story instead of my head, my mouth? Imagine that, if my legs and feet were to tell you of my life? Maybe they would not be so happy?" She made herself smile, which made me smile.

She picked up the page magnifier she used for reading and, laying her left hand palm-down on the table between us, placed the magnifier on the back of her hand. "See, Jesús? Every leetle break of the skins, every tear from the thorns of Papá's roses, burn from the cooking, all still here." She emphatically pointed with her right hand, then paused to examine her skin, peering through the magnifier, and murmured, "And I do not remember many of them. Leetle accidents. This one here," she pointed to the base of her third finger, "big accident with scalpel. Dr. Hernando at the Naval Hospital, gave it to me to take but he did not let it go. He too was not thinking, not of the scalpel." She sat upright.

"The record of everything I have done and seen is here in my body. Lou says we are born with everything inside of us, the blueprint he called it, and now we die with the, hmm, copia inversa."

"Reverse copy."

"Sí, yes, having lived the blueprint as best we can, at eighty-nine we get to look back on it all."

I sipped my coffee. There was nothing else except to listen.

"I think I have done okay, Jesús. I try to think who will meet me up there and say: Rosa, that was not nice." She chewed on a little ginger square.

"Angelina Carillo, I pushed her over at the school. She took my el pasador, hmm … ." She brushed her hand through her hair. "Barrette. I got angry. But I got angry because she does this to many leetle girls. No tienes que ser un bravucón para conseguir lo que quieres."

"You don't have to be a bully to get what you want?"

"Sí, yes. But I should not have pushed her. She was hurt, then I was sad."

"Guilty, for causing harm?"

She smiled and nodded. "Oh, Jesús, I don't think Angelina is waiting for me in heaven to get what, hmm?"

"Revenge?" I suggested.

She laughed. "Sí, but you know, I hurt someone. I should not do that." She stopped, sipped her coffee. "I used to sometimes get angry with your grandfather. Maybe I get tired, small baby crying, no more babies coming, long hours nursing, Mamá passing. You know, all the things."

"Life. Life every day, Abuelita."

She nodded, picking ginger crumbs from her plate. "I cheated la patología exam, my, hmm, maybe second-year nursing studies. Mr. Moreno, he knew. He called me to the office to say my paper was very good but too good. He knew I was not that good. I was avergonzada, sí, ashamed. But he say, 'Why you not tell me? Ask for help? I can help you more.' He say, 'Go home to think, have the holidays, and next term ask for help when you need the help.'" She shrugged. "I am not the one usually to ask for the help."

There was a pause. I sat there with her on a fine mid-summer day in Cork, in what is now of course, a lifetime ago.

"There was a seester, at the convent, you know. She loved your grandfather. Not love, you know … the first steps."

"Attraction? Infatuation?"

"Sí, infatuation. El encaprichamiento te hace actuar como loco. Make you crazy. Attraction, but he played her along. Did nothing to stop her." She was silent then, clicking her tongue against her teeth, rooting for stray ginger.

"He used to laugh when he told me of her, of her hiding around a corner, pretending to be busy near where he was working, building. Fainting in the heat, all of those things." She grimaced and waved her hand vaguely to indicate offensive behaviour. It seemed I had yet more to learn of my grandfather.

"Then few weeks, maybe months, he stopped telling me the stories, or maybe his stories were a leetle not so recto, not so straight." She nodded sagely. "I knew he was over his head."

"He had acted upon her attraction?" I could hardly hear myself.

"No, no, no. Had not acted at all. This is just as bad."

"Let it continue?"

"Sí, but for too long. Silence, this is not honesty, Jesús; it is just silence. No use to anyone. She was young, a young seester. Foolish, even with all those prayers. He needed to be the wise one. Wisdom, I tell you, it is the other side to ignorance."

She sat a while, watching the birds feeding. My father filled a bird feeder year-round and placed it where Rosa could see it.

"Beautiful chaffinch."

"Yes, Abuelita, beautiful." Beyond the chatter of tits and finches, the harbour hummed, traffic rhythmically thrummed on the distant tar, faraway sounds of dogs and children, an excited blackbird yakka yakka yakked behind the roundhouse.

"I say these things because this is life, Jesús, these stories, sentimientio, emocíon. This is what makes the eighty-nine years a very long movie." She smiled again. "And it is not a thriller, or very exciting. St. Peter will not be well entertained."

We laughed together. The image of St. Peter waiting at the heavenly gates was a favourite of Abuelita Rosa and Mamá. Many times watching something silly on television, she would say, "Wait until St. Peter hears what they did." Or, if there was soccer or rugby or golf, one of them would say, "Wait until they have to tell St. Peter what they did with their life and the leetle ball." Papá would chide his womenfolk with "Doesn't someone have to be the entertainer or sportsman?" And the discussion would ensue as to whether anyone actually did have to entertain others, or whether a sport should ever earn anyone a million dollars. I am certain every home has a similar vein of discursive thought. We were, however, all agreed that meeting St. Peter for a life de-brief was a given. The concept often gave me the pause required, before speaking or acting.

Rosa sipped her water. "I say we will have a holiday, Sean. We took María down the coast for a week to Barbate, fishing village, quiet. I have a nursing friend there so we had a good time. Before we go, I walk to the convent with María, maybe she is cinco or seis or so. I bring churros for Sean and lemonade and see him at his almuerzo. Lunch. We sit together and he is showing María to break the stones with the hammer and put it in the wall. I see the seester, I see her inside, looking out. I smile and nod to her. I go inside to her and I say hello, I am Rosa the wife of Sean O'Soolivawn." She stopped her story there. Her hands clasped to her chest. "We are all feeling, Jesús. All of us have hearts. I did not want her to be sad or bad. She needed to let the feelings go."

I understood. There was no need for confrontation, for discourse, just a simple exhibition of how family life was for Sean, and removing him from sight for a week was enough to burst the young bubble of desire.

"Abuelita? Your heart. Takotsuba?"

"Octopus trap," she cast her eyes heavenwards. "I cannot wait to tell Sean I am now a fishing vessel."

"You knew of this condition?"

"No, I had not heard it. Lou he always say everything we know is so tiny." She squinted as she pinched her thumb and forefinger together. "Tiny bit of what there is to know."

"You know why?"

She smiled. "Why this happen? Hmm … I am not sure, Jesús." She paused, her tongue clicked against her teeth. "Lou is in California, yes?"

I nodded. I had visited him a year or more previously and spent time with his family again. We had met in Cadiz several times over the years and I had assisted him fifteen or so years ago to dismantle his Spanish life, to finally retire to the U.S. I remained in reasonably regular contact, through e-mail and messaging, with one or other of his children.

Rosa closed her eyes. "In my dream that afternoon, ah! I was so tired that day, Jesús, like my body is heavy, it needs the rest. Your Papá made me the lunch, I came to my bed, then the dream. Oh, Jesús! I still see it, it is so clear. Sean on a not very big boat."

I laughed spontaneously. "The very last place he would ever want to be."

She smiled and nodded. "Exactemente. And," she stressed, "the boat is going down." Her hand swung wide from her side, drifting slowly downwards to the leg of her chair. "He is shouting, he is screaming. I hear him clearly. I remember once him like this, at la playa, a person swimming and in trouble, maybe drowning, and he was like a wild animal screaming for someone to help."

"Because he could not help."

She nodded. "Yes, helpless. For Sean, the sea is for the looking at."

"Yes, I remember."

"In the dream, I am swimming but no moving, no getting there. It is like swimming in el lodo. Mud. And so very real, Jesús. I was trying, trying, but no moving near him. Then ppfff!" She snapped her fingers. "There is Lou, he has Sean's hand and my hand and he is pulling, pulling, up, up, up, like a long light." Her hand lifted to her brow and slowly trailed down her cheek. "I could even feel the water, Jesús, on my face, then up, up, up we all go." Her hand now rose upwards with the memory, her eyes were bright with vision.

"No sound, just light. Then I woke up." She shrugged. "And bueno, you know the rest."

The roundhouse door was slowly pushed open, a faint wheeze of a stiff hinge, a fhlap as it passed across the doormat. Sunny, the almost-black tomcat, sidled towards Rosa's chair, looked at us both, then sat to lick his whiskers. Rosa clucked and tut-tutted, calling to him.

"See? He nearly ignores me." She clicked her teeth to call again. "But not quite. He will be mine when it suits him."

I smiled at Rosa looking at the beautiful graceful creature that was nonchalantly licking a paw while calculating his next move. It was a given in our household that cats were fortunate to be mute, fortunate not to have or express an opinion.

"I was left alone, Jesús. My mother, my father, all gone. No aunts or uncles, no family. Sean came, my mother went. So my life has been everyone you have known too. I have so many friends always—the Naval Base, Cadiz, mothers to María's school friends. Always talk and life and noise." She paused, chewing the soft ginger square, lowered her arm, rubbing her finger tips together to coax the cat.

"Then here in Ireland I find I am from Cork. The line of my peoples back to here, then there." She waved her biscuit towards the sea. "Now I am here too. Many lovely people here, I like them."

The swallows hooped and looped across the garden, chattering and calling. At the back door of the cottage, I saw Mamá pull on her gilet then come our way.

"Here comes Mamá, Abuelita."

"Mi hermosa María," she smiled. A tear came to her eye.

"They have been everything to me, Jesús," she whispered. "You have been everything to me." She reached for my hand. "You truly are my family."

I cried then. Just then the tears came, for there is no measure of the time I have shared with this soul. The wisdom, knowledge, love, laughter we have exchanged. We both know it is nearly spent, that this is natural and not conclusive, but it brings sadness.

"Estaré contigo por siempre. I will be with you," she is saying to me. "I will be with you, lovely Jesús. I will always be with you."

I nodded through tears. "I know Abuelita, I know this so well. I have heard Abuelo Sean for thirty years now."

She smiled. "But not so much of late, I am guessing? Because I think I am hearing him more."

I was surprised, for it had not consciously occurred to me, but she was right. "Yes. You are quite right. He has been quieter in the last year or so."

"More content, or moved on to another life perhaps, learning again. Maybe no smoking this time," she added. "Maybe this time he listens to those who love him."

The door opened, Mamá looked in. Sunny sprang onto Rosa's lap, startling us all, rubbing his head against her breast.

"Well, look at you lot." Mamá smiled. "My favourite souls in all the world."

∞

It was very late in what we called summer, for crisp mornings were truly autumn on the wind. From my hilltop pondering on Iona, I had returned to Cork and carefully listened to the progress of Abuelita Rosa's health, knowing that she chose to fade and did not intend to fight. I would now leave her again once more.

When I was about to depart again, Abuelita Rosa assured me that she was well and happy, and would be with us for some time yet. "I am not ready, Jesús, to see them up there," she had said, jerking her leetle head skywards. "They come to me sometimes, you know, but we smile and I say, Not now, not yet, I like the summertime."

"Oh!" I was surprised, "You can choose your time quite specifically, Rosa?" I queried her. "Sí Jesús, I ask for a leetle longer. " I pleaded the empty pledge of not being too far away on the island and ready to return within a few hours.

I had continued my research with the early saints and wrote follow-up essays on early Christian Ireland. My first series of saintly tales had the Boston publishers seeking more—more depth of conviction that drew the heart and soul into the very roots of Ireland, the crossover from pagan to priest, the retention of essential practices, rituals and how they were disguised by the new church. The readership was chiefly American and I felt the soullessness of a planted population in a soil that was not theirs, endlessly seeking their own roots.

I heard the story of the day from Papá. Mamá had been playing music with her friends. If I close my eyes, I visualise his words, playing across my mind like a stage show, a drama in which I am the lone audience of one, seated in the theatre of souls, drawn to every moment of unfolding upon the stage, to the final curtain. These are the thespians whom I love best and this is the script:

Abuelita Rosa was awake, attempting to attune to my father's presence in her bedroom.

"Rosa? Good morning."

"Daniel. Sweat at night, Daniel, not good. Heart not close the skin, so out with heat. Siento mi propio pulso. I feel my pulse, Daniel. It is full."

"Is that good, Rosa?" My father, not medically minded, could do nothing except listen carefully, to know when to call for help, or what to tell Mamá.

No, no good. It is too big today. The vessels are weak and see here." She reached for a hand-mirror on the bedside table; she stuck out her tongue. "Red, see? Red at tip."

"Yes, I see. You know what this is?"

"Sí, I am at the dee-solution of yin and yang, little finger not feeling right, numb, no deqi today, Daniel."

"Deqi, Rosa?"

"Deqi, arrival of qi. Life force. I am nearly usado."

"Spent? Empty?"

"Sí, Daniel, nearly now. I will get my clothes on and go to the garden if you will help me?"

"Of course, Rosa. I will bring you some toast in the roundhouse. Let me help you to the bathroom first."

"Thank you, Daniel."

My father hovered between the hall and kitchen while she washed and toiletted, checking occasionally to see that she was okay.

"I need you now, Daniel, please."

He barely heard her. He found her sitting on el vater, tears in her eyes.

"I just cannot do it, Daniel. I cannot get myself up again. Me disculpo. I am so very sorry."

"Sshh, sshh, Rosa. It is not a problem at all. Let's see now, if you are all finished there. Are you finished? Do you need a wipe or cleanup at all?"

She shook her head.

"I can maybe lift you? Or would you prefer to stand on your own feet?"

"I will try the standing. I am not sure I am ready for the carrying."

He recalled how light she was, how light in frame and stature—like the birds she loved to watch—yet she could not lift herself. He dressed her, wrapped her in wool blankets, and wheeled her to the roundhouse, where he had lit the Caledonia Queen, a tiny wood-burning stove rescued from an abandoned gypsy caravan.

"I am okay now, thank you, Daniel. I will just sit for a leetle bit."

"I will bring you some toast maybe and some tea?"

"That would be so lovely. Thank you, Daniel."

He turned to leave and she called to him.

"Daniel? I have been thinking some of the things. It is so many years since I gave you breakfast in my kitchen, you remember? When you were the leetle English boy María found?"

"Of course I remember, Rosa. You cooked eggs for me."

She nodded, smiling. "Many years. María found the very best boy. The angels brought you from Cyprus to Cadiz, Daniel. Do not forget that."

It is right here, this moment, this is the very moment that in my solo place as the audience, I can hear from the theatrical orchestral pit, the sound of Pachebel's "Canon in D." I know Dr. Lou Zhao would be in a splendid white tuxedo, surrounded by a heavenly choir of angels. He would conduct the friends and neighbours of the East Cork Orchestra: Mamá playing principal violin, Joyce Byrne on second, Cousin David on third, Paul Whelan on cello, old Jack Thurston on the harpsichord he built for his demented wife. Tony Willis would be at his baby grand piano, followed by the resounding French horns and Arthur's trumpet. A tall Scotsman would pump his trombone, Cousin Frank and Julia O'Brien pulling accordions and, somehow, although not an orchestral regular, the strain of an Anglo concertina would follow along, in honour of the sweetest leetle Abuelita anyone could ever have been born to.

Tears of love and grief squeeze through my eyelids, for the curtain is about to fall on the last act of her final chapter and the stage door will soon close.

∞

Mamá came home at lunchtime then did not return to her dancing children. Rosa had spoken several times with her, then desired only to sleep, just sleep in her own bed. They drifted in and out of the room. Sometimes Rosa opened her eyes, acknowledged them; sometimes she used the bathroom; sometimes she smiled yet seemed not to see them. Occasionally Papá heard her voice, conversing, like hearing her on the phone, a one-sided chat. He watched her from the door and she was quite content. She very clearly said, "Jesús is coming from Val-en-see-a."

I did arrive later that evening from Valentia Island. "Val-en-see-a," Abuelo Sean had also said. We lit a candle, Mamá prayed with her beads, my father sat quietly in a chair at the foot of her bed. Mostly there was silence among us in those first hours. I made a playlist for background sound, a mix of Irish, Ambrose's jazz, Philomena's swing, Papá's occasional American country or Nashville-Irish, and Lou Zhao's classic hits that she might have liked.

Papá brought tea and Philomena's fruit brack. Ambrose and Philomena had visited from Cork a day or so previously, laden with tasty treats from the Two Spoons, exchanged for pots of blackberry and apple jam, red currant jelly, and bunches of heavenly sweet pea for the café. Rosa had been well yet quiet. Ambrose called me in Kerry to tell me of the visit, saying, "I hope y'have all yer saints lined up, Jesus. I'm thinking they may be doin' the guard of honour quite soon."

Now Mamá was the nurse, sitting, assisting, holding hands. During those watching hours, we exchanged stories in low voices, remnants of our lives shared. Occasionally Abuelita Rosa would open her eyes, even smile at our words.

Mamá spoke quietly. "Do you remember, Daniel, when we got married in Cadiz?" My father raised his eyebrows, nodding his assent, giving her way to memory.

"We were to have the ceremony in the Naval Base Chapel, Jesús. This was easiest for everyone as many lived on the base and the church at the convent was so big for our small wedding. My Papá would have liked it there with the sisters; he could show me off to all his nuns and brothers. But Mamá insisted on the Naval Base, where, of course, all her work colleagues and friends would be. They had this ding-dong, argy-bargy for weeks. I was teaching in Seville and then near Jerez, so I only heard sometimes at the weekend. Neither Daniel nor I had said anything about where we would have the marriage, nor had we given them even a date, but they did what, hmm, atrapados … …."

"Got caught up in it?" I suggested.

"Yes! Caught up in it. Somehow this became the focus. Which church for the wedding. I am sure they did not argue all the day every day but somehow this thing was like a volcano between them. Ya, ya, yada-yada back and forth."

My father harrumphed quietly. "Your mother could be quite feisty, María. I did occasionally see her with her hackles up."

Mamá smiled. "And my father did not at all like being argued with. What's this they say here, he was like a dog with a bone."

Rosa smiled, turning her head on her pillow.

"Who won?"

"We did!" declared Papá quietly. "We organised the whole thing one quiet weekend when Rosa and Sean didn't even know your mother had come from Jerez. We spoke with the padre from Convento de Jesús Nazareno in Chiclana de la Frontera; he agreed to marry us on the Saturday morning and the nuns would provide almond pastries and coffee. And that's what we did. We had a beautiful simple ceremony, a lovely time in the sunshine with our coffees and then we all walked down the town to a restaurant, Santa Ana. No gazing at us by half of Cadiz or the whole Naval Base. Oh no, no!"

Mamá laughed. "Yes, that is how it went. But let me tell you, Jesús. We came home to Cadiz from visiting Padré Ignacio that first weekend, you know, when we were making the arrangements.

My father and Rosa started the ya ya church discussion, then Daniel gave one shout that silenced them both. He told them very calmly, 'María and I have sorted this.' " She smiled. "You remember, Daniel?"

Papá grinned mischievously. "I told them, Jesús, I told them we were hiring a yacht and we would all sail from Cadiz harbour across to the Naval Base at Rota. It would only take a couple of hours with a bit of time for some music and the captain would marry us en route. That way anyone who wanted to see us, could see us, and if they were bad of sight they could use binoculars."

"Well, Jesús," continued my mother, shaking her head, "if you saw the face of Papá."

"I bet he went white?" I laughed.

"And then green. And that was the end of any discussion. We gave them the date and I said I would look after inviting the guests when I was free and on school holidays at Christmas. We were married at Easter holidays." She smiled at Papá. "How long ago my love?"

"Sesenta y quatro," came a small, soft voice from the bed. "Todavía estoy escuchando."

She could hear us. Mamá took Abuelita's hand and smiled. "And we are hearing you, Mamá."

∞

My mind wandered past the nearly twenty years in Cork, back to their departing days in Cadiz, when my parents and Abuelita Rosa had embarked on a new phase of their lives and I set forth on mine. Leaving Dr. Zhao in Cadiz had been painful for us all, Mamá and Papá included, for the impact he had made on all our lives. My miraculous presence was solely attributed to his curing Mamá of amenorrhea. He had cried when Abuelita Rosa and I together had told him of impending plans to emigrate, to sólo para ver, just go to see a new life. What Rosa and Dr. Zhao had shared was not enough to keep Rosa, at nearly seventy years old, in Cadiz without her beloved María and Daniel. Soon after learning the news, Dr. Zhao left for San Francisco—before he might possibly witness them pack their belongings and drive away from southwestern Spain.

Those early days in Rostellan, we made new friends, established connections with family and neighbours of Abuelo Sean. There was a surreal element to meeting those who remembered him, played music with him, and his family who had mourned his departure. It was sometimes difficult to bridge the gap of the intervening fifty years, when so few in 1980s Cork would have experienced Cadiz, or even had a wider knowledge of Spain.

I would walk the Rostellan estate garden walls with my grandmother, her petite presence dwarfed by limestone giants. "Why they so big, so tall, Jesús?" I could only surmise that they offered the most elemental protection and perhaps growing height for greenhouses. I could not in truth calculate in my non-mathematical mind the sheer volume of stone contained in their structure, the hewn slate as Abuelo Sean had told me, atopping their formidable rise. This was the work of human hands, the hands of my forebears.

We poked around the perimeter of these great walls covered in creeping ivy and lesser celandine. We uncovered some of the dislodged slates that had slid from their mortared beds through a process of age or disturbance by falling trees. Perhaps they had lost the desire to hold on any longer, sliding through the silence of a moonlit night to the forest floor. Papá, Ambrose, and I had removed some of these ancient slabs, ferrying them awkwardly by wheelbarrow and a certain amount of naval language, stumbling over tree roots, sliding down beech-leaved tracks to manoeuvre the wheelbarrow to Ambrose's van. Their new home was to form the Caim path. Blue slates from Bangor imported by Anglo-Irish gentry, laid to trace a Celtic way in a foreigner's garden. It was just magical.

Abuelita Rosa would often walk the stony shoreline alone, past the aviary remains, from the old boathouse to the crumbling Siddon's Tower. She was not interested in the history, not cognisant of the story, just content to touch the mortared walls, humming her own tune, her own sound, scanning her own harbour.

∞

By the early hours of the morning I had relieved my Mamá of her vigil, suggesting she get some sleep on the couch next door. Papá had retired an hour or so earlier, but she protested, wishing to be with her mamá to the end. I could only agree that when the time came, it would be my wish also. I wedged an easy chair into the bedroom between the bed and the wardrobe, making Mamá as comfortable as possible under a woollen blanket and within hand-holding distance of her mother.

I make another playlist—elemental, soothing, harmonic sounds. My mother snoozed, curled in her chair, their hands touching on the sea-blue and green bedspread. My meditative gaze follows the lines of woven blues, intertwining greens. I see seahorses, seaweed, trees, climbing roses, a multitude of flowing waves and green rocks, until I reach the end of the circle and am carried again to seahorses, seaweed, trees, climbing roses. I lift my eyes from the covers to her face. Sometimes Abuelita Rosa is animated, occasionally she frowns, sometimes she mutters. Her breathing stays steady.

My mind returns to Dr. Zhao, what they might have shared together, what I had shared with him, long hours of knowledge and learning in old Cadiz. Into my drifting head came a memory of when he once handed me a child's drawing of what appeared to be a tree in assorted colours.

"A tree?" I asked of him, thinking perhaps it had been the work of a grandchild.

"Yes," he drawled, "looks like, eh?" He rotated the page twice.

"A lung!" I exclaimed.

He laughed. "Indeed, but just like a tree, roots, branches, and leaves."

"Needing our carbon dioxide, giving us oxygen."

"The simplest but most glorious of all miracles, eh?"

"Aorta," he had said to me once, of our main human blood-carrying vessel. "Ay-or-ta. From the Greek aorte "a strap to hang (something by), to lift up. Perfect." He had a way of standing still, an imperceptible nod of his head as he listened carefully to something, himself probably. And that may have been it, my nugget of wisdom for the day.

I once had seen him cry silently after he opened and read a letter. I had often kept myself removed as the occasion arose, aware I was in the privacy of his home. If the phone rang, I would retire to the porch or take time in his backyard under the vine leaves to give him space. This particular day he had looked at me and beckoned me to join him at the table. He folded the letter into its envelope and said simply, "My son, the electrical engineer." I waited for him to continue.

"I have fretted and worried for him for several years. He is a homosexual in San Francisco, which is a centre of the AIDS epidemic. Any father would be worried."

"Is everything okay, Dr. Zhao?" I asked.

He nodded and gestured to the letter. "He has fobbed off my concerns for quite some years, kisses me, and tells me I'm being silly, that he is careful, he is sexually careful, you know. But one never does know. At least, one's father never does know." He laughed.

"He has written me to say that he is going to have a civil partnership in the fall. He and his partner, Harry, have been together for some time, and has asked if I would arrange perhaps to be in San Fran in October so I might give him away."

With a heartfelt smile, I took the hand of this man I had grown to love.

"I couldn't be happier for him, Jesús. Experiencing love. I loved my girlfriends when I was young. I loved my wife until she died. I truly loved your grandmother and, although we drifted apart, I am eternally grateful she has returned to me, for I truly still do."

My wandering mind next came to rest with the Terry's of Cork, the ancestral lineage of my lovely Abuelita, here before me in her last hours. Some five or six years ago we had visited a new museum of the seventeenth-century Wine Geese families of Ireland, housed in fifteenth-century Desmond Castle, standing on one of those narrow Kinsale streets. She had spent time reading, looking, taking notes. "Look, Jesús," she pointed and I read:

> *Fernando A de Terry y Brucet, who was born in Cadiz in 1783, had stocks of maturing wine by 1816 in both Cadiz and El Puerto de Santa Maria.*

"Different Terry family," she said. "You remember the Cartujano horses in El Puerto? That was Terry business too. Everywhere they were near me in Cadiz and I did not know it. I think perhaps I only knew a leetle bit of me, all of my life? I am, hmm, avergonzada de mí mismo."

"Oh, Abuelita," I could only exclaim, "there is no need for shame. How could you have known when you had no family around you, no one to ask?"

"But I never asked the question, Jesús. Never once thought who is my mother? Concepcion Herrera y Terry, what is her name? She left Madrid after the fire, came to family in Cadiz, and said not again anything I remember." She clicked her teeth and shook her head. "Soy un idiota. What will I tell her when I meet her again, Jesús?" She laughed then. "I think I know I will meet her again."

I nodded. "For sure, Abuelita. And she will probably not question why you did not ask about your family history. She will most likely say, 'Oh lovely Rosa, you have done so many loving things for people. You have been so kind, so caring for so many others. You have saved lives. You have helped lives. I am proud of you. You truly were a wonderful daughter.' "

She pushed against me playfully, "Jesús, parar ya. Stop now." She laughed a leetle. "I only always did the best I could."

"And that is why you are so loved, my Abuelita."

∞

I watch for signs, for death is not just a moment, not just the final breath after nearly ninety years of breathing, and the soul is eternal. Towards the bewitching hour between four and five, her hands move outward, reaching. She smiles, then frowns and says, "Necesito esperar." I need to wait. I am curious what she needs to wait for. Her head tosses, then she is asleep again.

Towards dawn, my heavy eyes open, aware of vehicular sound outside. Mamá stirs in her chair, awakens and, touching her mother's brow, frowns, smiles, and whispers to me, "She is still with us."

I nod. "Yes Mamá. We have visitors." I rise to kiss her and help her out of the chair.

I stretch, loosening cramped joints. I hear the robin shrill in the hawthorn, a wren hops furtively to the hebe outside the window. Papá is in the kitchen—morning sounds, the filled kettle spitting and hissing on the hotplate, the back door opening for the dogs, the fridge door rattling bottles and cartons, the hum of the oil stove. The sounds of the familiar hypnotic rhythm of daily life in the cottage by the water.

Abuelita Rosa stirs, opens her eyes, and smiles widely toward the ceiling. "Ah! At last. They are here at last." She has not heard a car, she is not looking at me but past me, somewhere to the wall behind me, smiling at the wooden carving of Virgin and Child, hung by the mirror.

"Mamá, una vida tan larga. Llevo mucho tiempo viviendo acá."

I know she does not see me. She sees her Mamá. It has been such a long life, she says to her, I have been here such a long time. She looks at the window, reaches forth, lifting herself off the pillow.

A toilet flushes, the dog yaps and yowls, sounds from the yard. Mamá's voice from the kitchen, muffled, quiet, coming down the short hall. I hear the quietest of Scottish voices, "Came to be with ye at this time, María. Och hush, hush, there, there my love, what are family for, eh?"

My mother is crying as Ambrose follows her into the leetle bedroom. Philomena's large frame fills the doorway behind him, my father at the rear. Philomena presses my tired self to her bosom, kissing the top of my head. "Well now, Jesus, 'tis been a long night for you all," she whispers. The room is full of love. Mamá is back in her chair by the pillow, holding her mother's hand. Abuelita Rosa is peaceful, her breathing shallow, her pallor sallow.

Philomena blesses herself and quietly says to Papá and Ambrose, "I know you two are nearly heathens unless there's a horse involved, but I think we might have just a quiet prayer for the lovely lady on her journey. Just a simple one."

With her free right hand, Mamá reaches for Philomena, who holds Ambrose, who clasps my father, who reaches for me. I stand to close the circle, gently lifting Abuelita Rosa's left hand. I think she squeezes mine—or maybe it was just a reaction? I look to Mamá. She is smiling and I see Rosa's hand grip hers. She is still with us.

It occurs to me that should my grandmother open her eyes just now, it might just be the Transfiguration she would be witnessing—with three six-foot-tall bodies holding hands at the foot of her bed. I think of Sr. Dolores in Cadiz, reading the Sunday gospel to us on a Thursday, then we would take out our paper and pencils and draw the gospel scene on a Friday, so we were well-versed before attending the church on Sunday. For some reason in the Transfiguration, Jesus, Moses, and Elijah were conveyed as giants.

"Our Father, who art in heav'n, hallowed be thy name," Philomena had started quietly. We join her in The Lord's Prayer.

"Hail Mary, full of grace … ." The Angelic Salutation. We are about to refrain when a soft clear voice from the dying bed responds, "el Señor es contigo, bendita tú eres entre todas las mujeres." Philomena smiles and continues quietly in English, "blessed is the fruit," as my mother and her mother say in Spanish, "y bendito el fruito de tu vientre," then altogether, with bowed heads, I hear, "Jesus, Jesús."

There is a pause in which my vigil tears rise unbidden, the beauty of the moment is suspended over my grandmother's bed and my hands are held in a circle of love. The candle flame bursts high, shining a thousand reflections on glasses, the mirror, the dawn outside. I am sobbing.

Philomena smiles to me and in her broadest Cork accent says, "Lovely Jesús. Everybody's miracle."

Mamá is smiling and crying and praying, "Holy Mary, Mother of God, pray for us sinners, now and at the hour of our death." My mother pauses.

"Amen," chorus the heathen horse-men.

Our hands held, from deep within me I feel the rise of an 'ohm,' the sound of the universe being born, the universal frequency. I let it flow out loud, inhale, Papá joins me, 'a-a-u-u-m-m' the reverence of sound vibrates through our clasped hands, Abuelita Rosa no longer gripping, yet still held in mine. Once more, we chant, 'a-a-u-u-m-m' and we are joined by Ambrose, Philomena, and Mamá, the final note drifting around us, through us, before settling quietly and, just before it fades, a gorgeous Scotsman in the lowest of voices starts to sing ...

> *Amazing Grace*
> *How sweet the sound*
> *That saved a wretch like me ...*

His eyes lift to look at us all, a smile at the edge of his lips, and with streaming tears his Cork-accented wife of endless years joins him ...

> *I once, was lost, and now I'm found*
> *Was blind but now I see.*

A loud sigh from Abuelita Rosa startles us, a small cough and, taking her hands from mine and Mamá's, she raises them slowly above the bed, palms open to the heavens, "Sean, Lou," she sighs with a whisper and I know, and maybe it is only I who knows, that

Lou has them both by the hands and he is lifting them from the water on a bright path to the sky.

And she is gone.

∞

It is lunchtime, although that human marker for midday means nothing today. There has been endless tea, coffee, cake, and sandwiches; and my long night is wearying me. I excuse myself and escape to the garden with the dogs. The damp path draws me towards the shore, to the garden house beneath the rowan tree, empty now on this chilly September morning. I am bereft.

My phone buzzes in my pocket. My heart sinks, this is not the time for any more words with anyone. I glance at the screen, Steven Zhao, +1 831-238-4912. How can it possibly be at this very moment that Dr. Lou Zhao's son is calling me from Carmel, California?

"Steve! Hi."

"Jesús? Hi."

"Steve, it must be four in the morning there?"

"Ya, Jesús, just about that. Listen, this isn't text material and I just needed to tell you myself. Dad passed away late last night. He hadn't been so well these last few weeks, just kinda faded away."

A late swallow who should have been en route to South Africa swooped past me. Maybe she had forgotten something in the shed roof.

"Steve? Oh Steve! My grandmother passed away five hours ago. She just faded away these last few months."

The silence fills the eight-thousand-and-something kilometres that separate us.

"No way? You're kidding me? Jesús?"

"No kidding at all, Steve. They must have made a plan."

He laughed. "Well I'll be darned."

"Me too, Steve. Darned. Like a worn out pair of socks."

∞

We waked Abuelita Rosa where she lay, in her leetle room. Mamá and Philomena attended to her physical needs, then dressed her in the flowing purple gown of the Millennium Party. Her bed was made in bright white sheets. Mamá brushed her hair and I lifted her into place, laying her head on her pillow. A circle of five candles lit her bedside table, with a vase of the straggling last of the lilac-and-white sweet-pea. Through the window ajar, the robin with a white spot on his wing sang from the hawthorn.

The kitchen took on the appearance of the Two Spoons on a Thursday lunchtime—boxes and trays of cakes, sandwiches, pots of jam, scones, apple tarts. I washed cups for Ireland. I like the sound of that, something I learned from the café when Philomena would quip, "Oh I've made scones for Ireland today." Or Bridget would say, "You can talk for Ireland, they still won' listen."

We laid out the trestle tables in the garden. By mid-afternoon, Ambrose and Michael returned from the city with Maureen and Shy Sheila, a Burco boiler, folding tables, chairs, and an extra fridge-freezer. Another box revealed tea towels, cutlery, extra cups, glasses, plates.

"We're having a party, Ambrose?"

"Och aye, Jesus. Funerals can be like that around here. You wait 'til the music starts."

My memory for the remainder of that day is a continual stream of friends and neighbours, some well acquainted with Rosa over the years. I shook countless hands, and to a one they felt genuine affection for Abuelita; to a one they mourned our loss. She had ingrained her leetle self into this place and she had passed on, belonging to a community, being a part of their lives. There was a concertina-playing stone-mason who had lived amongst them a very long time ago, and we all carry his-story.

Sometimes I would leave the garden, go to the bedroom where she lay, meet someone she knew saying a prayer over her body. Someone brought Holy Water in a font. There were smiles, tears, rosary beads, every fashion of the Sign of the Cross. Sometimes I would find Mamá in a huddled embrace, Papá shaking hands with a local. There were children from the schools, young musicians and dancers clutching a parent's hand.

I walked to meet Sue from the doctor's surgery as she wheeled Morna Doc down the avenue. Morna had tears in her eyes for her lost friend. She took my hand as I walked beside her and held me tight as I helped her across the threshold and into our home. In Rosa's bedroom she kneeled by the bedside, touched the cold face, pressed the folded hands with hers, fingered the blue glass beads in Abuelita Rosa's clasped hands.

> *I had a friend, the greatest gift*
> *The Lord has shown me yet.*
> *When life was low and needed a lift*
> *You were the one I met.*
> *In my eye I see your smile*
> *It lights my every day.*
> *And though you maybe gone for a while*
> *For God's gift … I humbly … .*

Morna Doc lay her head on the bed and cried. I gently touched her shoulder, stroked her hair, the unspeaking care I had learned from my passed-on grandmother. After a moment, she lifted her head, "For God's gift, I humbly pray," she cried into the sea of blue-green seahorses, seaweed, trees, climbing roses, flowing waves, and green rocks.

∞

I watched Maureen and Sheila deliver pots of tea to neighbours gathered outside, chatting in September sunshine. Somewhere we met and spoke with the priest. At one time we met the undertaker. Somehow, underneath it all, I felt the strength and guiding presence of Philomena Sowersby. In the evening cool, she had a further dispatch arrive from the city in the guise of Con and Majella: trays of lasagne and fish pie, a portable bain-marie to keep food warm so hunger could be assuaged at anytime. Michael arrived in the Two Spoons van with Bridget McCarthy nodding and bobbing in the passenger seat. He hooked up a portable washstand beside the Burco boiler to wash dishes. I am in awe.

"Oh, you know, I think I might just give up on the city," quips Philomena. "This mobile catering is a piece o' cake."

"Oh, Jesus. I'm so sorry. I'm jus' broken-hearted ah the though' tha' she's gone." Bridget climbed from the Two Spoons van and hovered and jittered, well, jihhered, in my vicinity but out of reach. I stepped towards her and took her two hands in mine, holding her so at least she stopped moving.

"Thank you, Bridget."

"Oh she was the lovlies', she was always so kind to me Jesus and you know I haven' meh too many tha' would be bothered with me ah all, ah all." The pathos of Bridget, that she didn't see as pathos but as reality, that really didn't bother her in the slightest, other than a factual representation of her whole life.

Mamá joined us and gave Bridget no time at all to be ill at ease, putting her arms around the waif-like woman, "Oh, Bridget, thank you for coming all this way to see us. It is such a sad day for us, for me, losing my lovely Mamá."

"Oh I los' mine when I was nine Maree-ya. I often wonder wha' ih woulda been like, y'know, to have a mammy. A real mammy of yer own. I had me aunts, good 'n' all as they were, Philomena's mammy was the bes' to me." She dabbed her eyes. "Buh your mammy was lovely to me too. I jus' wish I had some one of me own. Anyone ah all."

We were silenced again.

"It is a real comfort to me that you are here, Bridget," Mamá said quietly. "Would you have some tea with me?"

"Oh I'd love tha' Maree-ya," Biddy smiled. "Thank you, thank you so much for inviting me."

They moved away, my mother leaning on Bridget's outstretched arm. I released my held breath.

I escaped again; I ran dogs along the shoreline, the sliver of waning moon shining amid the first stars. The oystercatchers took flight, pip-pip-pippitting crossly at their disturbance on the ebbing tide.

As the night falls on this first day of mourning, Papá lights the brazier, bodies ranging in and out of heat and light and hearth. We take turns to keep vigil with my lovely grandmother, a succession of neighbours and friends, who, as if by Irish magic, seemed to have formed a rota to accompany her on her journey. Around the trestle table in the garden as the last cups of tea are drained, Philomena takes my mother's hand.

"We'll have a decade of the Rosary now while we're all here, if you like, María?"

Mamá smiles her gratitude. "That would be lovely, Philomena, thank you."

The Rosary, the 'Crown of Roses', a spiritual bouquet of roses for Mother Mary. Just some of the descriptions of this ancient practice. The rose of all devotions, the first cultivated flower. Papá's emigrant gardening dream. Alfred Lord Tennyson drifts to my mind:

> *More things are wrought by prayer*
> *Than this world dreams of.*

On my travels with the monks of the early saints, I remember 150 pebbles in their pouch, or knots in a piece of hide string, the Celtic infatuation with the number three—trinity. They shortened the rope to 50, recited three times. In persecuted Catholic Ireland, after Henry's Enormous Protestant Boot stamped out all resistance, the string became shorter again and 10 knots would suffice, eventually tying it off it to a prayer ring, easily concealed. The smallest religious rebellion.

"Saturday, so it'll be the Glorious Mysteries," Philomena is saying, "isn't that right, Biddy?"

"Oh, I think, I think tha's righ', Philomena. I couldn', couldn' be exackly sure, buh I'm certain She won' mind."

"Let's have the fourth, the Assumption of Mary into Heaven. Our Father who art in Heaven … ."

There must be six, seven of us around the table. Julia O'Brien is keeping vigil with my leetle grandmother, Papá is hovering near the brazier, the long legs of Ambrose are spread to the westering sky. His bass Scottish voice murmurs with the ladies, Shy Sheila is beside Michael and holding Philomena's left hand. I see their lips move in nearly mute murmur, Michael nodding at the rhythm of chanting prayer, counting down the Hail Marys on his left hand. I see Bridget, her head bowed, intoning softly with Philomena, then the deep inclination at "Jesus," then she lifts her head heavenward, eyes closed and prays fervently, "Holy Mary, mother of God, pray for us sinners, now and ah the hour of our death, Amen," as she strikes her skinny breast.

"Totus Tuus," Pope John Paul had said. "I am all Thine," inspired doctrine expressing total abandonment to Jesus through Mary.

"The Irish tenacity of faith is unexampled in the history of the whole world." I think that was the British Secretary in Ireland after the Easter Rising, 1916. The tenacious Irish, the wonderful, loving warmth of them, who have embraced us foreigners and taken us to their heart; and I am sitting with them and my lips have moved with them for ten Hail Marys, "… now and at the hour of our death. Amen." The world stops. I inhale.

"Glory be to the Father," Philomena says quietly. "And to the Son and Holy Spirit, as it was in the beginning, is now and ever shall be, world without end. Amen." She smiles at us, squeezing my mother's hand. Sunny, the cat, sidles unseen and jumps into her lap, sending Bridget into a startled tirade.

"Jesus, Mary an' St. Joseph, wha' was tha'?" she shrieks.

Ambrose laughs. "Och keep yer hair on, Bridget, 'tis but the wee cat."

Sheila elbows her. "He's coming to pray with us, Bid."

"Oh my saintly hear', I goh a woeful frigh'! I though' ih was a ghos'. After all the prayin' 'n' all tha'." Biddy giggles in her relief.

"Maybe my mother has come to see you, Bridget?" laughs Mamá, tenderly touching Bridget's hand.

Ambrose unwinds his length from the table, nods to Michael, they go to his van, returning with a box of glasses. He uncorks the Powers whiskey. Mamá reaches under the table, lifts the box and unclasps the concertina.

"Now 'tis the first night of travel for her soul," Philomena cautions her husband. "Let's respect that please."

"Och now, whisht my fretting pet. Just a wee dram for us all, after a long day. Anyway I'm sure these folk could use some sleep and some privacy for their grieving."

A long deep sob rises in my body. "This IS our grieving, Ambrose, and I cannot think of a better way to live it."

∞

It is a very late hour when I leave the little group of storytellers and musicians to sit with Abuelita Rosa. Cousin Ken kisses my cheek as he leaves the room, blessing himself carefully from the font as he bows out through the door, which he closes behind him, leaving me alone now with the physical remains of my beloved grandmother. My first thought is for the outer layer of her onion, which makes me smile. A breeze stirs the curtain and carries the sound of Mamá's fiddle to me, with Ken working up and down the scale on his. Leaning over the bed, I kiss her cold forehead.

452

"Thinking of your onion layers, lovely Abuelita. I am with you while you peel back to the Divine. I am here for you and Lou now."

I sit in the chair where I had spent the greater part of the previous night and which has since seated a procession of vigil bodies. The circle of five white candles blaze until the flames dance and diverge and merge into one light. I breathe the leetle room, the light breeze of the night freshening the still air, carrying music and muffled voices or song. I close my eyes and, from the quiet of my heart, ask Leah and Lawrence to stay with me on my spiritual accompaniment. There are the hushed notes of a concertina.

"Physical, ethereal, astral, mental, soul, spirit, and Divine. Different frequencies," Dr. Lou Zhao would say. And eight-thousand-and-something kilometres away, someone else is sitting by his cold body, praying for his soul to be carried to the Light.

∞

By the dying embers of the brazier fire, Papá plays his guitar. Mamá places her fiddle on the red silk scarf in the cracked wooden case, releasing the tension in the bow, smiling at Julia and saying that perhaps it is time for bed. The city folk have departed, for tomorrow is another long day in the waking of a deceased loved one in Ireland. Papá strums, carefully plucking his tune and, raising a tired head, looks at Julia, saying, "Just one more perhaps? Help me out on this one, Julia, please?" He coughs to clear his throat and begins to sing. "La, la la, I'm sure I dreamt you were back again."

Julia picks up his lead, looking at Mamá, leaning over her fiddle case. I stand behind my mother and place my hands on her shoulders. My father is crying, tears streaming through his broken song, 'Past the Point of Rescue.' Mamá's shoulders heave with sobs, her cheek falls to my hand, her hand rises to mine. I lean over her leaning over her fiddle, and we cry together. Papá has no words left in him, Julia softly hums the chorus and we are together, united by heart-wrenching words and grief.

∞

On the second day of Rosa's journey I awake, remembering that I do not like whiskey and I should not have liked a second one. My own idiocy, yet I am somehow grateful that I am not yet as evolved as my now-passed grandmother and now-passed mentor, who would both have known better. Oh the joy of life learning! I take to the sea on a cold October morn, springers prancing beside me through the crashing waves, early rain.

The day passes as the one before. Washing crockery for Ireland, breathing my task, the solidity in which I take refuge, the consistent flow of air in and out of my body. I see the smile of Thich Nhat Hanh, his peaceful gaze, his quiet response to any question. I breathe slowly, and doing so keeps me together. I have not yet mentioned the passing of Dr. Zhao, for this is Rosa's time, so I carry my grief for him silently in my heart. We greet, smile, shake hands, nod, embrace, listen. My body and mind united with my breath, mindfulness in as many moments as I can manage.

We have funeral arrangements to make, prayers to be apportioned, gifts to be carried. At the kitchen table we sit together and tick off a list, adding a name after each task.

"Is every funeral like this?" my father asks of Michael, or Ken, or someone, anyone Irish.

"More or less," answers Michael, enough words for an answer but not enough for an explanation.

∞

In the late afternoon, my parents, Philomena, and I gather in Rosa's bedroom, when from the short hallway comes the muffled sounds of the undertaker and his assistants. My mother unwinds the beads from cold hands, placing them in the cloth bag, as Philomena rolls back the bed clothes. Dressed in splendid purple, as she was for the Millennium party, Abuelita Rosa looks as if she is having an afternoon nap before partying. Mamá blesses herself slowly and blows out the candles, murmuring the Light and Love to whomever needs it. We stop and pause.

"C'mon now," Philomena whispers, "let's leave the lads to their job."

I am first to walk from the back door through the porch to the garden, where the yawning, gaping hole of the undertaker's hearse is ready to swallow the coffin. Looking up, I see neighbours standing in twos and threes in the meadow, around the caim, lining the avenue of hawthorns to the gate. I stare incredulously for they are all here, our community, every soul who met her, knew her, knew us.

"Papá." He is behind me in the doorway. "Papá, look."

He is quizzical until I gesture outwards to the garden.

"Oh my dear God! Oh dearie me. Well, well. I have never seen anything like it."

He turns to Mamá about to step from the kitchen. "María! María, look. Everyone has come."

She walks silently towards the hearse, slowly taking in the crowd of mourners who await the final journey of her mother. She climbs onto the picnic table, faces them all, raises her hands towards them, pulls inwards towards her heart, then bows her head in thanks.

"Holy God," says Philomena behind us. "That's a great turnout. Fit for the Queen Mother herself."

I do not know who I am, the grandchild of this honoured being, one who thought the world was simple enough to understand when all actions arose from the heart with love and love could outdo all fear and anger. I climb to the picnic table beside my mother and take her hand, raising my free hand to my lips and blowing a kiss outwards, upwards, carried on heaven's breath, showering heartfelt gratitude on my neighbours and friends, on those who have taken us in and embraced us and made us theirs.

The evening is for us at home. Abuelita Rosa lies alone in the vastness of the new church in Aghada. As we left her, Papá quipped amusingly, "That's the biggest room she has ever slept in. I hope she doesn't wake in the night for the loo."

In the garden I find Michael and Sheila by the Two Spoons van.

'Hiya, Jesus," Sheila greets me, kissing my cheek. "Are you getting on okay?"

"I'm doing all right, thank you."

Michael scuffs his feet in the grass, head lowered then looks up at me, tears in his eyes. He hesitantly extends his hand, which I grasp then pull him into my arms and hold him tightly.

"She was so lovely, Jesus," he cried. "She was like my own granny. My mam says to say hi an' she'll see you tomorrow."

I release him gently. "That will be great, Michael. Thank you."

Sheila is fussing about the back of the van. "I think we have left everything we'll need for tomorrow. 'Tis all clean and ready to go. Mrs. S has gone now to meet Maureen at the café and make the sandwiches. We'll head off now and see ya in the morning, okay?" She cast her gaze downwards, sweeping a stray strand of hair behind her ear.

"Sheila," I stop her flow. "Sheila. Thank you. I have seen you pour tea for two days now. You are the best. You both are. I am so lucky and Philomena is so lucky and my grandmother was so lucky to have known you both. Now be gone the two of you, drive safely and God bless you until tomorrow."

In the kitchen there is quiet, other than the hum of the oil stove warming the autumnal night. Mamá sits before a lighted candle; the scent of rosemary wafts around the room.

"Rosemary for remembrance," I remind her.

She shrugs. "I do not even know who left it, who to thank. It was just here, on the table."

Papá comes through from the middle room, carrying an uncorked bottle of Tempranillo. "Quiet glass of red perhaps?"

I nod and reach for three glasses, while Mamá prepares nuts, crackers, some cheeses, olives, cherry tomatoes from her greenhouse, cucumbers pickled at the end of summer. The last of the evening sun shines from the harbour as we sit in our now quiet kitchen.

"Mamá, Papá," I start, then stop, then start again, "you should both know, now that Abuelita Rosa has left our home. Dr. Zhao has," I pause and swallow the lump forming in my throat. It takes several moments to continue. "Dr. Zhao also passed away on Friday night," I finish in a rush.

"No! Jesús? No!" Mamá utters, her hands flying to her face, to tired and reddened eyes. "I cannot cry anymore!"

I nodded. "Sí, Mamá. Steven said," but no words would form, no sound utter and I had to stop and breathe deeply. "Steve said 'desvanecido'. Faded away, just like Abuelita."

Papá stares at me. "Oh Jesús! The day gets stranger and stranger. All those people. It's like every cow yard and parochial outpost I took her to in the ten years she nursed here, every one of them came to see her. I have never seen anything like it. When did you hear about Lou?"

"Lunchtime yesterday. Steven called me. I could not tell you. It was just too soon, too close to living with Abuelita Rosa's last hours."

"Oh Jesús, Jesús," Mamá's sobs are dry, her breath catches in her throat.

"Do you know, Jesús, I came to the kitchen this morning to find a crow sitting on the windowsill?" Papá says. "He jumped about a bit, caw-cawing, tap-tapping at the pane. Gave me the most awful fright, then flew off. It was like he was, well, calling me really. So I went out with the dogs and walked around to see if he was still there and, goodness me, about thirty of them just lifted off the garden, flew around the roundhouse a couple times, then took to the trees. It was ... well, quite odd really."

"The crow is a strong symbol in Celtic mythology of death and transition, Papá." I hold my mother's hands across the table where we have shared so much of our lives. "What you witnessed would not be surprising to many folk. I can nearly hear old Timmy O'Brien say, 'They come to guide the soul.' It is also believed that they are messengers, caw-caw-calling to us about creation and the magic that is alive and all around us, all the time."

We are silent. My mother shakes her head. "Dear Lou. Such a wonderful man. He loved her so much. He loved you so much too, Jesús."

I nod. "He told me." I squeeze her hands. "They are all together now, Mamá. There'll be music up to heaven tonight if Abuelo Sean has his way."

We laugh amid our tears, clinking glasses through rosemary-laden scent.

∞

The final day of the journey of Rosa's soul: the day we congregate, remember, celebrate. Another day in the stream of my consciousness, moments merge with moments, faces, smiles, and tears.

In the church, Kenneth and David read the liturgy; grandchildren of Philomena and Ambrose say Prayers of the Faithful, carry offertory gifts to the waiting priest. Mamá's musician friends play hymns, repeat incantations and responses. My father and I stumble through designated kneeling and standing or sitting. Ambrose, of utterly no assistance, on Papá's left; myself, from the corner of my eye, following the lead of Mamá and Philomena to my right. In a muddled moment of comedic proportions, I stand and my father sits. He stands and I sit, I stand again, until we both eventually kneel with the rest of the congregation, our shoulders shaking in silent mirth. Behind me, I hear a stifled snort from Con and a whisper from Majella Sowersby, "Cool moves there, Jesus. She woulda liked that."

At the consecration bell, my head lowers and I am returned to the monks of Plum Village where the sound of the bell carries me to my true home.

Bridget McCarthy fervently bows and prays, climbing the steps at her appointed time to a private audience with the priest to receive the host, drink from the chalice, and minister communion to the faithful. I watch her flutter and bow at the altar, and hear her a decibel or so above the priest, "Body of Chris', Body of Chris'."

At the end of the service, the priest announces that there is no burial, that the tiniest Spanish woman in the whole of Cork will travel by hearse to the crematorium in Dublin, to return thereafter as ashes in a leetle casket in an aging VW van. He invites friends to our home for light refreshments and I smile, knowing that Philomena doesn't do light.

We are blessed. Feet scuffle as we rise to await the priest's departure. The hair on the back of my neck stirs, sounds in my head fade away, a faint ringing rises in my left ear and a concertina awakens. Across the expanse of nodding, bobbing heads, Catherine O'Brien rises to stand as her sister Julia raises her violin to play the opening notes of Jimmy McCarthy's 'Bright Blue Rose' to fill this sacred space. I reach for my mother and pull her to me and my father pulls me to him and we are three now, in this place, in this holy and precious time we share. We hold each other as the beautiful voices of our congregation carry us through the forget-me-nots in the snow, to the one 'Bright Blue Rose' that outshines them all, pondering death and life and eternal notes of love.

I look to the high ceiling as a bright white light travels slowly across the panelled expanse and hovers above the suspended cross, on which the real Jesus hangs.

∞

Cottage by the Water, Rostellan

In the weeks following Rosa's passing, a stillness descended on the cottage by the water. I stayed close, working from the 'whole upstairs,' as it was in its entirety both my own sleeping space and the home office with the strongest Wi-Fi signal. If any one of us were entirely adrift, it was my father. Mamá outwardly continued with life, her music schedule of playing, attending for dancers, and teaching music in the primary schools where she had once taught the curriculum. In the short dull days of November, my father sank inwards in silent grief, so I grasped the lead in our lives.

"Come, Papá, let's do some research together."

He eyed me over the top of his book. "What are you planning, Jesús?" The flat grey winter light reflected on his reading glasses, the oil stove hummed behind him.

I cleared the kitchen table to spread a map then opened my laptop at his elbow. "I have a conference in two weeks time in Bristol. Would you come with me?"

His eyebrows raised. "Bristol?"

"Yes, I thought I would book four nights here," I gestured to the screen and he leaned in, laying his book aside.

"A houseboat?" Papá was duly surprised by my choice.

"Yes, moored in Welsh Back, centre of the city. Handy though. Thirty-two feet, easy to handle and manoeuvre."

"That's very marine of you, Jesús, but you are not a sea-pootler at all?" he laughed.

"No, but you are. I can manage four nights on Bristol's Floating Harbour, Papá. And you could do some sea-faring, poking about the inner reaches of the harbour or the outer reaches of the Avon Channel? I will be busy during the daytime; you would be there in the evening when it is the early dark of winter. It would be perfect for us both."

"And I could travel up the canal to Bath. Splendid!" He paused to peer up from the laptop at me.

"And Mamá?"

"She is busy here and happy to stay at home. She will begin to sort Rosa's possessions and is content to be on her own." What I didn't add was how she had seemed somewhat pleased at being alone for this task. I understood her need to mourn privately her mother's passing.

"Well, if she is sure then, yes. Yes, thank you. I will be with you, Jesús. I will welcome the change."

"That's great, Papá! After Bristol, we will take a car south to the Somerset Levels, here," I showed him on the open map. "I want to see the spectacle of the starling murmurations at dusk, here at Shapwick. We will stay there, for I also fancy seeing where Timmy served his time at the radio station in Highbridge, which is not far, just here." We pored over the map together.

"Oh, wonderful idea! That would be just lovely. Thank you, Jesús. You will of course give me good notice as to how many pairs of socks I should pack?"

I kissed his head. "Seven, Papá. Seven is a good number."

∞

"How is Papá, Jesús?" We were sitting in slow traffic and pouring rain, the ticking of the turning indicator our metronome of life.

"Good, Mamá. He will come with me to Bristol."

"Oh, Jesús! Thank you. Thank you!"

She surprised me. For although we had discussed the possibility of the trip before I spoke with Papá, I had underestimated her concern. "Mamá? Are you okay?"

"I have been so worried about him, Jesús. I know he keeps busy but he also keeps silent. Somehow losing Rosa was like losing a part of himself, if that can make any sense?"

I nodded, having observed the same. My heart was listening, my mind watching the lumbering traffic and sloshing wiper blades, an empty crisp packet blown by the foul winds.

"I think I had not realised how much of his routine was caring for her. In my absences, you know? She was not as strong as I had thought. Daniel never said, never spoke of what he did for her every day. They just, well, you know, Jesús, you know what they were like."

"A couple of old odd socks, sharing the same drawer."

"¡Exactemente! Both of them happy doing what they were doing every day, scheduling lunch, or teatimes in the round-house, birds at the feeders, seeds and berries for collecting. Then I come in, or go out, and we just flowed along like that for so many years."

"He has been with her for a long time, Mamá. Remember, since he was ten? I am sure he was closer to Rosa than to his own mother."

She pursed her lips, nodding. I negotiated a roundabout in silence amid background noise of wheels and wet roads.

"I had to stop after her heart trouble and think, my mother is eighty-nine. We had wondered if Philomena would do a birthday party for her ninetieth celebration." Mamá dabbed her eye with her sleeve.

"Join us, Mamá? In Bristol," I suggested. "The last day of our stay in the city would have been her ninetieth birthday."

"Yes, I know this, Jesús. I thought perhaps that was the day I would be alone." She picked at flecks of dust on the dashboard, occupying her hands as her mind deliberated. As she wiped the foggy window, she whispered, "Let me see. Okay?"

I touched her hand. "Of course, Mamá. It's November. There will be no difficulty getting you a flight."

∞

As is the way with the Universe, I stumbled across the next story in our lives through a series of Internet browsing connections. Descending from the top floor, I handed my mother a sheaf of printed pages.

"What is this, Jesús?"

"For you, Mamá. I found it on the whuh whuh whuh."

She chuckled as she always does at the www. Her eyes widened, her smile broadened. "Oh my word, Jesús! It never occurred to me to ask. Look, Daniel!"

Papá reached across for the pages, pulling reading glasses from his shirt pocket. "Charles Jeffries: The Man and his Family." He looked at me and asked, "C. Jeffries. Maker?"

"That's it, Papá. The Maker of the Sound. His whole life story, wonderfully written by several authors and posted to concertina. com."

Papá handed back the pages to my mother, who scanned through them and said, "I shall take my time and enjoy this, Jesús. Thank you. What a wonderful surprise."

"You know, Mamá, when I imagined C. Jeffries asleep in his bed all those years ago … remember I told you? I always imagined him in Cork, where Abuelo Sean came from. I had no imagination for London or anywhere else. As it turns out, I have been to the London suburb of Willesden where they lived and made concertinas. All of the Jeffries family are buried in the vicinity."

"Someday we will go there maybe, Jesús? Next time perhaps you need the London airport?"

I nodded. "Yes, that could be a plan." I was pleased for her, for them, for the concertina was such a part of their lives, of all our lives, just a leetle thing on its own, yet so much more than its size.

"There is also lots of information on cleaning and maintenance, Mamá." Many times I had watched my own father perform simple cleaning tasks on the concertina, but he was wise enough to leave deconstruction to an expert. "I remember Abuelo Sean taking off the end plate to fix a reed a few times or a stuck button. I remember him oiling the leather so it wouldn't dry out in the sun. 'Feed that leather,' he said. I think of it always when I am cleaning my boots."

She nodded in agreement. "That's just why it was always closed in the case, always pushed under his bed. In the cool and the dark.

That's where I used to sneak it from when he was out at work, so I could play. I was like you, Jesús. 'Little fingers, not for you, María,' he said to me when I was very small and he never changed that, so I had to steal my turn. My mother would hear me and leave me for a little while, then come into the bedroom with this great surprise, clucking and tutting and saying, '¡no es para ti niña!' and we would close the bellows and the studs and carefully put it for sleep. This happened for maybe, hmm, two years. I thought he did not know but of course he did. He wanted to see how I learned without him."

The concertina had just always been there. I had never thought to ask my mother when she began to learn to play it. It was in the house before me, an integral part of our existence. Abuelo Sean played, Mamá played. Questioning anything of its story previous to my own had escaped me.

She paused, remembering, nodding and smiling. "Then one day a reed stuck open with this terrible wailing noise and I was ¡aterrorizada! I did not know what to do."

Papá smiled. "I remember that day! I arrived, called to your house for you, and could hear the wail. I thought it was your Papá, but that was puzzling, for we had spoken to him at the convent when we were leaving school. And there you were, my love, with Rosa, in an utter flap."

"So what did you do, Papá?" I laughed. "Tell me you saved my mother's skin?"

"Indeed I did! I took it from her and I can definitely say that was the first time I had ever touched it. I gave it the slightest of shakes and whatever had jammed, unjammed. Blessed silence!"

Now Mamá was laughing. "There we were the three of us, on the floor of my parents' bedroom staring at this instrument like it might now decide to bite us. I quickly got it back into its bed and under my father's one."

I looked at them both, my parents together as children, while I was still a faraway star in the sky.

"I left it alone for a long time. It was his, you know, Papá's sound, and I was afraid to break it. But then after I had watched him one Sunday, in the taberna of your Mama, Daniel, I just had to try again. When I pulled out the case from under his bed and lifted the lid, there was a little note on top of the end plate that read: Maria, lessons at 7. One hour, two days a week. Papá. And under the note was the little figure carved from wood, playing a concertina."

"Ah! The one on your dresser? I used to play with it as a child. I just thought it had come from Abuelo, that maybe it was his."

"He made it for me before we started to play together, before I began my lessons."

"Then I watched him opening the end plate," Papá chimed in.

"That was the bit I liked. I wanted to see how it worked, what was inside." Papá smiled. "He had such steady hands. He always laid a white sheet or towel on the kitchen table so it could be clean and safe. The first thing he told me was that he couldn't do this job in his workshop because of the dust. Everything had to stay spotless. Any screw he removed was laid on the sheet in order. He would roll up a two-peseta note to clean the steel reeds. It had to be quality paper and there's nothing better than currency."

A moment of silence descended.

"He had such careful hands, Papá," my mother mused. "Whether it was stone, or wood, or the concertina. So gentle. Mamá used to rub them with aloe vera and a little olive oil when he had washed after work."

My father nodded. "Working on the concertina, that was the only time he did not smoke."

I looked at him quizzically. "I thought he smoked even when he slept?"

It was easy for us to laugh now; so many years had passed since his rasped and tortured departure.

"No, he never smoked when he was disassembling the instrument. Imagine a spark, Jesús, or wafting paper ash drifting down inside the bellows? Disaster!" Papá paused, recalling, "Until he taught me to do it. Then he would sit over in the chair swilling and puffing and say 'do this' and 'do this' and 'can you see that?' He was good at giving orders."

He sighed as he remembered. "He had an incredible way of teaching you something, do you both recall? He would make you watch him, talk about it as if it was a story, then the next time ask you to do it. He never, ever lost his temper or got, well, as the Americans would have said, 'shitty' about anything. He would calmly take you back a step or two and talk you through that stage again. He never seemed fazed."

"Ah!" cried Mamá. "He didn't look worried, but of course he was drinking and smoking himself to the death watching you."

∞

I descended slowly and sat on the bottom step, drawn downstairs by her music.

"This is 'Trip we took over the Mountain' Jesús." She glanced up at me as she fingered the notes and I watched her play a few minutes while she studiously concentrated on her moving hands.

"I often think of Papá while I play. He taught me all the early tunes I know. This is one of them. I remember how he sat with the concertina saying, 'That's it, María, 3/4 time waltz—dd, ggg, ab, ab, gg, gg, aa, gg,' and he'd jig and play along the chords. Giving me the knowledge. I like to give it to the children." She lost herself in her sound as I listened and waited until she drew the bow for the final note.

"Fly to Bristol, Mamá." I urged her. "Join us for the Somerset Levels, to see the starlings swoop to their nests in their millions, and hear the bittern cry. Then we will drive to London and see the Jeffries Makers in their graves. Be with us and not alone."

Mamá studied me intently over the neck of the fiddle, then frowned briefly, firelight glinting off her glasses. "I will have three days at home and then fly. I think that is enough. I think that is what Rosa would tell me too. She would say, 'Why you alone, my lovely girl? If I was to be ninety, I would be here to blow out the candles.' "

I smiled at her. "Wonderful, Mamá. Papá will be happy. We will have the candles for her in Bristol. We will sing and be merry even though you and I will be afloat."

"Oh yes! One night of the floating is just okay for me, Jesús."

"Yahoo!" I cheered. "I'll book your flights."

"Jesús?" she called after me as I turned to climb the stairs. "I want to see the big cathedral and the big bridge. Will you have the time?"

"For you? Most certainly! And Mamá?" She raised her eyes again from the bow. "Bring your fiddle, Mamá. There is a music night at the Nova Scotia pub, just by the water."

∞

Bristol, England 2009

Our trip to England was memorable, unfolding beautifully from day to day, swathed in the novelty of being tourists in the wintertime. Papá and I wandered again around the centre of his father's birthplace; this time I was the strong, fit adult and his was the pace of a young child. His feet were the first to weary of man-made paths and lanes, so we sat with coffees and pondered the differences since our trip of 1977. "No macchiatos or skinny lattés back then," he quipped. In my absences, he did enough pootling and poking to satisfy his own curiosity. I hear Dr. Zhao in my early days of study: "Curious people ask questions, read, and explore." My father does that, even now in his later years he explores, asks questions, nosing the thirty-two foot cruiser up canals and into waterways.

The first day was spent in all things marine, talking ships and sailing craft the length of Bristol Harbour, nosing about warehouses and boatyards, helping to steady sleek rowing sculls while the crews launched off a slipway. While his hands and head had been nautical, his heart had been lifted. I was joyfully reminded of the spirited sailor I once delivered to Monkstown for his first MK Voyageur cruise from Cork. As I left Papá the following morning, he cast off on another adventure, navigating Cameo to the great Bristol train station at Temple Meads. Papá meandered waterways through Wapping Wharf, to explore the M Shed Bristol Museum, finally spending hours on board the reconstructed steamship SS Great Britain. Indeed there was a further hour over our evening meal recounting the genius of Brunel. I did wonder why I was indoors at a travel trade conference and as to where I might be better serving my time. Something in me rejoiced with his rejuvenation, his deepest interests rekindled, a ready smile returned.

On the third day I slipped away at lunch time and met him in the foyer of the At-Bristol Museum of Exploration, where he was watching a group of school children in flashy neon vests.

"Why do they wear the vests, Jesús?"

"To be more visible to their teachers I would guess, Papá."

He nodded thoughtfully, lips pursed. "I just had a memory of us children in Captain Jack's air shelter in Cyprus, learning our three R's. There must have been fifteen or so of us, I think, of all ages. We repeated everything Captain Jack said, we were just so excited to be learning and speaking English. No books you know? He stole paper pads and pencils from the RAF base office, where he did some work to stay on the payroll. This was probably '45, so everything was falling apart at the seams anyway. He taught us whatever came into his head, anything that took his fancy. He had been a teacher, you know, before he had to join up, and he was one of those chaps who always fell between the cracks or took the desk job no one wanted. Not a military man at all, at all. No desire whatsoever to be anywhere near the action, and his mother thought he would last longer in the RAF than if he joined the army. That kind of irrational thinking that so many succumbed to in wartime."

The noise level rose a few decibels as the tour guide's lecture came to an end and the group of children dispersed to interactive displays—boat models, a lift powered by water pressure, kinetic energy simulators. It was a playground.

"Forty-five, and we considered ourselves lucky to be in a castoff air shelter with a half-cracked British Naval officer. I don't wish to be mean; he was a bit bonkers, but I think everyone was by then." He paused, surveying the moving masses in the foyer. "Do you think this lot will look back and think themselves lucky when they are seventy-something, Jesús?" He waved his hand at the chattering children. "Do you think they will go home from here and say, 'Mummy, guess where I was today? I am so lucky, so fortunate.'"

"They may not, Papá, but it is not the world of 1945, of war. Isn't it wonderful that they can be here? Here, in a huge emporium of learning where they have been given so many things to experience?"

He nodded thoughtfully. "It is like, well, just like every day is Christmas," he declared crossly.

I playfully punched his shoulder. "Every day is Christmas, Papá, when you have what we have. Now remove those surly glasses and look again with a smile."

He sat upright, shaking his shoulders and head vigorously, then grinned at me. "Yes, of course, my child! What on earth am I thinking?"

A young girl in a neon vest walked towards us where we sat. "Excuse me, sir," she spoke to Papá, "could you please tie my shoelace?"

"Why of course!" Papá replied good-naturedly. "Would you like to put your foot here beside me on the bench? I'm not so good at bending all the way to the ground."

The child raised her foot as requested. "My mummy always says I will trip on it and have to go to the hos-table. I'd be sad to miss all the fun things here with my friends."

"Well let's make sure you don't need a hos-table." Papá nodded sagely, double-knotting the child's lace.

"Why don't you bend anymore, sir?"

"Because my body has got old and tired from lots of work and gardening; but you know, doing fun things too."

"My grandad is old and tired sometimes. So is my mummy, she says, after her work. She works at the hos-table." She dropped her bag on the ground beside her, rummaging momentarily before producing a Tetra-Pak carton of orange yoghurt drink. Proffering it to Papá, she said, "I have this if I get tired or hungry. You can have it, then you will bend all the way to the ground. Thank you for tying my shoe."

The child smiled and skipped towards the oncoming teacher, who was busily locating her missing charge. My father sat mute, staring after her, the juice carton in his hand. He took a moment to recover himself.

"What's this you say, Jesús? About seeing things clearly?"

"Ah! Which bit, Papá? Here is the first that comes to mind from Thich Nhat Hanh, which I will paraphrase as I recall the sentiment:

> *Every day we are engaged in a miracle which we don't even*
> *recognise:*
> *a blue sky, white clouds, green leaves, the curious eyes of a*
> *child—our own two eyes.*
>
> *All this is a miracle. For things to reveal themselves to us,*
> *we need to be ready to abandon our views about them.*

He nodded. "Thank you. That will do. I can stop being a miserable ass now."

"Children will always be children, Papá, no matter if they are in an air shelter in a world war, or a wonderful playground. And here is one more nugget for you to ponder: 'If you truly want to be at peace, you must be at peace right now. Otherwise, there is only the hope of peace some day.' "

"Ah, yes! And try this one, Jesús. 'I will practice coming back to the present moment, not letting regrets and sorrow drag me back into the past or letting anxieties, fears, or cravings pull me out.' Did I get that somewhat right?" he laughed.

I nodded, smiling. "Let's walk for lunch, Papá. There is so much we can do together."

∞

Mamá arrived to the city centre by airport bus, early morning lights still glimmering on foggy cars. We took her first to the Cameo for coffee and croissants before a walking tour of the city centre, through Queen Square, Pero's Padlock Bridge, meandering down Harbourside, eventually to the great old cathedral.

"No history, Jesús. I do not need to know anything. I just want to feel it here."

"You have an hour-and-a-half for feeling, María," my father answered, somewhat sharply. "We need to be back on board Cameo at exactly two o'clock." I was paused in myself, for I had not heard my father's commanding military voice for some time.

Mamá looked at him curiously, pulled a comical child's face, and playfully retorted, "Aye, aye, Captain Daniel." I smiled, for she did not know the next adventure.

"I'll be poking around in the dark corners, Mamá. See you by the main organ in thirty minutes perhaps? I know you will like to hear the sound. And the Eucharist bells will be at 12:30, okay?"

"You will most likely find me in the café or asleep in the garden if the sun shines," Papá announced.

We did our wanderings until I noticed a teacher who was leading a small group in school uniforms enter by the nave door—followed by another group in different uniforms and yet another moving up the main aisle. I sensed a gathering, possibly of choristers, so sent a text message to each of my parents: "Come now. Choristers gathering."

There was scuffling and whispering, a shuffling of hymn sheets throughout the church for a few minutes before silence descended. The organist carefully watched in her mirror through the warming chords and pit stops, then poised for the conductor's baton. A hundred heavenly voices raised:

> *The Lord's my Shepherd I'll not want.*
> *He makes me down to lie.*
> *In pastures green*
> *He leadeth me.*
> *The quiet waters by.*

My mother took my father's hand and tucked it into the crook of her elbow, leaning against his shoulder. She smiled at me, tears gathering at the corner of her eyes. "Oh Daniel! Psalm 23, Rosa's favourite. Oh! Happy Birthday, Mamá."

George Herbert rises to my mind: Wherefore with my utmost art, I will sing thee. And I return her smile. "Happy Birthday, Abuelita." I think of Mamá Tia's passing, when I drank coffee in this very cathedral in 1986, unknowingly watching her light flicker across my cup and dazzle my eyes—and now as I look at my parents as they are rapt with wonder, hearts and senses full of chorister sound, a shaft of sunlight breaks through the stained glass above them and pierces a strong line to their clasped hands. "Noventa es sólo un número, Jesús." I hear Abuelita say in my ear: Ninety is just a number. "Estoy contigo para siempre." I am with you forever.

∞

Our cathedral time curtailment was dictated by a lock-through we had reserved, to leave the Floating Harbour of Bristol city centre and mosey west up the Avon Channel to the big bridge that Mamá had requested, the Clifton Suspension Bridge. And from her seat in heaven, Abuelita Rosa called out the angels, for the grey November day lifted with warm winter sunshine, the waters were bright, the tides aligned, and we were joined in the lock by three smaller craft. Papá was in his natural element, water and waves, wind and weather, fellow mariners hailing and calling, all sharing together.

"Just a short sea-pootle, Mamá," I assured her, reassuring myself.

"It's a river, Jesús," Mamá said, playfully squeezing my arm. "Do not be so concerned; it is not the open sea." She smiled at me. "It is nice to still be your Mamá, Jesús, and soothe your fears. You do not have this need for so many years now. It is nice that you are always my child."

I kissed her greying head. "I can hear Sean and Rosa laughing, Mamá. You? Soothing my sea-sickness fears! Abuelo Sean would say, 'In the name of God, what are you doing out there? Shur couldn't you see the bloody bridge with the earth under yer feet?'"

Mamá joined my laughter, two Spanish landlubbers born smelling the sea, living nearly on the water, surrounded by all life and work marine and absolutely earth-bound in our every fibre. Mr. Onions' etymology is calling, as lock water rushes around our floating home. Land: Old English lond, land, ground, soil. Old Norse, Old Dutch, Old German: a definite space belonging to a person or nation. The lubber is of Scandinavian origin; just a lazy lout. Cast out by the sea-faring folk.

And then we are there, floating on muddy brown waters with high banks of oozing mud, littered with the cast-off shreds of city life, amongst twisted trees and drifting wood. Above us the towering bulk of iron and rivets, steel shimmering, bolted and built into blocks of brick, fashioned as if from the earth itself, gracefully spanning the Avon Gorge.

"My father would have sailed here," Papá calls from the wheel. "He would have left Bristol on this very river."

I think of the Buddhist monks, their acceptance of the changing atoms of air and water, the cyclic motion of movement, of time and space, when nothing is consistent yet everything remains connected, constant. My four grandparents shedding their own layers to their own divinity; I know they are watching us, floating on the tide of now. The words of Sarah Doudney, a Portsmouth girl, come to mind:

> *Learn to make the most of life,*
> *Lose no happy day;*
> *Time will never bring thee back*
> *Chances swept away!*
> *Leave no tender word unsaid*
> *Love while love shall last—*
> *The mill cannot grind*
> *With the water that has past.*

I lean backwards against the grab rail to stare up at Brunel's engineering feat, and see a tiny figure of a stranger on the bridge above me, waving to us below. The stranger releases a helium balloon—in the shape of a red heart—to drift on November sunshine.

∞

We ate simply in our floating home. Papá and I prepared the meal while Mamá slept soundly in the aft cabin, her long travelling day catching up with her. We had moored at the western end of the harbour, close to the SS Great Britain, as the cold and dark descended, days shortening into winter nights, the lights of the city dancing a thousand tunes through every window of Cameo, motor traffic above us on city streets.

"Come, Mamá, get your fiddle; we will have a quick walk."

"Oh, Jesús! Really? I have to stand up again?"

"You can do it, Mamá. One last squeeze of the batteries and then you can sleep for the night, rocking on the Bristol waters."

We walked the short way on the Hotwells boardwalk, crossing the Plimsoll Swing Bridge to the Nova Scotia pub, where from a reasonable distance we could hear the music.

"Ah!" she declared, " I hear the session!"

"Just a few tunes, María," my father warned sternly, "or you will be too tired to enjoy tomorrow." He turned to me and whispered, "That was quite hollow, wasn't it?"

"Yes, Papá, that was all about you!"

An eclectic mix of musicians had squeezed themselves together into snugs and benches, raising their eyes to welcome a newcomer uncasing her fiddle. We stood with our beers, away from them, amongst the drinkers not fiddlers. Papá leant towards me. "You know Jesús, the music playing in the taberna or these sessions have never been my comfort zone. This, to me, is what sea-pootling is to your mother."

"Relax, Papá. I would guess Mamá has a dozen tunes and she will be done for the night." I was nearly right, for just about the end of the tenth or so tune, a flurry of laughter arose from one end of the bar, a glass was clinked loudly to call for a moderation of silence, and an older lady with purple and blue in her hair laid aside her accordion and stood up to sing. Her progress was checked, though, by a loud voice from someone near to my mother, "Just a minute, missus. I've got something to sing for you, m'love." Then his broad voice cleared, his Bristol accent sang strongly:

Appy Birthday to you
Appy Birthday to you

—from there, the entire gathering joined his rousing song:

Appy Birthday dear Rose.
Appy Birthday to you.

I turn to Papá, who is looking at my mother amongst her fellow musicians, all strangers to her, all friends through their sound.

"Well goodness me! I say, what a coincidence!" Papá exclaimed. "Oh! I do miss her, Jesús. I miss Rosa. She was as constant in my life as your mother is, and it is a very long time since I was ten years old." He paused in his memories. "We had our moments, for she could be incredibly obstinate," he reflected, nodded, then wiped his eye with a finger. "She would set her mouth in a line you could not cross, so I learned not to, to wait and she would meet me halfway. We had our own way of doing things, for María was often absent. Rosa was never my mother-in-law, she was another human being who looked kindly upon me and treated me with utter respect. I loved her for that."

The lady singer smiled and bowed her thanks, awaiting quiet to begin her song.

We were far enough removed at the bar for Papá to continue.

"What María didn't appreciate for a long time was that Rosa and I worked together at Rota. We would have known the same people, the same commanding officers and, although I would have had little to do with the hospital, there is always cross-communication somewhere like a Naval Base. I was there when I was sixteen years old and Rosa was already there as a nurse. I grew up with her in every aspect of my life, just as María did, but in a different way. So although I married her daughter, Rosa was already like a mother to me. My own mother owned a taberna. I did not have the eh, well, relationship with her that I had with Rosa. Does that make sense?"

"Yes, Papá. Perhaps like a birth mother and an adoptive mother?"

"Well, yes. Two very different personalities. Both strong players in my life. Grieving Rosa is very different from grieving my own mother. I never lived with my mother again from the age of sixteen but I have lived all of my life with Rosa."

"If we take ourselves outside of the obvious, Papá, the characters, the players in our show, we look at our ancestral lines and behind every one of us are personalities, beings that we may meet lifetime after lifetime, incarnation after incarnation. This may not be the first time you have shared with Rosa and Tia, or María, or me. This time you are in a different role, learning a different way. Does that make sense?"

Papá nodded. "More and more as I age, Jesús, more and more."

Our discussion was silenced by a guitarist who stood tall on a bar-stool in front of Mamá and plucked the opening notes of "¡Volaré!"

His musical companions, familiar with this exhibition, called and whistled their encouragement before joining in the rousing chorus, as my mother smiled and clapped along. The guitarist put a finger to his lips, the resident singers subsided and Mama carried the song in Spanish—joined solely by the birthday girl Rose—singing: "Nel blu dipinto di blu".

The entire gathering including my father and me from the bar, joined with them as they flew and they sang in the blue painted skies of happiness and stars. Happy Birthday, Abuelita Rosa and Rose the singer, from us all in a pub in central Bristol in which we have landed this moment on our journey.

∞

We departed the city southwards, each of us in our own way rejuvenated by the experience, whether it was the change of scene or country, the poking and exploring, the children, the water, the air, the music, the singing. Who could say?

Papá leant from the rear seat and pointed at the in-built SatNav screen on the dashboard of the vehicle. "I know this sort of stuff isn't quite your thing, Jesús, but humour an old star-gazing naval man, if you please."

"Your star-gazing knowledge has inspired many of my column inches, Papá."

"In 1919 there was a solar eclipse, and the great astronomer Sir Arthur Eddington knew that was the chance to test Einstein's Theory of Relativity. You know this one, of course?"

"Ah Papá! Let me drag that one from the recesses of my non-scientific mind. $E = mc^2$. I know that much; I couldn't explain it to you though."

"Or me," agreed Mamá from her reclined front seat. "I shall sleep through this lecture, Daniel."

"Ha-ha, you both. Anyway, Einstein's predicted theory was that mass causes space to curve, which was all looking good on paper but no one had experimentally proven it. If his theory were right, the light from stars should be bent by the gravity of the sun and appear displaced. An eclipse, where the moon blocks the sunlight enough for stars to be seen near the sun, was the perfect opportunity to test this. By observing how the stars near the sun were displaced from their normal positions during the eclipse, Eddington wanted to show that this apparent change happens because the path of light is bent by gravity, when it travels close to a massive object like our sun. Okay? Still with me?"

"Hmm, sort of, so far," I ventured. Mamá feigned a loud snore.

"Eddington's predictions were spectacularly correct. The theory fundamentally changed the understanding of physics and astronomy. Einstein shot to stardom, pardon the pun, and Eddington was the man who helped get him there. We could not have any of this," Papá gestured towards the screen again, "without it. Or weather forecasting, or phones, or satellite-based technology, or any GPS-based systems. All of which are now critical to us every day. Eddington was the man to prove it." He paused a few moments, his fingers drumming on the headrest of my seat. I heard vague murmurs and could see his lips moving in my rearview mirror. "Yes, here it is, I have it. Eddington composed this ditty for the non-astronomers like you two:

> *Oh leave the wise our measures to collate.*
> *One thing at least is certain, light has weight.*
> *One thing is certain and the rest debate.*
> *Light rays, when near the sun, do not go straight.*

"We used to chant that in naval college, learning our sextant work."

"So ninety years later, we thank Albert Einstein for the clear directions to our farm guest house?"

"Yes. Oh wouldn't it be fun if some clever clogs programmed that thing to speak in Einstein's voice?" Papá mused. "He himself was always quick to thank those around him, you know, those who made him think, to extend himself. That is very gracious."

"Papá, I have made my living all my life by those around me, who make me think and extend myself. I thank them daily."

Papá sat back in his seat, nodding sagely to himself, before quoting again from Eddington:

There is a moon which appeared on the scene before the astronomer; it reflects sunlight when no one sees it; it has mass when no one is measuring the mass; it is distant 240,000 miles from the earth when no one is surveying the distance; and it will eclipse the sun in 1999, even if the human race has succeeded in killing itself off before that date.

"That bit of Eddington must appeal to your Buddhist thinkings, Jesús? Although I am not sure he meant it in a spiritual way."

"Yes, that's much how I see it, Papá." I recalled something Dr. Zhao had paraphrased regularly for me:

Trees are moving for us, water is flowing for us, it is in us, in all of nature, the elementals are not inferior to us, they are us, we are them. Our mistake is to think we are better. We are the guests not the keepers.

"I prefer that science," came a sleepy voice beside me.

∞

Somerset, England

On the Somerset Levels we spent a lazy day meandering to our guest house, not far from where we could observe starling murmurations at sunset. Our host, Ben, was to drive us to the marshes; so, swathed in jackets, hats, and boots we were ready. I thought I was ready, but truthfully I was not. I had watched recordings of this spectacle on a screen, or YouTube clip, yet I was unprepared for the sensory wilderness overload I witnessed. Several tens of thousands, or millions of little birds swooping, and gracefully, flawlessly pulsating in a giant bellows-like manner, preparing to roost in the reeds. In my joy I thought of leetle Abuelita Rosa in the roundhouse watching her feathered friends. We were silenced for many minutes by the majesty unfolding before us.

"But why, Ben?" Mamá asked. "Why do they perform like this?"

"Well, ma'am," replied Ben in his West Country accent, "it's thought theys swoop like tha' as a giant signpost, attractin' all the starlings in an area to flock together. Once together, the swirling mass of birds makes it 'ard for predators, like them peregrines, to get single birds. Tha's a proper job," he nodded, "them there birds then roost together for safety 'n' warmth."

"Spectacular," my father agreed. "Just spectacular. And all these people coming out in the freezing cold to watch. We silly humans are still silenced, awestruck you know, by our natural companions."

"Aye, sir." Ben handed binoculars to my father. "Clever little things, theys stay in time, synchronised like, with five or six others abou' them. Tha's why it seems like a movin' cloud. There aren't nothin' better to be doing of an evening 'ere, but watchin' these little beauties. Been doin' this all me life."

Mamá inhaled deeply, sighing with awe. "Not superior, not in charge, we are the guests, not the keepers." She smiled at Ben.

"Aye, ma'am, aye. Come now, you're my guests this night. Let's get 'ome and get tha' dinner down us."

∞

"Jesús?" My mother whispered to me in the hallway outside my room.

"Mamá?"

"I think tomorrow I will stay just here in the warm room with my book. You take Papá to the Big Naval Place?" She was referring to RNAS Yeovilton, the Royal Navy Fleet Air Arm Museum, to satisfy my father's military history inclinations, which included a much anticipated viewing of a British prototype Concorde aircraft from 1969.

"Why yes, Mamá. There is plenty there you would find interesting. Are you sure?"

"Oh sí, I am sure. I can do birds or walks and no learning or looking for the day. That is quite fine."

"Okay, Mamá, we can do that."

"And, Jesús?" I looked at her, waiting. "No London, no driving, no need for graves of concertina makers." She smiled and stroked my arm. "I am happy with C. Jeffries Maker all of my life, I do not need to see where he is dead. I am certain this will upset your plans for which I am arrepentida, so sorry, but it is a long drive from here, no?"

"Sí, Mamá." I shrugged. "But I would have made it for you." My monkey mind moved to reorganising the forthcoming days, noting the calls I needed to make, until I stopped myself in the moment, pausing into stillness to bring my mind only to here, whispering in a hallway with my mother. To really hear her.

She shook her head steadfastly. "I am here, lovely farm, lovely Ben and Alison, with my living loved ones, the beautiful birds, and my mother's presence. There has been enough death for me."

∞

Blackrock, Cork

The years passed, yet another decade of our lives—coming and going, boating, writing, playing music, maintaining our home. My father cheerfully grew roses and taught himself husbandry, filling shelves in the greenhouse with cuttings in various stages of propagation and growth, filling shelves in the shed with rooting hormone, homemade insecticide remedies, fly-spotted handwritten notes, and copied articles about leaf weevils and black spot. My mother pruned shrubs, germinated perennial flowers, and they both continued to grow and harvest edible foods. Between them, or when my hands could be in the task, we would pot seedlings in the shed, deadhead pansies, weed the potato row, pick slugs off lettuces. As the decade came to its final quarter, they engaged assistance from Mark. Every home needs a Mark or a Bob, or a Mags, or an Alan—eyes to the ground, cutting, strimming, mulching, weeding. His every visit was a series of collected tasks graciously, efficiently, and effectively carried out: eyes sweeping boundary lines for stray thistles, overgrowth on the Caim stones, brazen dandelions radiant in the gravel driveway. The lives of my parents remained simple yet busy, in a beautiful place by the sea.

Life in the Two Spoons continued, Philomena's erstwhile self only occasionally complaining as age and girth made things a little harder. She succumbed to a hip replacement and to the energetic programme of weight loss that was required preceding it. A certain amount of fun was given to all by this enforced vigour.

"Pill-ah-tays."

"Wha? Wha's tha' then? Sounds like a jug. Are you doin' jugs, Philomena? Don' be doin' jugs, they're very bad for yer health."

"Drugs? What are ya on about, Biddy?" Philomena retorted crossly. "Pilates has nothing to do with drugs! Or pills of any kind. It's a form of exercise."

"Buh why? Shur you never done any exercise ever, why're you starting now?"

Philomena raised her eyes to heaven beseechingly. "Oh dear Jesus," she started, to which I felt compelled to intervene.

"Yes?" I responded.

Bridget tittered loudly, "Tee hee hee, Jesus is no use to you, Philomena. Shur wasn't ih the Lord Himself who said, 'Blessed are those who hunger and thirs' for they shall be filled'? I'm sure he said ih jus' for you. He shoulda told you when to stop eating! Tee hee hee."

I looked at my cousin, who sighed and looked at me. "Will you tell her or will I? Or could you be bothered? I might just kill her myself."

I laughed and replied, "I'm not sure I could explain righteousness. Well, not in a simple way."

"Righ' who? Wha'? Who's righ'?"

"Oh shut up, Biddy. Just this time. Please. The pilates is killin' me. 'Tis worse than the gammy hip."

∞

"She nearly met her end y'know, Jesus."

"Bridget? How so, Philomena?" I steadied her elbow as we slowly walked to the Blackrock River. She leaned heavily on a crutch on the side of the new hip.

"Did you not hear? I thought your father might have told you?"

"No, there was no time. I had only a brief stop and he was in the garden with Mark. I will return to him tomorrow for I was eager to see you first."

"Aw, sweetheart, Jesus. Thank you. Your care lifts my spirit."

"I can hear singing in the flat key of Biddy, 'Sweethear' of Jesus, fon' of love and mercy, today we come, la la la la le lala.' She's a minx."

Philomena paused to flex her stiffening knee. "She just loves crooning along with Daniel O'Donnell and, yes, she is rightly a minx. But let me tell ya, she was nearly a dead minx last week."

"Oh! How so? I'm not sure I could imagine life without Bridget?"

"Well, you nearly had to. She apparently came to the hospital to see me after the hip op but it was late and she was told visiting hours were over. Don't ask me how she got to my room or any of those rational questions. She seems to have been through every stairwell in the Regional Hospital and somehow found me. I was out for the count, had pulled the sheet up over my head, and she got it into her tiny little mind that I wasn't breathing, that in fact, I was dead."

"Oh dear God. Oh dear God, this can't end well."

"No indeed! Having got herself in there unnoticed, she then thought she'd be in trouble for saying anything, so she hightailed it outta there and made her way straight back to Ambrose, where he met the most awful caterwauling and going on at the back door and Biddy sobbing, saying I was dead, she'd seen it with her own eyes, the sheet over my head, not breathing. Well she put the heart across him, Jesus. Ambrose lost all his sense. Didn't stop for one minute to think this is Bridget McCarthy! What are the chances of this being truthful or correct?" Philomena paused, resting on her crutch, her bosom shook, and she whispered, "Dear Jesus, don't let me laugh, don't let me start laughing, it hurts so much."

"Come and sit here, Philomena. Try and think of her crossly and then you won't laugh. God won't mind bad thoughts in order to protect your poor self."

She gingerly lowered herself onto a bench, paused then snorted, grimacing, " 'Tis funny now, 'cos I can imagine the two of them in Church Lane in that moment. But I tell ya, there was no mirth in Ambrose!"

"What happened?"

"He quieted her enough to puh, put, his hand on the telephone to ring the hospital, and right then the phone rang. Shur that was a shock enough, he could hardly lift it 'cos Biddy was wailing in his ear, saying, 'That's them now, tha's, tha's the hospihal calling ya and Phi-Phi-Phi-Philah-Phil-ah-she's dead,' with, well, as you can imagine ... ."

"The awful Bridget wail. De-de-de-ded."

"Exactly. Well he had to push her into the chair to shut her up and when he answered the phone of course it was me, as right as rain after my drug-induced stupor and waiting for tea and toast from the night nurse. I was a bit surprised when he said, 'Ooh, thank God, you're alive.' I had to remind him it was a hip op and they do hundreds of them, there was little chance I would actually be dead. Then I heard herself in the background and had to ask him why Biddy was there, was something wrong?" She paused to chuckle a bit, wincing with each ripple, her guffaws reduced to a "Wh, whu, whu." "So he says in a kinda strangled voice, 'Just a minute, my love.' Then he didn't even cover the mouthpiece and I heard him BELLOW. I mean BELLOW, Jesus, he hollered at her, 'Would you just shut up, Bridget, NOW!' I was a bit taken aback for of course I still had no idea why she was there with him, or what was going on. It was fortunate though that I knew them both well enough that she must definitely have crossed a line this time."

I held her elbow as she gave into mirthful temptation, squeezing gasps through clenched teeth, tears watering her seeds of incredulity. "What will become of her, Jesus? She's a liability to her very self."

∞

Blackrock, Cork & Pembroke Dock, Wales, 2020

"Where are ya, Jesus?" Philomena's voice broke in and out of coverage.

"Pembroke Dock. Are you okay?" I knew she would have the phone in front of her face, the speaker off, and would be shouting at full volume.

"Oh, Jesus, 'tis the end. Leo put us in lockdown. For two weeks he says."

"Yes, we heard. We couldn't get back from Stranraer, so we drove to Wales." It had been a toss-up between Fishguard or Pembroke Dock. Ambrose had blankly refused to try Liverpool or Holyhead to get to Dublin.

"Is Ambrose okay?"

"I'm okay, pet." Ambrose was also shouting, though in the confined space of the cab of his van, I did wince. " 'Twas a quick and quiet affair, the funeral. No one was allowed to pay their respects. He'd have been tickled at that, the old man."

"Will you get back tonight, Jesus?"

"I hope so, Philomena. They are loading the freight now and there are many police about. We do fit the essential travel category and I don't think anyone here wants a Scotsman and a Spaniard stuck in Wales."

"Oh Jesus. Jesus wept. What a turn of affairs. I think now I'm ... ." The connection trailed away, the searching, searching wheel.

"I didn't hear that, Philomena?"

"I said I think I'm done now. Time to retire."

"Arra, hould yer whisht woman. We'll talk when I get back." Ambrose retorted loudly, and quite crossly, but it had been a very long drive from Brae Knap, with little other than motorway services sandwiches and tea. And long days before that, of sanitiser and the new unfamiliar world of face masks in his familiar world of the estate. He had hoped to stay there for a while; I could have flown back from Glasgow, but pandemic events had tumbled us all in a heap.

"Philomena? Can you hear me?"

Her voice crackled and hissed. "Yes, Jesus?" came loudly in my ear.

"We will be back in twelve hours. But you know your own heart. Listen to it well. Right now Leo has given you an unexpected two weeks off work."

"Oh I'll be happy forever in my garden, Jesus. No more teas for me."

∞

Church Lane, Blackrock, Cork

"Biddy just didn't get it." Philomena was in her little yard at Church Lane, looking well during her summer of freedom. "You know, Jesus, I have never not worked. This is the first time ever, ever, I think I can say, that I have not worked."

I smiled and touched her hand, murmuring platitudes like "Well deserved I'm sure, you really earned a break, bidden or unbidden."

"Bad choice of words there, Jesus—Biddy or un-Biddy."

Ambrose heaped spoons of sugar into his tea. "Builder's brew," he had once said to me as Philomena had looked to heaven despairingly "It's just not fair. He gets to inhale sugar and stay as skinny as a rake. I get to look at it from across the room and put on the poundage."

"No," she continued, "She just didn't get it, or should I say, 'geh ih'."

"I could understand that. I met you when we got back from Pembroke, remember?"

"That's right. She wanted to know where it was and would there be a bus. Y'know, Leo was 'puhhing' us in Lockdown. It had to be somewhere. That was very exciting for her. She got it into her head it was near Kinsale. Wanted to know if Fr. McSweeney was running a bus, that everybody seemed to be going there."

"I remember! 'Is there a bus to Lockdown and can I geh a cuppa tea there? Won' ih be awfully busy if everyone's goin'?" My Bridget accent was pretty good after thirty-plus years of stories.

" 'Is Father Mulcahy puhhin' on a bus? Can I come with you, Philomena? Is ih Lockdown, Tipperary, or Lockdown, Wexford?

Is ih near Fiddown? When'll we all be coming back? I won't go if Ambrose is goin'. That'd be too much for me.' "

"Oh dear, it didn't improve then?"

"Ah hear now, Jesus, you're hardly applying rationale?" Philomena shook her head. "Biddy hasn't an ounce of rationale in her body. No, this was definitely going to be a difficult one."

I smiled, "Yes, I am sorry. For a moment the gravity of the situation for the rest of the human population eclipsed my understanding. I realise of course the difficulty of applying it to Bridget."

"Oh 'tis serious all right, but it took some explaining. First line of defence was The Friendlies. No more tea and biscuits in the Day Room, in fact no more Day Room. It was only a short time then and Jennifer rang me to ask very nicely if perhaps I might have a word with Bridget, as she just didn't 'geh ih'."

"No Day Room?"

"Oh no Day Room. No visiting, no visitors, no shopping, no bus, no chats, no one in shops, no one talking. Face masks. Sanitiser. Groceries by delivery only to their front doors. And no snooping to see what the neighbours had in their delivery. But worst of all, wait for it … ."

"I can hardly guess."

"No Two Spoons!"

"Ta-ra!" Ambrose chuckled.

"She came stomping up to Church Lane and near shouted at me, 'Wha' on earth has gohhen inta you?' I couldn't even ask her into the house. In the end Ambrose brought her into the backyard and HE told her."

"How did that go, Ambrose?"

Ambrose sucked his pipe, smiled and coughed, "Och you could probably guess, Jesus."

"Oh dear, Jesus," Philomena interrupted gravely, "She was a picture."

"That's right," Ambrose continued. "I have not often seen Biddy exercised in the last forty-five years but the Two Spoons closed on a Monday morning was the end for her. She managed the weekend at home, wondering what time the bus might be going. But to find the Two Spoons locked tight was a watershed moment. There really might be just something not right in the world. Where would she go? Who would she talk to? In the end I had to draw pictures for her, like for one of the little grandies, y'ken?"

"Behind you there, Jesus, under the newspapers and the knitting patterns." Philomena jerked her head towards the table.

"Knitting?"

"Och, I had to do something."

"You were knitting, Ambrose?" I tried bravely to disguise my disbelief.

"Well yes, for a wee while. Thankfully they put the construction industry back to work after a couple of weeks. So that was me and Michael sorted."

I must have looked askance for he exclaimed loudly, cracking his pipe off the paving stone beside him, coughing and spluttering.

"You're right, Jesus. I'm stitching you up. Not really my kinda thing at all."

I leafed through and pulled out several sheets of paper from the stack fluttering in the breeze, the corner weighted down by a catering can of baked beans.

"That's them there, Jesus. The first one is the alien virus attacking the planet, then that one is the alien landing on her nose and another in her mouth as she's standing agape in the shop yawing with Mrs. Flynn. And there, see?" He pointed with a long trombone finger. "There it is going into her lung. The red spider's web is her lung full of bad stuff and she can't breathe." He paused momentarily. "She actually wasn't sure where her lungs were, or what they did."

"Oh if you had seen her, Jesus," added Philomena. "I thought the eyes would pop outta her little head. God love her." She shook her head sympathetically.

"Then I got to the masks, see there? Green for good, red for virus."

"Then the hand-washing," chimed in Philomena. "She's a bit of a germaphobe without it registering consciously anyway, so that wasn't so bad. She got that. Then we had a problem of, em, Ambrose?"

"Yes." They both stopped and were solemn.

"Social distancing."

"Two metres."

"Go away and stand away two metres," Ambrose commanded in a military manner.

"From who?"

"From everyone."

"Buh you mean like no one, ah all?"

"No one."

"Noh even you?"

"Noh even me." Philomena was quiet. "She nearly cried. It upset me greatly to see her so."

"Aw. Oh, that's so difficult for her," I sympathised. "For you all really?"

"Yes. My heart went out to her. She really is just a waif." Philomena nodded.

"Och, I just had to get her to know the worst case scenario and then we could build it up from there."

I was puzzled.

"If she couldna see anyone else and couldna be within six feet of us, or well Philomena to be precise, then things couldna be much worse, could they?"

"No," I agreed. "I don't suppose they could."

"So I laid out all the lovely artwork there and made sure she got it and THEN I said okay, here's what we'll do now." Ambrose stopped, changed the cross of his leg and jigged a bit.

"And?" I encouraged him, but it was Philomena who answered.

"Well, we had already decided talking about a bubble with us would just drift over her head," Philomena said. "And we still hadn't tackled the no Mass, churches all closed situation, so we had a bit of a ways to go with her, educating her like." She looked at Ambrose.

"Och, it was hard work, Jesus, it really was. As I say, forty-five years of the poor woman and all that goes with her but I just couldna face her living with us, or being here every day and short of me moving out and her being with the missus, we dinna have an answer. And I don't think poor Jennifer and Johnny had one either."

There was a silence in the yard. Swallows swooped across the field above the wall where I watched two tortoise-shell butterflies on the valerian. "Well, you all survived lockdown, so she must have got the message somehow. Well done."

Ambrose began to laugh. Cough and laugh. Philomena did her best to keep a straight face, then she too began to shake. Her substantial garden chair scraped and creaked against the paving stones.

Ambrose pulled himself together enough to continue, "We offered her a position at the Two Spoons, as security. Y'ken? No one on the premises during the day 'cos of the Great Lockdown and it might attract the wrong attention. We just needed someone to keep an eye on things, keep the lights on and off at regular intervals. So we suggested she install herself in the apartment for the duration. Philomena would stay with her every second night or so, and as long as she wasn't within two metres of anyone ever, or indoors in anyone else's place, she would be able to stay there. In the apartment."

"Like it was her own place," added Philomena.

"I even got her a TV. To keep abreast of things, y'ken? To know what the virus was doing in the world."

"And," added Philomena, "Ambrose got her a two-way radio, connected to us here at the house. For emergencies of course."

Ambrose beamed, "I quite liked that touch maself. All she was missing was the cammo gear and a machine-gun. The skinniest birdy-like woman in the whole of Cork on security detail in downtown Blackrock. Rata-tat-tat, boom!"

"Ah Ambrose!" Philomena exclaimed. "Be kind!"

"It obviously worked?"

"Like a dream." Philomena nodded. "She took it all very seriously. No one was there to bother her and she could walk where she liked in Blackrock and keep an eye on everything that was going on. It got her outta Jennifer's hair, away from all the other residents. And best of all?"

"What?"

"Philomena's undivided attention. No customers. No family or grandies looking for her." Ambrose peered over his glasses at me. "I was very nearly jealous, Jesus. Very nearly."

"Then we had a little mishap," Philomena added. "All jokes aside."

We fell silent. I could not imagine what could be next in the Lockdown Life of Bridget MacCarthy.

"Aye." Ambrose was quiet. "Where were you anyway, Jesus?"

"In East Cork. For the full duration. I returned from England with you on April first and that was that. I know there was suffering and pain, Ambrose, but I liked lockdown. I was fortunate to be in a beautiful place, with my parents and the dogs. We were endlessly in the garden, in the roundhouse, watching the birds. I filed or dumped countless photos on my laptop, cleared old documents—all those, what Uncle Jerry used to call 'back-burner tasks.' Everything that stood still was painted. We tackled 'the hole upstairs,' shredded all sorts of out-of-date documents. Mamá finally cleared the remaining few boxes of Abuelita Rosa's possessions. You know? It was that kind of time."

"Aye, same here. Hours strolling around ma field and the garden, eh Philomena? Had to see to the horses, so I was allowed to travel for that."

She nodded. "And all of ours were healthy and well wherever they were. Stan and Lilly had the closest call in Boston, weeks off the building, and he has thirty or forty contractors working for him. Dan said they too tore the office asunder and cleared and filed. There must be shredded paper to cloak the globe. Dan does all the bookwork for Stan's firm." She fiddled for her chin hair, plucking and twisting, pushing her glasses up her nose.

"We saw Con and Majella and the lads there at the gate, tea in the garden, and in the end Ambrose took them into the field to play. That was normal enough for me, Jesus, so we were okay. We have our health though. We're blessed." She did her Sign of the Dotting Cross.

"And Bridget had a mishap?"

Ambrose nodded, ponderously refilling his pipe with tobacco from a red cloth pouch bag. "Aye. The apartment plan went south after how long, Philomena? Three weeks maybe? Four perhaps?"

"South?"

"Aye, common enough phrase for down the toilet, or down the drain, y'ken, failed."

Philomena nodded gravely. I sensed that it could not have been too disastrous or we would have heard before now. I also noticed a slight tickle at the corners of her mouth while Ambrose seemed to be studiously occupied with his pipe and tobacco.

"She called me all of a dither one morning, very quiet in herself, saying something was wrong, could I come down, that she thought she had 'ih'." In recalling, Philomena's voice trailed off to a conspiratorial whisper. "Yes. All very serious. 'Ih', of course, being the plague. And you can just imagine the drama that erupted."

"Oh Dear Lord."

"Indeed," puffed Ambrose, "indeed." He remained solemn, if not more than a tad interested in his feet.

"Oh come on you two," I eventually burst.

Philomena reached through a series of pockets for a tissue to pat her eyes and diligently blow her nose.

"What, Ambrose? What was it?"

"Och, very serious actually, Jesus, but now that the time has passed, we can laugh. Bridget, possibly because she didn't speak to many people for three weeks, sucked far too many liquorice allsorts, wore the face mask until she got into bed every night, what else, pet?"

"Never drank any water because she thought it might be contaminated by the council somehow unknowingly, held her breath for as long as she could if she ever DID venture into a supermarket or to Sue's News, took everything Ambrose drew on those pages," said Philomena, gesturing to the pile beside me, since replaced under the bean can, "so seriously that she made herself sick."

"And," stressed Ambrose, pointing with his unlit pipe, "stopped brushing her teeth, in case the virus had got from the tap to the water to her toothbrush."

"Sick with what?" I dared ask.

"Quinsy."

"Quinsy? That's what exactly?"

"Peritonsillar abscess."

"Tonsils?"

"Och yes, very bad infection. First, had ta go to the north side of the city for the virus test. That near scared the bejaysus outta her, sticking the cotton bud way up her nostril. No hospital then because of the bloody virus, so the doc went to the Two Spoons." He smiled a little. "Aye. Aye. Poor, poor little birdy Bridget."

I could imagine his Scottish phrase translating into an Abuelo Sean tune. For a moment I was a child in Cadiz, scuffing dust across the cobbled harbour, the crying gulls and hot sun shining on Sean's sweat-lined hat as he played his concertina. I pulled my mind back to Cork.

"We sat her in the middle of the kitchen," continued Ambrose, "and Doc Kelly, of course, is in all the plastic gear and big face mask in case there is the bloody virus about. He had to give her the local anaesthetic jab, then a quick little nick to let out the poison. Then all she had to do was stay quiet and gargle every half hour for three days." Ambrose was silent.

"But," wheezed Philomena, "to get that little jab, she had to stay still, quite still, with her mouth wide open for ten seconds. Now, Jesus." Philomena chuckled and wiped her eyes.

"Oh! I can just imagine."

"That took three of us, forty-five minutes. Every time the doc went near her, she'd clam up, shivering and squealing like a little banbh."

"A what?"

"Banbh, little Irish piglet."

"I threatened to lay her out on the countertop and give her the needle into her buttock," Ambrose added in the stern voice he had obviously used at the time.

"Yes, that certainly didn't help. Then he threatened her with a bigger needle that he uses for the horses. Doc Kelly got her in the finish."

"Oh? Some fabulous new trick of medicine?"

Ambrose chortled. "No indeed. One he uses on the kiddies. I took the head-torch and worked above his head, spoke very slowly to her in my nicest, kindest voice. Like those fellas Philomena has been listening to on Meditate Dot Net."

My eyes widened as I looked at Philomena. She waved her hand vaguely, crinkled her nose derisively, and mouthed, "He's joking."

"And," Ambrose continued without pause, "I told her to count with me to ten, dazzled her in the eyes with the head-torch, while Doc shone the iPhone into her gob and got the needle inta her. I did a little dance with the torch so her eyes followed the light in a circle and that gave him enough time to make the incision." He nodded. "Very satisfactory indeed."

"Poor Bridget. What a disaster for her."

"Children and horses, Jesus. They're not for working with. You gotta have a trick or two up yer sleeve."

"I take it she recovered?"

Philomena nodded, then shook her head as she said, "I couldn't bear it, the gargling and spitting and tissues, the yawning in front of the bathroom mirror to see what the Doc had done to her and trying to ask me at the same time." Philomena opened her mouth widely and mimicked her friend. " 'Oh Hilomeha, a cah' shee wha' ya dochur di in me mou? Wha' che do t mhe?' " She laughed. "Oh Jesus, it was more than anyone should have to bear, so I said she needed rest and quiet, not to forget to gargle and that she was still infectious, so take the antibiotics and call me if she needed to, but that she wasn't to be speaking or she would open the wound and maybe die of the poison."

"Oh Lordie, Philomena, that was quite harsh?"

Philomena looked chastened. "Oh? Do you think so? It was mostly true."

Ambrose poked at me with his pipe. "Easily said, Jesus Josephus, when you were safely twenty-five miles away in East Cork. You didna get an eyeful of the McCarthy sack of quinsy and the babbling brinsy that came with it."

"Too true, too true, Ambrose, and my apologies, Philomena, for my rash judgement." I bowed my head over prayer hands.

"Och, stop now. I don't know whether to laugh or cry sometimes when I think of that woman. She certainly has had a fair dose of my time and energy over the years. What will ever become of her?"

There was no answering that.

∞

Two Spoons Café, Blackrock, Cork, 2020

In the rollercoaster unworldly order of the universe, along with the rest of the human population, Philomena had to adjust to the world of pandemic. She thrived as she relaxed in her garden, the sun shone on her corner of Cork and she listened carefully every day for news of the possible return to business. When it finally came, it was all-hands-on-deck to reconfigure the Two Spoons to new operational guidelines. The team, led by Ambrose and Michael, with my father, myself, Kathleen, and Robert assisting, gathered in Blackrock in high spirits one Saturday morning. The very thought of a gathering was enough to lift one's humour, after long days of uncertainty and relative isolation. Determined not to ruin her lovely café, Philomena clucked and tutted and directed as we moved and removed chairs and tables into a workable, practical fashion that would adhere to a long list of health and safety criteria. Exasperated by her motley team and no visible results after half an hour of cacophony, she stormed through to the kitchen.

There were hoots of laughter from Kathleen and Robert, both wearing face masks; Robert's sported large red lips like that of a circus clown. Unusually, neither Kathleen nor Robert seemed to be paying much attention to the situation, or to the needs of their workplace. I watched in amazement as Kathleen jived across the cleared section of the café, singing along to Paul Simon's "Kodachrome" playing on Cork's 96FM. "Mama don't take my Vodafone away, mama don't take my Vodafone, get your own and leave me alone, mama don't take my Vodafone away-ay-ay." She and Robert howled with laughter, lost in their own little world.

In later moments of clamour, hustle, and bustle Ambrose suddenly cried out, "Och girl, turn up that sound, Kathleen. Och love it, Kool & The Gang, 1971. Perfect. 'Cos who is really gonna clean it all up eh? 'Who's gonna take the weight?' "

Ambrose pulled himself up onto a chair, which brought him to near ceiling height, playing his air trombone. "Och listen you lot now, sing it, who's gonna take the weight? Who's gonna take the weight? Ba, ba, ba, ba, baba bat, och what a sound. Baw, baw, baw, bat. Oooo, ow! Ya!"

The melee continued. A mask-grinning Robert placed chairs in a row, the radio blared at high volume, and the rest of us rushed about Ambrose, playing musical chairs as and when Kathleen turned the noise to silence. My poor father, in his eighty-third year, was on the verge of hysterical collapse.

"Now, now, now, this WON'T DO!" roared a tightly wound Philomena, charging through from the kitchen, bellowing above the clattering noise and bass beat. She banged a large saucepan lid on the counter-top. "I need a solution! I do NOT need live entertainment. Stop. Stop this nonsense NOW," she hollered.

We silenced our mirth, shuffled, and respectfully stopped our antics. Kathleen switched the radio off at the wall, then looked away embarrassed. Robert hung his head, nervously rocking to and fro on his feet, then pulled a chair towards him in order to be occupied. We were not sure of this version of Philomena or how to respond. The adjustment to sanitiser, acrylic screens, two-metre distancing, don't breathe out, wear your face masks, wash your hands, 'the whole shebang' as she would say, had sent her to her edge. I had certainly never seen Philomena raise her voice to anyone, even on the very hottest of carvery days.

Ambrose climbed off his chair, unhurriedly. "Arra will ya whisht up woman," he chided. "Isn't it better than keeping the shop closed up any day?"

We were quiet, mollified, for other than Michael we had probably not witnessed Ambrose and Philomena in such a personal way;

yet Ambrose alone could defuse her mood. Philomena glared at him angrily, then suddenly, removing her glasses and rubbing her eyes, quietly said, "Ah Ambrose, I've got to get this sorted and I just don't know how. I don't know where to start." She very nearly sobbed. "There's no live health official here to even begin to explain how all this is to become a reality." She shook a sheaf of printed rules at her husband.

"Och my love, it's okay pet." Ambrose lovingly pulled her to him.

"We are here to give you the help you need and you couldna have a better bunch about to get it sorted. You know tha'. We were having just a wee bit o' fun."

A palpable relief descended, a conversational chatter arose amongst us, our crew not yet aware that Robert's star was about to shine.

"So, if I could, Mrs. S, if I could just suggest something, I think I have an idea. If you don't like the idea of having booths and small tables, I have a possible plan that will fit the rules."

"Och, quiet, you lot." Ambrose silenced my father, Michael, and me. "Tell me more, son?"

Robert chattered and measured, nervously pulling at his own lower lip through the smiley mask knowing the wise old eyes rested on him. "Why don't we put the acrylic screens on a pulley system?"

Kathleen caught my look, her eyes revealing a broad smile behind her neon pink mask, and signalled a big thumbs up for her buddy.

"Fixed up to the beam, 'cos we have the ceiling height," Robert explained to Ambrose. "Pulley them up to move two tables together for four or more, down to separate them into tables of two. Cinch the leverage, to the left, here and here and here on cleats, easy peasy."

Ambrose listened intently and was clearly impressed. "Hmmm. Yes I see. Hmm. And drill holes through the acrylic sheets, clean bit o' sailing line to the pulley?"

"Yes sir, that's easy enough with the right drill fitting."

"Och yes, that might just do it. Yes, might just be the trick. What do you think, Daniel? And tell me, son, will it be Jimmy Jack proof?"

Philomena belly-laughed at her husband's question, "Whuh, whuh, whuh," releasing the tension from hours of pondering, weeks of wondering, nights of restless sleep. She leant against her husband's shoulder, playfully swiping her paper rules at him.

"Meaning if Jimmy Jack gets it, anyone will?"

"Aye surely," said Ambrose, eyes twinkling. "I think you have a first-class winner here in this lad, my love. Hang onto him." He looked at Robert fondly. "Do you think this'll be the end of it, son?"

Robert laughed nervously, flicking "lockdown" hair off his forehead and smoothing it with his hand. He jigged from foot to foot, eyes bright and searching above his sporty lips. "What if we already did this on another planet, Mr. S? What if we actually already made a complete mess somewhere else and then we had to move to another planet? What if we actually were the green men on Mars and moved to earth half a million years ago to start again? So maybe now, maybe this is the chance for this particular planet to shake us off, like fleas off a dog?"

My father smiled at the young man. "Ah, Roberto! A true and questioning young mind. You will never go wrong when you continue to ask such questions."

"Och, but that's not an answer, Daniel, for the wee fella. Do you have an answer, Robert?"

Robert reddened, then offered, "No sir."

"But ye have a thought on it, eh?"

"Yes sir. It's not an answer to what is happening with the virus but it must make us think. We're just so many in a very fragile existence. Maybe this is the time for the survival of our fittest? Maybe the next inhabitants of this earth will be designed to live in a carbon-rich atmosphere, and they won't know that the poles were once covered in ice. Or that the mean temperature was once 2.5 degrees cooler."

It was a joy to hear the heartfelt opinion of youth, although Kathleen and Michael's attention had already drifted away and turned to the task at hand.

"Aye, son. Aye indeed." Ambrose scratched his chin thoughtfully, his long leg resting on the seat of a chair. "You might just be right, son."

My father leaned in towards Robert and placed an age-spotted and visibly veined hand on his shoulder. "What if cats are humans, who are smart enough to become cats, so everyone will just feed them and let them be?" His eyes twinkled with mirth and I knew that behind his mask, Robert smiled. "You keep that big smile, Roberto. For wherever you go, that smile and that mind will look after you. You will survive and you will be needed, for it will be small groups like this one around you now, that will need to work together." He wagged his finger. "Find the Spaniard Valverde, from Doñana, on that Mrs. Google thing. Survival is for the one to make the most use of their energy." Papá patted Robert gently, sat back in his chair, then added, "I perhaps am glad it is at the end of my energy. I do not wish to be the one working out a solution."

"Och, Daniel, I don't think you are going anywhere soon. Unless Kathleen and those musical chairs get to you." Ambrose grinned at my father. "We have horses to keep fit, in case the next species in charge needs transportation."

They laughed together, we joined them through the generations, students to octogenarians.

Work commenced, shifting and lifting, Ambrose and Michael with drill and hammers, following Robert's directions. The change of energy, change of leadership became apparent, Ambrose poking Michael and saying, "You're not listening to the boss," nodding towards Robert. "He's our man today, Michael."

∞

In the reconfigured café, a rejuvenated Philomena busily implemented changes. The Four Anns got their large table and with it new instructions which included a one hour maximum stay. For good measure, they got Bridget McCarthy perched on her stool, pencil in hand, with a beady eye on the comings and goings and the ticking clock. Justice finally, Bridget in charge, and along with her came the unwitting reorder of the ladies.

"Five minutes to go, Mrs Doyle," she would cheerily sing. "Two more outside, Kackleen, whenever Mrs Doyle leaves. Ladies," she turned to the Four Anns, "have you everything you need? For your time is tickin' now. I shall let you know when you are close to your final furlong." There was little doubting a certain smugness in her voice.

No one disputed, no one complained, for the atmosphere was warm and genial in comfortable control. A semblance of normality in an abnormal world. Robert quietly and efficiently manoeuvred screens and tables, creating space for twos or fours.

∞

"Oh 'twas mayhem the first few days, Jesus," Philomena told me over Thursday afternoon tea.

The carvery had been cleared, Friday's baking lay ahead, and I was en route to West Cork then farther to the west coast, to write about the pandemic in small communities. I would camp with Brown Dawn and his family on Bere Island to begin my work and was sure that what I met in West Cork would be the mirror of the world-wide-web of confusion. For although cases were low, effects were high. Away from hospitals and urban living, daily case numbers and WHO statistics, the rippling pandemic was slowly rocking the foundations of everyday life. I had never before witnessed an event that affected every living human being.

"Mayhem," she repeated. "The screens are a great idea but it all needed to come together with customers. Maura Flanagan nearly died when Robert pulled the screen beside her up into the air and it slipped down again like a guillotine. Biddy took her role a bit too seriously, demanding phone numbers, how long they intended to stay, had they been in close contact with frontline staff. 'Twas more of an interrogation than a contact record," conceded Philomena. "Biddy McCarthy behind a face mask, behind a sheet of plastic, screeching instructions at anyone who moved. She would have been an asset in a war zone; she was a liability in a café. I sent her out to the shops."

I laughed, delighted to see a well-rested Philomena back in her space. "And unflappable Kathleen?" I queried.

"Oh, even she was a tad ratty at times. She had lockdown at home with her family and of course couldn't see the boyfriend 'cos he got stuck in the college digs in Galway. But we got it together all right and d'you know, Jesus? We were all-to-a-one grateful. Grateful to be well and healthy and alive and able to talk more or less normally to each other again. Grateful to catch up. Grateful for living. A cup of tea was the icing on the cake."

She paused, nodded, and said, "Did you ever wonder how much time we spend talking about the weather, Jesus? I thought I would time it once, in the Two Spoons, you know, count the seconds while someone is going on about the rain, or no rain, or the sun or clouds or forecast, the will it, won't it. Were they right or wrong?"

I cheerfully speculated, "Oh I can see you getting worked up on this one, lovely cousin!"

"Well Packie Flynn is one of them, on and on you know, lovely sun, rain on the way, the forecast said, blah blah and I was actually counting the seconds. In me head, I thought. Then Kathleen asked me afterwards, 'What were you counting, Mrs. S?' She heard me! So then I told her and, d'you know, I only then noticed that she never, ever answers weather questions, or comments about the state of the day. She told me she just looks at them and nods until they finish, then asks them what she can get them. She's not rude or anything, just does not talk about the weather. She will ask about their granny, or their cat, or their bus journey. How did I not know that?"

"I didn't either," I admitted, "and I like to think that is the kind of thing I would notice. She's quite the girl Kathleen."

"So now I'm practising it, Jesus. 'Tis hard enough after lockdown an' all the fuss. The weather is the only safe topic, for you certainly can't ask about their holidays, or weddin's, or God forbid there were ten at a funeral. I can't do the silent bit, like Kathleen, but I just say, it is what it is, Mary or Pat or Sandra or whomever. And d'you know, Jesus, I'd say I'm saving minutes of my life every day. They're not long drying up, ha ha, d'you get that, drying up? They're fairly short of weather-related chat when they get no response. We get to the real things of life much quicker now. I ask them if they are getting out and about, walking, if they have a dog. Lots of them took up the sea-swimming, in all weathers y'know? That kind of thing. Things that are real to them. Make sure they are keeping body and soul together. There are so many fragile people, Jesus. So many on their edge. Shur the weather is just the weather."

We enjoyed our slow tea. Philomena hummed quietly to herself. "Brain fog. That's a new one on me. That's one I've heard bandied about a bit. Is it the long-term effect of the virus or something?"

"I'm not sure it's anything new, Philomena. Seems to me the virus is being held responsible for all sorts of things that already existed."

She agreed. "I get brain fog at the thought of the carvery now. We're doing okay but lots of places are still only doing the ould takeaway. Customers carry off their food or sit on the river wall, or there at the new benches. Oh 'tis heart-breaking! All that good food eaten with plastic knives and forks? All that plastic, 'tis a fright to God! An' the masks! Dearie me! If you can keep a phone or a purse or your handbag, for the love of God how can you not keep one mask? Or one spare? They're everywhere! Thrun about like confetti. They shouldn't be allowed to make them disposable except for the hospitals. We don't have disposable knickers do we? Or car keys? Or any of those things we use every day?"

"Gosh you are well exercised by this one, Philomena!"

"Ah, Jesus! You think we woulda learned all the things we're getting wrong, living the way we do, and it seems all we have done is create another layer of mass confusion on top of the mess we already had. I just don't know where it will end." She ran her hand around her neck and collar, airing her steamed-up self.

I stood up and went to her, gave her a big hug. "Lovely Philomena. Just look after yourself and your own and teach your children and grandchildren what's good and right. You can't fix the whole world but you can help it every day."

∞

Cottage by the Water, Rostellan 2020

The next creek from the cottage by the water is called Poll na Badhb. Badhb, Bibe, being the battle goddess of the pagan Irish. The late summer sun was still warm, the terns rose and dived, dropping carelessly to make a faint splash behind the cormorant's cry. Every bird for themselves, feeding furiously on exposed mud from the outgoing tide and the flush of fresh food on the incoming. Everywhere, birds doing their natural inclination. Eternally, no Monday or Friday or Bank Holiday or half-past anything. No viruses or disasters, no March or November, no marker other than tide and weather, sun and moon.

My father came to this, this slow unfolding of his days; his working life behind him. His house was home, his wife and mother-in-law had kept their own schedules. He checked the sun, listened to the wind and the sounds of the stars and the moon. Phut-phutting about in the Lily Kathleen, he was lifting pots, watching weather, unwrapping egg sandwiches from paper bags, pouring hot coffee from a flask. The simplicity of life was his haven.

Sometimes in the late evenings, when I was with them there, we would take the VW to the village of Whitegate, hugging the inner lee of the southern harbour. "Oh ho!" he'd say as we rounded the bend, "It's New York!" The tower lights of the refinery, like metropolitan skyscrapers, lit up the sky above the village, the white lights of the storage tanks of industry.

We would journey to the coast: Guileen, Inch, Ballybrannigan, Roches Point to watch the lighthouse flash, walk a dog, observe the sky, eat picnic cake. Often Mamá would accompany us. Sometimes she would play the fiddle or concertina at the back of the van and we would attract attention, conversation, opinion, exchange in the Irish way. Anything sparked connection: the dog, the VW, the music, Mamá's accent. My parents would often remark on how it was impossible to find life dull.

Late in Papá's life, this September day, the newer version of the VW climbs the hill, past endless yards of black crude pipes, past vast yards of gleaming orange propane tanks at the gas-bottling plant, and into the blackness of the headland beyond. We walk the last fifty metres to the gates of the fort, to survey the breadth of Cork harbour below. A waxing crescent moon slips below the fort of Camden on the opposing western shore, pink in the autumnal glow.

"Equinox," he says, "equal night."

Jupiter shadows Saturn in the southern sky, a gas flare from the refinery tower glows yellow or as orange as Mars hanging above it. We settle into camp chairs on the path, a green and blue wool blanket over his knees, our fingers stained blackberry-purple from earlier foraging.

"My Very Educated Mother Just Showed Us Nine Planets," he recited.

He had first told me this when I was only six or seven years of age, lying on the sand dunes of Doñana watching the skies. "Mars, Venus, Earth, Mercury, Jupiter, Saturn, Uranus, Neptune, Pluto," I return in a Spanish sing-song voice that makes him laugh. I like to hear him laugh.

"Pass me that flask, Jesús, and we'll see what's what in the world."

Ever the engineer, he snaps a digestive biscuit carefully in half, biting off a quarter, while watching the water flow below. There's a pilot boat, the nav lights of a late yacht, a fishing trawler heading out. The whoosh-whoosh of wind turbine blades on the northern industrial shore cause a slow flash of green-and-white light amongst a string of lights from Ringaskiddy to Cobh, a sodium glare, save for the dark bulk of Spike Island. The jetty lights draw the eye to a waiting ship full of crude, dwarfed then by the red chimney stack lights of the electricity generating station.

"It is somehow beautiful," he says, "a hive of industry, humming away. But I do like to sit above it now and observe. I have had my time of busy-ness. What's between the wind turbines and the dark spine of Spike Island, Jesús?"

"That would be the Naval College at Haulbowline. The crematorium is there on the causeway across to the island. I thought it novel that the old Naval Powder Magazine became Cork's first crematorium. You can be cremated right where they kept twenty-five thousand barrels of gun-powder in its heyday."

"Oh that is clever! Send me there when it's my time, won't you? Burn not bury, please. How splendid! An old naval site indeed." He sips coffee, coaxing biscuit residue out of his teeth with his tongue. I sit quietly awaiting him, the constant low industrial hum of oil refining, electricity generation, and liquid-gas bottling seeps over the hill behind us.

"How did I get to here, Jesús? So far from all I knew?" The crunch of digestive, a slurp from a cup. A faraway dog barks. "The world over, so many people everywhere they didn't belong, for so many reasons. Tell me this, Jesús: How does a man of Greek birth speak like a public schoolboy, grow up in Spain, and grow old in Ireland?"

I was not meant to answer this. The silent moments pass.

"I hardly knew my father, you know. I was a war baby and he was simply never there. The Med was busy in the war years, he largely worked out of Alexandria, or Crete when it wasn't being battered. I sort of remember anxious days for my mother, when he would have been in the action somewhere, but it was impossible to keep up with development. Cyprus got away with a lot of the bombing, Crete wasn't so lucky, and Greece got hammered," he muses.

"There was an RAF base on the island, lots of wartime activity there, that even I remember. But thankfully the Germans chose not to blow us all to smithereens. I remember my uncles coming back from serving, my grandmother in her little village taberna. They farmed goats. Oh! How I hated the smell. And the heat made the smell worse. My father would come on leave and my mother was happy with her dashing young Englishman. Then he would go, and life was just ordinary. Just Cyprus again."

His shoulders shrug. "We didn't have school until I was seven, maybe eight, then Captain Jack from the RAF base started a school in his old shed. There was such chaos in the war and it didn't stop with the end of it. Oh no sir! Chaos reigned for a long time afterwards."

The bow lights of a container ship slip into view to our left, the thrum of engines coming louder until the bridge passes us, as she pulls to starboard through the shipping lane. I could have reached out across the dark to shake the captain's hand.

"When we arrived in Cadiz, Jesús, it was like they never had a war. The Americans were everywhere, you know. They worked hard after the war, almost skilfully, to establish permanent strategic military operations, where temporary war ops had been based. To keep their fingers on the pulse of Europe. Here they were, a second time in twenty-five years, bailing the English and Europeans out of a sorry mess. My father was a good officer, but his Bristolian English rankled the Yanks. They always carried themselves with an air, like they were somehow the champions, the superior beings, and we should forever be grateful that they showed up." He sips his coffee. A herring gull sweeps past with the faintest of wing beats. "There I had school with the naval chaps. Good public-school English."

I recall my father in his uniform coming home from work at the Rota Base in Cadiz, or from extended time at sea. For many years I had never really considered exactly what he did at the base, for my life was shaped by Mamá, Abuelo Sean, and Abuelita Rosa. Papá had become a cadet in 1953, when he was sixteen, by which time the British Royal Navy were nearly shipping out of Cadiz and the Americans were in new negotiations to rebuild the Spanish military.

My father slipped between stools, a Greek-born British Royal Navy cadet, in what became a largely American and Spanish base. The Americans took him on their payroll eventually; his command of Spanish and English was invaluable, notwithstanding his capabilities and training as a naval officer. Of course, equally invaluable was his intimate knowledge of the Cadiz environs and the operating systems of all three naval forces. Someone had to bridge the gap between the rapid-fire Americans and the not-so-hasty Spaniards.

In 1959 the Seabees, a mobile construction battalion, arrived to Rota Base from Rhode Island, U.S.A., and built Quonset huts—a school, gymnasium, library, service club, gas station, dry-cleaning plant. The base expanded and became more complex. In 1965, another construction battalion for more modern houses, each unit pre-packed in twenty-two crates from Georgia. The Seabees built houses like jigsaw pieces around a waiting foundation. My father had commented sometime to me, "I watched everything, and learned so much. These Americans always arrived with something new, like beings from another planet. I was in awe of them."

I returned my attention to a clifftop in Cork.

"I was there for the Falklands War in '81. I am so glad I got out when I did. 1988, wasn't it? Yes, missed all the '90s Gulf action." He jerked his thumb towards the harbour below us. "Busy pootling about in Cork, eh?"

"Pootling indeed, Papá. You catch lovely crabs though."

"Indeed!" Then he shook his head. "For what? All for what?"

"I can't say, Papá. I don't think anyone could ever say that war solved anything. I am certain it endlessly created more misery."

My father nodded, inhaling deeply then a long, slow exhale. "He was a bit of a drinker, my father."

I nodded. I knew this.

"He was hoping for a big promotion, the top Royal Navy post in Spain, but he clipped a gun boat off the harbour wall one night, coming into berth. Cosmetic, but enough of a scrape to be noticeable and damage to the bowline housing. One of the officers ratted on him and, essentially, he lost the promotion. It was already complicated by the Brits and Yanks working with the Spanish, not to mention the postwar tension for everyone. And this was before what we know as the Cold War had even started to chill things down."

He munches awhile, his eyes sharp enough to follow the returning yacht heading towards the container ship.

"It wasn't too long after that, you know, when he drowned in the bath. I always thought my mother, despite all her moaning, was quite relieved. She was never exactly cheery of course, but that seems to have been her nature. She got along happily enough in the taberna. Look, look!" he exclaimed. "To the eye it seems that the yacht will be mowed down by the container ship."

We watched awhile, remarking on this and that.

"I remember a funny comment from one of the other RN officers in the taberna after his funeral. I overheard him say, 'Well timed eh? He slipped us out of a sticky London enquiry.' It meant nothing to me; I was so young, but he was referring to the docking incident of course."

I was silent, for my father wasn't usually so eloquent with tales of his own.

"He was a real naval man. All business, all naval business. He never had much time for me. It was like he didn't notice me. Never saw I was there. We upped sticks and moved to Cadiz because that is what the Navy said. My mother and I just, went with him. Like chattels, the inventory of his belongings. He bought her the taberna to keep her busy and not homesick. And I?" His head shook sadly. "I was lost there. Lost. Ten years old and lost."

I poured a hot drop into his coffee, handed him another biscuit, then fished a naggin of Powers whiskey from the picnic bag and sloshed a drop into the hot drink.

"Until I met your mother." He watches the container ship slip between the channel markers, moving silently up Cobh Road. "When he drowned, I felt nothing. Even when I was there in the bathroom with the physician, you know, finding the cause of his death. He was just this person, this voice demanding this or that." He waves his digestive biscuit vaguely, then pinched between his forefinger and thumb, wags it at me. "Get this, fetch that. Fetch more sticks, boy."

There is silence between us. I have no memory of this grandfather. In a short passage of time, my other grandfather more than adequately filled the space. We watch the quiet scene beneath us. A slight southwesterly drifts over the hill behind, rustling biscuit wrappings, flapping his anorak drawstrings. His old hand pushes up his glasses, wipes his eyes, pushes stray hair behind his ear.

"I hope I have been a better father to you, Jesús. I know you know that I love you immensely. I think I have read, or I have most definitely tried to read, every word that you have written since you were six years old. You have taught me so much."

Hot tears rise unbidden through the lump in my throat, burning the back of my eyes, then breaking through my closed eyelids, flowing unabashed down my cheeks.

"Papá." I manage, after a long silence. "Papá."

I take his hand, on a clifftop in Cork, late on a September evening.

"Now, now, don't be upset, no need for that." He does not hide his own tears, fiddling his anorak hood and catching the stray hair again behind his ear. "You know if we stay here a few more hours we'll see Orion and Venus to join the others for a fine display. But I am certain my old bones would never again get out of this chair." Extending his hand towards me, he exclaims, "Look! Here comes the pilot boat." I held his hand in mine. "Slosh some more of that Powers in here would you, Jesús, then I say we can toddle on home."

∞

Not long from that time, through undulating, uncertain waves of pandemic rules, the winter solstice was upon us. I walked with my friend Lal, my very wet springer and her wetter collie-cross—racing, looping, and playing—on a windswept beach scoured by winter rains. Channel markers sequentially flashed below the lighthouse, as the surf crashed upon the ebb-tide shore. A fishing vessel winked green and white lights, yellow light glowed from cabin windows as the vessel pitched and rose, riding the rocking sea. We were alone—darkening sky, in a place far removed from pandemic and fear, while yet in a world that faced looming viral restrictions at Christmastide. Even more so, we both knew the separation, basked in it, cherished it, stood quietly to it, conversing about life.

The solstice had passed earlier in the day, the moment our Celtic forebears believed the wheel of life paused for the briefest of breaths, as a new cycle of the sun began. There is a power in this liminal position in our time. Above the wind I sang a verse of "The Halsway Carol" for my friend, the lyrics capturing the kairos moment in which we were suspended, biding the fading light of the shortest day, giving thanks to the heavens for the winter sun, as we looked to the longest night. We shall sing the world into a new existence. The earth had turned into herself since the onset of winter at Samhain, the beginning of November. Yet already, the cycle was renewing, regenerating, the sun acknowledging a cosmic glance to spring. A cock's step every day, old Timmy had once told me.

I had written an article on folk music in Bristol some eight or so years ago and had happened upon "The Halsway Carol" and the hurdy-gurdy on which it is played. The simplicity of the music and the instrument, wedded with the harmony of voices had moved me. Perhaps it is my winter birth that brings me resonance with this low point in the calendar? Having never been a player, music has always had an important role in my life, my mother of course, the musician with whom I am most familiar, and every day in some way I feel the presence of the long-deceased concertina-wielding grandfather.

Returning to the cottage by the water in my saturated state, I knew it wasn't going to be possible to observe the great conjunction of Jupiter and Saturn, much to my father's disappointment. As my mother prepared a meal, I went to Mrs. Google on my father's iPad. In our many discussions about pre- and post-internet world, we had all agreed to use our beautiful brains before consulting the www or "whuh, whuh, whuh," as Mamá says, chuckling. "It reminds me of lovely Philomena laughing." Papá coined the term

"Mrs. Google," quantifying, "No one could be that thoroughly knowledgable in such a short space of time, and be male."

In the bright warmth of a wood fire with a glass of Chianti, we watched a livestream connection with Italian astronomer Gian Luca Masi on a rooftop in Rome, as he followed the planets in their miniscule movements. A German musician, Arvo Pärt, played De Profundis in the background, the 113th Psalm. This was not the experience of those who observed the last conjunction, eight hundred years ago, and there is no future plan. My father watched in wonder, firelight dancing on his glasses, his hands bridged under his chin.

"It's so real, Jesús. It's outside our window right now, Jupiter and Saturn aligning to zero degrees in Aquarius."

"Zero, Papá. Moving from an earth zodiac to air. Zero. The number of infinite potential. The one which holds the energy of limitless possibilities. Dr. Zhao would have been so excited at this. A new world."

"Well, I hope he's up there helping. I have lived through all those bloody wars and useless fighting and I have never seen this one in such a mess as it is now. We can only hope for better."

"Come. Eat," commands Mamá. "Leave the music, Jesús. It is soothing."

My father sits in his chair by the fire, snoozing over Tim Severin's *The Brendan Voyage,* half-open on his lap. All of Severin's books line the shelf above his head, thrilling stories of endless voyaging around the planet by a staggering variety of means. The story of Brendan's journey remains Papá's favourite, even above the Grecian hero Jason and his team of Argonauts. We once visited Craggaunowen Castle in County Clare to see the actual leather boat Tim Severin had built in 1976 and in which he had successfully recreated Brendan's journey. He examined every detail of the craft, shared his knowledge with visitors who happened into the space, became overwhelmed by the energy. He had once hoped the intrepid crew of the Voyageur might attempt to follow this ancient route to Newfoundland.

"Papá," I say quietly, "are you awake enough for something new?"

"Of course, Jesús," he smiled, his eyes opening and slowly refocussing. "I'm always ready for something new, you know."

For post-dinner tea and cake, I had stumbled upon "A Journey Around the Earth in Realtime," YouTube time-lapse video footage from the International Space Station. On a digital screen, my octogenarian parents and I watch the earth unfold from space while listening to the harmonics of Phaeleh.

"No es eso algo?" my mother queries out loud.

"Truly spectacular," my father agrees. "I am glad I have lived to see it."

∞

Through the roof light in my attic room, I cry to the clouded sky. "What is happening on my planet?" I hear myself, my confusion. "We may probably deserve it, but oh my dear Lord, the mayhem. Please, please help!"

In the nearby woodlands a barn owl hoots, while the harbour gives up the cries of night-time birds. With the oystercatchers and whimbrels on the whistling wind I hear: *20, 25, 2025. Change more change 'til 2025.* The universe of course knows itself. The worst wars were longer than that. In the artificial bluish light of white walls and winter darkness, I search Mrs. Google with varying terms—the mayhem on our planet, the variant, virulent, virus, the backdrop of madness that has gripped our world. Is there something that would help me to understand? My own belief in anything I have held fast seems in the moment to be spiralling away from me.

I close my eyes and imagine Dr. Zhao in his house full of books; Abuelita Rosa holding the hands of her patients; Abuelo Sean and Timmy, eyes closed and smiling, their fingered music filling my head. What would they say to guide me through this maelstrom? Mr Onions would say: mael-strom—Dutch, grinding-stream [from malen to grind and strom stream]. I hear hu-bris—from Greek hybris—wanton violence, insolence, outrage, a presumption toward the gods, an anagram of rubish. Rubbish, all rubbish. We have made a world of rubbish and wanton carnage. Is this our lesson?

What would my guides tell me to learn from this? Dr. Zhao would clasp his hands and lower his head recounting memories of serving on a hospital ship, young lives damaged, destroyed, extinguished by suited politicians and medalled military. Who gives one man power over another? Who wrote boundaries of ownership, divided nations according to ethnicity? Who took that power? Who deemed us superior to any other species, gave us the illusion of power, the power of illusion? Challenge that illusion, I hear. My own truth will not dissolve. Be strong, be true, follow your own heart, Jesús. Stay close to the earth, all my ancient wise ones speak clearly to me.

The Universe guides me, the rotating search engine wheel directs me, finds me—the Ancients at Uluru, Ayers Rock, Australia, in the centre of an old, old landmass. Click here, the page suggests, and I read "The solar plexus chakra of Gaia, the Earth, our living planet." Dr. Zhao whispers in my head. "You found it, Jesús." It is there on my screen, "The Magic Box," the Elders and Keepers of Lore telling me that the earth will change its vibrational frequency, splitting the human race into two separate pulses. Each soul will automatically gravitate towards the frequency that reflects their current stage of spiritual development. I am drawn to the esoteric value of the text, the references to new beginnings, to the race dividing into those who believe and know, to those who refuse to change. Mother Earth is not unhappy with us, she will be free for her own journey. We can help her sing the earth into a new existence.

I read into the darkness of the longest winter night, no one to share with, no one but me, alone in my attic room. I lie awake to rain beating on our roof, running down my skylight onto the world. Kept in by foul weather, fortunate to be looking out. And into my headphones, Damien Rice sings "Cold Water."

∞

In the still, early morning hours, by the humming oil stove with a cup of tea, sleep evades me. My father comes softly from the hallway, stands near, tousles my hair. "No sleep for you either, Jesús? It's not the dark moon, you know?"

"No, Papá, well past it and into the first quarter. I am not sure what to blame for this insomnia. Perhaps the incredible pandemonium on the planet."

"Well, what would your Buddhist buddies say to you, Jesús?"

I look up at him, his wise old greying head that I have loved forever, nighttime hollowed eyes defied by the olives, wine, and sun of his very being.

"Not just the Buddhists, Papá, all of the spiritual leaders would have tried to teach us that the Earth is Herself, Gaia. She too is on a journey, she too must survive. She was being and turning in the cosmos a long time before we evolved. Everything is as it needs to be, Papá. Mother Earth is somehow looking after herself. We are carried also on her journey, or lost on the way."

Papá nods and briefly smiles before kissing my head. "That's it, Jesús. And isn't that all you need to know?" he whispers.

∞

It is Christmas Day. "Every day is Christmas Day," says Mamá cheerfully, "when we have everything we need, and always we have each other."

I hear the iPad playing random music from the kitchen and I pause on the stairs as cello strains fill the room. The Piano Guys play Christina Perri's "A Thousand Years"—just glorious.

My mother hums as she busies herself with culinary tasks for the day ahead, which we will share with our Cork relatives. In the strange times of pandemic, there isn't any Christmas Mass, so Mamá and I walk a leetle bit along the path in bright winter sun, smiling and greeting our neighbours. She is slower, more careful in her movement, wonderfully well for eighty. We leave my father feeling slow and low in his bed. He joins us later to open gifts, laid on the red tablecloth. The centre-piece is a holly-trimmed Christmas candle, fashioned by Mamá with greenery gathered from the woods.

In the Two Spoons, there is bustle and noise, decorations glinting and sparkling in warm firelight. The generational gathering is large and merry; Christmastime carried on the cheer of children, stories of Santa, fun, and festive foods. In this midst is my father, who is quiet and picks at his plate, smiling wanly at my mother's prodding, grinning somewhat cheerfully at Ambrose's Christmas cracker jokes.

"Why did the skeleton not go to the ball, Daniel?"

My father eyes him balefully, "I cannot in truth possibly say why, Ambrose."

"Because he had no body to go with! D'you get that eh? No body." Ambrose laughs loudly, squeezing my father's shoulder. "Och, I am working hard to reach you today, old boy?"

Under his crooked green cracker hat, my father smiles at his friend, replying somewhat woefully, "I hear you, Ambrose, but seem unable to lift my spirits. I have caught the winter blues."

"What d'you think eh, Jesus? What does daddy need? What about a wee dram, Daniel? Would that help?"

I stop in my thoughts, my response not reaching my sound, for all I can hear in my own head is What is it my Daddy needs? Papá, Papá, a Spanish child calls from somewhere deep within my adult self. Papá! In this matrix of connection, absolutely nothing ever stays the same.

"I have a cup of tea for you, Daniel, a lihhle sugary tea. Geh tha' in ya and you'll be grand. You'll feel behher in jig-time." Bridget MacCarthy fussed about my father, sensing things were amiss. "Oh saints preserve us, wha' are y'like, yer half-frozen. Leh me warm yer hands there." She sits beside him and slowly rubs his hands between hers. "Poor Daniel, poor Daniel," she mutters, "I never seen ya ouh of sorts, never."

From along the table I see Philomena and Mamá anxiously looking our way, for Daniel "out-of-sorts" Joseph was a new being to us all. Philomena raises her large self and jerks her head towards the door, signalling a hastily called conference, from which the consensus is agreed: Daniel needs to be at his own home.

"Take care of yourself now, go with God and Christmas blessings." Philomena kisses my father's cheek and he eases himself into the front seat. As we depart Blackrock mid-afternoon, the knot of relatives watching our leave-taking fills my rearview mirror, the tall Scotsman standing apart; and I am aware that beneath the cheery farewells is a sense of trepidation and gloom. I hear Dr. Zhao in my memory, as we once dissected myriad causes of illness, "Anxiety is always prevalent, flushing underneath."

∞

As I dress to leave the cottage by the water to walk the dogs in the waning light, the aged Springer looks at me sheepishly from in front of the crackling fire. Her gaze follows me around the room, from the log pile to the grate, coat-rack to the door. She shifts to look to my father in the chair, moves to sit determinedly, then nudges under the arm and finds his hand. He laughs, scratching her ears. "No moving this one today, Jesús. She's only for me this afternoon."

"Lovely creature art thou mine, thine eyes hold me Divine." I fabricate lines for him.

My father responds, "Thy heart remains true, thy soul dost keepest due." He smiles briefly, catches my hand as I pass the chair.

"Goodbye, my child. Enjoy your walk."

I kiss him on the head. "See you soon again, Papá."

"And Jesús?" he calls after me.

"Yes Papá?"

"Will you walk the Caim? For my Christmas prayer, you know;

May You be a bright flame before me,
A guiding star above me,
a smooth path below me,

I join him for the final refrain:

a loving Guide behind me,
today, tonight and forever.

∞

Returning to the cottage well after dusk, kicking off boots in the porch, hanging my coat, towelling the young Springer dry, preparing food for both dogs, I am surprised the older creature has not appeared. At least she could show some guilt for abandoning us on this Christmas Day. I find Mamá in the dark, at the red-clothed kitchen table, seated before the lighted holly candle. She reaches for my hand. Her eyes are bright with tears, her cheeks streaked, candlelight dancing a thousand times on her face.

"He left us, Jesús." A mournful sob escapes her. "He asked for tea, ate some fruitcake, I helped him to the bathroom to relieve himself. He climbed into our bed and once more smiled at me. He said 'Thank you so much, my love. It has been the most wonderful adventure with you.' Then he closed his eyes, oh so peacefully, Jesús. And in what seems like a moment, just passed away. Ppff! Gone from me. Gone from me!" she cried.

Sobbing, wrenching, heart-wracking sounds, burying her face in my damp clothing. I stare at her head, her hand clenching mine, mine clenching hers, not knowing. Not hearing. Not seeing. Extraordinarily, I think of Dr. Zhao: "All of your senses are in your head, Jesús. Sight, smell, taste, hearing. All of your body feels, touches. All of your heart is love."

We are crying together by candlelight on a darkened day.

Epilogue

In my headphones, Leonard Cohen sadly sings. I smile inwardly, for no outwardly part of me feels a smile, and Abuelo Sean would say, "Shur in the name of the Lord God himself, what kinda nonsense is that fella talkin'?" I hear my father, "Cohen was a genius, a poet." He would have plucked away at his guitar and Mamá would stroke the fiddle for this same tune I hear, "Hallelujah," Papá's raspy American sing-song voice, germinated at Naval Base parties and flowered at Cork social gatherings.

Mamá would sway over the fiddle neck, her hair swept out of the way of the bow, her eyes would raise enough to smile at him. I used to wonder if my father missed these moments, with his half-closed Cohen eyes, but I knew of many occasions when a smile was all the exchange they needed. I hear him say to me now, "Oh, Jesús! It was my time. The blueprint of my heart beats, right?"

In the early half-light of the woods, pigeons clatter and rustle skywards, disturbed by our presence. The clover leaves curl in early frost. A blackbird trills, a robin calls clearly. The seagull answers in a raucous chord. In celebration of another year treading carefully upon this earth, together they all cry, "Haa-ppy Biii-rthdaaa-y, Jayy-ssuss."

"What? What?" I ask of them. "What is it? Who am I now?" I shout fiercely to the wind.

In the turning of the seagull framed by the dancing sky, I see my father's eye. I see him soar, I see him glide.

Then I can smile. I know all this. And this is all I need to know.

∞